Ten Things I Hate About the Duke

By Loretta Chase

LORETTA CHASE

Ten Things I Hate About the Duke

A
**DIFFICULT DUKES
NOVEL**

AVONBOOKS

An Imprint of HarperCollins*Publishers*

TEN THINGS I HATE ABOUT THE DUKE. Copyright © 2020 by Loretta Chekani. All rights reserved. Printed in the United States of America. No part of this book may be used or reproduced in any manner whatsoever without written permission except in the case of brief quotations embodied in critical articles and reviews. For information, address HarperCollins Publishers, 195 Broadway, New York, NY 10007.

First Avon Books mass market printing: December 2020
First Avon Books hardcover printing: December 2020

Print Edition ISBN: 978-0-06-295263-9
Digital Edition ISBN: 978-0-06-245741-7

Avon, Avon & logo, and Avon Books & logo are registered trademarks of HarperCollins Publishers in the United States of America and other countries.

HarperCollins is a registered trademark of HarperCollins Publishers in the United States of America and other countries.

FIRST EDITION

20 21 22 23 24 LSC 10 9 8 7 6 5 4 3 2 1

In memory of Isaac Mann

Acknowledgments

This book would not be possible without the support of:

May Chen, my editor, who encourages, inspires, keeps me from running off the rails, and brings out the best in me;

Nancy Yost, my agent, who's always there for me, keeps me going through good times and bad, cheers me on or gives me a hard time as necessary;

Larry and Gloria Abramoff, who once again provided a writer's refuge in a warm clime, along with meals filled with laughter and mental stimulation;

Jessica Fox, who provided invaluable assistance with riding scenes and matters equine;

Claudine Gandolfi, whose beautiful photographs of London sites have not only enhanced my collection of images but offered inspiration;

Patricia Henritze, my incredibly cool sister-in-law, who assisted me with theater history and found me experts I wouldn't have known how or where to look for;

Bruce Hubbard, MD, who once again helped me navigate between the worlds of nineteenth- and twenty-first-century medicine and explained the changing views about taping fractured ribs;

Mark Hutter, Master Tailor, the Department of Historic Trades and Skills, and Neal Hurst, Associate Curator of Costume and Textiles, both of the Colonial Williamsburg Foundation, whose expertise has helped me better dress my gentlemen;

Pamela Macaulay, my researcher extraordinaire, who found the elusive Baron de Bérenger, *The Long Finn*, and other obscure materials to satisfy my obsessive mind;

Susan Holloway Scott, my friend and general consultant on all matters writerly, fashionable, and all the et ceteras, who, in addition to friendship and moral support, provides me daily doses of images to fire my imagination;

Dave Walker and Isabel Hernandez of the Kensington and Chelsea Central Library, London, who not only provided a vast store of useful images and resources, but introduced me to the Baron de Bérenger's rifle and the fascinating fellow who invented it;

Cynthia, Vivian, and Kathy, my sisters, who are always there for me—

—with bonus thanks to Cynthia, for standing at my side at public events and keeping things moving smoothly, and for the ideas, the shopping, and the talking;

Walter, my husband, who is a genius and a prodigy among spouses, who took over my responsibilities to allow me to complete this book, and whose patient guidance has made him the major part of every book I write.

The blunders are mine, all mine.

"The aristocratic world does not like either clergymen, or women, to make too much noise."

—Edward Bulwer Lytton,
England and the English, 1833

Ten Things I Hate About the Duke

Prologue

—It is many years since so great a sensation has been excited in the gay circles by the beauty of a *débutante,* as by that of the Hertfordshire beauty Miss Hyacinth Pomfret, second daughter of Lord deGriffith. At the Drawing Room on Thursday, this young lady was the admiration of everyone present.

—*Foxe's Morning Spectacle,*
Saturday 4 May 1833

—Not long ago we reported the excitement of Miss Hyacinth Pomfret's debut. This week her sister Miss Pomfret has unexpectedly returned from abroad. As our readers will recollect, Lord deGriffith's eldest daughter has instigated more than one sensation since her own debut some years ago. On two occasions, the Riot Act was read. The second, shortly before her departure for the Continent, followed a dispute with Lord Nunsthorpe regarding the Factories Regulation Bill. Consequently, news of her return has been greeted, in several quarters, with trepidation.

—*Foxe's Morning Spectacle,*
Thursday 30 May 1833

Chapter 1

Lecture Hall of the Anti-Vice League, London
Thursday 13 June 1833

*P*apa was not going to be happy about this, Cassandra thought as she rose from her seat.

But it had to be done, and the Andromeda Society had agreed that she would speak for them. Her father was a powerful member of the House of Commons, where Mr. Titus Owsley seemed to be gaining more support than he ought for his ill-conceived bill. He might ignore other women, but he couldn't afford to ignore Lord deGriffith's daughter.

Owsley was one of the younger members, handsome, well-spoken, and, according to her father, far more ambitious than his apparent humility suggested. Parliament's generous supply of hypocrites didn't hurt the gentleman's cause.

She'd dressed so as not to call attention to herself. No flowers or birds sprang from the modest hat perched upon her dark red hair. No mounds of ruffles and furbelows adorned her pale lavender dress. She had dressed, in fact, in the way moral crusaders like Owsley approved. She had sat quietly through his lecture and listened. He was not entirely without sense and compassion, but he, like most of the upper classes, understood essentially nothing about ordinary people.

Her face its usual mask of calm, she said, "Mr. Owsley, in recent weeks some pieces have appeared in the London journals regarding your bill for the better enforcement of the Sabbath. I and many others have patiently awaited your response. Since Sabbath laws and practices have formed the substance of your lecture today, I trust you will answer the critics now."

He gave her a puzzled frown. "Critics? I'm not sure what journals you mean, Miss Pomfret."

This she doubted very much, but she played along.

"I mean this sort of thing." She waved the clipping she'd taken from a recent edition of *Figaro in London*, a satirical paper with a radical slant.

Though by now she'd memorized the words, she looked down and read:

"'The introduction of a bill by Mr. Titus Owsley, which, under the plea of enforcing the observance of the Sabbath, is calculated to withhold on that day the supply of their necessities from the poor, without curtailing the rich of any of their luxuries, is one of the grossest pieces of senatorial humbug that we can remember for a very long period.'"

Gasps and titters from those about her. A crack of masculine laughter from the gallery. She kept her gaze on the clippings.

He said, "Th-that is n-n—"

"'He wishes nothing to be done on the Lord's day,'" she read on, "'but such work as may be necessary for the existing state of Society. Splendid dinners may still be cooked and eaten in mansions, but necessary food may not be procured at an eating house. Private carriages may throng the roads as usual, but there are to be no public conveyances tolerated on the Sabbath. In fact the alteration is to affect only the poorer classes, while the same license that hitherto has existed is still to be permitted to Society.'"

Hisses, boos, and laughter now.

She looked up at him. He'd pasted on his red face the condescending smile men customarily awarded women who attempted to reason with them. He cleared his throat and tightened his grasp on the lectern.

Before he could compose a response, she said, "Is it or is it not a fair characterization of your bill? Or would you find it easier to answer the questions the editor asks?"

She read from the next part of the *Figaro* piece:

> "*Mr. Titus Owsley do you think,*
> *That on a Sunday 'tis discreet*
> *The poor should neither eat nor drink ?*
> *That food on that day is not meet ?*
>
> "*That private carriages may go*
> *Without the smallest fear of evil,*
> *While stages—*"

"Thank you, Miss Pomfret," he said through clenched teeth. "This is typical of the impious journals, which delight in ridiculing everything and everybody." He looked out over the audience. "Other questions?"

"Before you have answered mine?" she said.

"Let her finish the poem!" somebody called out.

"Answer the lady's questions!" somebody else shouted.

"What lady? That's deGriffith's Gorgon."

A collective gasp at this.

Then a chorus of "See here!" and "Who said that?" and the like.

More voices joined in, opposing, agreeing, daring, threatening. Men rose from their seats. Women began leaving theirs and starting for the doors.

Fists waved. The shouting amplified to a roar. In a moment, the lecture hall erupted into pandemonium.

deGriffith House, St. James's Square
Later that day

"IN A MATTER of hours I have become a joke among my colleagues," Lord deGriffith said as he paced his study. "My daughter could not leave it to me to deal with Owsley and his defective bill, but felt obliged to raise questions herself, in a public place, to make us the laughingstocks of London."

Cassandra had expected a severe scolding. What she had not prepared for was her father summoning her sister Hyacinth into the study as well.

But lately, Papa had been behaving oddly regarding Hyacinth. This started when he, Mama, and Hyacinth arrived in London for the sitting of Parliament and the social events connected to it. Shortly after they settled into the town house in St. James's Square, influenza had begun to rage through Town, and he'd used that excuse to postpone her debut again and again.

Once she was presented at Court, he curtailed her social life, refusing countless invitations. She could attend only the most exclusive affairs, among only the highest of the haut ton. She was not nineteen, and relegated to the stuffiest of stuffy parties.

Hyacinth hadn't complained. She never did. But Cassandra could read between the lines of her letters, and the last note from Lady Charles Ancaster, their aunt Julia, had only hastened Cassandra's return from France.

She'd hardly arrived when her brother Augustus's wife, Mary, fell ill, and Cassandra had gone to Hertfordshire to help look after her and manage the family. She'd no sooner returned to London than she needed to deal with Owsley's sanctimonious drivel.

"Mr. Owsley invited the public," she said. "I spoke because *somebody* needed to point out—in simple terms, in public—his duplicity." The papers would report the to-do at the lecture hall. Among other things, this would attract the attention of eating houses, transport companies, and others whose businesses would suffer. With them in an uproar, the bill was doomed, she hoped.

"Papa, he lectures about pious behavior and claims to be helping the poor while his bill actively seeks to increase their misery."

"The Sabbath bill—or any other bill, for that matter—is not the issue," her father said. "You are not a member of Parliament. You're a young lady. Episodes like these will make you unmarriageable."

"For having an opinion? For caring about more than what frock to wear?"

"There are other ways to care, as I have told you time and again. If your little social club isn't enough for you, you've scores of other ladies' charities to choose from."

As though she'd never lifted a finger to help those in need. How many fêtes and fairs and other fund-raising events had she been part of since she left the nursery? Hadn't she joined the Andromeda Society—her "little social club"—precisely because the others weren't enough?

"That is the way a lady offers service," Papa said. "Not standing up at a public event and quoting from the radical journals."

"But you have quoted from *Figaro*—"

"How many different ways must I say this?" he said. "It is not the belief. It is not the caring. It is not the journal. It is the standing up in public and making a spectacle of yourself."

It was her refusal to be silent, in other words.

He went on, "I had hoped this time you'd returned from your travels with greater maturity and patience. I had hoped your efforts with Mary signified a change. But you seem determined to make a harridan of yourself, and place yourself beyond any possibility of marriage."

Uh-oh. Cassandra saw a chasm yawning before her. Her father was a wily politician. She said cautiously, calmly, "I am unable to see the wisdom of changing my character in order to please a man."

"Not your character. Your *behavior*. Can you not see the difference?"

"I know I cannot pretend to be somebody I am not."

He stopped pacing and looked from her to Hyacinth and back again. He drew a deep breath and let it out. "Very well," he said in milder tones. "Do as you like. You always do. But."

He paused and bent his head and appeared to study the floor.

Cassandra and Hyacinth exchanged glances. The word *but* uttered in that particular tone, followed by the pause and the bowed head, was famous. On several occasions it had preceded the death and burial of a piece of legislation. It had led to the untimely demise of four political careers. It had made the previous King cry more times than anybody could count.

"But," Papa said, "be aware that I am unable to see the wisdom of continuing Hyacinth's Season if you are going to undermine it."

"Undermine—"

"Your behavior reflects on her, on all of us. You came out years ago, and you're still unwed. You do as you please, with no checks on your behavior, thanks to my overindulgent parents."

Their hands full with an abundance of sons, her parents had more or less transferred the upbringing of their difficult eldest daughter to her paternal grandparents, a most fortunate turn of events. Grandmama and Grandpapa Chelsfield understood she wasn't like other girls, and they didn't try to mold her into that sort. However, they remained in Paris, and she was obliged, for the present, to deal with her parents on her own.

"It does not occur to you," her father was saying, "that eligible men as well as their families may wonder whether Hyacinth will follow in your footsteps."

"But Hyacinth is nothing like me, Papa. She never has been."

Neither younger sister was like her. Helena was away at school, not getting into any trouble, so far as Cassandra knew, and Hyacinth . . .

Oh, she was beautiful, inside and out, sweet-natured, kind, forgiving, tolerant, patient.

Cassandra was *Medusa* and *deGriffith's Gorgon* and *Cassandra Prophet of Doom*. The world saw her as unwomanly because she did not keep her opinions to herself and, worse, she said what she had to say plainly and directly.

In short, she was a shrew.

Nobody wanted to marry a shrew—except the swaggering bully Petruchio in the Shakespeare play, hardly her ideal man. Not that the ideal man existed.

Marriage was tricky enough even with relatively rational men like her grandfather or father or her brother Augustus. Even intelligent women made fatal errors in this regard. Look at her dearest friend, Alice, now bound forever to the Duke of Blackwood. And

only the other day, Lady Olympia Hightower had a narrow escape,
she having the abundant good sense to run away minutes before
she was to marry the Duke of Ashmont.

"I had deluded myself that being in Society with other girls would
soften you," Papa said. "But Season after Season passed, and you
only became more fixed in your ways. I cannot allow you to continue
to set a bad example for your younger sisters. I cannot allow you to
continue to distress your mother. As I have pointed out to her more
than once recently, it is ridiculous to bring out a daughter of eighteen
when the one so rapidly approaching thirty will not settle down."

Thirty! She would not reach that dire age for another four years
and some months.

"Papa, it is not a matter of—"

"It would appear very ill for Hyacinth to be wed before her sister,
who is quite as handsome in her own way and could be equally
agreeable if she would only make the effort. And so, that is the end
of it." He paused, and looked from one daughter to the other.

"The end of . . . ?"

"I will not give Hyacinth permission to marry until you are wed,"
he said. "Since she may not marry, I see no reason for her to spend
another minute on the Marriage Mart. No dinners, dejeuners, fêtes
champêtres, balls, routs, picnics, water parties, plays, ballet, opera.
In short, as of this minute, Hyacinth's Season is over."

Putney Heath
Midmorning of 15 June 1833

LUCIUS WILMOT BECKINGHAM, the sixth Duke of Ashmont,
slowly lifted his head from his folded arms. He'd been called the
most beautiful man in England. He'd been called other things, too,
but that's for later. At present his fair, curling hair stood in ragged
corkscrews. His excessively blue eyes were bloodshot. Bruises, a
few days old, adorned one.

While he struggled to focus, the clamorous world about him

tipped up, down, and sideways, the whole time turning like a fog-filled ship in a swirling sea.

He closed his eyes then opened them again, and the haze thinned a degree. These weren't sailors, only yokels shouting at one another. The din arose not from creaking ropes in a storm but from the thump of feet and the clunk of ale pots slammed on tables. Not a ship or anything like a ship. A public house.

Right.

The Green Man. Putney Heath.

That's where he was.

After the duel.

With his best friend.

He looked down at his hands. They'd finally stopped shaking.

It had taken only—what? A dozen brandies and soda? Two dozen? Why not three?

No matter. He'd done what he had to do. His Lying, Traitorous Grace the Duke of Ripley, miserable, rotten cur of a so-called best friend, had stolen the girl. Not just any girl, but Lady Olympia Hightower. And not the usual stealing-the-girl business—normal fun and games for him and his two alleged best friends—but Ashmont's bride-to-be. In her *wedding dress*! Minutes before the sermonizing and *I wills* and what's-its.

But no, it was all right now. All for the best. He and Ripley had done what they had to do and . . .

Ashmont shook his head, trying to shake off the image. But all the brandies and sodas failed to wash away the nightmare stuck in his skull: Ripley's arm upraised when it oughtn't to have been, a fraction of a heartbeat too late—the same instant Ashmont pulled the trigger.

He'd come within a gnat's eyelash of killing his best friend.

No thanks to the friend. Bloody idiot. Deloping, of all things.

"More." Ashmont raised a hand to signal the barmaid. "Another."

Then he remembered he wasn't alone.

Not yet.

Humphrey Morris. Other side of the table. The Earl of Bartham's third son. Known at school as Morris Tertius. Tall fellow. Nearly as tall as Ashmont. But younger. Lankier. Better behaved.

Which explained why he wasn't one of Ashmont's best friends. Before. Now was different. Morris had acted as his second when His Bloody Grace the Duke of Blackwood refused, traitorous swine. Another so-called best friend who wasn't. Bugger the lot of them.

Ashmont cast a bleary gaze at the man sitting opposite, who looked to be loading a pistol.

"Didn't we already do that?" Ashmont said, his heart sinking. Had he only dreamt the whole ghastly duel?

"Not yet," Morris said. "You went asleep there for a bit. But before that I said you couldn't shoot a tankard off the top of the window frame over there without breaking the glass and you said you could and now it's ten guineas whether you can or can't. Only first I need to go out." He jerked his head toward the back of the public house. "Do a piss." He pushed up clumsily from his seat. "Don't start without me."

Ashmont watched him move, like a ship in rough seas, out of the room.

He stared at the table in front of him, where the pistol case lay. He considered the proposed target, to the right of the pub's entrance.

Easy shot.

"You lying whoreson!" somebody roared. "Say it again and I'll learn you something you won't forget."

"*Teach*," Ashmont muttered. "Not *learn*, you sapskull."

Nobody heeded the grammar lesson. Somebody shouted back at the sapskull. Then everybody was shouting, banging mugs, scraping chairs over the floor.

The noise set Ashmont's head vibrating.

"Stow it," he said. "Stow it, goddamn you all to hell. Stop your bloody row."

He didn't raise his voice. He was a duke. When he spoke, people leapt to attention.

Not this lot. Too busy with their— Oh, and now louder shouting, some funny oaths he hadn't heard before, chairs falling over, and a table. Somebody leapt onto somebody else. A rush to the door— Good. Let 'em go. But they left the door open, and the uproar— Louder and louder. Inside. Outside. Men spilling out of the back rooms.

What were they all doing here at this hour? He flung open the pistol case and grabbed a pistol. Shoving men out of his way, he staggered to the door.

He stomped through it, through the covered entryway, down the steps, and onto the footpath. He cocked the pistol.

Meanwhile

THERE WAS A limit, and Cassandra had reached it. Mama had wept for two days, Papa wouldn't listen to reason, and Hyacinth couldn't find a reason to blame anybody for anything.

"Papa wants you married," she'd said last night. "He wants someone protecting you. He doesn't mean to be harsh. He worries. About both of us. You didn't see what it was like after I made my debut. The gentlemen would make a crush about me, and it made Mama anxious and Papa angry. And to tell you the truth, I had rather be able to spend time with the other girls, but it isn't pleasant for them, when men make such a fuss, wanting my attention."

She'd said, too, that she wasn't ready to marry anybody, and Cassandra wasn't to fret about it. She urged Cassandra to visit their ailing former governess in Roehampton. Mrs. Nisbett was preparing to move to Rome, on doctor's advice. This would be Cassandra's last chance to see her.

The proposal, for once, met with no parental objections beyond the usual grumbling about her driving herself, and it got Cassandra out of London, at any rate, and into the fresh scenery of the country.

And so this increasingly cloudy June midmorning found her driving her demi-mail phaeton toward Putney Heath. Her maid, Gosney, sat beside her in front, and her tiger, Keeffe, behind in the dickey. For a journey of not seven miles from London, in broad day, Cassandra deemed this escort more than sufficient.

Though inside her head turmoil reigned, the world about her was quiet. The only other living creature she saw was a stray cow, sole occupant of the cattle pound that stood in the heath opposite the Green Man Inn, not many yards ahead. Given the hour, the weather, and the number of other vehicles about her (none), she assumed she'd reach Mrs. Nisbett's place in short order.

But.

As she neared the Green Man, two men tumbled through the door.

From behind her came Keeffe's voice: "Miss, you'll want to—"

"Yes, I do see."

She saw the combatants scramble to their feet and go on with the fight they'd begun indoors.

Other men surged out of the inn behind them, shouting—encouragement and bets, no doubt. She saw a brawl in the making, about to spill into the road.

While the way was narrow, she had it to herself at present, and could easily move farther to the left, closer to the heath. She expected to slip by the imminent melee easily.

But in the same instant she turned her horses, another man staggered out of the inn, aimed a pistol at the cloudy sky, and fired.

The explosion reverberated through the rustic scene like the start of battle. Gosney screamed, squawking birds rocketed up from the trees, and the horses took off at full speed. Having begun turning toward the heath, they ran straight into it.

Gosney clung to her seat while Cassandra kept to the job at hand: Quiet the animals, stay in control, as Keeffe had taught her. She could do this.

She hadn't time.

The reins broke, a wheel struck the edge of the cattle pound, and the vehicle went over.

ASHMONT RAN, ON unsteady legs, but he ran. A host of men, equally unsteady, went with him.

When he reached the scene, he saw three bodies on the ground.

Two women, near the carriage. A man, farther away.

Though he needed to cover only a short distance from the steps of the Green Man to the cattle pound, an eternity passed while he approached, sick and dizzy, looking from one motionless body to another. Then he saw movement from the heap of blue clothing. The woman sat up. Shook her head. Looked about her. Her hat had fallen to one side of her head, revealing dark red hair coming loose from its pins.

He was moving to her even as he took this in, but the ground was rough, he could barely focus, and his legs didn't want to work.

The other woman lifted her head then. Still alive. Good.

He crouched by the one who was nearer, the redhead. His mouth was dry. His tongue was stuck. With some effort he managed to croak out, "You all right?"

She looked straight at him, her eyes stony grey.

"You," she said. She jerked the hat this way and that and pulled it off, tearing a ribbon. She hit him with it, hard. It was only rice straw but she took him unawares. His reflexes sluggish, his balance swimming in brandy, he went over.

She scrambled to her feet and picked up the whip lying nearby. "*You,*" she said, looking down at him.

Ashmont decided to stay where he was.

She walked over him, her skirts brushing his trousers.

"Yes, you, of course," she said. "It only wanted this."

HIM.

The knowledge had been there, certainly, somewhere in the commotion of Cassandra's mind: a flash of recognition in the same instant the horses bolted.

But he didn't matter.

Her servants mattered. The horses mattered.

Keeffe.

He'd taught her to ride and drive. He'd been with her from the time she was a troublesome girl of fourteen and he a crippled ex-jockey of six and twenty. For nearly twelve years she'd relied on his wisdom, and not only about horses.

She would have to attend to the cattle later. The first glance told her they weren't obviously injured. Further examination would have to wait. "See to the horses," she called, and several men hurried to the animals.

Gosney was clambering to her feet. Scratched and bruised, and—oh, bleeding a little. She walked a few steps and took hold of one of the cattle pound's rails. She was damaged, yes, but alive and more or less in one piece.

The cow, in no wise discomposed by recent events, moved to that side of the pen to regard her with the usual mild bovine interest.

Cassandra walked swiftly on. She knew where Keeffe was. She could see him, too still, near the foot of a tree.

On the outside, she was fully composed. No matter what happened, the person who held the reins remained majestically calm. He'd taught her that. She resisted the urge to run. The ground was rough, and she'd be no good to anybody if she sprained an ankle.

Her mind was on Keeffe. Her world was on Keeffe.

Her mind made pictures of him: his neck broken, his skull cracked, this time beyond repair.

"Keeffe!" she called.

"Miss!"

She let out a shaky breath she hadn't realized she'd been holding and went to him.

He started to struggle up to a sitting position, and his face twisted.

"Don't," she said. "You're hurt." She knelt beside him.

"Not a bit of it, miss," he said. "I'll be up in a minute. Had the wind knocked out of me is all."

"Damn and blast!" Breathing alcoholic fumes, the great, worthless ox who'd caused the trouble pushed in next to her, and knelt by Keeffe. "Not dead?"

"No, Your Grace. Not broken, neither. I'll do well enough in a minute."

Your Grace. Yes, everybody knew who he was: the Duke of Ashmont, degenerate par excellence.

Cassandra rose. Rage swept over the first wash of relief. Never had she wanted anything so much as she wanted to bring the whip handle down on his head. Hard. Repeatedly. Not that he'd feel it.

Then she realized she was looking at his bare head, a mass of tousled pale gold curls. The duke was hatless.

And drunk, but that went without saying.

"You lot!" he called. "A litter for—for—"

"Keeffe, Your Grace, and I don't need carrying. I'll be right in a tick."

Years ago Keeffe had been carried off a racecourse, so badly broken that most believed he was dead, or as near as made no difference.

"Keeffe." The duke paused, swaying. "Don't I know you? Not Tom Keeffe? The jockey?"

"Was, Your Grace. Long time ago."

"Saw you ride at Newmarket that time. Me and some friends. Mere lads then, but we knew all about you. Damned shame about the last race."

Damned shame didn't half cover it.

And now . . .

Something was dreadfully wrong. Keeffe was trying to hide it, but Cassandra could see it in his face, in the set of his mouth.

She turned her Medusa stare upon Ashmont. "If you would be so good as to save your reminiscences for later—or never," she said, "I should like to have my groom looked after."

"I'm all right, miss." Keeffe tried to get up. He gasped and his eyes widened. "Maybe one of you fellows'll give us a hand," he said to the surrounding gawkers.

"I'll do it," the duke said.

The Duke of Ashmont, of all men.

Once upon a time, he'd loomed large in Cassandra's life. Among other things, he was the boon companion of the present Duke of Ripley, brother of her dearest friend, Alice—unfortunately, and perhaps tragically, the Duchess of Blackwood now. For a good part of Cassandra's girlhood she'd seen Ashmont nearly every summer at Camberley Place, home of her aunt Julia.

These days she knew him primarily by repute. He featured in newspapers' and magazines' gossip columns, indignant letters to editors, and satirical images in print shop windows and print sellers' umbrellas.

Though Cassandra had had little to do with him—or Ripley or Blackwood for that matter—even in her girlhood, she was well aware of what he'd become. Ashmont, along with the other two, was one of Their Dis-Graces and, in the opinion of most of the Great World, the most reprehensible: a hard-living libertine with a puerile sense of humor and the combative instincts of a gamecock, who created chaos wherever he went.

Ah, yes, this was exactly what she needed: a badly damaged carriage, no acceptable vehicle in sight, the peerage's most disreputable member with an entourage of idle, drunken locals, and Keeffe in severe pain he couldn't hide as well as he thought he could.

She quickly reviewed the situation.

Until recently, Augustus and Mary had lived in Putney, and Cassandra knew the area reasonably well. She knew the Green Man, after a fight, was no place for an injured man. The same applied to other nearby taverns.

However, the White Lion, a large and busy hostelry in the High Street, stood not a mile away. There was a competent surgeon in the High Street as well, if he was still there, after the three dukes' depredations. They had provided more than usual excitement in Putney and elsewhere in the past week, according to *Foxe's Morning Spectacle*.

Ashmont rose uncertainly and put his hand out to help her tiger.

"On no account move him yet," she said sharply. "Keeffe's broken something, and I won't have him jolted."

"No, miss! It's only bumps and bruises, and you know I've taken harder falls."

"Don't move," she told Keeffe. "Don't speak."

"Miss, I vow—"

She looked at him. Keeffe subsided.

She turned her gaze to Ashmont and found him regarding her in a puzzled manner.

A few stray beams of sunlight broke through the morning clouds and glinted in his fair hair, like sparkles in a glass of champagne. He smiled, and his bruised, dissipated face changed and became ethereal.

In her mind's eye arose a long-buried memory of an autumn night at Camberley Place and a ten-year-old Cassandra looking up in wonder at the heavens. Beside her stood the Duke of Ashmont's beautiful son, a few years older than she. He was her brother Anselm's age, but not as obnoxious. At the time he was Lord Selston—Selston to the other boys—but her aunt Julia called him by his given name, Lucius.

From *lux*: light. Cassandra was learning Latin, mainly on her own.

He was showing her how to find the constellations in the great mass of stars that formed the Milky Way.

"And there is Andromeda," he said.

"Where?" she said.

Unlike her brother, he didn't snort or sneer that girls didn't know *anything*.

Lord Selston showed her how to pick out the relevant stars. "Do you know her story?" he said.

"No." She looked up into his face and imagined he'd come from there, from the stars, while he told her the myth of Perseus and Andromeda.

His Grace with the Angel Face.

Alice called him that, among other things.

Years and years had passed since that night of stargazing. The boy who'd once seemed a celestial being had vanished a long time ago.

Cassandra swallowed a sigh. Such a waste. Such a great waste.

Still smiling down at her, the Duke of Ashmont swayed gently one way, then the other, and toppled to the ground.

Chapter 2

*H*er eyes were grey, like the clouds overhead. They had flashed silver lightning. Her eyes, that is. When Ashmont opened his, the clouds he gazed up at were calm, shadowy things, big as elephants, marching slowly across the heavens. Here and there between the fluffy elephants, one caught a glimpse of what might be sky, or clouds farther away. No hint of blue broke through the elephants and their world.

Her eyes were grey, and Ashmont felt as though the elephants had been dancing on him.

He became aware of voices. Hers said, "I don't have time for this. You men, get the duke up from the ground."

What seemed like hundreds of outstretched hands appeared above him.

"It's all right, Yer Grace," said one.

"You was took sudden-like, is all," said another. "Coming out straight into the air, and running after Miss Pomfret and all."

Pomfret. Didn't he know that name? Never mind. Thinking hurt.

"All the fresh morning air overcame him, no doubt," came her voice. "And why he should be awake at this hour is no mystery. There was a duel, I collect."

Chorus of voices: "Oh, no, Miss Pomfret!"

"Them's illegal, them duels."

"Nobody does it anymore."

"Not here, leastways."

Ashmont waved a hand. "Stop your bloody row. Go away."

They retreated. He was a duke, after all. When he waved his hand, people did things, like get out of the way.

He was the only one who didn't.

No matter what he did, he didn't get out of the way.

He wasn't sure what that meant. Never mind. Didn't care.

He lifted his head from the ground and shook it. Into his line of vision came a pair of lady's half boots. Blue. And the bottom of a dirt- and grass-stained blue skirt. His gaze traveled slowly up a line of bows to a belted waist and up over a rumpled lacy bodice— not the most ample one he'd ever seen—framed by wrinkled wide lapels, and up to the face and the silver-flashing eyes and the dark red curls. No hat. She'd hit him with it.

All the effort of looking made his head tired.

He let it sink back again.

She said something to somebody. He heard footsteps, thudding hurriedly over the heath and fading away.

She held out a gloved hand. "Get up."

Ashmont didn't want to get up. His head was a great, throbbing, lead mountain.

"Get *up*." The gloved hand remained, waiting.

He ignored it.

He closed his eyes. Time passed.

Cold water sloshed over him. He was drowning, gasping, bolting up so suddenly from the ground that he very nearly cast up his accounts. The world went round and round, green and brown and grey with bright blobs of color here and there.

"What? What?" His vision cleared and he saw her holding the bucket.

"Feeling better now?" she said.

He was distantly aware of laughter, abruptly stifled.

Mainly he was aware of her, standing tall and straight, chin up, grey eyes daring him . . . and was that a hint of a smile at the corners of her mouth?

"I did not have time to wait for you to come to your senses," she said. "I strongly doubt that will ever happen, in any event."

For an alarming moment, he couldn't remember. Everything before this moment was lost in a heavy haze. Clouds.

"My man needs help," she said.

"Miss, there was no call for that. He's a *duke*. I'll be right as rain in a wink."

"Save your strength, Keeffe," she said. "You'll need it."

Ashmont looked in the direction the male voice had come from. It all came back.

The gun had gone off, then everything went wrong . . . but nobody dead. Yet.

She moved nearer, and he resisted the strong and unusual temptation to retreat. She said, her voice much lower, close by his ear: "You are so intoxicated, Lucius, as to be a danger to yourself, not to mention everybody in your vicinity. Regardless of my personal feelings—and personally, I find your condition and behavior disgusting and disgraceful in the extreme—"

"Never mind the sweet talk, m'dear," he managed to croak. "Say what's on your mind."

"Horrifying as the thought is, I need your help. Now. I need you to throw your weight and your money about. You must collect yourself and try, for once in your misbegotten life, to make yourself useful."

SOMEHOW THROUGH THE haze and the nearly overwhelming desire to lie down and die, Ashmont made sure a litter was produced in short order, along with transport. He saw Keeffe carefully loaded onto it, then onto the cart, where he was secured, to reduce jolting as much as possible. Miss Pomfret insisted on walking alongside the cart to the inn, and warned the driver of every bump and rut in the road ahead. Ashmont walked on the other side. By the time they reached the White Lion, the surgeon he'd sent for had arrived, and Ashmont was ready to have his head amputated.

Though a young man, in practice for only a few years, Mr.

Greenslade had immense experience with concussions, near drownings, broken bones, and divers other injuries, all thanks to Their Dis-Graces. He could have performed admirably in wartime. Likewise, neither plague, pestilence, famine, nor cannon fire would daunt the proprietor and staff of the White Lion, the three dukes' favorite stopping place in the area.

They'd done some damage here and elsewhere, but Ashmont and his friends always balanced the scales. They paid for the trouble, whatever it was, and paid handsomely, wiping the slate clean of pranks, fights, seductions, and destructions. As a result, the dukes' return met with welcome instead of pitchforks, blazing torches, and snarling dogs.

The surgeon had Keeffe transferred to a table in one of the private dining rooms. This was the same table and room in which Ashmont had seen more than one fellow stretched out, awaiting Greenslade's ministrations. Miss Pomfret was determined to remain to supervise, but this once she was overborne. Though he'd submitted to everything else, Keeffe would not submit to her seeing him undressed. He became so agitated that she finally left, to prevent his injuring himself further.

At the surgeon's suggestion, Ashmont took himself to the coffee room.

Shortly after the waiter took his order, Morris Tertius arrived, carrying the pistol case and Ashmont's hat.

Only then did Ashmont realize he'd lost the hat. And a fine dueling pistol. What had he done with the weapon?

"Where'd you get to?" Morris said. "One minute you were there, and then you weren't and then I woke up under a table and nobody knew where you'd gone, and then they did, only it was ten different directions. Somebody said you were shot, and somebody else said it was a servant, and then I looked down on the table and there was the pistol case and only one weapon in it. 'What happened to the other one?' I wondered."

Blackwood had said of Humphrey Morris that he had tongue enough for two sets of teeth. At the moment, Ashmont didn't mind the talking. It stopped the thinking.

Drink did that, too, but oddly enough, the duke felt he might have drunk enough for one morning.

Two women injured. And the little fellow, the little fellow. Of all the men in all the world Ashmont had to damage, it had to be Tom Keeffe. A hero of the turf? Hell, a hero of life. Born in a workhouse. A child of the rookeries. Somehow he'd escaped, to find his calling and climb to the very top of jockeydom.

. . . until that day at Newmarket, when he'd been all but trampled to death. In fact, he'd been reported dead at first. Yet here he was. He'd survived, against impossible odds, much in the way he'd won his earliest races.

If he didn't survive this . . .

It didn't bear thinking about, and so Ashmont wouldn't think about it.

He said, "While you were gone, the locals started brawling. Wasn't in the humor for it. Went out and fired the pistol. Didn't you hear it?"

Morris shook his head. "Heard something. Don't know what. Don't actually remember very much."

Ashmont told him.

Morris's eyebrows went up. His light brown eyes opened very wide, as did his mouth. "Did you say Miss Pomfret was in the carriage?" His facial expression softened and his voice became hushed. "Not Miss *Hyacinth* Pomfret?"

"Miss Pomfret," Ashmont said. "Red hair. Grey eyes. Five and three-quarter feet tall or thereabouts. A Boadicea sort of female. Threw a bucket of water on me."

Called him *Lucius.* Whoever did that?

Morris's dreamy expression sharpened into horror. "Oh, no! Cassandra Pomfret! *Here!*"

"You know her, I take it."

"You don't? How can you not know her?"

"Someone said she was Miss Pomfret, and most of Putney seems to know who she is."

"One of her brothers has a place here," Morris said. "Lets it now. Lord deGriffith's family. Earl of Chelsfield's heir. There're ten of them. She's the eldest of the three girls. Also known as Cassandra Prophet of Doom, which is, she opens her mouth and horrible nightmare things come out. You must know her. Ripley's sister's friend. Lady Charles Ancaster is Lord deGriffith's sister."

Lady Charles Ancaster: Ripley's aunt Julia. She'd always treated Ripley's two friends as though they were his brothers and she was their mother. She'd called Ashmont by his given name only the other day, in the course of a sharpish dressing-down. Having grown up without a mother, Ashmont didn't mind the tongue-lashings. They seemed to go with the affection she supplied with equal generosity.

Lucius.

No one else called him that anymore.

Except Miss Pomfret, on the heath, when she also called him *disgraceful* and *disgusting.*

It came back then. The redheaded girl. Camberley Place. So long ago that was, ages and ages. A lifetime.

"No genealogy," he said. "My head isn't right and I haven't the stomach for fourth cousins six times removed on the mother's side or wherever it is."

"Lady Charles Ancaster," Morris said patiently. "Ripley's aunt."

"Yes, yes, I know."

"Also Miss Pomfret's aunt, but from the other side. How can you not know Miss Pomfret? She and Lady Alice—the Duchess of Blackwood, that is—have been as thick as thieves since they were in the nursery."

"Seem to have lost touch," Ashmont said. "Good girl? Good family? Unwed? What would I have to do with her, then?"

People had introduced him to eligible girls, and he'd bowed and gone the other way. He'd avoided the species when he first entered London's social whirl, and he'd kept on doing so. Respectable misses were boring. Chaperons everywhere. No privacy allowed. You certainly couldn't have any fun with them. If you did, you had to marry them.

Olympia, the girl he'd decided to marry, was a good girl. Not that he'd been looking for a wife at the time. He'd found her by accident.

She wasn't boring.

But his best friend had stolen her, the thieving, lying maggot.

Now Blackwood and Ripley had wives and Ashmont didn't. Ripley hadn't even had to work for his! He hadn't spent weeks courting her and persuading her family he wouldn't ruin her life. No, all Ripley had to do—

But no, not all Ripley's fault, the backstabbing swine. Women were unpredictable, and respectable women were especially troublesome, because they didn't play by the rules of trade, as the fallen sisterhood did.

No, Olympia had gone her own way, tossing aside vows and signed papers as though they were old gloves. And he and Ripley had fought this morning, as they were obliged to do, and cleared the slate. Friends again. And that was that.

Always best to clear the slate. Saved endless botheration.

And best to clear it as quickly as possible.

If it could be cleared.

But Keeffe wouldn't die. He couldn't. He'd live, and Ashmont would pay whatever it cost.

He returned his attention to Morris, who was rhapsodizing about one of Miss Pomfret's sisters.

ACCORDING TO CASSANDRA's watch, more than two hours had passed by the time Mr. Greenslade entered the small private dining parlor on the first floor, where she waited. She'd tended to Gosney's lacerations and sent the maid to the public dining room to settle her nerves with tea and something to eat.

Cassandra had occupied the time since either watching the doings in the courtyard below or the darkening and swelling clouds above while she considered her situation and entertained fantasies in which the Duke of Ashmont made his way slowly and painfully through all nine circles of Dante's Hell.

"Two fractured ribs," said the surgeon. "While the fractures appear to be clean, it is, as I'm sure you understand, impossible to be certain of the fact."

She'd suspected broken ribs, and though the injury was not as bad as she'd feared, this wasn't the best news. Surgeons, in her experience, were inevitably sure, all too sure.

"What's wrong?" she said.

"A fever."

Her heart sank.

Shattered bones could result in fatal infections, affections of the lungs. She'd seen it happen in impoverished families. Even among the upper orders, one heard of all too many cases. She told herself that Keeffe had survived a great deal worse—but he'd been a younger man then, undamaged and in prime strength.

"He claims he's ready to return to work," Greenslade said. "I don't doubt he feels better, and in the usual way of things, having wrapped him securely, I would say you might continue your journey—albeit with caution. But peripneumony is a concern in these cases, and in the present circumstances I would urge you most strongly not to move him farther than the nearest bedchamber. A day or two of rest, with a cooling diet and careful nursing, will tell us whether the fever is simply the body's immediate reaction to the injury, or a deeper complication. I attempted to explain this to him, but he became so wrought up that I was obliged to administer a dose of laudanum, to prevent his injuring himself further. For the moment, he has quieted."

"If we want to keep him here, we'll have to strap him to the bed," Cassandra said. After the racing accident he'd spent months immobilized, told he'd never walk again. Small wonder he'd reacted so forcefully to the surgeon's recommendation.

"What I would suggest—"

The door flew open. The Duke of Ashmont filled it, all sunlight hair and celestial blue eyes and big shoulders and too much of everything. He stepped into the private parlor, which seemed to shrink in consequence.

"They told me you were out of the sickroom," he said. "How's the jockey?"

ASHMONT HADN'T EXPECTED a warm welcome and he didn't get one. The lady folded her arms and looked at him, her face impassive, while the room's temperature sank several degrees.

"Two fractured ribs," she said before the surgeon could respond. "With complications."

He felt sick. He ignored it and said, "Ribs, yes. Tendency to go to pieces. But Greenslade here's wrapped him up good and tight, I daresay, and—"

"Mr. Greenslade, kindly step out of the room," she said. "I should like to have a word with the duke. In the meantime, I must ask you to look at my maid. Some lacerations. I cleaned them, but she needs a stitch or two, and she resisted my offer to do it."

The surgeon looked at him, eyebrows raised.

"Do as the lady says," Ashmont said. "If I need help, I'll scream."

Greenslade went out, closing the door behind him.

"Remember you now," Ashmont told her. "Camberley Place. You and Lady Alice and all the other little girls. The cousins."

Her expression remained as cold and blank as stone.

"You know, not sure you ought to be alone with me," Ashmont said. "As I recollect, it isn't done. Respectable lady. Infamous rakehell. That sort of thing. Maybe, for instance, we could adjourn to the courtyard, where I might get a running start. Or at least witnesses, in case of murder."

"Keeffe has a fever," she said.

"Ah."

"He is not to be moved. He is supposed to lie quietly in bed for a day, perhaps two or more, while we wait to see whether the fever worsens, and then, whether he survives."

"Not to be moved. He won't like that." He caught a flicker of surprise in the grey eyes before the Mask of Death came down again.

"No, he won't. He dislikes it to the point that the surgeon has had to dose him with laudanum. That won't quell Keeffe for long, and it ought not to be repeated often, in any event, where there is a possibility of lung infection. He would never have let himself be carried here had he not been in extreme pain. Now, his ribs secured, he'll be wild to get moving again. Even if he's in pain. Even if it threatens his recovery. He won't be reasonable."

"I'll speak to him," Ashmont said.

She stared at him.

"Man to man," he said. "I'll offer to break a few more ribs if he doesn't follow orders."

"Break a few—"

"Manly pride," Ashmont said. "No shame for him if I offer violence. I'm three times bigger and a duke. He can grumble then do what I give him no choice but to do."

He went out again.

She went after him.

ASHMONT HAD SOMETHING to do. He'd been waiting for it. He'd ordered an inn servant to keep watch for the surgeon.

The lady had told him to make himself useful. He was happy to. A piece of the amends he needed to make.

He should have known he wouldn't be allowed to get away easily.

He paused. "I won't hurt him. You needn't worry."

"If you do, I'll shoot you," she said. "One of the few enjoyable actions I can perform to universal approbation."

As though he'd lay violent hands on the little fellow. What kind of blackguard did she think he was?

Stupid question.

The more interesting one was whether she'd shoot him.

No, that one was easy, too. He'd seen her handle the runaway horses. From what he'd been able to make out, she'd kept as calm as any man—no, calmer than most—even when the reins broke. She'd taken a bad fall and not let out so much as a whimper. She'd hit him, and walked right over him, and then when he didn't get up quickly enough, she'd emptied a bucket of water on him.

Yes. She'd shoot him, and her hand would be as steady as that stony gaze of hers.

"I'm not going to hurt him," he said. "I'm only going to *look* like I'll do it."

She lifted the hard, grey gaze to his face. "Ordinarily, I wouldn't believe you capable of playing the ugly brute. At present, however, given your wrinkled and muddied splendor of dueling black, coupled with the bruises, dirt, and general air of not having bathed in a week, you appear fully qualified."

"That bad?" He bent his head and sniffed at himself. Well, more than a little sweaty, with overtones of spilled brandy. Grime and grass stains marred his "dueling black." He'd better send somebody for a toothbrush and tooth powder. "There you're wrong. Had a bath this morning." He ran his hand along his jaw. A trifle stubbly. "And a shave."

"Wanted to look your best when you sent your dear friend to eternity, did you?"

"How did you . . ." Another stupid question. It didn't take a giant brain to do this sum. All the world knew about Ripley and Olympia. Miss Pomfret knew Ashmont had fought a duel this morning. Who else would he have fought it with? "Thing is, it was an even chance he'd send me."

"You didn't kill him." Her voice was lower now. "If you had, I expect you'd be on your way to France by now."

He shook his head. "Nobody dead, no thanks to him."

"Any injuries? You didn't fall and hit your head on a rock, by any chance, and have a concussion?"

"You like to look for the silver lining, I see."

"Is Ripley all right?"

Ashmont truly did *not* want to talk about the duel. He'd fought half a dozen, but it had never been like this. The scene played over and over in his mind, an endless series of encores. If he didn't look out, he'd have nightmares.

He started down the corridor, and she went with him.

He touched the side of his head. "Trifling head wound. Skull too thick. Bullet bounced off, I reckon. Bled like a pig, though."

Any of a hundred well-bred maidens would have swooned at this.

"Scalp wounds do," she said. "You're both idiots, by the way."

"Olympia pointed that out."

"I cannot decide whether she had a narrow escape or jumped out of the pan into the flames."

"You do know how to lift a fellow's spirits."

"I don't care about your spirits," she said. "You came within ames ace of killing my dearest friend's brother. He's as worthless as you are, but Alice is unaccountably fond of him. Within hours of that piece of pointless behavior, you nearly killed three other people and two horses. My carriage is in pieces, and my father will never agree to replace it, because he hates my driving it. He'll wish now he'd thought to crash it himself. Thanks to you, I am obliged to remain here for I don't know how long with only my maid, who will never qualify as a proper chaperon. Even with a chaperon . . ." She trailed off and took a deep breath.

Out of the corner of his eye, he watched her bosom rise and fall. It wasn't easy. The enormous sleeves of her carriage dress mostly blocked the view, already half-hidden by lace and big lapels. Maybe the bosom was a degree fuller than he'd at first supposed?

Was she pretty? He wasn't sure. Though his head had cleared to a great extent, he still had a sense of moving in a fog.

She hadn't been a pretty child. Of that he was certain. He remembered vividly his time at Camberley Place. So many memories of the warm and welcoming old house. And the fishing house—possibly his favorite place in the world.

"One thing at a time," she said. "Keeffe first. It isn't manly pride. Not all of it. You need to understand."

"No, I don't. It's simple enough."

"It isn't what you think."

"I wasn't actually thinking."

"It's the accident at Newmarket," she said. "Months and months. All that time when he was told he'd never walk again."

Ashmont didn't need to hear this. He wasn't happy, and for the present, he couldn't cheer himself with drink or any kind of carousing. He had things to do. He needed a clear head. This was only the start. He knew that.

"He can't abide the idea of being immobile," she went on. "That's why—"

"It makes no matter," Ashmont said. "I'm not going to reason with him. I'm not going to *understand* him. I'm going to be a great bastard of a duke who tells him to do as he's told."

"Very well, do it your way," she said. "But it had better work. If he hurts himself—"

"It'll work." It had to. He had to clear the slate. Whatever else anybody said of the Duke of Ashmont—and that would fill volumes—he paid his debts, and generously. Always.

"If it doesn't, I'll shoot you," she said. "That won't solve anything, but it'll make me feel better."

CASSANDRA DIDN'T FIND her maid or the surgeon in the public dining room.

"He's in the coffee room, Miss Pomfret," a maidservant told her. "Don't know where she's got to."

Cassandra found Greenslade standing by a box compartment where sat an alarmed-looking Humphrey Morris, the third of the unpleasant Countess of Bartham's sons. That was to say, Morris didn't appear alarmed until he looked up and caught sight of Cassandra.

His alarm grew as he watched her approach. Coffee rooms, generally, were men's domains. Cassandra usually observed such proprieties, because men became hysterical when women trespassed, and that was tedious. Not to mention it was precisely the sort of thing gossips would use to smear her character and shred her reputation. Not that she had much of a reputation at present, or saw how it would survive this day's events. But one thing at a time.

"Ah, Miss Pomfret," the surgeon said. "I beg your pardon for putting you to the trouble of seeking me. I have been looking everywhere for your maid. It would appear that Mr. Morris was among the last to see her."

She looked at Morris, who hastily rose and slid from the seat and bowed, his face crimson.

"Didn't know who she was," he said. "Didn't see—you know—the crash—and Ashmont told me to hang about in case he needed me. I went out into the courtyard to find out if anybody heard where his pistol got to."

A dueling pistol, beyond a doubt. Morris must have been Ashmont's second this morning.

"The fellows reckoned one of them from the Green Man picked it up wherever Ashmont dropped it and took it inside for safekeeping. He left his hat as well, but that was only on the hook, and I got it back to him, along with the pistol case and the other weapon. I've been worried about the thing lying in the damp, or run over by a wagon. So I was thinking whether to send somebody to the Green Man when the coach came, and we all stopped to watch."

People invariably did. Crowds gathered at London's General Post Office to watch the night mail depart. Departing and arriving coaches always had an audience at the White Horse Cellars in Piccadilly as well, and at other London coaching inns. The entertainment was sometimes as good as a play. Even she enjoyed the sight of the night mail setting out. Any driver would appreciate the coachmen's expertise and flair. It was one of the things she'd missed about England.

"Saw the girl burst out of the office, waving her ticket," Morris said, reclaiming her attention. "Only an outside place left, but she took it. Climbed up and went. Last I saw was her ducking her head and holding her hat when they went out under the arch. Didn't know she was yours until Greenslade here asked me did I see a female in a drab green dress."

Cassandra gazed at him for a very long time while her mind digested this and ran through the implications. "Did you find the pistol?" she said.

"Not yet." He swallowed. "Sorry about your jockey, Miss Pomfret."

"Let me know when you find the pistol," she said. "I may need it."

Meanwhile

A SMALL DOSE of ducal dominance and a large dose of "You're worrying Miss Pomfret" worked better than the laudanum to settle Keeffe. In short order, a contingent of inn servants and local volunteers gently transferred him to a bedchamber. After the men left, Ashmont, who never apologized, except by way of coins and bank notes, apologized.

Looking embarrassed, Keeffe thanked him. "I'm not like to die, Your Grace. That quack got me wrapped up like one o' them Egypt mummies. You could drop me off the topmost gallery and onto the courtyard cobblestones and no damage done. The only thing could hurt me now is maybe if you was to shoot a cannonball straight at me, and then it might make a dent. If a pileup of racehorses couldn't do for me, a couple cracked ribs won't."

"Glad to hear it," Ashmont said. The man didn't look well. His face was drawn and his brown eyes were cloudy.

"Only thing worries me is my miss, and what's to become of her."

Ashmont took the chair by the bed. In spite of or maybe because of the laudanum, Keeffe wanted to talk. He was supposed to rest, but it seemed he wouldn't rest until he said what he had to.

Which made it Ashmont's job to listen.

He still couldn't see his way. He'd sobered, but the fog remained: Confusion; feelings that came and went; and scenes from long ago, mingled with recent ones, swirled in his head.

A somewhat overwrought Morris had told him about a to-do with some fellow named Owsley at a lecture and the rule Lord deGriffith made about one of Miss Pomfret's younger sisters as a result. Morris was privy to countless details, his mother being not only a notorious gossip but a friend of Lady deGriffith.

Keeffe had a view of the family even more intimate than Lady

Bartham's: Miss Pomfret loved her sisters dearly, and this business "cut her up something bad."

There was more, too, filling in Morris's gossipy sketch of Miss Pomfret: how her grandparents had taken over her upbringing. How her grandfather had found Keeffe, some two years or so after the accident, sweeping stables in Blackwater and the worse for drink.

"Those was bad days, Your Grace. But then his lordship hired me to look after his granddaughter. A bodyguard, he said, but discreet about it. And a tutor—me! But she was a strong-willed girl and he worried about her. He knew how I grew up, and he wanted me to teach her how to take care of herself. He trusted me with his granddaughter when nobody else would trust me with a horse. I was bad luck, you know."

Ashmont understood. The turf was rife with corruption, and Keeffe, who'd spent his childhood in the lowest dens of London, was famously incorruptible. His swift, unlikely rise to fame had made enemies eager to kick him when he was down.

"And me a cripple," the jockey went on. "What use was I anymore? But his lordship saw the use. She did, too. She never took no notice how lame I was. She listened—and oh, she has a sweet hand with the horses, Your Grace. You saw how she kept calm and steady. If the reins hadn't've broke, we'd've come through as easy as kiss your hand."

"I saw," Ashmont said. "You taught her well."

"It's easy when somebody wants to learn and is willing to work hard. I only wish I knew how to get her through this without harm. It's bad, you know, Your Grace. Not like if she was a man. Ladies got their reputations, more precious than them gold plates at the sweepstakes."

Ashmont knew all about ladies' reputations. Between his uncle and guardian, Lord Frederick Beckingham, and Blackwood's autocrat father, it was impossible not to know. The easiest solution was to steer clear of respectable women. The other sort were in plentiful supply.

"There's a rulebook for ladies a thousand pages thick, was it written down," Keeffe said. "And she breaks 'em. Lots of people got their knives out for her to begin with. Today—everything that happened—they'll twist it and blow it up so big none of us'll recognize it. And what's she to do? Run away back to Lord and Lady Chelsfield? Leave her family to face the jokes and insults? And all the while them knowing what's going on behind their backs is worse than what's said to their faces." Keeffe shook his head. "That's what worries me. I don't know how to mend it."

There was only one way. It hardly bore thinking of, but honor demanded Ashmont think it anyway.

"You see to mending yourself," he said. "You did it once. This is a trifle by comparison. Leave the rest to me."

The shrewd brown face cracked into a smile.

"I know what you're thinking," Ashmont said.

The Duke of Ashmont didn't mend things. He broke them. All the world believed it, and the world wasn't wrong.

Keeffe let out a short cackle, wincing as he did so. "With respect, Your Grace, I'll wager you don't."

CASSANDRA RETURNED TO the private dining parlor, ordered writing materials, and sent a note to Mrs. Nisbett, briefly explaining what had happened. A mangled tale would soon reach the lady if it hadn't already, and Cassandra didn't want her to worry. Word would reach London, too, but with any luck, her family wouldn't hear until tomorrow.

By tomorrow she'd be ruined.

"One thing at a time," she told herself.

She did not write to her parents. She still cherished a frail hope of salvaging the situation, or at least minimizing the damage, and didn't want to cause more upset than absolutely necessary.

She wanted strong drink. She ordered tea.

A servant brought it in wondrously short order, considering how many travelers came and went from the inn. The Dis-Graces effect?

When she'd left the coffee room earlier, a group of coach passengers swarmed in, claiming all the tables except the one where Humphrey Morris was sitting. That was Their Dis-Graces' place. When any of them were in the neighborhood, their chosen table was barred to other customers.

The three dukes were gods here. It didn't matter who or what Ripley, Blackwood, and Ashmont broke. It didn't matter what outrages they committed. They were dukes. They threw their money about. Money was their holy dispensation for all manner of bad behavior.

She shrugged. That was the way of the world—and hadn't she acted promptly to take advantage? Ashmont had barely to lift an eyebrow to get whatever he wanted, without argument or delay or any of the other obstacles she'd face without him.

She'd seen Keeffe transported to the White Lion more gently and in a fraction of the time it would have taken otherwise. All the inn had hurried to accommodate them. Other customers had to give up their private spaces because Ashmont required them. Having him about was like having a magic wand.

The door flew open.

Gods didn't knock, did they?

There he stood, with his sun-gold hair and sky-blue eyes, in all his bruised, dirty, and dim-witted glory, like some drunken Apollo who'd fallen out of his chariot.

Beautiful, godlike, and hopeless.

He was a great, tragic waste—of looks, position, everything.

Once upon a time . . .

Remember you now. Camberley Place. You and Lady Alice and all the other little girls. The cousins.

Yes, dozens of Pomfret and Ancaster cousins and their friends. She was only one little girl among many, while to her he'd been the sun and the moon and the stars.

She remembered too well, the scenes breaking out of the mental trunk in which she'd locked them years ago. They crowded into her mind, all the way to the first time, the night before he and the other boys left for school, when he'd pointed out the constellations.

The next time, a year later, she'd had a good look at him, in daylight. He'd miraculously appeared at one of the many bad moments of her youth, stepping out from the crowd of boys, so utterly unlike the others. He was a golden being, the most beautiful creature she'd ever seen: the fair, fair hair that curled in soft ringlets and the bluest eyes in all the world . . . and the face, too impossibly perfect. Like an angel's.

This angel had taken her side, bringing Blackwood and Ripley with him. He'd even fought a monster, which, in her child's view, made him a warrior angel joining her battle against the world's wrongs. Ever after, for years, in the face of contrary evidence, she'd believed he'd grow up into—what? Sir Galahad? The prince in the fairy tale?

Yes. She'd believed he would do great things.

She'd stopped believing, eventually. In time, she realized that the celestial creature she'd all but worshipped had existed only in her imagination. He'd never become what she wanted him to become.

She knew how to mend some kinds of damage. She knew how to help those to whom life had been unkind and unjust. But the Duke of Ashmont had traveled too far down the road of self-indulgence and self-destruction to be brought back. The amount of work he needed to turn into a semi-acceptable human being was far beyond her scope, practically beyond her imagining. An angel or a saint might tackle him. She was neither.

He was beyond help or hope, and the grown-up Cassandra Pomfret had more serious matters and more deserving persons to occupy her mind.

All she could do now was use him.

He stepped into the room and closed the door. "I have an idea," he said. "Marry me."

Chapter 3

Ashmont ducked. The teapot crashed against the door, exploding into chunks of blue and white.

Though he'd braced himself with brandy and soda, as one would for a duel, it wasn't enough to numb his reflexes. He'd seen the warning signs, and dodging missiles was second nature. At least she hadn't a pistol at hand.

He looked down at the shattered pieces of crockery and the tea puddle spreading at his feet. "I know it's sudden but—"

"Your bride bolted five days ago," she said. "Have you lost your mind?"

"She did. True enough. And if you would only—"

"You haven't lost your heart, that's certain."

"Here's the thing. From what I've heard, you need a husband. I was planning to have a wife. That didn't go well, but—"

"Didn't *go well*! She ran away. Do I strike you as less intelligent than Lady Olympia? Not that one wants above-average intelligence to recognize a bad bargain—and if *bad bargain* isn't the euphemism of the year, I don't know what is."

He wasn't used to explaining. He wasn't sure he knew how. That was something other people did. All the explanation he ever needed was coins. Bank notes. Charm, sometimes. Persuasion. But he hadn't time for persuading.

A misadventure was enlarging and worsening by the minute. No matter which way he turned it—this way, that way, right side up, and upside down—the consequences of this morning's events would be . . . very bad.

His reputation wasn't pretty. He'd done some things. A great many things, far from virtuous or well behaved. But he was a man and a duke and the only consequences he ever suffered were to his purse.

She wasn't a man and a duke, and she'd stepped on too many toes, annoyed too many people.

Lots of people got their knives out for her, Keeffe had said.

Like Ashmont, she shrugged off the gossip and naysayers. But a girl like that wouldn't shrug off trouble she brought to her family.

He didn't have a family. Thought he would. Starting with a wife. But no. Joke was on him. Ha ha.

He had Ripley, Blackwood, and a smooth-tongued busybody of an uncle.

Smooth. That was it. He needed to try to think like Uncle Fred.

"Why don't we send for another pot of tea," he said. "Or better yet, brandy and soda. And talk this over like sensible fellows."

"You couldn't be sensible if your life depended on it. I want to see Keeffe."

"Best not. He's sleeping. In a proper bed in a bedchamber."

Her eyes narrowed.

"I said the magical words," he said. "All I had to say was, 'You're worrying Miss Pomfret.' He quieted wonderfully. We talked. About horse races and such. Greenslade stopped in to look at him. Keeffe's feverish, but his mind never wandered, all the time until he fell asleep. Greenslade's sent for a nurse to look after him. Everything is in hand."

"I am perfectly capable of looking after my own groom. I know how to nurse. You have no idea how many sickbeds I've sat beside."

"Keeffe does, and he made a point of saying I wasn't to let you nurse him. He said you had enough to manage. If I were you—"

"Indeed. Exactly what I need. Advice from *you*."

She went to the window, which overlooked the courtyard, and

turned her back to him. She shook her head, and a pin slid out from her hair and caught in the embroidered white lacy thing that filled in the low neckline of her dress. The cloudy sky had darkened, but even in the parlor's gloom he could make out bits of twigs and grass in her hair, deepened to mahogany in the gloom.

If he tried to pick out the debris, something bad, possibly fatal, would happen to him. Of this he had no doubt.

"You don't know," she said. "You simply don't know."

He knew a few things now. The man he'd broken was more than a former champion jockey. Keeffe was her bodyguard and mentor and probably closer to her than any family member, except perhaps the sister who had Morris in palpitations.

Among other concerns, Ashmont knew that if he didn't act, her brothers would be fighting for the privilege of shooting him at thirty paces. He didn't want to fight her brothers, who'd never done him any harm. He didn't want to cause her family trouble. He was an arsehole. He knew this. All the same, even he had lines he didn't cross. Precious few, but there they were.

This morning he'd come sickeningly close to killing Ripley, two women, and one of England's greatest jockeys. Even now, it was even odds Keeffe would make it.

All of it done with the same pistol.

Nobody dead yet, but the consequences were sweeping down and piling up like an avalanche in the Alps.

"Tell me you've a better idea," he said. "I'm all ears."

Silence.

It went on for a while.

"I can hear you thinking," he said. "Nothing comes to mind, does it? So here's my idea—"

"Your ideas lead to people screaming and things exploding." She turned to him. "I was there, you know, the night you and your friends smuggled the goat into Almack's."

"You were there? Really?" At close quarters, he noticed the little black cravat she wore under the lacy collar. It must have come undone, and she'd made a bad job of refastening it, because it was crooked. The collar was wrinkled and the lacy something-like-a-shirt it was attached to was smudged with dirt. One of the belt buckle prongs had torn a large hole in the silk belt or ribbon or sash or whatever it was. His hands itched—to right matters or make them worse, he wasn't sure. It was distracting; that much he knew.

"It was my first Season and my first Almack's ball," she said. "I'd heard stories. After that personal experience of your gift for chaos, I stopped dismissing them as exaggerations. When it comes to you and your accomplices, the papers don't need to exaggerate. They can't. It's impossible to claim anything more outrageous than what you actually do."

"Which is why this will work. I'm outrageous. You're outrageous."

She stared at him. "I? Like *you*? You're not yet nine and twenty. You've had every advantage: power, rank, money, looks, not to mention your gender. What have you done with them? What have you accomplished, besides dissipation and destruction? All I did was cross your path unwittingly, and now everybody I care about is in trouble, and the man who helped me keep my sanity is likely to die."

She brushed past him, yanked the door open, and stalked out, slamming it behind her.

He stood for a moment, debating: persevere or give her temper time to quiet?

He'd waited too long five days ago and let a promising future get away.

He went after her.

FEELING HEMMED IN on all sides, Cassandra strode along the gallery. The air was oppressive, the clouds auguring a storm. Dust rose from the courtyard below, where another coach was on its way out. Still, she was outside. She was not in a small room with the Duke of Ashmont. She could breathe properly. Think properly.

Almack's. She had to bring that up—as though he'd remember her. He hadn't remembered her then, when she stood in front of him, resplendent in a grown-up, blue striped satin dress, and long-ing to dance.

And he . . .

She couldn't remember what he wore. She'd been bedazzled. She and Alice, eighteen years old, with three years' Continental school-ing and travels behind them, were vastly more sophisticated than any other debutantes. All the same, Cassandra reeled when she came face-to-face with him again.

She saw him, some sort of glittering deity, approach to pay his re-spects to Aunt Julia. Cassandra was standing next to her. She could hear her aunt's voice, so clearly: "Ashmont, you will remember my niece, Cassandra Pomfret, I'm sure."

And he, obviously not knowing Cassandra from Adam, bestowed upon her a smile that could melt rocks and glaciers, let alone ado-lescent girls, and said, "How could I forget? Miss Pomfret, your servant."

A graceful bow, a moment of chitchat with Aunt Julia, then he was gone, disappearing into the crowd and leaving Cassandra so dizzy that the crushing disappointment took some time to settle in.

Minutes later, women began to scream. Turning that way, she saw Lady Thurlow standing stock-still, shrieking, while a goat nib-bled on one of the satin roses at the hem of her dress.

Under the balcony, where the band had abruptly stopped playing, the three dukes were doubled up, howling with laughter.

Pandemonium. Attendants running to corral the goat. Women running out of the ballroom. Lady Jersey marching across the room, two other patronesses in her wake.

Aunt Julia shaking her head.

Alice and Cassandra looking at each other.

"It would seem they have not matured during our absence," Alice said.

"Not in the least." But what had Cassandra expected, after all the stories she'd heard? Had anybody detected the smallest hint of maturity previously?

"Got it in with a hoist, I expect," Alice said.

It was the way boys sneaked girls into their rooms at university. The trio had been the talk of Eton before they were dukes, then the talk of Oxford. Now London.

"I should have known," Cassandra said.

"You wanted to dance with him."

Cassandra could hardly deny it to her best friend, who knew *everything*. "One dance, Alice." One, that was all. She loved to dance. Men rarely asked her. She wasn't comfortable company. She'd been speaking her mind since she was a child. Not a popular quality, in children or in debutantes. But he—bold and reckless, caring nothing for others' opinions—he wouldn't be afraid of her.

"They never ask respectable girls. Too complicated, Ripley says."

"Complicated! It's one dance!"

"One dance too many. You're not a courtesan or a merry widow. That's all they need to know. Did you fail to notice that none of them asked me, either?"

It was not at all fair. She and Alice were *interesting*. "It's stupid."

"It's for the best. No happy endings with those three."

"He has *everything*—looks, money, rank. What is *wrong* with him?"

"He's drunk, for one thing. For another, he's an idiot. A gorgeous idiot, I grant you."

"Gorgeous, yes. Oh, Alice, that smile of his—"

"Could launch a thousand ruinations."

They'd laughed, and Cassandra had told herself to stop hoping he'd change. The unruly boy she'd heard so many wild tales about had only become the unruly adult she heard so many wild tales about. All the same, it took another two years' worth of Ashmont Incidents to bring her to her senses at last.

Today he'd dragged her into one of his Incidents, and she would be the one to pay. She and her family.

Your behavior reflects . . . on all of us.

She'd traveled out of London without a chaperon and outriders. People would say she'd asked for trouble. They'd say her father, one of Parliament's leading members, charged with making law for the country, couldn't control his own daughter.

She could see the satirical prints: Lord deGriffith's face on a bull wearing a nose ring, with Cassandra leading him. Her father pulling a cart, with Cassandra cracking a whip over him.

That was only the beginning of her family's humiliation. Within days an accidental encounter with the Duke of Ashmont would be distorted into an assignation. An orgy, for all she knew. They'd have her rolling drunkenly in the heath with him.

Her face was on fire.

Marry me.

There was a sure path to heartbreak and misery.

Misery he'd already brought. If the fever worsened and Keeffe didn't survive—

"Miss Pomfret."

The low voice seemed to promise everything. Like the face. So much physical beauty on the outside. So little of value within.

She didn't pause. "Go to the devil."

"I realize you're overwrought—"

"Overwrought?" She stopped and turned to face him. "Your drunken recklessness injured, perhaps fatally, a devoted employee. You've terrified a less devoted one into fleeing on the first coach that had room for her. You've destroyed my carriage. You've set off one of your exciting explosions, whose innocent bystanders, this time, are members of my family. Yes, indeed, I'm an overwrought female—because there's no cause here, is there, for me to be at all agitated."

As she spoke, she stalked nearer, until they were practically nose to nose. "I do beg your pardon, duke, for my *excessive*"—she poked him in the chest, wishing it was the barrel of a pistol, rather than her finger—"reaction"—another, harder, poke—"to these *trivial* matters." One last, hard poke. "Stay away from me." She turned to continue her not-very-calming walk along the gallery.

She was distantly aware of movement below, as people came out of the inn to watch. She didn't care. The day was bound to worsen. How could it not?

"Miss Pomfret, I wish you would give me a minute. A minute only."

She kept on walking.

"Would you stop?" He tried to take hold of her arm.

While not new, her dress was French, and fashionable, with enormous sleeves. His big hand sank into the folds of fabric and crushed the puff supporting the balloon-like structure.

She whipped about, acting instinctively. Not a poke in the chest this time, but a shove, the kind she'd learnt from Keeffe, her body balanced to give her maximum leverage.

The gallery was narrow, the rail low, and the duke had his back to it. He let go of her sleeve to grab the nearest baluster, but not quickly enough to stop him from going over, more easily than she could have supposed.

AT THE LAST instant, Ashmont managed to grab the post.

He hung there for a time, his knees over the balustrade's rail, one arm about the post.

Had he been a less fit man, he'd be on the cobblestones below by now.

But he boxed, fenced, and rode. He walked more often and greater distances than other men of his class. He liked testing his strength. He liked fighting. And while he might be idle in some senses, he was, possibly, all too active in others.

Still, he'd had a sleepless night before the duel and more brandy and soda than was good for him after it. He'd eaten, but not much, his stomach not being up to it.

Not at his best, in other words.

And so he hung there uncertainly for a short time, while gawkers gathered below and while he listened to Miss Pomfret's footsteps, firmly going away, not toward him to help. Her footsteps stopped, a door slammed shut, and a latch clicked into place.

Very well. Not a ministering angel, then. Not to him, at any rate.

He would have laughed, but he needed the breath to keep his balance, then pull himself up and back onto the gallery. This took two attempts, while the audience grew, people hurrying out from the inn to stare. A few male voices offered encouragement while others mocked him.

When at last he was safely upright, he wiped his hands and bowed. The onlookers applauded and laughed.

"MARRY HER?" MORRIS said, eyes threatening to pop from their sockets. "Did you shoot the pistol off close to your head, by any chance? Went deaf for a bit? Smoke got in your eyes?"

Having decided to recruit his strength before tangling with Miss Pomfret again, Ashmont had returned to the coffee room. He'd scarcely sat down before a waiter appeared to take his order. A moment after the waiter left, a fresh group of travelers entered, along with some of the courtyard loungers, Morris among them.

Ashmont didn't mind the hubbub or Morris's talking. He lacked Ripley's and Blackwood's wit, true. However, what Ashmont needed at this point wasn't wit but information, as much as he could get—and Morris was a walking, talking *Debrett's Peerage* and encyclopedia of gossip. He was like his dragon mother in that regard. Happily, this was their only point of resemblance.

"Do you take me for the sort who'd marry a milk-and-water miss?" he said. Had Ripley married that sort of girl? Had Blackwood? Not even slightly.

"There's milk and water, and then there's girls who push you off a gallery," Morris said. "I thought sure I was going to see you lying at my feet, your brains all over the courtyard."

Ashmont shrugged. "I've been knocked about worse."

Morris sat back and gazed at him.

"Don't know what you're fretting about," Ashmont said. "You fancy her sister. You won't have a chance of getting near her if Miss Pomfret doesn't marry. Considering how afraid of her everybody seems to be, what do you reckon the odds of that happening soon? If I were you, I'd be cheering me on. I'd be saying, 'You lucky dog, Ashmont. Your bride bolts, and not a week later, another one, even better, practically falls in your lap.'"

"No, no, no, no, no." Morris shook his head with each *no.* "Not to bring up painful memories, but—" He held up his spoon. "Lady Olympia." With the other hand, he held up his knife. "Miss Pomfret. Different kettle of fish altogether."

Ashmont held up a fork. "Me."

Morris reddened.

Ashmont watched this with amusement. He couldn't remember when last he'd blushed.

"If you'd fallen onto your head, I could blame it on a concussion," Morris said. "Anything else happen when I wasn't looking? Surgeon drilled a hole in your skull, perchance?"

"I like a lively girl," Ashmont said.

This was absolutely true. If he'd had any qualms about marrying a young lady he knew almost nothing about and whose existence he'd forgotten until this day, these had dwindled to nil under her ungentle attentions.

"She got thrown out of a carriage," he went on. "Did she lie there, moaning and groaning and waiting for help? No. First thing she does, she sits up and knocks me over with her hat. Then, I'm lying on the ground, only wanting to be let be for a minute or two, so I don't cast up my accounts. She throws a bucket of water on me and makes me do this and that and march a mile with her, while she fusses over her tiger. I ask her to marry me and she throws a teapot at me."

Morris closed his eyes. "Yes. Charming."

"Then, I make a lunatic move, and try to lay hands on her—and she knocks me back over a gallery rail and leaves me dangling."

Ashmont laughed at the recollection. Whatever else Miss Pomfret did, she wouldn't run away.

He'd bungled this. Should've known better. Would've known better, maybe, had he not endured the harrowing night before and the meeting at dawn. Remembering that still made him queasy.

He turned his mind elsewhere.

"Remember when you asked didn't I know her?" he said. "I did, but it was a long time ago. I was still at school. It was during the long holiday."

Morris's despairing expression sharpened into interest. He sensed a story in the offing, one more to add to his vast mental library.

"That was where you and Blackwood and Ripley met, I know," he said. "Eton."

The three dukes' sons had instantly become fast friends. So much in common.

"This was early in the autumn, shortly before we were to return to school," Ashmont said. "Camberley Place. I was fourteen."

Morris set down the cutlery and settled back to listen.

ASHMONT SAW IT clearly in his mind's eye, the way he recalled most of his time at Ripley's uncle's home in Surrey. Not having much of a home to go back to, Ashmont was thrilled to be invited once more for a long holiday visit.

He was the Earl of Selston then, Ripley was the Earl of Kilham, and Blackwood was the Marquess of Rossmore. These courtesy titles eventually ended up among all the other lesser titles they inherited with their dukedoms—Ashmont first, then Blackwood, then Ripley—all while they were still at school.

Near the end of his visit Lady Charles organized a party for her numerous young relatives and their friends. Mainly the boys went their way and the girls went theirs. But at one point, he and his two friends heard shouting and laughter coming from the area set up for the girls' relay races.

Curious, the three friends sauntered over, to find Godfrey Wills and his company of arse-kissers teasing a little redheaded girl. The elfin creature seemed vaguely familiar, although Ashmont couldn't place her.

"Stick insect, can't you go faster?" Wills screeched. Then it was, "Faster, faster, Freckle Stick!"

The girl was thin, and no beauty, but hardly freckled, as far as Ashmont could see. Still, Wills's cronies took up the taunt, shouting, "Run, run, Freckle Stick!" and the like, and laughing fit to bust a gut at how witty they were.

"Bullying little bastard," Ashmont said. "I'd like to take a stick to him."

"You don't know Cassandra Pomfret," Ripley said. "Wait."

They waited.

Even after the races, Wills wouldn't stop plaguing her. In the manner of a stick insect he crept after her while his friends egged him on.

It wasn't fair, picking on a girl, and Ashmont was practically dancing with impatience to take Wills apart, when at last she came to a place where the crowd of children was thickest. She stopped suddenly and turned to face Wills. He grinned, expecting her to beg him to stop, the way smaller children did when he bullied them.

She put her hands, palms down, under her chin, fluttered her eyelashes, and said, pitching her voice high and loud, "Oh, Godfrey, you're always following me. I know you can't help loving me, and I'm truly sorry. But alas, I cannot return your love."

It was so unexpected and so apt, Ashmont let out a whoop. An instant later, others did, too.

Wills's face turned bright pink.

Then Ashmont couldn't resist. "Oh, Godfrey," he called, his voice pitched high, like a girl's. "Poor Godfrey's in lo-o-o-ve."

Boys and girls, all laughing then.

Ripley moved to Ashmont's side, put his hand on Ashmont's shoulder, and made a pretend sad face, saying, "But she doesn't want you, Wills. How tragic."

Blackwood said, "Unrequited love. I could weep for you, Wills, old man."

Wills was the target now, even his friends mocking him. He turned as red as a boiled lobster. "Stow that!" he said.

"Maybe you could try getting down on your knees and begging her to love you," Ripley said.

"Yes, do," Ashmont said. "Down on your knees, Wills, and beg the lady's favor and forgiveness."

That was when Wills invited Ashmont to get on *his* knees and perform an act that wasn't to be thought of, let alone mentioned in mixed company.

Ashmont remembered the burst of joy he'd felt then. He'd waited, and here was his reward. He'd said, "Yes? Would you like to try and make me?"

What a splendid fight that had been! Wills so much bigger, who thought he could make short work of puny Lord Selston—for Ashmont hadn't finished growing yet.

He came back from the past to meet Morris's puzzled gaze.

Ashmont touched the corner of his eye, where it was bruised. "Wills gave me a black eye that day, but that's nothing to what I gave him. Don't remember when I've had so much fun. Well worth the whipping afterward, courtesy Uncle Fred."

There was a short silence, then, "Ashmont, she makes men cry," Morris said. "Grown men. Seen it with my own eyes."

"Don't fret about me, lad," Ashmont said. "I can look after myself."

The storm broke then, finally. Having darkened to ebony, the elephant clouds dissolved into torrents that turned the world dark, outside and, until the lamps were lit, inside as well. The courtyard emptied.

For a time the two men simply watched the rain pound the cobblestones, sending up waterspouts that splashed against the windows. Ashmont caught a distant flash out of the corner of his eye. Shortly thereafter came the crack of thunder. Through the glass he could hear, though faintly, horses whinnying in alarm and dogs barking.

He remembered the ugly lout, a few days ago, in this same court-yard, raging about a dog he claimed Ripley had stolen. He'd said other things as well, and Ashmont had felt compelled to teach him some manners.

The black eye had happened afterward, but how was a question. Ashmont had done some drinking. Fallen down some stairs.

He frowned.

"Second thoughts, I hope," Morris said.

Ashmont touched the bruise again, the one at the corner of his eye. Looking as he did, he wasn't going to make much progress with a lady. He sniffed at his coat. Didn't smell so pretty, either, as she'd pointed out.

"I need a bath and my clothes cleaned," Ashmont said. "Can't court properly in this state."

Morris rolled his eyes.

"Didn't bring a change of clothes," Ashmont said. "Expected to be back in London by now."

"You can be back in London in an hour or less, as soon as the rain lets up. I recommend it."

"Doesn't have the look of stopping anytime soon. Might as well get a room, and quickly. Nobody here's going anywhere for a while."

Nobody but the mail and stage, and maybe an express.

A waiter hurried in. "Begging Your Grace's pardon," he said, "but the lady's gone out to get Mr. Greenslade."

"In a rainstorm?"

"Didn't want to send anybody else out in this weather. Her groom's fever has worsened. My master and mistress tried, both of them, but nobody could stop her. They said to tell Your Grace."

By the time Ashmont caught up with her, at Greenslade's surgery, Miss Pomfret was drenched. She'd had sense enough to take an umbrella, but the wind had made short work of that. Her carriage dress was stuck to her undergarments and the giant sleeves had deflated a great deal, the wadding soaked through. She was obviously wet to the skin, which meant that her clothing weighed several times what it did normally.

A debate ensued, but she was too tired to put up much of a fight. At both Ashmont's and the surgeon's urging, they drove back to the inn in Greenslade's hooded carriage.

Ashmont ordered a fire made up in one of the best bedrooms, and tried to get her to dry off there, but she wouldn't cooperate.

"If he dies, I shall be there," she said. "If he lives, I shall be there. I shall be with him throughout, whatever happens. I must.

Greenslade seems a competent bonesetter, but I've had more experience of fevers than he can dream of. Furthermore, I know Keeffe."

She had only gone for the surgeon because she knew the patient must be bled, and that, she admitted, ought not to be trusted to inexperienced hands. "Leeches I can manage," she said. "But this is not a case for leeches."

And so she let Greenslade take some blood, then sent him on his way. She stayed in the sickroom, keeping watch over Keeffe, and now and again ordering this and that.

While she harassed the surgeon and inn servants, Ashmont sent two messages express to London, one to his valet and one to Lord Frederick Beckingham.

Uncle Fred was a great pain in the arse, and Ashmont would as soon consult with the devil. But he seemed to be out of his depth, Morris wasn't helpful, and the men Ashmont would have turned to normally were not available. Ripley was enjoying his purloined wedded bliss and Blackwood wasn't speaking to Ashmont.

Lord Frederick was a wily old courtier.

True, he might have washed his hands of his troublesome nephew, and Ashmont would have to fend for himself.

In any case, given the miserable weather, one might expect a good wait for a reply, if any came.

But the storm wouldn't last forever, and the messenger was handsomely paid to endure it. At worst, Sommers, the valet, would come, bringing a change of clothes and all else needful to make Ashmont presentable.

Miss Pomfret, in a soaked dress stuck to her undergarments, appeared in his mind's eye. As soon as the storm abated a degree, he sent one of the maidservants out to a local dressmaker for fresh clothing. At his sister's urging, Ripley had done Mrs. Thorne a great favor at one time, and she, like so many in the area, would drop everything to assist Their Dis-Graces.

Ashmont also claimed additional bedchambers, for himself and Morris.

After making sure somebody brought her something to eat,

Ashmont adjourned to his bedchamber, wrestled himself out of his coat, and hung it on a chair to dry. He washed his face and combed his hair. He lay down, intending only to rest, but fell instantly asleep.

CASSANDRA MUST HAVE dozed, because she woke abruptly to Keeffe's muttering.

"All right," he said. "Gently, there, my girls. Gently."

"That's right," Cassandra said softly. "Gently now."

"Good girls. You did right, miss. Did you see her? Never turned a hair, did she? Gently, gently. Another minute and not even that, and they'd've quieted. The reins. Not your fault. Reins broke. It happens sometimes. Even the best. The horses?"

"They're well," she said. "Rest now."

"Where'd he go?"

"The duke?"

"He was here. Did he tell you? Amphion. Oh, he was a one, wasn't he? Come along once in a lifetime, if you're lucky. I was lucky. Unlucky. Don't know which."

Amphion was the horse he'd ridden on the fateful day. The great racehorse had survived, though. Not to race again, but he'd been well tended and put to stud. The thoroughbred had fared better by far than Keeffe.

"You were lucky," she said. "You rode that splendid creature."

"Aye, he was a one, wasn't he? Something wild, you know. Tricky, too. Full of the devil. You couldn't look away even to blink your eye. But how he could run. Loved to run. I told him. Said they was one of a kind. He laughed. He said he wasn't that quick. I said, 'You'll do, but mind your paces.'"

He quieted, but remained feverish.

She waited.

Chapter 4

The day wore on, the storm continuing—now intense, now seeming to drop back, like a racer gathering power for the next length. Keeffe slept fitfully, but without stirring much. When he did, muttering incomprehensibly, he seemed to be dreaming rather than delirious.

Cassandra felt as though she were in a delirium.

The past crowded her mind: The night she'd looked up and seen the heavens filled with stardust, and Ashmont had shown her the mythical beings who lived there. The day she'd faced a bully and Ashmont had turned the tide in her favor. All the times thereafter when she'd been invisible to him, one among dozens. Almack's, when she'd finally begun the rather long process of giving up the fantasy.

Then, oh, as recently as last month, when she'd learnt he was to be wed to Lady Olympia Hightower, and wondered if he'd changed, because Lady Olympia, to her knowledge, was a sensible and intelligent young woman.

Alice had cleared that up, in her letter.

You ask if he's suddenly reformed. So far as I know, he's only grown worse, but that isn't what he shows her or her family. She saved his life, and got his attention that way. I

*hope he cares for her, truly, but I suspect he's only trying
to get the marrying over with, now that Blackwood's done
it. There she was, right at hand—pretty, good family, vir-
gin, but not boring. She spared his having to go out in the
normal way and find a bride. Horrible thing to say, but I'm
horrible, as you know.*

*Still, Ashmont may come to love her. She deserves to
be loved, in my opinion. As to her feelings, I can't say absolutely. Let us bear in mind, however, that her father's
debts are nothing to sneeze at and the family is large, like
yours, and also overburdened with boys. Self-sacrifice? I
wish women wouldn't do such things, yet I understand the
compulsion to protect those nearest and dearest. (I trust
it's understood I except Blackwood? He needs nobody's
protection.) Only think, if Lady Olympia proves a difficult
wife, who better deserves difficulties than Ashmont?*

Cassandra had laughed at this conclusion, though other parts
of the letter troubled her. Mainly the parts relating to Alice and
Blackwood. As to Ashmont, five or six years ago she might have
grieved for something lost. But whatever she'd lost had been gone
long before she admitted it. She'd loved a boy, then an illusion.
The boy no longer existed. The illusion had crumbled under the
weight of evidence.

She had only wished his marriage would not go so badly awry as
Alice's had done. Though she didn't know Lady Olympia very well,
what little she knew she liked. She'd hoped Ashmont would treat her
kindly.

But none of that signified now. He'd behaved stupidly, as usual,
and Lady Olympia had decided not to risk it, after all. The man
had been blind drunk at his own wedding. Cassandra shook her
head. He was simply incapable of doing the right thing, even on his
wedding day.

At some point—time meant nothing at present—a maidservant
entered, bearing a tray of tea and sandwiches that Cassandra hadn't

asked for. She shook off the past, to discover that she was hungry. She'd be no good to Keeffe in a weak and famished state.

She found she was shivering as well. Her clothes. Her overnight case. She'd planned to return to London after a few hours' visit. But Gosney had packed a small travel case, anticipating mishaps on the road. She'd borne a few.

She didn't approve of her mistress's manner of travel, and she'd seen little value in journeys to foreign parts. Still, she'd lasted longer than previous lady's maids. She did try to prepare for every eventuality. She couldn't have foreseen this, poor girl.

Cassandra explained to the servant about the case, which might still be with the damaged carriage. Otherwise it was on Putney Heath, covered in mud by now. Fixed on Keeffe, she'd given it no thought whatsoever.

"We'll find it," the maid assured her. "But meanwhile, I'll tell my mistress, and we'll see what we might have for you to wear." She shook her head over Cassandra's still damp, wrinkled, and dirt-spattered dress. "That won't do. You'll catch your death, Miss Pomfret."

No, it wouldn't do. When the maid left, Cassandra moved to a chair nearer to the fire Ashmont had insisted upon, and fortified herself. The day—and the coming night—promised to be long.

MORRIS WOKE ASHMONT to tell him Sommers had arrived—in a post chaise, of all things! He brought with him no valises, not even an overnight case.

The valet confirmed this when he entered empty-handed.

"What?" Ashmont swung his long legs over the side of the bed.

"I do beg Your Grace's pardon," Sommers said. "I pray this explains."

He took out from the pocket of his tailcoat a piece of writing paper bearing a familiar seal and gave it to Ashmont.

He broke the seal and unfolded the paper.

In Lord Frederick Beckingham's clear, decisive hand the duke read the following:

You were never there.

Pay whatever is necessary.

I've written to Lady Charles.

Leave as soon as you can, and take Bartham's boy with you.

Come directly to me.

*If you truly want to help the girl, for once in your life,
do as I say.*

If you don't truly want to help her, I wash my hands of you.

Ashmont stared at the single sheet of paper.

No greeting. No closing. No signature. Nothing else.

He turned it over, as though expecting invisible ink to suddenly become visible, in a language he could understand.

He looked up from the note to the two men standing in the bed-chamber.

Morris was all curiosity. Sommers wore a pained expression.

"Sommers, did I not tell you, plain as plain, what I wanted?"

"Indeed Your Grace did, and it grieves me to see Your Grace in this—this—" Sommers shook his head. He waved a hand, taking in Ashmont's stubbly jaw, the coat hanging crookedly on the chair, the wrinkled neckcloth, shirt, and trousers. The manservant's eyes glistened, boding tears.

Sommers was a brilliant valet. He took his work perhaps a trifle too seriously.

"No weeping," Ashmont said.

"No, Your Grace. But it's most vexing."

"I agree."

"His lordship your uncle sent for me, Your Grace, or else I should have been here an hour ago or more."

"He told you to bring me nothing. He told you to hire a post chaise."

"Yes, Your Grace. He'd already ordered it. The vehicle arrived while I was at Beckingham House. I had barely time to catch my breath before his lordship sent me on my way."

"Dammit, Sommers."

"Indeed, Your Grace. It is most distressing."

Ashmont read the note again. He walked to the fire. The faint glow told him nothing.

He walked to the window, which looked out onto the gallery, as did those of the other rooms in this part of the inn. Each had a door as well, opening onto the gallery. Where she'd left him hanging.

The rain still came down, less fiercely at the moment.

He opened the door and stepped out into the gallery. The courtyard was deserted.

You were never there.

The narrow walkway offered poor shelter from the downpour. The capricious wind blew the rain this way and that across the courtyard's open space while Ashmont mentally turned the message this way and that, cursing his uncle.

He wished Blackwood were here. Ripley, too, confound them both. They were better at riddles.

A small closed carriage rattled into the courtyard.

A footman climbed down from the back, opened an umbrella, let down the step, and opened the door. A lady stepped out into the umbrella's shelter and hurried into the inn, a female servant close behind her.

Distantly Ashmont wondered what would bring a private carriage out in this weather, so late in the day.

But the main part of his mind wrestled with the message. He read it again and again. It took a while, but at last he understood, as he should have done instantly. There it was, as plain as the horses being led away to the stables.

Pay whatever is necessary.

Money—enough of it, and he surely had enough—performed magic and miracles. He still wasn't clear about what this would accomplish, but his annoying uncle, no doubt, would explain.

To Cassandra's consternation, Mrs. Nisbett arrived with her maid.

She was in poor health, and she'd come out in the storm, in spite of Cassandra's written assurances that all was in hand.

"You can hardly pass the night in a public hostelry unchaperoned," the former governess said. "I am not so frail as to be unable to lend you countenance at least, until Keeffe is well enough to travel."

Though Cassandra knew her reputation couldn't possibly survive the day's events, she was glad to have the company of a sensible lady.

Matters seemed to be improving somewhat.

The nurse had turned out to be not only sober but also more competent than average. With Mrs. Nisbett here, Cassandra might leave Keeffe in trustworthy hands from time to time and take some rest.

She took the time not long after her governess arrived, and went to a room the innkeeper's wife had made ready for her. There she found a lady's walking dress, in a deep purple, and all the necessary undergarments. She wasn't sure the color suited her, and it wasn't a perfect fit by any means, but it would do well enough until one of the maids could thoroughly dry her own clothing and make it relatively presentable.

This was more than one could say of the contents of her overnight case, which had been trampled, run over, and rained on.

The purple dress showed no signs of wear, likewise the undergarments. Both were of good quality. Perhaps a traveler, pressed for time, had left the clothing behind and failed to claim it? She told herself this wasn't her worry. Her concern was looking after Keeffe, a task she couldn't perform if she developed a lung fever. She'd asked for dry clothing. Someone had found it for her. That was all she needed to know.

She summoned a maidservant, stripped, and washed. With the maid's help, she dressed.

She felt no qualms about her demands on the innkeeper and servants. She knew Ashmont's influence was at work here. He'd pay for everything, and pay more than amply, out of his pocket change, no doubt. It was a pity he couldn't pay to make this whole ghastly day vanish.

As the long summer afternoon faded, the storm dwindled to drizzling rain. She was sitting in the sickroom, she and Mrs. Nisbett by the fire, talking in low voices, when Keeffe called for her.

She went to the bed and felt his forehead. It seemed not so hot as before.

"No, no, I'll do," he said, gently pushing her hand away. "What a fuss over nothing. I do wonder at you, I do, fretting over a couple broken bones."

"You have a fever," she said.

"Had 'em before. Get 'em easy. Always did."

"The surgeon said it was pneu—"

"What he don't know would fill one of them encyclopeeders."

Mrs. Nisbett came to stand beside her. "Back to his ornery self, I see."

"You," he said. "What'd you let my miss fret for? Whyn't you send her to bed? She got thrown out a carriage, you know."

"Ladies' garments are thickly padded," Cassandra said, "as you well know." In his heyday, Tom Keeffe had quite the reputation with women. "I bounced a few times, but found my feet soon enough."

He laughed.

"Don't laugh," she said. "You'll hurt yourself."

"Not likely, miss. Like I tole His Grace . . ." He frowned. "Where'd he get to? We was talking. And do you know, miss, he ain't"—the former governess glared at him—"*isn't* half bad, once you get to know him some."

Marry me.

Cassandra's face was warm, and well it might be, with indignation. His wedding plans were hardly cold in their grave, and he was trying to snare another bride. When he sobered, he'd come to his senses, or as close to that state as he ever came, and celebrate the narrow escape with a tub of champagne.

She became aware of Mrs. Nisbett's considering regard.

"The world knows the Duke of Ashmont more than *some*," Cassandra said crisply. "And he's more than half bad."

"I need to tell him something," Keeffe said.

"You need to rest."

"I need to tell him something now. Before I forget. Before you dose me with laudanum again and it goes up in dreams."

"Keeffe."

"You might at least heed a dyin' man's last wish."

"You're not dying."

"I might, you aggravate me enough, 'n' work me up into a killing fever."

She looked at Mrs. Nisbett.

"I daresay he'll live," the older lady said. "But we might as well send for the duke. He'll want to know how the patient is faring."

Cassandra rang. A maidservant came.

"Be so good as to send the duke to us," Cassandra said.

The girl's brow wrinkled. "The duke, Miss Pomfret? What duke?"

IT WAS A fine joke, actually.

One of Ashmont's better pranks, though, if all went well, nobody would know it was a prank.

It was easier than some, certainly. Enough villagers had done well by the three dukes to return their generosity with ample goodwill. When Ashmont told the innkeeper and his wife, "I wasn't here," they only looked at each other briefly, then nodded.

"I'll leave it to you to pass the word," he told them. "And any coin necessary to encourage people not to have seen me. Oh, and we'd better not forget my pistol. When found, it's to be discreetly delivered to me in London, with a reward to be collected then. And if you'd be so kind, the same message to be communicated to the Green Man."

Given the sum he proffered, his hosts would be so kind to their worst enemy.

He left it to them to carry out his wishes. People hereabouts would assume it was one of his pranks, and more than a few men—and women—had acted as co-conspirators at one time or another.

Having done all he could to arrange Miss Pomfret's comfort

and peace of mind, though little she knew it, he hired a post chaise larger than the cramped, two-passenger one his valet had traveled in, and he, Morris, and Sommers set out for London shortly before sunset.

London

LORD FREDERICK BECKINGHAM knew about the duel this morning.

His lordship knew everything worth knowing, and more, about everybody, and most especially about His Dis-Grace the Duke of Ashmont.

As much as his lordship would like to close his eyes and stop his ears in this regard, he had a duty, which he'd never shirked.

Following the deaths, in quick succession, of a brother at Waterloo, then a wife in childbed with their stillborn daughter, the previous Duke of Ashmont had sunk into a melancholia from which he never recovered. He neglected everything, including his young son.

As a result, Lord Frederick, who had no boys of his own, had taken over the present duke's upbringing. Whether this was for good or ill, it was impossible to say. Even the best of parents and guardians might obtain unsatisfactory results, while the worst produce heroes and prodigies.

Now he looked at the last, best hope of the Beckinghams and swallowed a sigh.

A dirty, disheveled, bruised, and unshaven Ashmont paced the drawing room. His friend had been allotted a room where he might refresh himself after the journey, not to mention the long, arduous day of trying to keep Ashmont from getting himself killed, thankless task though that was.

Lord Frederick had ordered a meal sent to Humphrey Morris, and a bottle of good wine. For the time being, he was out of trouble and couldn't wag his busy tongue at anybody.

The valet had been sent on to Ashmont House, to prepare for his master's return.

"She's a fine girl, Uncle," Ashmont was saying. "A deuced fine girl."

He related a contretemps in the first floor gallery of the White Lion Inn, and Lord Frederick resisted the urge to sit down with his head in his hands and sob.

"Had you fallen," he said calmly, "you almost certainly would have died. And who would that leave us with?"

"You," Ashmont said.

Lord Frederick was Ashmont's heir presumptive.

"And after me?"

"Cousin Norbert."

This gentleman had all the present duke's worse propensities and none of the good ones, such as they were.

Lord Frederick knew he ought to have remarried years ago and produced acceptable heirs. He'd almost remarried, more than once, but for one reason or another, matters had never proceeded to completion.

"But I didn't die," Ashmont said. "And even if I had fallen—"

"Perhaps your skull is too thick to shatter."

Ashmont paused. "I think she said something like that. Or was it Olympia? Or did I say it?" His beautiful brow creased in perplexity.

"Miss Pomfret comes of good family," Lord Frederick said. "She's handsome, as I recollect."

"A great Boadicea of a girl. Profile like a queen on a coin. Long legs—"

"Yes, I don't doubt your judgment in that regard. However, fine girl or no, I recommend you pause in your wooing for a time."

Ashmont frowned at him.

"You were to be wed on Tuesday," his uncle said patiently. "Ripley married your bride yesterday, and you tried to kill him this morning. Do you not think it reasonable to wait a decent interval before pursuing another young lady? Without casting aspersions upon Miss Pomfret's charms, I believe we might safely assume that nobody else will snatch her from you in the interval."

If anybody did, Lord Frederick would have to assume it was for the best, though he did believe, wondrous strange though it was, that Ashmont had fixed his sights on suitable duchess material. Not only was the young lady not a courtesan, dancer, or actress, but she was the Earl of Chelsfield's granddaughter.

The Pomfret family was an old, highly regarded one. Equally important, her mother had produced seven males, and the mother's sisters had also done well in this department. Seven was perhaps more than a father would prefer to manage, but finding brides and/or places for younger sons was not Lord Frederick's concern.

His concern was a dukedom desperately short of satisfactory heirs and a nephew who needed taking in hand.

While Ashmont was far from satisfactory, he hadn't wasted his inheritance, as Norbert Beckingham had already done his. Whatever else one might say of Their Dis-Graces, they kept their finances in good order. This was more than one could say of perhaps half the peerage.

"Nephew, do you not see that you have fences to mend?" Lord Frederick said. "If you will keep away from Miss Pomfret for a time, you'll give her altogether reasonable indignation time to abate. It will not abate if you give people cause to talk—and talk they will, if you are so mad as to pursue her not a week after your first choice of bride deserted you."

He thought Ashmont needed the time as well. He couldn't be as sanguine as he seemed about Lady Olympia's desertion and the related public humiliation.

"Miss Pomfret made that point," Ashmont said.

"I have often found it useful to listen to women. Sometimes one must pay close attention, because they tend to talk in riddles. In this case, however, the lady seems to have made her position clear."

Ashmont pondered this for a time.

While he exercised his brain, Lord Frederick poured two glasses of wine. He crossed the room and gave his nephew one.

"I recommend you curb your natural impetuousness and give the lady time," his lordship said. "It will work greatly to your benefit, I promise."

To his astonishment, his nephew took only a sip of the wine then set the glass on a table. "Don't know. I did what I could, but it's not the easiest or surest thing, making oneself not be where one's been. I've sworn Morris to secrecy, as you'd expect. The trouble is, sooner or later, in all the talking he does, he's bound to let something drop. And there were so many witnesses."

"Most of whom will hold their tongues," his uncle said. "As to the few who don't, it's their word against many others'. Word may get back to London eventually, but by the time the story gets about—if it does—it will be old and garbled news. In another week or two, somebody will get into trouble of some kind, and fresh scandal is more delicious than stale."

"Can't say, Uncle. I hope you're right. But people don't like her, and so they won't treat her fair." The duke gazed into the empty grate. "I have to make it right, you know."

His uncle gave him a searching look. "Are you quite well, Lucius?" he said more gently than usual. He'd lost a brother to a dark world Lord Frederick had never experienced and could hardly comprehend.

Ashmont straightened and laughed. "Flourishing. Only a trifle blue-deviled. Long day. A good night's sleep and I'll be myself again." He must have guessed what his uncle was thinking, because he added, "It isn't in me to brood. If I'd killed Ripley . . . well, it wouldn't be pleasant. Rather not think about that. But I didn't. And there's an end of it."

It DIDN'T TAKE Cassandra long to understand what had happened. The servants' and innkeepers' faces were too innocent, too mystified at her mention of Ashmont.

As soon as she understood, she stopped asking.

She was impressed, certainly, by what wholesale bribery could do. Furthermore, as in the case of clean clothing, she chose not to look a gift horse in the mouth.

She wasn't sure this would solve her difficulties. Word was bound to reach London. The tale was too exciting to be suppressed for long. But Ashmont had given her a reprieve of sorts. She wrote to her parents, telling them she'd had a mishap with the carriage and Keeffe was hurt, but Mrs. Nisbett was with her, and Cassandra only awaited the surgeon's approval before returning home.

Not a word of the message was a lie, except by omission.

When she told Keeffe what the duke had done, he grinned and said, "I knew he'd bring us through. Whatever faults you find in him, he's a true gentleman, born and bred."

"A gentleman! He! By birth, undoubtedly. As to character, he's a fraction of the gentleman you are."

"Well, you know, miss, nobody's as perfect as me."

"As I," Mrs. Nisbett murmured.

"Very well, you, too," Keeffe said. "But that duke of yours, miss—"

"Not mine by any means," Cassandra said.

"He plays fair and sporting. Like one of them knights in the stories, you know, protecting your honor." Even with his ribs bound up, Keeffe managed something like his normal cackling laugh. "Put up a great shield of money to keep off the scandal."

THOUGH DISCOVERING THAT the Duke of Ashmont had quietly gone about fending off scandal had shaken Cassandra's view of the universe, it wasn't until late on Sunday afternoon that she saw her world entirely upended.

That was when Lady Charles Ancaster, her aunt Julia, arrived at the White Lion in her landau.

She was Papa's youngest sister, and he doted on her. Following her husband's death three years ago, she had gone into seclusion at Camberley Place in Surrey. In the past week, Cassandra had heard, all three of Their Dis-Graces had landed on her aunt's doorstep, along with the Duke of Ashmont's uncle, Lord Frederick Beckingham—though not all at the same time.

By early evening, Mrs. Nisbett was on her way home and Aunt Julia had taken charge. Still a handsome woman at six and forty, she was as sure of herself as she'd always been.

"I grieve at her leaving her home in bad weather," she said, after they returned to Cassandra's room. "It was brave and kind of her, indeed. Had I known, I should have made greater haste. But by the time I learnt of your mishap, it was too late to set out."

"Learnt of—"

"As it was," her aunt went on, not heeding the interruption, "I was in the last stages of preparing to return to London. I hesitated to journey back and forth some thirty miles."

"Return to London," Cassandra said. "But how— Wait."

"Yes. Back to London. I've sent the baggage and servants on ahead. I shall put up at my father's house while my town house is being refurbished."

"Refurbished." Cassandra felt dizzy. "You mean to stay in London, then."

"Really, my dear, after all that's happened in the past week, do you wonder at it? Charles and I did what we could for those three boys, but I daresay they were more to one another than we ever were to them. I know their boyhoods were difficult, but that's hardly an excuse. It would be laughable were it not so infuriating. Dukes' sons, with every advantage in life, not to mention friends and family who truly cared for them. And what have we now? Grown men, close on thirty, busy making chaos of their lives. Stealing brides and fighting duels—with each other! But nobody's dead, it seems."

"How did you—"

"Everybody tells me everything, though there are times I would prefer they didn't. I had one express after another yesterday. The ball couldn't penetrate Ripley's thick skull, it seems. Then there's the business with Alice and Blackwood. I should like to understand what's gone awry there, but Alice has always been inscrutable." She looked at Cassandra.

"I can't enlighten you," Cassandra said.

"Can't or won't?"

"She doesn't tell me everything."

"I'll get to the bottom of it," Aunt Julia said. "But Alice can wait. At present I wonder what on earth has possessed my brother. One would think it simple enough for a clever politician to manage his daughters. But you may be sure I shall deal with that as well. Now, my dear, be so kind as to order sherry. I daresay our landlord will have something drinkable, for the dukes if for nobody else. And a bite to eat. I'm famished as well as thirsty. In the meantime, let me have a look at Keeffe. Then I'll rejoin you, and we shall see what we'll make of this business."

And out of the room she went, like a general going out to view his troops before battle, while Cassandra sat staring at the door and trying to make sense of a world in upheaval.

The Duke of Ashmont, master of pandemonium, had not only taken his scandalous self out of the picture and stifled gossip with great lumps of money, but apparently had summoned the one person in all of England who might help Cassandra out of her predicament.

Marry me.

No. Never. Out of the question. She mightn't look a gift horse in the mouth. That didn't mean she was blind.

Chapter 5

By Monday, Mr. Greenslade pronounced Keeffe well enough to travel. This was fortunate, because Keeffe was determined to travel in any event. He was obliged, however, over his strong objections, to make the journey in Aunt Julia's well-sprung and cushioned landau.

Even Keeffe was no match for Lady Charles Ancaster. He submitted at last to riding with the ladies, rather than at the back in the servants' place, where he belonged. He hid his face, though, tipping his hat low over his forehead, for fear of being seen in this shameful position.

In London, Aunt Julia gave Papa an expurgated account of events. The missing maid required little explanation: She could have been killed, and was wise enough not to risk it again. Since Lord deGriffith disapproved of Cassandra's driving herself—it terrified him, actually—he could understand the desperate act.

If he suspected he wasn't being told the whole truth, he kept it to himself. He was far too glad to see his sister out in the world again to scrutinize every word, as he usually did.

The rest of London was pleased as well. Her abrupt reappearance caused a sensation that swept aside other, more commonplace news, like rumors about dueling dukes and drunken sprees thereafter.

On Tuesday, Lord deGriffith, his lady, and his sister were summoned to the royal presence. Lady Charles was a favorite of the Royal Family, and Their Majesties were impatient to see her.

Their parents gone for the day, and no social engagements in sight while Papa's rule was in force, Cassandra and Hyacinth settled in the library.

By now, Hyacinth knew everything, which was a great deal more than their parents did. She took an overly romantic view of matters, but then, Hyacinth was young, and less cynical than Cassandra had been at the same age.

"I still believe it was gallant of the duke to propose," Hyacinth was saying. "If he were as wicked as everybody makes him out to be, he wouldn't have done half the things he did, to protect you."

"If he weren't as wicked as everybody makes him out to be, it wouldn't have been necessary," Cassandra said. "He tried to kill his best friend. He was drunk. I don't doubt he was drunk when he ordered me to marry him. By now he's thought better of it."

"By now he's pining for you," Hyacinth said. "He saw for himself how beautiful and strong and confident you are. He didn't let other people's opinions color his judgment."

"My love, he has no judgment. No discernment. No sense of propriety whatsoever. He was jilted only a few days before."

"I'm sure that was for the best, and I don't doubt he sees that, too. Only think if he'd married Lady Olympia, and met you afterward." Hyacinth's great blue eyes widened. "How tragic that would be!"

Cassandra gazed helplessly at her sister. The girl's Season had ended because of Cassandra, yet she never made so much as a murmur. She wanted Cassandra to have everything Hyacinth was being denied: admiration, flirtation, appreciation. Even love.

All of it was denied to Hyacinth because her elder sister couldn't be like other young women.

Hyacinth was so beautiful, inside and out. A paragon among sisters. Cassandra did not deserve her.

But Hyacinth was excessively romantic. And naïve.

"I can only hope that Aunt Julia can make Papa see reason," Cassandra said. "Talk of making spectacles of us and setting tongues wagging. But even if we disregard the gossip, it is completely unfair. This is supposed to be your first Season, and the influenza and Papa's fussing and draconian rules have made it too short as it is."

Though the Queen would hold her last Drawing Room on Thursday, Parliament still sat, and the entertainments would continue, albeit in diminishing numbers, until Parliament rose and the remaining families left for the country. Hyacinth ought to be the center of attention.

At this point the butler, Tilbrook, entered. The footman Joseph followed, carrying a rectangular parcel about the size of a quarto volume.

"From Ackermann's, Miss Pomfret," Tilbrook said. "The servant said it was something you forgot there, as is explained in the note."

Ackermann's Repository in the Strand sold prints, paintings, paper, art supplies, illustrated books, and various articles for the fashionable home.

The note, which bore a plain seal, was addressed to Cassandra in a masculine hand, big, bold, and barely legible.

She told Joseph to put the parcel on the table by the window.

"I did not forget anything at Ackermann's," she said after the servants had gone out of the room. "I haven't entered the shop since before I went abroad."

She gazed at the parcel, then at the note in her hand. "What do you make of this?"

Hyacinth drew nearer. "Costly paper," she said. "But Ackermann's sells fine stationery. They're not likely to use inferior paper for correspondence."

"The handwriting," Cassandra said. "Does that look to you like a shopkeeper's or a clerk's?"

Hyacinth shook her head. "They're usually neat and precise."

"How much do you want to wager it's a prank?" Cassandra said.

Her sister clapped her hands. "A mystery. A gift from a secret admirer."

"Not likely."

"Oh, for heaven's sake, Cassandra, read the note. I'm dying of suspense."

Cassandra walked to the window, broke the seal, and read:

Dear Miss Pomfret,

I hope you will allow me to tell you how sorry I am for breaking your tiger. Keeffe is a game 'un, that's certain. I wish you would give him this little gift from me. He'll recognize it and will understand, I trust, that he's still a legend and a hero to some of us. I send it in hopes that the picture will cheer him while his ribs knit back together.

Yours sincerely,
Ashmont

She read it twice over, then gave it to her sister, who read it and smiled. "Oh, my goodness. A love note. From the Duke of Ashmont. I knew it. He's pining."

"Very amusing," Cassandra said. "Did I not tell you this was a prank? What should you like to bet he's sent a naughty print, or a set of them?"

"Like the ones in the portfolio at Chelsfield House?"

"Yes. He supposes I'll be shocked and faint dead away. At this moment he's laughing himself sick, telling his friends about the clever thing he's done."

Another one of Their Dis-Graces' famous pranks.

Cheeks pink, Hyacinth found scissors in the table drawer, gave them to her sister, and stood beside her while Cassandra cut the strings. Unwrapped the paper. And caught her breath.

"Oh, my," Hyacinth said. "Not a naughty print, then."

Cassandra didn't speak because she couldn't. Her throat was tight.

What Ashmont had sent was a small, expensively framed, exquisite oil painting of a man on a horse. In the lower right corner was inscribed "Amphion." On the lower left, with the artist's name and the date, was "T. H. Keeffe." It had been painted not a month before he was trampled at Newmarket. This was the horse he'd loved more than any other.

She sat down, the painting in her shaky hands. She stared at it.

"For Keeffe," Hyacinth said. She laid a hand on Cassandra's shoulder.

"If this were somebody else's gift," Cassandra said tightly, "I'd be touched by his sensitivity and compassion. But Ashmont has neither. He's merely paying, as he always does. Generously, as he always does."

"He wants forgiveness," Hyacinth said.

"He's a charmer," Cassandra said. "He charmed Lady Olympia out of her wits, I don't doubt, else she'd never have consented to marry him. She came to her senses in the nick of time."

"That's as may be, but this seems kindly meant. To think of Keeffe in this way. Why, who'd look so carefully for the perfect gift for a servant? The duke put thought into this. And care. You must give him a little credit, Cassandra."

Cassandra laughed. "As little as possible. But Keeffe will be pleased, I expect, and the duke is welcome to turn him up as sweet as he likes."

Tuesday night
Drawing room of deGriffith House

"But Lady Bartham's daughters will be there on Thursday," Mama cried. "One always puts the prettiest girls at the front of the stall."

On Wednesday would begin the Grand Fancy Fair and Bazaar for the Benefit of the Society of Friends of Foreigners in Distress. To be held at the Hanover Square Rooms, the event would continue through Saturday. Thanks to plots and intrigues Machiavelli's prince would have envied, Mama had secured a stall in which the art and needlework of the ladies of the family would be offered for sale.

As the *Court Journal* had reported, the Queen meant to attend, and "Several members of the Royal Family will also be present, as well as the whole of the principal Nobility and the Foreign Ambassadors and their ladies."

"You are more than pretty enough," Papa said.

"We'll do for the first day, when the Queen is to appear, and the crush will be dreadful, I don't doubt," Mama said. "But nobody wants to see nothing but mothers and grandmothers. We must have Hyacinth on Thursday, when Lady Bartham's daughters will be there. We cannot change all our arrangements at the last minute. This is for charity!"

"As much for competition among women as charity, I think," Papa said, taking up the paper he'd been reading when the dispute began. "I made a rule."

Cassandra looked up from her embroidery. Hyacinth was pink with excitement, longing to attend, deluded creature that she was. She'd never been to a grand fancy fair before, only village fêtes and the like.

Mama was close to tears.

"As I recall, Papa," Cassandra said, "you said, 'No dinners, dejeuners, fêtes champêtres, balls, routs, picnics, water parties, plays, ballet, opera.' Your rule did not mention fancy fairs or any charitable events. In fact, you recommended charity as a proper occupation for me."

Once more her father put down his paper. A deadly silence ensued while he regarded her from under his eyebrows, a gaze known to terrify junior MPs. "Will you split hairs with me, child?"

"I should never attempt such a thing," Cassandra said. "I merely pointed out a deprivation you'd overlooked."

She turned to her sister, who sat, hands tightly folded, looking from her to each of their parents. "Mama wants you at the fair because all you need do is stand there to sell every last article in the stall, and at exorbitant prices. If you are not present, Lady Bartham will crow and lord it over Mama in an unbearable fashion. This is because, having two young, unwed, and attractive daughters on display, Lady Bartham will make more money."

Mama moaned. "Oh, my dear, it is all too true."

"But only think," Cassandra told her sister. "You'd be trapped in a hot hall with a seething mass of people. These sorts of things are like Smithfield on market day—and in summer, I daresay the smell is much the same. No, no, you've no idea what a gift Papa has given you. You're far better off at home, as I'm sure Mama wishes she could be. A fancy fair out of doors is not so bad, but this is another article altogether."

"No, it isn't altogether pleasant," Mama said. "The crush will be appalling, and the heat disagreeable. But one must make sacrifices for charity! And Lady Bartham—"

"Has two daughters," Papa said. "Not half so pretty as ours. It upsets you, imagining her lesser offspring getting all the attention."

Mama dabbed her eyes with her handkerchief. "She will be quite unbearable, as Cassandra says. That woman is so jealous of Hyacinth."

The Countess of Bartham was a discontented woman, jealous of everybody she could find the slightest reason to be jealous of. Among other sources of bile, she resented other mothers' handsome daughters. Poison barbs laced her conversations.

Papa sighed. "I see how it is. We cannot let Lady Bartham get the better of you, my dear, and we cannot let you make this great sacrifice without support. Fortunately, Cassandra allows me to save face. Since I failed to make a rule in this regard, I can hardly break it by consenting to let Hyacinth attend. *But*."

He paused and bowed his head.

They waited, Hyacinth trembling.

"But only if Cassandra is with her."

Hyacinth's face lit like the sun, and that, Cassandra decided, was worth the tortures of the damned she'd endure on Thursday.

Wednesday
Ashmont House, Park Lane

ON THE TRAY bearing the Duke of Ashmont's morning coffee came two pieces of personal correspondence.

He opened the one from Ripley House first, read it, and laughed. The new Duchess of Ripley invited him to a ball on Friday night.

Clearly a head wound wasn't going to stop Ripley's celebrating his nuptials at the earliest opportunity.

"Sommers, bring me pen and ink."

Casting one anguished look at the bedclothes, as though he could already see the ink spatters, the valet obeyed.

On the invitation Ashmont scrawled, *"Delighted to attend. A."*

After ordering it delivered to Ripley House, Ashmont opened the other note.

Dear Duke,

Since Keeffe is ashamed of his writing (his hand, as you may know, along with other parts, was broken in the racing catastrophe), he has asked me to communicate to you his thanks for the painting. Had you given him one of your champagne banquets, complete with the usual bevy of insufficiently clothed opera dancers, he could not have been happier—or so he assures me, but since he is a man, I strongly doubt it. In any event, you have succeeded in pleasing and flattering him and raising his spirits to a surprising degree. For this I allot you one point. When you accumulate another five thousand nine hundred and ninety-nine, I shall begin to consider you a tolerable human being.

Yours sincerely,
Cassandra Pomfret

"One point?" Ashmont muttered.

"Your Grace?"

"Nothing."

Nothing, indeed. It wasn't much. Still, it was a point. And here was a note, in her own hand. It was a woman's hand, certainly, but rather more sharp about the edges than the usual.

That she'd written to him was no small thing. Unmarried gentlewomen didn't write to gentlemen who weren't relatives or affianced husbands. She'd done it, though, and had it smuggled out of her father's house and delivered to his.

Was this encouragement or simply evening the score, as he'd tried to do?

He was still unhappy about the damage to Keeffe, for all that she and the jockey made light of it in the letter.

Ashmont wasn't happy about his uncle's advice, either, though for once he couldn't help admitting the sense of it.

The Duke of Ashmont rarely had difficulties with women, and in those odd cases, he seldom had trouble winning them over. He was handsome, rich, and gifted with natural charm. These qualities had helped him win a young woman who felt a powerful responsibility toward her financially ramshackle family.

In the end, though, his looks, money, and charm hadn't been enough to keep her, and they'd made no impression on Miss Pomfret.

Admittedly, conditions on Saturday hadn't shown him to advantage. The opposite, rather. Their encounter had happened on one of the worst mornings of his life. Among other things—like the long hours leading up to the duel, the duel itself, and a few terrifying minutes afterward—he'd had a great deal too much to drink, no sleep to speak of, and almost nothing to eat.

Now, days later, with a clear head, he could see what a muck he'd made of it.

He needed to keep away, and let the unpleasant memory fade from Miss Pomfret's mind.

His pistol had been discreetly returned. Even Morris hadn't heard any rumors about Putney, apart from some talk about the duel. Word was bound to leak out eventually, but as Uncle Fred had said, it would seem like idle gossip—and stale at that. Not likely to cause a sensation.

All Ashmont had done to protect her reputation would go for nothing if he sought her out now. Not that he'd be able to get near her, in any event. The King had banned him from Court. Almack's patronesses had banned him from the weekly assemblies. All but a very few daring hostesses had crossed him off their invitation lists.

But she . . . she'd written to him, of her own free will. That boded a softening, didn't it? She'd given him a point!

Yes, possibly, but if he rushed his fences, he might find himself back in her bad graces.

Stay away, he told himself. And he remained firm in this wise resolution until after he bathed, shaved, dressed, and sat down to breakfast. That was when he read *Foxe's Morning Spectacle*.

HUMPHREY MORRIS ARRIVED at Ashmont House early on Wednesday evening, while Ashmont was in his dressing room. This was built on the ducal scale, and the portion devoted to dressing was only one part. A large part, true, for it is a duke's duty to keep as many people employed as possible, and as regards tailors, haberdashers, hatters, bootmakers, and the like, His Grace of Ashmont did his duty.

The space held, as it ought to do, a handsome dressing table. Since the duke used it as a writing desk, drinks tray, and general depository, it usually looked as though the Goths and Vandals had paid a visit. It was his valet's despair.

The dressing room also contained a small table and three comfortable chairs. These stood near the fireplace. Along a wall a sofa reposed. Several shelves held books and magazines. Other shelves as well as the walls displayed a collection of erotic art of remarkable variety and a changing series of satirical prints, many featuring the duke.

Although Ashmont House boasted a fine study, its master tended to loiter in the dressing room, much to Sommers's dismay. At present the servant moved among the drawers and cupboards of the adjoining light closet, engaged in the exacting process of assembling his employer's attire for the evening.

His Grace, in his dressing gown, sat at the small table, nursing a glass of wine and brooding over a lengthy entry in *Foxe's Morning Spectacle*. He waved Morris to the chair opposite.

Morris sat and said nothing.

"Carlotta O'Neill's," Ashmont said. "Tonight. After the play.

She's promised dancing girls. Naked ones. Or was it rope dancers? One or the other. But naked."

Carlotta was the most popular courtesan in London, for more than the usual reasons. Her entertainments were famously bawdy or comical or exciting or all three. Ashmont was looking forward to this evening. One could count on naked dancers to wipe one's mind clean, at least temporarily, of everything else—such as the three columns in *Foxe's Morning Spectacle* and, in particular, a handful of words therein.

He became aware of the peculiar sound of his visitor saying nothing. Silence? *Morris?*

"*Naked* dancers," Ashmont said. "Are you ill?"

Morris sighed.

"Take some wine." Ashmont poured. "You've lost your rosy glow. Got into the moneylenders' hands?"

Morris shook his head. "No, no, nothing so simple. Only . . ." He frowned down at the paper. "You saw?"

"Saw what?"

"There." Morris jabbed his index finger at the relevant column. "The fancy fair thing."

"Grand Fancy Fair? Hanover Square Rooms?"

"Yes. You saw?"

"Hard to miss. A lot of aristocratic ladies playing shopkeepers, selling their bits and bobs of handiwork. Queen promised to attend. Yes, that'll draw a mob, in a stuffy hall in midsummer London." Ashmont feigned a yawn. "No wonder you're wan and sickly. Saps a fellow's vital energy, merely picturing it. Now, if the ladies planned to have a wrestling match in a mud pit, that would be worth seeing."

"Are you blind? *She'll* be there." Morris took the paper and gently, reverently traced with his finger a place halfway down the second column. "Miss Hyacinth."

"Who?"

"Miss Hyacinth Pomfret," Morris said tenderly. "She'll be there."

"Ah, yes. Ladies of Lord Chelsfield's family. Stall Nine on Thursday." The temptation was powerful: public gathering, Miss

Pomfret in a stall she couldn't easily get out of . . . if she was there. She mightn't be there. The paper was unusually vague in this case. Dozens of women qualified as "ladies of Lord Chelsfield's family": aunts, in-laws, cousins.

All the same, his mind had gone to work imagining the possibilities. It couldn't help itself.

But his uncle had warned him to keep away. The lady needed time.

Yet she'd sent Ashmont a clandestine note. She'd given him a point, and it nagged at him. Did she give other men points? How many men? How many points?

He realized Morris was waiting for something.

"Well, then, there's your chance," Ashmont said. "All you have to do is buy a trinket of some kind and gaze adoringly into your adored one's eyes."

"Are you mad? I'll never get near Miss Hyacinth with Medusa standing guard."

"Why can't you get . . . Medusa, did you say?"

The Duke of Ashmont wasn't aware of his voice dropping a dangerous octave. He certainly wasn't aware of the demon within, crouched at the entrance of a deep inner cave, waiting to spring. He was only aware of a familiar surge of excitement, the joyous prelude to violence.

He wasn't aware, but Morris, like anybody else who'd spent any time with him, caught the signal. His face reddened. "Yes—meaning no offense, but—"

"Do you mean *Miss Pomfret?*" Ashmont's tone was mild, but Morris edged his chair back a bit.

"Exactly what I meant," Morris said.

The demon crawled back to wherever it had come from.

"How do you know?"

Morris looked at him. "How do you think?"

"Your mother."

"It was a last-minute thing," Morris said. "My mother says they did it on purpose to spite her—"

"But Miss Pomfret will be there."

Morris nodded. "And how am I—you know—with *her* there?"

It took Ashmont a minute to comprehend, his mind being very busy now. "You're afraid of what Miss Pomfret will say to you? Scared she'll embarrass you in front of everybody? Make you cry?"

Morris nodded. "In front of Miss Hyacinth. Everybody else can go to the devil. But, you know . . ."

Ashmont couldn't possibly know. The kinds of women he'd always spent his time with didn't humiliate him. They didn't speak harshly to him. He wasn't one of the Earl of Bartham's irrelevant younger sons but a wealthy and attractive duke. He knew this was why these women treated him the way they did, spectacular arsehole that he was. He didn't care. He'd always seen it as a fair exchange for what he wanted from them.

Two exceptions, and these were respectable young ladies. Good girls. The bane of a man's existence.

"Courage," he said.

"Miss Pomfret nearly knocked you off a gallery!"

"She was annoyed with me." Ashmont couldn't believe he'd been so lost to reason as to lay hands on her. Louts grabbed women. He was an arsehole, yes. He wasn't a lout.

"Annoyed? She could have killed you!"

"She won't kill you at a fancy fair," Ashmont said. "No weapons on offer. She could throw a pincushion at you."

Morris's shoulders slumped. He drank the wine Ashmont had poured for him. "Never mind. Lost cause. There'll be hundreds of fellows, all with the same thing in mind. Don't have a prayer."

Hundreds of fellows.

What had Uncle Fred said?

I believe we might safely assume that nobody else will snatch her from you in the interval.

Maybe not. Then again, not all men were as fainthearted as Morris.

"Giving up too easily," Ashmont said. "All you need is a diversion."

Morris, lost in misery, only looked blankly at him.

"Something to call Miss Pomfret's attention elsewhere," Ashmont said. "That'll be me. I'll take the abuse and you can make sheep's eyes at Miss Violet."

"Miss *Hyacinth*."

"Yes. We'll do it, then. Tomorrow." Ashmont already felt better. Something to do at last. And nobody had to know what lured him to a fancy fair. A prank. That would be enough. Easiest thing in the world to create one. And she'd simply happen to be where it happened.

"Erm . . . yes."

Ashmont looked at his friend, who did not appear as enthusiastic as he ought. "Now what?"

"How will you get in?"

"Through the door."

Morris said, patiently, as to one of slow comprehension, "Royals expected to attend. Foreign dignitaries."

"And?"

"You and any of them in the same room? Remember what the King said about you after that prank with the rabbits at the fête for the Grand Duchess of Volldenham?"

"Don't remember. Don't know. Don't care."

"He said, 'I'll hang that goddamned Ashmont by the yardarm if he comes within a mile of any member of the Royal Family.'"

"Sailor Billy's way of talking, that's all." King William IV had been a sailor, and he swore like one.

"Ashmont."

"It's a *fancy fair*, not a boring damn dinner at Windsor Castle. I'll get in. I'll stay as long as I like. Ten guineas says so."

Thursday 20 June

THE FANCY FAIR fulfilled Cassandra's predictions. Instead of Smithfield's animal smells, expensive scents permeated the Hanover Square Rooms' stagnant air, not fully masking the fragrance of a multitude of sweating aristocrats and gentry.

The attendees complained about the crush but didn't leave, and when they finally shoved enough people out of the way to reach a stall, they dithered over what to buy.

After two hours of it, the conditions had tested Mama's spirit of sacrifice. She'd gone down to the refreshment room minutes ago. Aunt Elizabeth must be expecting again, because she'd been snappish from the start. Even Hyacinth's good humor was on the wane.

Cassandra was about to step out of the place herself. This was not so much for refreshment or change of air as for a respite from keeping a civil tongue in her head despite gross provocation. She was halfway to the door when she spotted him. Not that this required any unusual feat of identification.

The Duke of Ashmont, in all his radiant satanic beauty, stood in the entrance.

He. At a fancy fair. No drink, gaming, fighting, or loose women to be had. The last event on earth, in short, to attract him.

With him was Humphrey Morris, and a small boy of indeterminate age and deficient hygiene who looked like an animate pile of rags and smelled like the Thames at low tide.

The aroma reached her from where she stood, nearly halfway across the room.

She could smell—literally—a prank in the offing.

One would think everybody else could, too. However, since nobody could have expected Ashmont—any more than they'd expect Genghis Khan or Attila the Hun—the organizers had failed to provide, say, a pack of rabid dogs or a cavalry regiment to keep him out.

Yesterday, the fair's first day, the directors had ordered the doors closed for a time, due to the crush of attendees and ladies fainting left and right. Nobody, however, had thought to order them closed against *him*.

Nobody had told them to say the fair was not at home or suddenly canceled, which was the way the duke was often greeted at the doors of aristocratic establishments.

Still, he was not a reasonable person, and such methods wouldn't necessarily work with him. If he wanted to get in, he'd do it, one way or another, and he could be rather a mastermind in that regard.

Furthermore, he was a duke. Born and bred to inherit the title, having inherited young, and being a Beckingham, he exuded authority even when he was half-seas over . . . which, oddly enough, he didn't appear to be.

Not that it made a difference. He was trouble, no matter what.

Yet sober, or something like it, and sauntering into the great concert room, he seemed like a deity come down from Olympus to walk among mortals.

Whether blinded by His Grace's angelic beauty or overcome by the boy's *eau de sewer* or simply terrified, the guardians at the gate failed to stop him. Everybody else only stood staring.

Morris trailing behind, the duke and the malodorous child made their way through the strangely hushed sea of distinguished persons. As the boy's fumes reached aristocratic noses, the sea parted, and the trio went from stall to stall unhindered.

Given the duke's reputation, one would expect persons of any sense to leave, and come back tomorrow. But no. They were like the people who hung about the rim of a rumbling volcano, waiting to see if it would erupt.

Cassandra had sense, but she could hardly flee. For one thing, running away was against her principles. For another, she couldn't abandon her sister and aunt to whatever hell was about to break loose. And finally, she was possibly the only person ready and willing to act. She wasn't sure what, exactly, she could do, but she'd solve that when the time came.

Head down, keeping herself concealed within the crowd, she followed him.

He introduced the boy to the ladies—who were stuck in their stalls and couldn't escape—as "Jonsatovickya, distressed foreigner," and looked on benignly while the child pawed silks and laces and chattered at the ladies.

Though too far away to hear what the boy said, Cassandra recognized the Cockney speech. The ladies, thoroughly confounded, stood as far back in their little prisons as they could . . . until Ashmont took out his purse.

For the sake of the Distressed Foreigners, not to mention intense rivalry among themselves, the stall-keepers held their noses and took the duke's money.

As a prank, it wasn't bad, and rather amusing, actually—

—until Ashmont and his entourage started toward Stall Number Nine.

At that moment she discovered that Hyacinth stood alone, with no Aunt Elizabeth in sight, and the gentlemen had begun to wash up about her, like the detritus that washed up on the riverside.

Cassandra thrust her way through the crowd and hurried round the back into the stall. As deGriffith's Gorgon hove into view, the masculine flotsam and jetsam oozed back into the throng.

"Where is Aunt Elizabeth?" she said.

"She left suddenly—to be sick, I believe," Hyacinth said.

Pushing her sister behind her, Cassandra moved to the front, to stand guard over her wares, a moment before the duke's leisurely circuit brought him and his minions there.

He smiled at her, all blue-eyed benevolence. "Miss Pomfret."

She put on her best dealing-politely-with-fools smile. "Duke."

"Look what I've brought you," he said. "A distressed foreigner of your very own. Will you allow me to present Master Jonsatovickya."

She opened her eyes wide, fluttered her eyelashes, and said, "Just for me? How sweet. You shouldn't have." She dropped the smile and narrowed her eyes. "Truly, you shouldn't."

He beamed, and it was like Apollo shedding golden light upon little, mortal her. For a moment, she teetered, mentally off balance.

Ye gods. He ought to be locked in a deep, dark dungeon.

He truly was dangerous, a soul-shatteringly beautiful monster.

Fortunately, she was a monster herself.

She leant over the counter.

The boy grinned up at her.

He had not bathed in a very long time, if ever, and another woman might have fainted dead away from the fragrance alone. But Cassandra had grown up with seven brothers, their boy cousins, and their friends. She had spent time in low places. Her stomach was strong.

"If Master Jones or whatever his real name is puts his hands on *my* goods," she said, "he'll lose his fingers."

The so-called distressed foreigner put his hands behind his back. He seemed familiar, but it was hard to be sure. His overlarge, stained yellow jockey cap shadowed a face wearing ancient layers of dirt. The upper orders found street children hard to tell apart, a fact the children were happy to take advantage of.

"Don't I know you?" she said.

The boy shook his head.

She scrutinized his features. Under the grime appeared to be a not-unhandsome child, one she'd seen before. "It *is* Jones, isn't it? Or Jonesy, as your young confederates call you."

She lifted her gaze to meet Ashmont's dazzling sapphire one. It made her a little dizzy, but she didn't blink.

Not blinking or backing down was something a girl in a large family of boys learnt early on. It was her brother Julius who'd first called her *Medusa*.

"Such elegant company you keep," she said.

Jonesy looked up at Ashmont accusingly. "You didn't say it were *her*."

What came out of the child's mouth didn't resemble these words. But she'd learnt Cockney, among other things, from Keeffe.

"Well, he wouldn't say, would he?" Cassandra said. "How much is the duke paying you to do this?"

She was aware of people drawing closer to the stall, in spite of the boy's stench. Out of the corner of her eye she saw handkerchiefs go up to cover noses and mouths.

The ragamuffin's dirty face instantly formed an expression of pure innocence. He pursed his lips and narrowed his eyes, appearing to think very hard, then, "I fink he give us a glistener," he said.

"A sovereign?" she said. "I think not. Two bob at most."

"A half crown."

Two and a half shillings was untold riches for a street urchin. It would be untold riches for any number of working people. But where Ashmont was concerned, this at least fell within the realms of possibility. Whatever else one might accuse him of—and the list stretched to infinity—he was no pinchpenny.

"I'll give you a crown," she said, "if you'll go straight to the nearest baths and get washed."

The boy grinned. He shoved under one arm the goods he'd collected and held out his filthy hand. She reached into the side slit of her dress, where the pocket hung, and drew out a small purse. She counted out five shillings and dropped them into his grimy little paw.

The boy closed his fingers tightly over the money. Then, still clutching the ladies' handiwork, he turned and ran out of the Hanover Square Rooms.

It was so far from what Ashmont expected to happen and it happened so quickly that he could only watch, in a sort of wonder, while his prank fell to pieces. Mouth hanging open, mind wiped blank, he stood blinking at Jonesy's rapidly retreating back.

Nobody tried to stop him. No surprise there. Nobody wanted to touch him.

Then he was gone, and Ashmont was left standing there, looking like—like—the goat. An ass. A great, slow-witted jackass.

"Good work," somebody said. "Bested her with that one, did you?"

"Was that supposed to be one of your cleverer jokes?" said somebody else.

"I had ten pounds riding on your emptying the rooms," said another.

"Nobody even screamed."

"Well, that went flat, didn't it?"

"Poor fellow. Could've warned you you weren't up to her weight."

"Look out, duke. It'll be you running next."

"Best get out while you can, with all your parts intact."

The men went on laughing and exercising their limited wit at his expense.

The image of Godfrey Wills flashed through Ashmont's mind.

He looked round to meet Miss Pomfret's gaze. Her face was set in a cold, blank expression, the one people called her Gorgon stare. But he discerned the glitter in her eyes and the faint hint of a smile at the corners of her mouth.

Many degrees more lucid than the last time he'd been with her, he realized how much he'd missed: the fullness of her mouth, for instance, not to mention the elegantly sculpted cheekbones, the slight upward cant of her eyes, and the overall effect of a face very much out of the common run.

She had a devil in her, too.

But of course she did. He'd known—sensed it, even when he wasn't fully himself. He'd sensed there was more to her, more than ordering fellows about and shoving them out of her way.

The hint of a smile. Amusement and a taunt. The same smile she'd worn after she threw the bucket of water on him.

Oh, yes, it seemed to say. *Go ahead. I dare you.*

One wrong move and he'd unbalance the scales, and the microscopic bit of ground he'd gained would vanish like a speck of dust in a high wind.

One wrong move and he'd destroy all the work he'd done to protect her.

The intelligent thing to do would be to acknowledge defeat and leave her in peace, with nobody the wiser as to any previous encounters.

But her face. The wondrous face, that made all the others mere shadows. The supposedly beautiful sister might as well be a china doll.

Yes, the figure, too.

Not to mention, there were hundreds of men here, and out of those hundreds, he couldn't be the only one who wasn't blind.

No. No retreat.

She'd dared him, and even now, chastened and wiser, he wasn't chastened all that much and he hadn't suddenly become a sage.

He'd hazard it.

Chapter 6

Ashmont put a hand up. "The lady's bested me. I bow to her." He made a theatrical bow. "Well done, fair lady. You've turned my joke upon me and made a fool of me in front of my friends."

The way she did to Wills.

He saw it so clearly in his mind's eye: the eyelashes fluttering; the clear, confident voice; and the handful of words that turned the tables completely.

She was a force to be reckoned with, and he was ready to reckon.

"Fair gentleman, it took no effort," she said. "Playing the fool is something you've rehearsed at length. All one need do is step aside and leave you to it."

"You've studied me?"

"In depth and great detail," she said. "In the way one studies strange life-forms. Have you never looked into a microscope, at a drop of some liquid, and marveled at the curious creatures wriggling about in it?"

He was aware of laughter, but more aware of her. "Never."

"You need to broaden your horizons," she said.

"I will," he said. "Most willingly. Show me to your microscope, fair philosopher. Show me anything and everything. I'm yours to command."

"Very well," she said. "I show you the door." She waved a dismissal. "Go away. And take your motley fool with you."

He glanced at Morris. "Now you mention it, my friend does appear a trifle motley at first glance. But he's a prodigy, he is, who can speak an infinite deal of everything and recite from memory your entire genealogy going back to the first Baron deGriffith, what fought at Bosworth Field or one of those places."

He clapped Morris on the shoulder. "Say something intelligent, my lad. Here's your great chance."

Morris didn't answer.

Ashmont elbowed him.

"Look at her," Morris mumbled. "I burn. I pine. I perish."

"What's he saying?" Eyebrows aloft, Miss Pomfret leant forward again, a pose that fastened Ashmont's attention upon her bosom.

Respectable women wore numerous undergarments, quilted petticoats and corsets and layers of linen, and over these intimate garments came more layers. The dress bodice wasn't enough. A lady must have additional armor, in the shape of mantillas and canezous and pelerines and such, covering her shoulders and bosom. Then there were the sleeves, enormous puffed things.

Still, he'd seen her in wet clothes, and the way they clung to the undergarments had offered a better-than-usual view of her figure.

Though at present she was dry and well covered—up to her throat—the bodice of her green dress was closely fitted. He took note of the way her bosom rose and fell, and didn't find it hard to estimate how much of that was fabric, and how much was woman.

He told himself to keep his mind on business. One wrong word, one wrong move, and he'd ruin everything.

"He's dumbstruck," he said.

"Good," she said. "The mute sort of male is the best sort of male. Strong and silent type. Or weak and silent type. But silent. Above all, silent."

"You're acquainted with the gentleman, I believe," Ashmont said. "Humphrey Morris, son of—"

A slight flicker in the grey eyes warned him he was treading on thin ice. "I know who he is."

"He begs to be introduced to the young lady." Ashmont leant in a little closer, and some delicious scent, fresh and herbal, rose to his nostrils. It took all his willpower not to lean in farther when he murmured, "He's infatuated with Miss Marigold."

"Who?"

"Miss Rose?"

"Do you mean *Hyacinth*?"

"That one," he said. "Have pity on him. Can't you let her sell him something?"

Her eyes glinted silver. She looked over her shoulder at the fair-haired girl. "My dear, this dubious person wants assistance."

The girl stepped up to the counter.

Beside him, Morris let out a curious sound, like a sheep being strangled mid-bleat.

"Hyacinth, my love, here is Mr. Humphrey Morris," said Miss Pomfret. "You know his mama, Lady Bartham."

She and her sister exchanged looks.

"In spite of the low company Mr. Morris keeps," Miss Pomfret continued, "we may reckon him relatively harmless, to the extent that any member of his gender is harmless. He wishes to buy something for dear Lady Bartham and his sisters. And his aunts and great-aunts. All of them. Perhaps you can help him make up his mind."

The girl's cheeks pinkened prettily, the way such girls' cheeks always did.

Morris stood like a great, stupid, scarlet-faced lump.

Ashmont gave him another elbow in the ribs. "There's the girl. *Do* something."

Morris moved toward the counter like a somnambulist.

The girl said, "Mr. Morris, perhaps you would like to look at this pincushion Mama made. Lady Bartham admired it very much . . ."

Leaving his besotted friend to sink or swim, Ashmont returned his attention to his target, who'd moved to one side of the stall to keep watch—and no doubt turn Morris to stone if he so much as breathed the wrong way.

As to Ashmont, if he didn't take care, he'd set off an avalanche that would bury them both.

They had an audience, listening avidly, and he couldn't make them go away. A fellow couldn't be private with good girls.

Very well. He liked a challenge, didn't he?

"The boy's not going to get a bath," Ashmont said. "That sort are allergic to soap and water. Probably for the best. Scrubbing off all those layers of grime might upset the delicate balance of his nerves."

"Are you still there?" she said. "Did I not expend vast reservoirs of patience and generosity in introducing your chatterbox friend to my sister?"

"He's going to buy every last article in the stall," Ashmont said. "That's why you cooperated."

"And now it's too late for you to buy everything, merely for the privilege of looking upon my Venus-like person and worshipping at my altar."

That, certainly, was part of the plan: Jonesy would scoop up everything he could reach, taking his time about it, and Ashmont would claim the remainder. While she was busy with them, Morris would make sheep's eyes at the younger sister.

The plan hadn't worked out as Ashmont had imagined, but he was flexible.

He hadn't much time. The more he lingered, the greater the chance of putting his foot in it. Still, he could give Morris a few more minutes with the sister.

A few minutes only, then Ashmont had better put temptation behind him.

"I shouldn't say Venus," he said. "I should say—"

"Scylla," came a voice from the crowd.

Ashmont had not been a dutiful scholar. However, like nearly everybody else, he was familiar with the *Odyssey*. After all, it was an exciting tale featuring pillage, eye-gouging, murder, man-eating monsters, and other thrills. He knew that Scylla and Charybdis were monsters who guarded a narrow strait. Charybdis was a deadly whirlpool. Scylla had six heads with three rows of sharp teeth in each head.

The demon irrupted from the deep inner cave, and through Ashmont swept a deadly combination of fury and joy and maybe the breath of the devil.

He turned slowly and smiled. In a low, mild voice everybody who knew him would recognize, in the same way they'd recognize the smile, he said, "Who said that?"

The audience shifted two steps back.

"Who said that?" Ashmont repeated, still smiling. "I should like for him to stand in front of me, instead of hiding in a crowd, and say it again."

Suddenly, everybody nearby found another place to be.

The demon flung itself back into its cave.

"Well, that was convenient," he said, turning back to Miss Pomfret. "The trouble with places like this is, no damned privacy."

"What I don't need with you," she said in a low, hard voice, "is privacy."

"I only wanted to say—"

"I don't care," she said. "This is a game to you, I know. I'm not playing. And may I point out, that if I were to stab you to death in front of all these witnesses, I should be applauded. They would carry away your corpse and clean up the blood and say it was an accident."

"Your imagination," he said, dropping his voice again, but not in the dangerous Come-Here-and-Let-Me-Break-Your-Face-for-You way. "Lively."

"Go away. And take him with you."

"You gave me a point," he said, dropping his voice lower still.

"You're about to lose it."

"You can't take it back."

"I gave it. I can take it back."

"But that wouldn't be sporting."

"Is it sporting to come to a charitable event, exploiting a street child, merely to disrupt the proceedings?"

"You call it exploiting," he said. "I call it gainful employment. I found him hanging about outside my house as Morris and I were leaving." The greatest stroke of good luck, he'd thought. "I hired the brat only to keep him busy with something that didn't involve housebreaking or pickpocketing. You ought to commend me for saving him from the gallows for ten minutes—which is about as much time as anybody can hope for in his case. If you think that crown you gave him will go for a bath—"

"I don't care what he does with it," she said. "I only hope larger and nastier boys don't steal his riches. I hope nobody cuts his throat. Still, he's cleverer than most, and he didn't live this long on the streets by being careless."

She knew the boy. How in blazes did she know him? Ashmont had met him on the day Olympia ran away. Jonesy had been loitering with a gang of other ragged children at a hackney stand in the Kensington High Street. He'd helped them search for the missing bride, then abruptly vanished while they were at Battersea Bridge.

"The constables will think he's stolen the things," Ashmont said. "They'll see him running from here and grab him long before he gets to whatever rookery he holes up in. He'll end up at the Great Marlborough Street police office, is my guess. Maybe Bow Street, if he's fast. Either way, I'll have to go to the bother of bailing him out. But that'll take a while. We've plenty of time. Never mind about him. You keep changing the subject."

"You and I don't have a subject," she said.

"First of all, what I should have said—before that ignoramus interrupted—was *Diana*," he said. "Not Venus, but Diana the Huntress, driving her chariot—"

"I must say, that was one of the more comical sights I've seen in some time," came a familiar voice behind him. "Your grand entrance with the ragamuffin."

Ashmont turned. There was the familiar sardonic expression. There

were the hooded eyes that made ladies' hearts go thumpity-thump—
ladies, that is, attracted to the tall, dark, dangerous type. "Blackwood,"
he said.

They had parted on very bad terms a week ago, and Ashmont
hadn't seen him since.

"But more comical still," Blackwood said, "was watching the
little beast flee, as though the hounds of hell were after him."

"He fled far worse than that," Miss Pomfret said. "I told him to
get a bath."

Blackwood smiled. "Smartly done, Miss Pomfret. You are done
with Ashmont as well, I hope? He wears an expression that tells me
you've demanded some brain work of him."

"As little as possible. I know he isn't used to it."

"Indeed not. He needs to be brought along by slow degrees.
Fever could result otherwise. With your permission, I shall bear
him away. His accomplice, too, if only Morris would stop gaping
at Miss Hyacinth in that stupid manner and pay up."

Miss Pomfret beamed at Blackwood, quite as though he had singlehandedly killed Scylla, Charybdis, and six or seven dragons for her.

Ashmont had experienced the Gorgon stare. He'd caught hints
of feeling now and again. But he hadn't realized how much she hid
until now, when she let go of whatever it was, and her smile seemed
to fill the room with sunlight, and the light left him breathless.

The smile wasn't aimed at him, which was provoking. More provoking still was the thought that she had just given Blackwood, the
treacherous swine, a point.

CASSANDRA WATCHED THEM go, her heart pounding, her face giving
nothing away.

She couldn't make sense of it, not now. It was too much. In a matter of minutes, Ashmont had thrown her world off balance. Again.

Sober, or something like it, he'd surprised her again and again.

The verbal sparring, which she'd not supposed him capable of, and
which she'd enjoyed more than she ought.

The sense of intimacy he created in a great crowd. The awareness of the secret they shared, and his care in giving nothing away.

Then the abrupt change in his demeanor when somebody called her *Scylla.* He'd made her see the boy again, the one who'd joined her battle against Godfrey Wills so many years ago. The same heart-stopping smile—oh, but that was only glee in the prospect of destroying another male.

For show, she told herself. He only wanted to drive away the onlookers, in order to . . . flirt . . . with her.

As though she were not a monster.

But he was one, too. Small wonder it didn't trouble him, if he even noticed.

And it was all part of the game, the prank. He couldn't resist causing an uproar . . .

Diana the Huntress, driving her chariot.

Not Venus. Not Minerva.

Diana, the mythical deity her much younger self had imagined she'd become: the Huntress, chaste and free and powerful, with her bows and arrows and her company of nymphs.

As though he could look into her brain, her heart, with that armor-piercing blue gaze.

"Oh, my goodness," Hyacinth said, drawing near her. "That was exciting. I've never seen him up close before."

"Who?" Cassandra pulled herself out of the haze of memory and jumbled feelings. The band was playing. Had they played all along? Or had the world stopped for a time? People were moving through the great room, slowly, as they'd done before. Into the open space about their stall, gentlemen were beginning to drift, though cautiously, looking about them, in case Ashmont suddenly sprang from the crowd again.

"You know perfectly well," Hyacinth said. "What did I tell you? Pining. He couldn't keep away."

You gave me a point.

Cassandra shook her head. "My fault. Stupid, stupid, stupid." She looked about her. A trio of elegantly dressed young gentlemen were making their way, in a determined manner, to Stall Number Nine. She smiled at Hyacinth. "More admirers, my dear. Have you anything left to sell them?"

"Not much. Mr. Morris bought nearly everything."

"His mother will be furious." Which meant she'd be sure to pass on every detail of Ashmont's intrusion, emphasizing the amount of time he'd spent talking to Cassandra and offering the most lurid speculation about the conversation. No doubt she'd see and hear things she'd neither seen nor heard.

Still, Ashmont had harassed others, and Cassandra would think of something to tell her parents. What truly mattered was Hyacinth. She was happy. The elegant trio were examining the pitiful remnants of what Mama had assumed would be enough goods for the duration. Cassandra discreetly withdrew to the back of the stall, so as not to alarm the customers overmuch. As long as they behaved, she was happy to see them admire her sister.

Meanwhile, nearby in George Street

"Sorry to spoil your fun," Blackwood said. "But I spotted Lady Bartham storming through the crowd, aimed your way. It occurred to me that Morris would probably rather his mother didn't embarrass him in that mob, with half his acquaintance looking on."

The mention of his mother roused Morris from his dazed state, but not by much. "Indeed, thank you," he said. He held to his chest the parcel his adored one had made up for him. "Grateful, yes. Very good of you."

"A week ago you said he was a blackguard," Ashmont said in an undertone.

Blackwood paused in front of St. George's Church. "Morris, be so good as to walk on. I must have a word with Ashmont. We'll catch up."

Still clutching the parcel as though it were a holy relic, still not quite free of the enchantment of Miss Flower, Morris walked on.

Blackwood looked up at the church. "I misjudged him. They're mainly an untrustworthy lot, that family."

"He's talkative," Ashmont said. "But he's harmless."

So Miss Pomfret had told her sister. That was a kindness she needn't have offered. She might have driven Morris away with a word or a look, but she hadn't. True, she and her sister had taken very great advantage of the poor fellow, but ladies could be ruthless at these charity affairs. According to one dashing widow Ashmont had known, the competition was brutal. Fighting cocks could learn something from them, she'd said.

"I should rate him higher than that," Blackwood said. "I'm told he made every effort to reconcile you and Ripley, and in other respects did all that was proper. He kept an eye on you afterward. You're not dead. Ripley isn't dead. Let's leave it at that."

A weight lifted that Ashmont hadn't realized was there. He and Ripley had made up promptly, but Blackwood had kept away, and Ashmont had missed him more than he'd ever admit.

"Fair enough," he said.

Blackwood's dark gaze came back to him. "Now that's settled, shall we take Morris out for a restorative beverage or two?"

"He does seem in need of a bracer."

"Not but what you could use some restoring yourself," Blackwood said. "You appear a trifle peaked. Not surprising, considering you spent fully ten minutes, perhaps more, conversing with Miss Pomfret. Does your brain hurt? I debated coming to your rescue early on, and in the end deemed it best you learn by experience."

"Didn't need rescuing," Ashmont said. "In fact, it was just getting interesting when you had to lumber in."

"No doubt you thought so. The trouble is, Lady Bartham swooping down in dragon mode wasn't all I saw. Miss Pomfret clearly wished to be rid of you. But I know there's no getting rid of you until you're good and ready. Detecting no signs of your being good and ready, and knowing she'd soon progress to drastic measures likely to be more injurious to herself than to you, I thought I'd gain myself a credit or two by hastening your departure."

"Credit!" Ashmont said. "She gives you points?"

Blackwood looked at him. "I meant credit with Alice, for saving her friend from herself. Or you. Or both. What did you think I meant?"

"Nothing," Ashmont said.

"I see," Blackwood said. After the briefest of pauses, he went on, "Going to Ripley's gala tomorrow night?"

"Wouldn't miss it for anything. Might steal the bride."

"That sounds like fun. But I recommend you do it discreetly. Ripley intends, as you may have already surmised, to establish his duchess's proper place in Society. Marriage calls for certain sacrifices, and this includes one's friends. We three, as I hope you realize, are to be on the very strictest good behavior."

"Certainly. No hard feelings. Wouldn't hurt Olympia for the world."

He wouldn't. She'd saved his life. She'd been kind to him. And he had not behaved well on what was to have been their wedding day.

"Indeed." Another small pause. Then, "His Royal Highness the Duke of Sussex is coming, I heard—dying of curiosity, no doubt, like everybody else. Especially with you there, the abandoned bridegroom. Everybody not invited is furious, as you can imagine. It's the talk of the town."

The party grew less appealing. Ashmont would have to do exactly the right thing at every moment. He'd be under scrutiny. No lapses allowed that might reflect ill on Olympia. At a party overburdened with respectable people.

But he had fences to mend, and he owed Olympia this much.

And maybe Miss Pomfret would be there.

"Alice going?" he said.

"Yes. My duchess is back from wherever she's been. She means to accompany her aunt, Lady Charles Ancaster—infinitely preferable to accompanying me." He studied one of the church pillars, as though trying to decipher a message there. "Miss Pomfret has been invited, to please Alice. However, even if Lord deGriffith allowed it, which is out of the question, Miss Pomfret would certainly decline."

Morris had said that she'd stopped going to parties and such years ago.

Ashmont couldn't blame her. He'd rather decline, too. But honor demanded he attend and make amends as best he could. "Too bad," he said. "I was hoping to get to know her better."

"A glutton for punishment, I see."

"She isn't boring," Ashmont said.

"That's one way of putting it," Blackwood said. "Let's collect Morris, shall we, before he wanders into trouble. In that stupefied state, he makes a prime target for pickpockets."

IT WAS GOOD to be Medusa. It spared one's having to suffer fools, gladly or otherwise, usually. It spared Cassandra a great deal of trouble following Ashmont's visit to the fancy fair.

It didn't occur to anybody, apparently, that he'd had any other object in view than causing an uproar, and people assumed that Medusa had frightened the little boy away and spoiled the prank. In the general view, Ashmont had lingered merely to test her patience, because he liked to tempt Fate.

No one was surprised at his departing with Blackwood—in search of more exciting sport, no doubt.

Certainly Mama had no complaints. When Lady Bartham tried to poison her mind, Mama shrugged it off as jealousy, because Lady Bartham's stall hadn't done a fraction so well. Mama even went so far as to twist the knife, asking if Lady Bartham had a few items to spare, since the Pomfret ladies were running woefully short of goods, and mightn't have enough for the remaining days.

The only one who didn't accept the general view of events was Alice. She and Aunt Julia came to dinner that evening. After the meal, while the older generation had their tea in the drawing room, she, Hyacinth, and Cassandra betook themselves to the sisters' sitting room.

"There's more to this than meets the eye," Alice said. "I can feel it by the pricking of my thumbs."

"Or maybe Aunt Julia dropped a hint," Cassandra said.

"Not a one. She can be mighty inscrutable when she wants to be."

"She says the same of you."

They both knew the reference was to the state of Alice's marriage. But Hyacinth was there, and she wasn't privy to even the little Cassandra knew.

Alice only smiled, and said, "Tell me."

Cassandra told her, all about events at Putney Heath and in Putney and after.

When she came to the painting, Alice's dark eyebrows went up. She and her brother shared the same green eyes, but where Alice was a raven-haired beauty, Ripley was a good deal more rough-hewn.

Not like His Grace with the Angel Face.

"Did not Lord Pershore's father own the horse?" Alice said.

Cassandra nodded. The present Lord Pershore's stud was as famous as his father's. Keeffe held both gentlemen in high regard.

"Then I wish I'd been a fly on the wall for that negotiation," Alice said. "Pershore was Ripley's second, you know, at the duel." She shook her head. "But Ashmont has never been one to hold grudges, and—oh, my dear." She looked at her friend.

"He wants to please her," Hyacinth said. "I told her, but she won't believe me."

Alice appeared lost in thought. No doubt she was turning over in her exceedingly quick mind all that Cassandra had told her.

After a moment she said, "I understand now why you're disinclined to attend Ripley's party."

"I'm sorry to disappoint you, but I dislike attending a party that Hyacinth can't."

"Oh, Cassandra!" Her sister drummed her feet on the floor. "All I want is to hear what happens there. It's as thrilling as a novel, I vow."

"So it is," Alice said. "But Cassandra's instincts are good. Ashmont throws himself headlong into everything. When it came to winning Olympia, he swept all before him. Swept the girl off her feet, no doubt. He can be extremely winning when he chooses, and he's especially dangerous in that mode."

"But she escaped," Cassandra said.

Alice nodded thoughtfully. "Which raises an interesting question. If he wanted her so badly, why didn't he exert himself more to retrieve her?"

"He was so drunk he could hardly stand up. Everybody knows that."

"Why was he drunk on his wedding day?"

"Because he's an idiot?"

"Because," Hyacinth said, "deep in his heart he knew he didn't love her and he'd made a mistake and he didn't want to go through with it."

Cassandra and Alice looked at her.

"It's possible," Hyacinth said.

"Some long-buried ethical impulse came to the fore for one brief, shining moment?" Alice said.

"It came to the fore when he tried to mend matters in Putney. He did ask Cassandra to marry him."

Marry me.

"Commanded, was more like it," Cassandra said.

"He's a duke!" her sister said.

"He was not entirely sober."

"Sober enough, apparently, to try to do his muddled idea of the right thing," Alice said. "Hyacinth may be correct in that. You did the right thing as well. Best to keep out of a highly fraught situation. Tomorrow night he needs to make amends with Olympia and Ripley and clear the air. Your being there would only distract him and complicate matters."

Cassandra allowed herself a sigh of relief. "I knew you'd understand."

"I don't," Hyacinth said. "I should give anything to be a fly on the wall tomorrow night."

"I promise to tell you both everything," Alice said.

"It won't be the same if Cassandra isn't there."

"It won't be the same, but it will be interesting," Alice said. "Of that I'm sure."

MIDSUMMER NIGHT. THE shortest night of the year. For Ashmont, it turned out to be the longest.

As predicted, Miss Pomfret didn't come, and he had what seemed like ten thousand duty dances, beginning with his hostess. He wasn't used to respectable gatherings, and he needed a clear head to keep all the old, half-forgotten rules in the front of his mind. In other words, getting drunk was out of the question.

He managed, somehow. What mattered was, he and Olympia settled the important issues, and she went back to Ripley looking relieved, while Ashmont went on to his next partner, knowing he'd been forgiven.

He danced with Alice, Lady Charles, and a few other matrons. On this occasion, the matrons vastly outnumbered the misses, and nobody was mad enough to try to matchmake. The ladies, it turned out, were as cautious about him as he was about them, which was rather amusing.

But he got through the evening without getting into trouble, and the following day, shortly after noon, his uncle called at Ashmont House to express his approval, an unheard-of event.

"You survived an entire evening during which you must have been very bored," Uncle Fred said.

"Don't know if the word *bored* is strong enough."

"Yet you never put a foot wrong."

Ashmont stared at him. Uncle Fred always found fault. Saints and martyrs would have their work cut out for them, trying to pass his inspection.

"You sure?" Ashmont said.

His uncle nodded. "Well done. I believe it will grow easier in time."

"In time? *What?*"

"You've taken the first step in making yourself acceptable to a respectable young woman. And her family."

"Being bored witless?"

"The news will be all over London over the course of the next few days," his uncle said. "It will cast your prank on Thursday in a new light. I despaired of you then."

Ashmont hadn't followed instructions. It wasn't something he was accustomed to do.

"Now I allow myself to hope you're not altogether a lost cause," Uncle Fred went on. "It is absurd, certainly, but you are often absurd. In any event, I cannot fault your taste."

Sometimes Uncle Fred could be painfully clear. At others, he talked in riddles.

"Do you refer to Miss Pomfret?"

"Who else?"

"What's absurd?"

"Your apparently miraculous recovery from the events of last week."

Ashmont hadn't recovered. Forgiven or not, he was still troubled about the duel. His conversation with Olympia when they danced had made him feel ashamed. He'd chased her and done everything he could to win her over.

He'd wanted her, or so he'd believed, but now he wasn't at all sure what he'd wanted. A wife. Because Blackwood had one and Ashmont didn't want to be the last one of them to marry? Was that it? And there she'd been. Pretty. And she'd been kind and treated him . . . like a brother.

But he'd been oblivious to what she wanted or truly thought.

If he'd won in the end, and she'd married him . . .

He would have made her unhappy.

The thought being unpleasant, he shoved it to the back of his mind, a crowded place.

He'd no sooner stowed Olympia in the mental lumber room than Miss Pomfret strode to the forefront of his mind: the steady grey gaze with its occasional glint of silver, the soft mouth, the clear, self-assured voice . . . the smooth skin, the fresh scent of herbs, the modest dress, with its layers of armor, that she'd worn at the fancy fair.

This was bothersome, in an entirely different way.

He remembered her stepping over him when he lay on the ground, her skirts barely—just barely—brushing his trousers.

He'd made the mistake of grabbing her and she'd nearly killed him.

Where had she learnt to fight like that?

The point she'd given him, because of Keeffe.

So many riddles, so much to discover about her.

His uncle broke into the crowd of recollections. "You may wish to go out of London for a time," he said.

"Now?"

"Now would be best."

"And let the other fellows steal a march on me?" Ashmont said. "Don't think so. As it is—"

"If I detect signs of another gentleman's interest in the lady, I'll notify you forthwith. In the meantime, I ask you to take a fortnight to be absolutely certain you wish to follow this course. You will make a better impression on the lady as well as her father. You cannot count on Lady Charles to take your part. She has been kinder to you than you deserve, but her influence with her brother goes only so far, and he is most definitely not predisposed in your favor."

"A fortnight," Ashmont said.

"Take Blackwood with you. He needs a change of scenery as well."

Chapter 7

*O*n Saturday afternoon, while Papa was out, Aunt Julia arrived with Alice, and invited her nieces to ride with them in Hyde Park.

As Cassandra pointed out to her anxious mother, Lord deGriffith's ruling had not included rides in the park.

"You are most welcome to join us," Aunt Julia said, "if you fear I should prove inadequate as a chaperon."

"Good heavens, no. Today is my day with my sisters."

Every Saturday afternoon while they were in London, Mama joined her sisters for tea. They took turns as hostesses.

"Ah, I'd forgotten."

"It's only that Henry may not like it."

"I shall answer to Henry," Aunt Julia said. "But I know the girls want to talk about the party last night, and they ought to get air and exercise while they do. Rule or no rule, you cannot keep Hyacinth in the house. She isn't a prisoner, last I heard, and I'm sure you don't want to add to the talk."

"No, no, I most certainly do not. Lady Bartham was altogether dreadful, as I told him. But what is one to do? A man must be master in his own house, and I'm sure I do understand. Still, it does try one's patience. Yes, go, go."

Cassandra and Hyacinth hastily changed into riding dresses, grooms and horses were sent for, and in short order the ladies rode out.

As promised, they received a full and detailed account of Ripley's party. They got more than what Alice had promised, in fact, since they had their aunt's perspective, too.

Both she and Alice agreed that Ashmont had behaved very well and must have been bored senseless. But there were no pranks of any kind. No explosions. No ladies fainting. No gentlemen demanding satisfaction.

"All terribly civilized," Alice said. "But nonetheless thrilling, because nobody could be sure, until the very end, how long Their Dis-Graces could contain their natural . . . Let's call it *exuberance.* But they went out of their way to be charming, and it was sweet, I thought, because it was all for Olympia."

"For themselves as well," Aunt Julia said. "The loyalty remains, in spite of the occasional attempts to kill one another."

"It was a relief to me, I will admit," Alice said. "It was made clear beyond any doubt that Ripley is over head and ears in love with her and she returns the feeling."

"Poor Ashmont," Hyacinth said.

"You may save your sympathy," Alice said. "I discerned no signs of a broken heart. He looked relieved, in fact, when he returned Olympia to Ripley."

"Oh, I didn't mean that. But even if he is over head and ears in love with Cassandra now—"

"I must stop your subscription to the Library of Romance," Cassandra said. "Either that or give you a large dose of Mary Wollstonecraft to restore the balance of your mind."

In her opinion, every woman ought to read *A Vindication of the Rights of Woman* before she turned eighteen, then once a year thereafter.

"I see what's in front of me," Hyacinth said. "I saw the way he looked at you. I saw the way his eyes lit when he was talking to you."

"I, too, see what's in front of me," Aunt Julia said, looking ahead. The others followed her gaze. A cluster of gentlemen, who'd been talking among themselves, were now turning their horses toward the quartet of women. "Well, well, this will be educational, I expect."

"They've spotted Hyacinth," Cassandra said. "Shall we ride on ahead, Aunt Julia, or do you want reinforcements?"

"I hope I shall never see the day when I cannot manage a group of eager young men."

When they'd passed the gentlemen, Alice said, "It's too bad about Hyacinth. What do you mean to do?"

"At the moment, I can do nothing," Cassandra said. "My father and I have been at loggerheads for as long as I can remember. He was angry with me about the Owsley business, and he wasn't altogether unjustified. But my fault or not, Papa made a silly rule, which I'm sure he now realizes, though his pride won't let him admit it. And so we're reduced to finding exceptions. The fancy fair. Riding in the park. But one can't get to know a gentleman in that way. A girl needs to go to parties, and compare and contrast what's on offer."

Alice laughed. "You put it well enough. It isn't called the Marriage Mart for nothing."

"My sister is a jewel who ought to be displayed in elegant settings," Cassandra said. "I wish you could have seen the way she sparkled at the hot, stuffy, fancy fair. It comes to her naturally. She's simply herself, and the men swoon. True, men see little else but the outside, and she is beautiful, but her nature makes her more so."

"Aunt has promised to help," Alice said.

They both looked back. Gentlemen on horseback now surrounded Aunt Julia and Hyacinth.

"How interesting," Alice said.

"You see? How unfair that she may not have the rest of her Season. I vow, Papa is—"

"No, no, I mean Lord Frederick Beckingham."

"Where?" Cassandra saw a cluster of men on horseback. It took her a moment to recognize Lord Frederick at this distance. Then he became all too familiar, so similar in build to his nephew. The way he held his head. And the shoulders, those big shoulders.

"He isn't there for Hyacinth, I promise you," Alice said.

Cassandra wouldn't be surprised if he were. Not a month ago, the eighteen-year-old daughter of Charles Manners-Sutton had married a man of nearly fifty. An extremely wealthy man.

"I could say nothing in front of our aunt, but I wish you might have seen them dancing last night," Alice said. "I'm certain they've a history of some kind. I've caught hints from time to time, but whatever the story is, it happened before you and I were born. All I can tell you is, one could practically see the sparks fly."

What Cassandra saw was the gentlemen dispersing, and Hyacinth riding toward Cassandra and Alice, leaving the older couple trailing a short distance behind.

"Did Lord Frederick frighten away all your admirers?" Alice said when Hyacinth caught up.

Hyacinth laughed. "Oh, no. He only waved his hand, like this." She gave the merest sketch of a wave. "And they began to fall away. Do you know, I think he fancies Aunt Julia."

"That, or they are two wily old courtiers plotting," Alice said.

"Perhaps both," Hyacinth said. "Not so old, either."

Cassandra said nothing. She was remembering a small dismissive wave of a ducal hand, and its effect on bystanders in Putney Heath. *Marry me.*

She glanced at her sister, then at the pair behind them.

No, she could never be so desperate.

If ASHMONT HAD to leave London—and he did see the wisdom of it, even if he didn't like it—he might as well do it quickly, and get it over with all the sooner. He sent a message to Blackwood, who agreed as promptly as he'd always used to do before he was married.

Since Ashmont couldn't take his leave of Miss Pomfret directly, he did it by proxy. He and Blackwood called on Lady Charles on Sunday, shortly after she'd returned from church. For the present, she was living at her parents' London residence, Chelsfield House. Her own town house wouldn't be fit for habitation, she said, for a month or more.

The more formal rooms being still draped in holland covers, the two dukes joined her in the morning room.

"I've left a skeleton staff at Camberley Place," she said. "You may wish to stop for a while to fish. As I recollect, you've never needed a great army of servants about you. Even Ripley, who's always liked his creature comforts, was content to live rough at the fishing house. More than content. None of you liked to leave, as I recollect."

Ashmont and Blackwood looked at each other, then at her. They had planned to go to the Stockbridge races, then on to other races in the July calendar.

But Camberley Place . . . the wonderful fishing house where they'd taken refuge as boys and young men . . . the atmosphere of the ancient place altogether . . . so many happy memories.

"Am I to understand we're still welcome?" Blackwood said.

"It will be quiet," she said. "I thought you would like a time of quiet."

"To ponder our sins," Blackwood said with a small smile.

"Fishing is good for the soul," she said. "That's what my husband claimed. He continued to fish until he couldn't anymore. You might as well go. I'm sure he'd suggest it."

That settled the question.

Lord Charles Ancaster, like his house, had been a refuge although, as boys, they wouldn't have understood it quite that way. They only knew that the place felt right, they liked him and Lady Charles immensely, they felt better when they were there, and they hated to leave.

The two dukes thanked her and, rather shaken, took their leave not long thereafter.

⸎

Camberley Place
Tuesday 25th Instant

Dear Miss Pomfret,

Blackwood and I are now settled at our favorite place, which Lady Charles most kindly offered us as a retreat for thinking. She seems to believe we can do this, although

Blackwood claimed that any attempt on my part was likely to unhinge me. He watches me closely for signs of fever. She told us to fish, and we've followed orders, as we don't dare to do otherwise where she's concerned.

We've moved into the fishing house, lock, stock, and barrel, and Sommers. He cries a great deal, though less today than yesterday. It wasn't what he expected. Primitive conditions, as you'll remember. He expected a grand fishing temple like mine at Selston Hall. But he turns out to be as adept at scaling fish as he is in every valeting skill. I reckon it's all the practice shaving me. You'll wonder how he's resisted accidentally cutting my throat. I can hear you saying that, actually.

We had planned to go to the Stockbridge races this week, but to our surprise, we find that we like the quiet. The quiet here, at any rate. This place was always different. Even with Lord Charles gone and Lady Charles in London, the atmosphere remains. If it rains, I daresay our mood will change. It's cramped quarters for three men. While we deal well enough in fair weather, we should be at each other's throats if forced to stay indoors for more than a day. The servants come and look in on us now and again, bringing this or that, while discreetly checking for broken furniture and such. But we are peaceful, and settled, for the present, at any rate.

I've written to Keeffe, but since he has difficulty with a pen, as you explained last week, perhaps you'll be so good as to let me know how he's mending. I hope it's quickly and well.

Yours sincerely,

A

Cassandra looked up from the letter.

She visited Keeffe at least once a day. Grandpapa Chelsfield, who'd hired him, paid for everything. He'd made sure the quarters in the mews were large and well appointed, more befitting a former champion jockey than even a head coachman, let alone a lowly groom.

Keeffe had hung the painting in pride of place over the chimneypiece.

"The duke is corrupting you," she said.

"Like you didn't use me to send a letter to him. It was you, miss, setting a bad example, though I grieve to say it."

"You asked me to write it."

"I was in a delirium from the pain, else I'd've realized it wasn't proper."

"You were perfectly in your senses, and I only wish I'd been in mine. I made an error of judgment, and he took it as encouragement."

A gross error of judgment. Giving Ashmont a point was one of the more idiotish things she'd done, and she'd done more than a few in that category. She knew as well as everybody else that he couldn't resist a challenge. She'd as good as invited him to get more.

"What's His Grace say? Or is it too precious to tell?"

"Precious, indeed." She read the letter aloud.

"Fishing," Keeffe said. "That'll keep him out of trouble."

"He'll very quickly grow bored with keeping out of trouble."

"Maybe. Maybe not. But long as we're on this improper course, maybe you'd be so kind as to write him an answer from me."

⤚⤙

deGriffith House
Thursday 27th Instant

Dear Duke,

I am to tell you that Keeffe is completely healed, only nobody believes him and he's a prisoner, practically, of quacks and worrying women. In fact, he is improving as predicted, and nobody locked him in, let alone chained him to his bed—although I have considered such measures more than once, because he doesn't know what "rest" means. "No exertion" might as well be a phrase in Sanskrit, for all he understands it. Lord Pershore was so kind as to send his own surgeon on Friday, and Mr. Williams echoes Mr. Greenslade's recommendations.

Keeffe has hung your painting in the place of honor above the chimneypiece.

I am to tell you he never learnt to fish, although he did try mudlarking when he was a lad, without much luck.

Sincerely,
Cassandra Pomfret

P.S. Don't write to me again.

deGriffith House
Saturday 29th Instant

Dear Duke,

I am desolated to interrupt your alleged fishing or debaucheries or whatever you are doing, and I would not do so, believe me, had I any satisfactory alternative. At present, however, I discern none, and upon applying to Keeffe, was advised to request your services.

I need a ruffian. This is the role Keeffe customarily plays for my club, when we turn our attention to self-protection for ladies. However, thanks to you, Keeffe is hors de combat. He seems to believe you would do best as a murderous attacker.

ASHMONT AND BLACKWOOD had been lounging under a tree by the riverbank when the letter was delivered. Express.

Ashmont's heart, which had started a wild beating at the sight of the familiar handwriting, had not altogether settled. Her previous P.S. had given him a fit of the blue devils. Still, he managed a veneer of amused insouciance.

"She wants me," he said.

Blackwood kept his gaze on the pages of a tattered volume of *A Vindication of the Rights of Woman* he'd found in a basket in the fishing house. "That I very much doubt, no matter who *she* is."

As though there could be any other *she*. "Miss Pomfret. She says she wants a ruffian and a murderous attacker for her club."

"Ah." Blackwood set down the book.

"Assassins club, do you think?"

"Not quite. I assume she refers to the Andromeda Society. A ladies' charitable club. They go to the rescue of Andromedas, as I understand it. From the myth."

"From the . . ." Ashmont looked up at the clouds floating overhead and saw a clear night, stars blanketing the heavens. In the darkness, he'd nearly tripped over her. A small, elfin girl. She stood by the fishing house, gaping up at the stars, and turning round and round.

"You'll make yourself dizzy and tumble down the riverbank and into the river," he said.

"I sneaked out," she said, coming to a rather drunken standstill. "Don't tell."

"I never tell."

"Did you come to spin in circles, too? It's fun."

He'd forgotten something at the fishing house—a glove, a book—he couldn't remember now what it was. But on an impulse, perhaps because she was misbehaving or perhaps because she was comical in her slow whirling and dizziness, he said, "I came to find the stories in the stars."

Andromeda was one he'd pointed out to her. He'd told her how Andromeda had been chained to a rock as a sacrifice to a sea monster or dragon, but Perseus had killed the monster and saved her.

But soon a nursemaid had come and dragged the elfin girl away, and the next day he, Blackwood, and Ripley had returned to school.

It was the same girl, the one he saw the next year in broad day, bravely facing Godfrey Wills. That was why she'd seemed so familiar. The way she stood. The way she held herself, straight and strong, as though she were much larger than she was. And the voice, the youthful version of the cool, self-assured voice.

It was curious, wasn't it, the way faces might blur or vanish from memory or get muddled with others, but a voice echoed so clearly, even years later.

"Andromeda," Blackwood was saying. "Surely you remember the myth?"

"Yes. My mind wandered."

"When does it do otherwise?"

Ashmont came back fully to the moment. The river below, burbling along. The quiet. The simplicity of the place. "A charity, you said."

"Alice says the club's meant to help women needing rescuing from 'the dragons of poverty and ignorance.'"

Ashmont returned to the letter.

My club meets on Friday next at two o'clock in Chelsea at the Baron de Bérenger's Stadium. The general meeting will take about an hour. During this part we usually discuss the subjugation of women, bills before Parliament relevant to our mission, letters to be written to the public journals, and progress in current projects. You will find it dead boring. The practical demonstrations come afterward, usually allotted half an hour. As I was reminded this morning by one of the members, I had promised a demonstration. This is where I require your services.

The club members are all women of some maturity. I am the youngest, admitted because my grandmother Lady Chelsfield is a founder and because I have useful skills, thanks to her and Keeffe. The ladies will be fully clothed and of large mental capacity. If you find the prospect too dull, too daunting, or inconvenient to your plans, and have no desire to make yourself useful—after having broken my

*tiger as well as my carriage, thereby curtailing the activities
in which I take pleasure—kindly let me know by return
post. Keeffe thought of you first, but I daresay he will be
able to recommend somebody else in the event you decline.*

Yours sincerely,
Cassandra Pomfret

＄

Camberley Place
Saturday 29th Instant

*Leaving first thing tomorrow. Will collect you at one
o'clock on Friday next. Leave it to me. Will arrange with
Lady Charles for chaperonage.*

A

Drawing Room of deGriffith House
Tuesday 2 July

"HAVE YOU TAKEN leave of your senses, Julia?" Papa said. "Ashmont is not admitted anywhere. Even the King won't have him."

"Really, Henry, I've been living in Surrey, not Siberia," Aunt Julia said. "I know as much as everybody else does. Not three weeks ago, when he came to the house, I hauled him over the coals. The fact remains, he is a duke, and he seems to be taken with Cassandra."

"Taken with her? Since when?"

"Well, you know, dear, Lady Bartham did imply as much," Mama said. "She claimed he lingered at our stall for quite some time, flirting with Cassandra."

Papa raised his eyebrows at Cassandra.

She shrugged. "It didn't seem like flirting to me, but then, I'm no expert."

"Why else bring a dirty street child to meet her?" Aunt Julia said. "It's the sort of thing little boys do. They bring dead spiders or mice or other disgusting objects to girls they fancy. They pull their hair. Even grown men use ridicule and insults to express affection for each other. Or fights. As to fighting, I'm told he took exception to somebody's slighting remark about her."

Not a word was a lie. The Duke of Ashmont did seem to be taken with Cassandra, for reasons as unfathomable as they were, surely, ephemeral. He had invited combat—though he did that at the slightest provocation. All the same, she felt deeply uncomfortable, and wished she had taken more time to think about Keeffe's suggestion for a substitute.

Alice would have done well enough, but she'd had to go out of Town again, which left Cassandra grinding her teeth over yet another aspect of her life that Ashmont had damaged. Not only could she not travel as freely as she'd done before, but she couldn't keep her promises to ladies who relied upon her and who'd helped make her time in London feel worthwhile.

It had seemed only fair that the man who'd caused the trouble should be summoned from wherever he was amusing himself and be obliged to put matters right. Now she suspected she'd been precipitate, and made one more error of judgment. Adding to her discomfort was the small, nagging voice telling her she wasn't entirely unlike him in this regard.

I'm outrageous. You're outrageous.

She didn't squirm, but it wanted all her practice in self-control not to.

"He'll fight about anything," Papa said. "I won't have that profligate near my daughter."

"I should have thought Cassandra was up to his weight."

"I daresay, in the right circumstances, she could knock him down," Papa said. "I should have thought that's what she'd prefer."

He returned to Cassandra. "Well, what have you to say for yourself? Will you try to persuade me that you are taken with—what do they call him?—Luscious Lucius, the gorgeous libertine?"

"It seems I must find a husband, if I don't want Hyacinth to spend her life as a spinster."

"If you think throwing that reckless blockhead in my face will make me change my mind about Hyacinth, I advise you to think again."

"I'd much rather throw somebody else in your face, Papa, but the Duke of Ashmont seems to be the only gentleman who doesn't run in the other direction when he sees me."

"That is a gross exaggeration of the situation," Papa said. "If you would only go out to the parties and stop playing the virago, you might have scores of admirers."

"Be that as it may, Ashmont has applied to me," Aunt Julia said. "Cassandra has agreed to his driving her out to her meeting. I shall accompany them. About three miles to the Stadium and three back here. That's time enough to discover whether she finds his company disagreeable. If so, that will be the end of it. If she finds him tolerable, we shall see what we shall see. When word gets out, it's more than possible that his fearlessness will stir the competitive spirit of other gentlemen."

Papa considered, his gaze moving from Aunt Julia to Cassandra to Mama. "Very well," he said. "But if I detect the smallest whiff of impropriety, I will kill him."

"Of that I have no doubt, Papa," Cassandra said. "And everybody will declare upon oath that it was an accident, even if you shoot him in the head at Crockford's hazard table in front of forty witnesses."

Friday 5 July

The Duke of Ashmont arrived at deGriffith House in a gleaming black hooded cabriolet, with the requisite very large black stallion and very small groom, smaller than Keeffe.

Papa, looking down at this spectacle from a window, made *grrrr* sounds, and muttered, "And in snow-white kid gloves, if you please, with his shirt wristbands turned back over his coat cuffs, like the veriest dandy."

The ladies stood with him at the window.

The cabriolet filled Cassandra with lust. It was a dashing vehicle, far more so than her demi-mail phaeton. She tried to persuade herself that this was why she felt overwarm and short of breath as she watched Ashmont alight with easy athletic grace. In exquisitely tailored glory of black coat, white trousers, impeccable white linen, and fawn-colored hat, the man crossing the pavement to the steps seemed another being altogether from the one she'd encountered on Putney Heath.

Though her father grumbled, he did not lock Cassandra in her room or throw chairs at the duke from the balcony. When Ashmont entered the drawing room, in all his diabolical golden beauty, Lord deGriffith was stonily polite.

Cassandra did not feel as stony as she wished.

She felt as though she'd crossed a bridge without realizing.

She told herself this was silly.

Ashmont was on good behavior, a pose he couldn't keep up for long.

A week or more at Camberley Place didn't change his character.

He was respectful to her parents and Aunt Julia. He made a little joke to Hyacinth about her singlehandedly saving all the foreigners in distress at the fancy fair. Then he came to Cassandra.

"Miss Pomfret."

"Duke."

"A fine day for our little journey." He glanced down at the sturdy green umbrella in her hand, and the devil danced in his blue eyes. "Not but what the wind might turn at any moment."

"Indeed it might," Papa said. "Yet no matter how the wind blows, I trust you to see the ladies to Chelsea and home again without mishap."

If Ashmont heard the unsaid *Or you will die in a painful manner,* he offered no sign, only expressed himself honored. Mercifully soon thereafter, Cassandra stood on the pavement in front of Ashmont's dashing equipage.

Then he was taking her hand, to help her into the vehicle . . . and holding her hand for too long.

"Don't do that," she said. "My father is watching from the window, looking for an excuse to drop bricks on your head."

"Don't worry about my head," Ashmont said.

"The last thing I should ever worry about is your head."

"I know what I'm doing," he said. "He knows why I'm here, and this is what a fellow does, protective father or no protective father glaring down at him."

"You are here as a substitute for Keeffe," she said.

"That, too," Ashmont said.

"That *only*," she said as he released her hand at last, and she sat, nerves jangling.

They hadn't had time to settle before he was in the seat beside her, whip and reins in his white-gloved hands. At which point she fully experienced, right down to her toes and with an odd feeling in the pit of her stomach, the vehicle's confined quarters.

Unlike the seat of a demi-mail phaeton, that of a dashing cabriolet seemed to allow room for one man of his size and one-half a woman of her size. Most of the right side of her body was pressed against the left side of his, a great, warm wall of male.

The body heat penetrated all the layers of their clothing . . . not that men wore as many layers as women did . . . and it was not at all intelligent to picture what he was wearing or not wearing underneath what he was wearing.

She pinned her attention to the tiny tiger as he moved away from the horse's head. A moment later he'd disappeared behind the carriage.

Aunt Julia, in a handsome green riding dress with white bodice and veiled hat, rode up then with her groom, and signaled Ashmont to drive on.

No turning back now.

THIS WAS THE girl, Ashmont thought, marveling.

This was the one who'd spun herself dizzy, gazing at the stars.

This was the little rebel who wouldn't be bullied. This was she, all grown up.

Not an elfin creature but a Boadicea in a simple green dress. A white lace pelerine, tied with light purple bows, floated over her shoulders. A few scraps of matching purple ribbon embellished the white hat perched upon her dark red hair. She carried a no-nonsense umbrella of a green darker than her dress.

In his fancy, it was a spear, exactly the sort of thing Boadicea ought to carry.

For a time, all he could do was enjoy the sensation of a shapely feminine body pressed against his. Until he extricated them from the crush at Hyde Park Corner, he needed to concentrate on driving. Only louts dashed headlong through the obstacle course of the London streets, whether or not the lady's father watched, hoping for an excuse to murder the driver.

The stallion, Nestor, was generally well behaved, though he had his quirks, as did any other creature. Managing him didn't require great effort. The truly interesting work was making one's way through a chaos of carriages, coaches, omnibuses, carts, wagons, riders, pedestrians, stray dogs and children, and, depending on the area and time of day, livestock of all kinds. All of these might, at any moment, do something unexpected.

Ashmont was well aware of Miss Pomfret seeing what he saw, and anticipating what he'd do and sometimes bracing herself in case he did the wrong thing. But he didn't. He'd learnt riding and driving from strict teachers, and he'd been taught to care for dumb creatures, if not for his own safety. Furthermore, he had five thousand nine hundred and ninety-nine points to accumulate, and causing another accident wasn't the way to do it.

Soon enough, however, they passed Hyde Park Corner and into Grosvenor Place. When they turned into the King's Road, Lady Charles gave a little wave, then rode past them and on a short distance ahead. He, too, picked up the pace, aware of Miss Pomfret tensing beside him.

"I'll do my best not to overturn the carriage," he said.

"That's the least of my concerns," she said. "You drive well enough."

"Tolerably well?"

"My aunt wouldn't have agreed to this, let alone ridden ahead, had she fears for my safety."

"She wanted to give us time to talk, I suppose," he said. "For instance, I'm wild with curiosity about your club, and what I'm to do. Perhaps I should have asked whether to bring a mask."

"You are not playing a highwayman, but a ruffian. It's very important, else I shouldn't have resorted to seeking your help."

She went on to explain about the club's work. They assisted families in debtors' prisons. They taught reading, writing, and sums; sewing, knitting, and other needle skills; basics of hygiene and nursing. Essentially, they did what they could to keep women out of workhouses and off the streets.

"What we do doesn't attract attention," she said. "No fancy fairs. No hiring grand concert rooms. Royals do not put in appearances. Nothing elegant about it. We go to lowly, often insalubrious, and sometimes dangerous places."

"Not the rookeries." Even he avoided certain parts of London. Taking risks was one thing. Begging to have your throat cut was another matter entirely.

"Not usually, but sometimes. Keeffe makes it possible for me. That's the world he grew up in. He knows how to talk to people, and he's skilled at dealing with troublesome persons."

Ashmont must have looked skeptical because she said, "He's crippled, not incapable."

"I assumed he must be made of strong material, to survive that accident."

"He's found ways to compensate for what he's lost, and he's never forgotten the survival skills he learnt growing up. He's taught me so much. And we're teaching the ladies—and they will teach others. That's what this is about. This is why I sent for you."

"To be a ruffian, you said."

"We'd promised a demonstration for this meeting. The ladies

were looking forward to it. Mrs. Roake, who started the club with my grandmother, visited Saturday last and asked about Keeffe and what we might do instead of the demonstration. But I couldn't bear to disappoint them. These ladies have done so much for me. They've helped me find a way to do something worthwhile and satisfying with my intelligence and skills."

She makes men cry, Morris had said, and Ashmont had assumed this referred to her plainspokenness, which might hurt a sensitive fellow's feelings. His hide being more of the alligator variety, he liked the way she put all her cards on the table. A fellow knew where he stood.

What he felt was altogether different—not hurt feelings but something else, the oddest sensation, a tightening in his throat as though somebody were strangling him.

They've helped me find a way to do something worthwhile and satisfying with my intelligence and skills.

He remembered what she'd written. He remembered easily. He'd read it enough times to have memorized every word.

. . . curtailing the activities in which I take pleasure . . .

He'd broken her tiger and her carriage, frightened away her maid, and spoiled everything important to her—the girl who'd whirled like some woodland nymph under the stars.

Five thousand nine hundred and ninety-nine points. To be *a tolerable human being.*

At present he wasn't sure ten thousand points would be enough.

Chapter 8

The Stadium, or, British National Arena, Chelsea
A short time later

*I*nteresting choice for your ladies' club," Ashmont said. "Rather out of the way."

He and Miss Pomfret were walking toward what had once been Lord Cremorne's mansion.

"Not two and a half miles from Piccadilly," Miss Pomfret said. "It's more convenient for some of the ladies who don't live in Town. For those of us who do, it's a pleasant escape into the country."

A few years earlier, the Baron de Bérenger had bought the property known as Chelsea Farm, and made an attractive combination of pleasure grounds and athletic arena.

Lady Charles had ridden on to make a tour of the place, which she hadn't seen since before de Bérenger took over. As she took her leave of them, her ladyship had reminded Ashmont that she was trusting him to behave as he ought to do.

It was a deuced lot of trust, given the temptations. In spite of the damper Miss Pomfret had applied to his spirits, temptation still tempted.

She was pretty and shapely and lively, and having her sitting practically in his lap had done nothing to stifle his appreciation. Taking the cabriolet had been an idea of genius, and not only because of the intimate seating arrangement.

He'd noticed the silvery gleam of excitement in her eyes and the wash of pink over her cheekbones when they came out of deGriffith House—and she'd been gazing at the vehicle, not him, at the time. She was a whipster, a good one, from what he'd been able to make out through the fog of drink and blind terror that morning in Putney Heath. Being a whipster, she'd regarded his vehicle with a longing even she couldn't hide.

She took up the dainty watch dangling at her waist and looked at it while he considered the white straw hat he wanted to take off. He remembered the way she'd looked, bareheaded, at the inn. He imagined taking out the pins and watching her hair fall down about her bare shoulders. And her bare back.

Patience. He could be patient. He fished, didn't he? This was something like fishing, wasn't it?

"We've arrived in good time," she said. "As I wrote, the first hour will be devoted to discussion. I shan't need you until three o'clock. In the meantime, I'm sure you can find something to do."

"I'm not coming to the meeting?"

"You are not required until the practical demonstration. As I wrote to you, the first part is boring. But there's plenty to do on the grounds. A pigeon shooting area and a carousel ring, where the gentlemen cut off imaginary enemies' heads, I believe. Cricket. Golf. Quoits."

"Yes, I know," he said. "I've been here before. But I'm interested in your club."

She treated him to the stony stare. "You know that's nonsense. I realize that the Stadium is not the most exciting place. No acrobatic females and nothing exploding or likely to and the only hazard hereabouts is the falling-off-one's-horse kind or getting an arrow in the neck or—"

"Drowning," he said. "There's a swimming school. They put you in a harness and drag you up and down the shallow little lake they've built."

She turned her gaze heavenwards. "Do you know, I'm having a happy daydream in which I drag you up and down a lake. A deep one. Filled with crocodiles. And sharks."

"Don't think sharks live in—"

"I see." Her stony gaze came back to him. "You're going to make a tick of yourself."

"You've aroused my curiosity," he said. "What does Keeffe do during the so-called boring part? Pigeon shoot? Quoits?"

"He helps us with tactics. Advises."

"I can do that," Ashmont said. "Tactics. You know. The pranks. That sort of thing wants planning and preparation and how to get in and out of difficulties without getting attacked by screaming women or angry townspeople."

She studied her umbrella, her expression speculative.

"Meant to ask about that," he said. "Sun's shining. Nothing in the air or sky promising rain. What's the umbrella for?"

"It's . . . an accessory," she said.

"To a crime?"

"It could be. Any minute now."

He smiled his second most winning smile.

IT WASN'T THE smile, even though that particular curve of his mouth, which made his eyes crinkle at the corners and seemed to deepen the blue, set off palpitations in Cassandra's bosom and tempted her to smile back.

That smile . . . But she could withstand it. She knew it meant nothing. He simply did it. He couldn't help himself.

The trouble was, he was going to come to the meeting, no matter what. When the Duke of Ashmont wanted to get into a place, he got in. She did not want to see him suddenly burst through a door or window or spring out from behind a curtain.

They'd reached the mansion. A footman opened the door.

She said, "Very well, but if ennui sets off an urge to jump out of a window, you must restrain yourself. We have important business to conduct, and not much time. Interruptions are unwelcome."

"No interruptions," he said. "I promise."

"I have a few more rules for you," she said. "If you break any one of them, I shall personally murder you. And nobody will care. In fact, the ladies will help me hide the body."

THEIR CHAPERON RODE on to the equestrian area, where the Baron de Bérenger had set up a carousel ring. There Lady Charles watched the gentlemen display their skill and elegance on horseback. And their manly physiques.

Lady Charles had mourned her husband for three years, a fact that would have shocked her much younger self. She had not married for love. She had married because Lord Charles Ancaster worshipped the ground she walked on, because he was the most suitable of all the gentlemen who courted her . . . and because the gentleman eighteen-year-old Lady Julia Pomfret believed she wanted didn't know she was alive. She'd married, believing that since her heart was irretrievably broken, it made no difference which man she wed. She'd turned out to be altogether wrong and extremely fortunate.

But Lord Charles had been gone for three years, and it would have distressed him to know she'd grieved for so long. Recent encounters with the three young men they'd more or less taken under their wing, combined with letters from her brother Henry's family, had only confirmed her intention to rejoin the world.

As it turned out, so did the elegant gentlemen demonstrating their grace and daring on horseback. She was a widow and a grandmother, true. On the other hand, at six and forty she still had a pulse, and a fine masculine physique had no trouble increasing its rate.

Meanwhile the gentlemen, also possessing pulses, were far from indifferent to Lady Charles. While she watched, the equestrians put on more of a show. After their turn at the exercise, three with whom she was acquainted joined her. Some mild flirtation occurred, which she enjoyed very much.

Not long thereafter, as she left the gentlemen and was debating where to go next, she did not pretend to be surprised when Lord

Frederick Beckingham rode toward her. He always knew where his nephew was.

Though both had been courtiers for all of their adult lives, in private, with each other, they wasted no time on polite chitchat.

"You needn't have troubled yourself," she said. "Nothing untoward has occurred."

"With him, one can never be sure," Lord Frederick said. "I'll admit, I'm terrified he'll bungle this."

"If so, it would be for the best. If he cannot rise to the challenge, then he doesn't deserve my niece."

"I hope you've told him this."

Her fine eyebrows went up a very little. "Do you imagine I am not capable of managing this sort of thing? Do you suppose I could not do it blindfolded, with my hands tied behind my back?"

"That sounds interesting," he said.

Lady Charles didn't blush. Not on the outside.

She only smiled. "And so it might be, I daresay." She glanced back at the equestrians.

"Indeed." He returned her smile. "As to my nephew, I believe, this once, he does know his own mind."

"That remains to be seen. Men often think they do—"

"And discover they're altogether wrong."

"True," she said.

"Most unfortunately true," he said.

A short, fierce silence ensued.

If Lady Charles believed a bridge had been crossed, she gave no sign. But when he suggested they ride on to the pigeon shooting grounds, she agreed.

Meanwhile

ARMS FOLDED, THE Duke of Ashmont leant against a window frame at the back of the room. He was not inconspicuous. For a six-foot-plus man who looked like a Greek deity, that was impossible.

But he contrived to remain quiet and did nothing to call attention to himself, and after the first few minutes, the club members went about their business, more or less as though Keeffe were there.

They'd heard Keeffe had been injured in a carriage mishap. Cassandra's simple explanation—that Keeffe had suggested the duke take his place—didn't surprise them. Neither did the duke's agreeing. They knew Ashmont was game for anything, even a group of bluestocking do-gooders.

To her surprise, he did keep out of the way, as Keeffe would have done, until wanted. Though the first and greater part of the meeting proceeded precisely as she'd described, Ashmont didn't fall asleep or prowl the room like a caged animal or climb out of a window.

Then, all other club business being dealt with, it came time for the ladies' favorite: the practical demonstrations.

Here was the great test. Keeffe had been so sure that Ashmont, a famous brawler, was the right choice.

Cassandra wasn't at all sure. Still, she'd assumed he was incapable of paying attention for more than a few minutes, had she not? Yet not only had he endured the bulk of the meeting without disrupting it, but he also seemed interested in their projects.

Seemed. The discussion must be leagues over his head, and so he'd taken his mind elsewhere for the duration. Behind a mask of apparent fascination he was undoubtedly contemplating scantily clad opera dancers or calculating odds for a coming horse race.

Not that what went on in his head was of any interest to her. He was welcome to think what he liked, she told herself. All she cared about was his doing what was required of him and not making her regret inviting him.

She glanced down at her notes. "The last time the Baron de Bérenger joined us, we touched on the topic of the umbrella as a weapon," she said. "He pointed out that it was not as strong as a walking stick or as adaptable as a whip. He had no suggestions beyond employing it as a shield. He'd used it to prevent an assailant's seeing him take out his pistol. He'd used it to keep a mad dog from biting him."

She held up her unopened umbrella, crook uppermost. "This struck us as a limited view. Hence today's topic: Is the umbrella a useful weapon for ladies? I suggest we begin with our fighting expert. Duke, what is your opinion?"

"What's yours?" he said.

"Mine," she said, taken aback.

She'd expected him to scoff at the umbrella, gently or otherwise. The Baron de Bérenger hadn't scoffed, but he hadn't been as enthusiastic and helpful as she'd hoped. She hadn't warned Ashmont because she wanted an unpremeditated reaction. Later, they would see who was correct.

This wasn't the only surprise. She tried to remember the last time a man had sought her opinion about anything remotely important. She tried to remember the last time a man had hesitated to offer his, whether he was asked or not.

Never. The answer was, never.

"Yes, yours," he said. "You're the one looking to defend herself from robbers and ruffians. There's the thing, in your hand. What do you believe you can do with it?"

He straightened away from the window in one smooth motion. "Here I am, a desperado, lurking in the shadows. I spring out at you, without warning."

Which he did. He was across the room in a flash, and coming at her.

She swung the umbrella up and at him. He grabbed it—or started to—but she moved in the nick of time and skipped backward. He started to stumble, but caught himself, and went for her again. Instinctively she slid her hand down the umbrella, farther from the handle, swung it up, and thrust it at his neck. With a laugh, he pivoted and danced back.

"Good, very good," he said.

He was quick, as quick as Keeffe. But she knew the former jockey. She didn't know Ashmont. She might be in trouble.

The duke charged at her.

She crouched and turned, bringing the umbrella point up under his neck, and he wheeled away—only to come back, in the blink of an eye, reaching for the umbrella.

She dodged and swung at his knees. He leapt out of the way. And came back again, fists out this time. He swung at her, and she dodged and bobbed the way Keeffe had taught her, and raised the umbrella to knock Ashmont's fists away.

She was aware of an inner surge of heat and a feeling she recognized—the fight feeling, Keeffe called it. She was distantly aware of murmuring and the sound of chairs scraping over the floor. But she had no attention to spare for anything else, because the duke kept coming at her and if she didn't fight with everything she had in her, she'd lose.

She lunged at him, aiming the tip of the umbrella at his groin. He spun away, and tried to come up behind her. She turned and went low and swung at his shins and hit at last, but he was so quick on his feet, she barely tapped him before he was dancing away, circling her, just out of reach.

On it went. He never stopped moving, and neither did she. He gave her no quarter, no time to think. He was always there, always coming for her, relentless.

She fought him off, but she couldn't get in a proper blow. For a man so large, he was amazingly light on his feet, and his reflexes were a match for Keeffe's.

Boxing. That was it. Ashmont was a pugilist.

"And I don't even have a weapon," he said as he evaded another blow. "What would you do if I had?"

She was tiring, breathing hard, and he seemed as fresh as when they'd begun.

"Give him a blasted weapon!" she said.

Somebody slid an umbrella across the floor toward them.

Cassandra stood back only long enough to let him snatch it up.

He came up swinging, but she'd expected that, and stepped out of the way, shifting her hold to grasp her umbrella with two hands, a short distance from each end, and blocked the blow. He drew back, assumed a fencing stance, and said, *"En garde*, Miss Pomfret."

"You idiot," she said, even as she struck.

He parried, and they fenced, more or less, with the umbrellas, but not for long. A bit of pretend swordplay, then he changed his stance and brought his umbrella down exactly where she was about to step, and she missed tripping over it by a hairsbreadth.

Misdirection.

She was the idiot.

She heard Keeffe's voice. *Don't signal.* Somehow she had, though. Ashmont had read her mind. But she hadn't read his.

Keep your head.

That was growing harder to do. She was tiring. Soon, her brain and body wouldn't keep up with each other. Time was running out. She had to bring Ashmont down and *quickly.*

He rushed at her, and she pivoted and raised her umbrella as though to strike the back of his neck, but when he stepped aside, she swung downward. Her umbrella's crook caught his ankle, and he wasn't quick enough this time. He fell with a crash and an oath.

As though at a great distance she heard first one, then another pair of hands clapping, and others joining in, but it seemed to be happening in another place. Her heart pounded so hard, it deadened other sounds. Her blood roared through her veins. Her chemise was damp with sweat and her legs wanted to buckle.

She looked down at him. His chest rose and fell fast enough to tell her he was catching his breath. His face was flushed and his blue eyes were very bright.

He laughed.

"Not bad," he said. "For a girl."

"Not bad," she said between gasps. "For a duke."

All Ashmont wanted to do was lie there, gazing up at her—the flushed face, eyes gleaming silver in triumph, bosom heaving, breath coming hard and fast.

Her hat had slid to a rakish angle and her hair was escaping, dark red tendrils dangling at her neck. A few damp wisps stuck to her cheek. Her dress hung crookedly. Her pelerine's bows having loosened, it was sliding from her shoulders. One sleeve sagged, and her belt had slid to one side.

Temptation, oh, the temptation—to hook his foot round her ankle and bring her down on top of him in a great heap of rustling muslin. To toss aside the hat and the lacy pelerine. To undo her hair. To undo everything.

. . . I trust you to see the ladies to Chelsea and home again without mishap.

The image of Lord deGriffith rose in his mind. It didn't take any thinking to imagine his reaction to that scenario.

Ashmont had only an instant to enjoy the view, in any event, because the ladies were bustling about, skirts swishing, and somebody said, "We're late!"

Pushing stray wisps of hair back from her cheek, Miss Pomfret said breathlessly, "We've gone over our time. The next ladies' group will be here at any minute. Pray hurry. Or did I injure you? Break something, perchance?"

"Sorry to disappoint you, but no," he said.

He rose, and if he was a little dizzy, it had nothing to do with fatigue and everything to do with their wonderful battle. She was quick and clever and unpredictable. And more fun than anybody could have guessed.

And unbearably inviting, in her present state, her businesslike ensemble all to pieces.

"You're a wreck," he said.

She looked blank. She was discomposed, obviously. He was far from composed himself, but he never troubled about such things.

He gave her a light push toward the door. "Never mind. Can't be helped. Take my arm."

"Certainly not."

"Only to steady you."

"I am perfectly steady."

"Doesn't look that way. You look as though you've been in a fight."

"I *was* in a fight."

"And a fine job you did, too. But you can't look like it. I'm reasonably certain of that. If your aunt sees you as you are at this moment, she'll trample me to death, and that will ruin everything."

No exaggeration. Good girls needed chaperons, and he needed one on his side, or somewhere in that general area. Lady Charles was the only one who qualified.

"Ruin everything for whom?"

Before he could answer, Miss Pomfret looked down at herself. "Oh, Juno!"

He drew her through the door and toward the stairs, down which the last of the ladies had disappeared. "That's what you can see. It's worse where you can't. But we haven't time to fret about it."

As they reached the staircase, women's voices wafted up to them, one strident one rising above the others.

Miss Pomfret retreated from the staircase. "I'll kill you."

"You tried, but—"

"It's *Lady Bartham*."

Ashmont swore mentally. Even he knew about Humphrey Morris's viper of a mother. Who didn't?

"She can't see me like this," Miss Pomfret whispered. "With you."

Footsteps on the stone stairs.

Miss Pomfret was scanning their surroundings, looking for a way out.

"Leave this to me," he said. An experienced troublemaker learns not only to run fast but also to be aware of suitable exits and hiding places. Depending on the trouble. Some he'd rather meet head-on. This wasn't the case at present.

He pulled her through a door into a large oval room opposite the one in which the club had met, thence to the nearest window and behind the curtains into the window enclosure. He loosened the decorative ropes holding the curtains open, which fell closed at the same moment the women reached the top of the stairs.

There they lingered, arguing about a charity event, the piercing voice indignant about something or other.

The window faced northeast, and tree branches obscured the view. Between their position and the curtains, some light penetrated, but not much. Beside him, Miss Pomfret was breathing hard, straining her bodice's confines.

He was not so calm, either.

Hiding was all very well, and fun, usually. Not today. The state of her clothes . . . and she with him, of all men. The consequences . . .

Very, very bad.

At last the women moved on, their voices fading to a distant hum as a door closed behind them.

He peered through the curtain opening.

"All clear," he whispered. "I'll step out. You put yourself to rights. If anybody else comes through, I'll keep them busy."

THIS WAS SUCH a bad idea.

The worst idea possible.

Cassandra should have held her ground.

She was only disheveled, and that was easily explained. She had witnesses. Her club members. Still, with Ashmont here instead of Keeffe—oh, she should never have listened to Keeffe! She should never have written to Ashmont. Ever since that day on Putney Heath, she'd done nothing but make one error of judgment after another. He'd infected her mind.

She looked down at herself and swallowed a groan. She was a wreck. Anybody who saw her would believe the worst.

But no one had caught them—yet. Hands steady, heart racing, she set about reassembling herself. So much easier said than done without a maid. She turned, hoping to use her reflection, but all she saw were leafy branches fluttering in the breeze and glimpses between them of the grounds.

She managed to get her hat straight—or what seemed like straight. She pulled her pelerine into place and tied the bow. Oh, but her sleeve! The puff had slid to her elbow and the now-deformed sleeve sagged. She must have torn the tapes during the fight.

The wonderful fight.

She tried to put it out of her mind and tamp down the heat that rose with remembering. She made herself focus on the job at hand.

Her belt buckle had snagged. She pulled and twisted and swore violently under her breath. It wouldn't budge. Furious, she had to summon all her strength of will to keep her voice to a whisper: "I can't see what I'm doing."

Ashmont darted behind the curtain at the same moment she heard voices coming from the stairs.

"They're going the other way," he said. "By gad, it's like the General Post Office at eight o'clock down there."

"You must help me with my dress," she said. "Otherwise it'll take forever."

She felt the pause, as though the air between them—what little air there was—vibrated.

"Help you," he said.

"Yes. Now. You said it was worse where I couldn't see, and I can hardly see a blasted thing as it is, and we need to get out of here before anybody else comes and before my aunt starts looking for me."

After all, maybe the hiding-behind-the-curtain trick wasn't Ashmont's cleverest idea.

People came and went, going up and down the stairs from the lobby below.

Keeping an ear tuned to doings nearby, he worked briskly. He tugged her dress straight and shoved the sleeve puff back into position as best he could from the outside. He smoothed the pelerine over her shoulders and retied it. He wrestled the belt back into position. She'd got her hat straight, but the ribbons didn't look right. He smoothed and fluffed them.

He put her to rights while trying, in distractingly close quarters, to stay alert to their surroundings. All the while he was disturbingly aware of her face, upturned toward his, and the brightness of her gaze. Or was that only a trick of the uncertain light?

He was all too conscious as well of his hands—on her dress, on her hat, tucking her hair out of the way.

He didn't want to do this.

It was intolerable.

And there she was, simply standing still, so very still, looking up at him while he played lady's maid.

He remembered her face in the starlight, gazing up at him so intently, while he told stories about the stars.

Don't meet her gaze. Concentrate on what you're doing. Points. Remember the points. Five thousand nine hundred and ninety-nine to go.

He made himself work quickly, quickly, all business, merely putting her into order, like—like nothing he ever did. He never tidied his dressing table or desk, let alone his clothes. He never put himself to rights. Somebody else always did that.

Yet here he was, fussing over ribbons and sleeve puffs.

"There, that'll have to do," he muttered.

She didn't move, only stared at him.

"What?" he said.

"I must give you a point." Her voice was so low, he barely made out what she said, and wasn't sure he'd heard aright. "It chokes me to say so, duke, but that was very well done, indeed."

"What, putting your clothes in order?"

"That, yes—but no. I mean the fight."

"The fight." He was trying to keep his mind on her clothing and nothing else. It didn't look right, and he didn't know what to do.

"Yes. You made no allowance for my sex or size or ignorance. You behaved as a ruffian would do. I had to fight for my life."

The glorious fight. Only minutes earlier, yet it seemed like a wondrous dream from long ago.

"I was not going to kill you," he said.

"I know, but you made me forget that. You made me work hard, and think quickly—and—and it was well done of you—and reason and logic demand I acknowledge this. I must give you a point."

She stood so close, he could feel her breath on his face.

His heart surged to racing speed. "Ah. Good."

Then, because old habits die hard—or not at all—his mouth went on speaking when it should have stopped and he said, "Does that mean I get a kiss?"

She went still again. "I said *point*, not *kiss*. Kisses do not come into it."

Stop! Stop! Go back! That was his brain. *Points. Remember the points. Lord deGriffith. Lady Charles. Too much at stake. Go back!*

But they stood inches apart in a small, warm space growing warmer by the second and he was breathing her in, and instinct and bad habits beat intellect all hollow. He was a man, and competitive; and she was a woman, and resistant; and, in short, he wasn't really thinking at all, but reacting, determined to win.

And so, he pointed to his cheek. "A peck on the cheek, to encourage me to do more good works."

"No."

"The merest nothing," he said. "Your lips touch my face. That's all. A token. Encouragement."

"Since when do you need encouragement?"

"Since I did something right for a change without realizing," he said. "Have you never tried to train a dog? A horse? Didn't Keeffe teach you his reward and encouragement method?"

"As though you're trainable," she said. "As though I would waste my time attempting it."

"As though you can't manage a mere male," he said.

An eternity of a pause followed. Through it he heard the faint hum of the women's voices in the room beyond. Below them, in the lobby at the bottom of the stairs, footsteps came and went.

She let out an impatient huff and rose up on her toes.

She kissed his cheek, as lightly as a rose petal might brush his skin.

But it lasted a fraction longer.

She was so close, he could feel her breast against his arm. All his senses took her in—the heat of her nearness, the whisper of muslin against his legs, the scent of her: a hint of sweat and a stronger hint of Woman.

And so, naturally, he leapt straight into trouble.

"I must kiss you now," he said.

CASSANDRA'S BREATH CAME faster. So did his.

"No," she said.

"Why not?"

In a dark inner dungeon a former self she kept prisoner there and tried to starve to death was asking the same question.

Why not?

In close quarters, he was inescapable. Every breath she took was *him*: pure male, musky, spicy, sweaty, and more, an atmosphere she was too dizzy to try to sort.

The air about her seemed to thrum with his physical power. Hers, too. She'd never before felt so aware of her body, its strength and agility and the life of its own it seemed to have taken on, as though her physical self and her brain had only a passing acquaintance.

She'd stood in a rare, electric state of mind, while he fussed over her clothes and her hat, and tucked in her hair. All done as briskly as could be, and yet. And yet . . .

The nearness of his big body. The heat and scent. The whisper of their clothing with each movement.

Feelings stirred inside her. Rebellious feelings. Why must a woman always behave? Why must she be the one to fight temptation?

The hidden self said, *When will you have another chance like this?*

She turned her head, presenting her cheek.

He leaned in, big and warm and inescapably a man and yes, a little mad and certainly bad.

His lips touched her cheek, like the brush of a butterfly wing, but then not like that at all. A kiss, not merely a touch.

Pressure, gentle and warm. She wanted to cry.

He stayed for the length of a heartbeat. Then another. Then another. And the feelings took over. All the irrational, useless emotions she'd tried to subdue after their wonderful fight, when she'd tried to pretend she was fully composed while inside her chaos danced, wild and dangerous and . . . happy.

Now, pretending was beyond her.

He was so much closer than he'd ever been before, even in the carriage. His breath, on her skin. His mouth, firm yet gentle, bestowing a kiss so sweet and so utterly unlike anything she could have expected from a bent-for-hell libertine. Sweet and gentle and soft, it set off a tumult inside her.

Old emotions, dreams, wishes were escaping from the mental boxes where she'd kept them locked up for so long, they ought to have crumbled to dust and she ought to have forgotten.

She needed to put them back. Now.

She brought her hand up and laid it on his sleeve.

Her brain—the sensible part—said, *That's enough.*

The voice of a wild, rebellious, and deluded girl said, *Don't stop now.*

She heard him catch his breath.

She told herself to take her hand away, but it only tightened on his arm.

Do it. Now. What other man will ever give you this chance? the voice whispered. *What other man will want you as you are, even for a moment? What does it matter if he's a rake and this is only a game to him? Why can't it be a game to you?*

She turned her head so that their mouths were inches apart . . . and then she closed the distance.

TIME TO STOP now, said Ashmont's brain.

But it's only starting to get good, said his cock.

A better man would have listened to his brain.

He wasn't a better man.

He cupped her face and kissed her. He meant to do it gently, and it started that way. And that was all right because she was new at this, clearly. The trouble was, new or not, she caught on instantly, and the first tentative and unsure response quickened into assurance, and that rocked him on his heels.

He forgot about her father and aunt. He forgot about points. He forgot everything he ought to have remembered. All he knew was *now*, and the instant surge of heat as their lips met and clung.

I burn. I pine. I perish.

Yes, yes, he should have pulled away. A part of him—the brain part—saw disaster looming. But he wasn't used to self-restraint.

He held her, his thumbs tracing the line of her jaw. He ought to have lifted his head and stopped then, but her mouth, so very apt at sharp words, was so soft and yielding, and he was hopeless, and so he went back for more: a slow, searching kiss, discovering the feel of her lips and the way she responded, the gentleness and willingness and the surrender that wasn't altogether surrender.

She held on to his arms and searched, too, making her own discoveries and learning from him, and inflaming him, because it was the same way she'd fought him, the way she'd picked up clues so quickly, allowing her to read him and respond to his every move.

More. And more. And more. The tip of his tongue touched the seam of her lips, which parted with a sharp intake of breath. But shocked or not, she let him in, and she tasted and felt like nothing and nobody else. Cool and sweet and clear, like her voice—while he wasn't cool or clear and never sweet. No, he was very far from cool, in a state of yearning beyond all his vast experience.

But he'd always flung himself headlong into everything, the riskier the better, and she did nothing to bring him to his senses. She answered his deepening kiss the way she'd fought, her tongue following his lead and using his own moves against him. She didn't—wouldn't—retreat or hesitate. She gathered knowledge as she went, learning quickly, and he was learning, too, lessons he didn't understand and didn't try to. His world was changing, whirling this way and that, and he was in a place he didn't recognize.

He didn't care.

He slid his hands from her face and wrapped his arms about her and pulled her tight against him. Her breasts pressed against his chest. Her long-legged body promised to fit his as though she'd been made for him.

A promise only.

He couldn't bring her close enough. So much between them. Bodice and stays and chemise and the rest of the feminine armor. He slid his hand down the curve of her spine, bringing her against his groin, but it wasn't close enough. Skirts and petticoats and other womanly whatnot barred the way.

Something thudded, loud enough to penetrate the haze of lust. A door slammed. Footsteps.

"It is perfectly absurd," came a strident voice. "I refuse to have anything further— Who is there?"

Thud, thud, thud. Footsteps drawing nearer.

Ashmont broke the kiss in the same instant Miss Pomfret put a hand on his chest and pushed, not hard, but enough. He released his death grip on her bottom—or as much of it as he'd been able to get to.

The curtain was flung open.

"Miss Pomfret!" the Countess of Bartham cried. Triumphantly.

Chapter 9

What did Keeffe always say?

You're in charge, miss. It's not up to the horses. It's up to you. They need you to be calm and to know what to do. You don't let nothing surprise you. You stay calm because you're ready for anything.

When Lady Bartham pulled open the curtain, Keeffe's training program took over: Remain calm in a crisis. Behave as though nothing out of the way has happened, even if your horses are running straight into the ruts and mudholes of a heath, a cattle pound on one side and trees on the other.

Metaphorically speaking, Cassandra took the situation's reins, though she placed no confidence whatsoever in this pair of horses.

"Lady Bartham." She nodded politely.

The duke bowed gracefully, the beau ideal of the English gentleman. She had no idea what he was thinking or what he'd do. She could only hope he'd follow her lead.

A short, taut silence followed while Lady Bartham put up her glass and surveyed Cassandra's ensemble.

"Calisthenics?" the countess said sweetly. "I understand the classes are vigorous."

"No," Cassandra said. "Not calisthenics."

"It's deuced hot in here," the duke said. "Ready for some air, Miss Pomfret?"

"Yes."

She watched him pick up the umbrella she hadn't realized she'd dropped. One end must have stuck out from under the curtain. That was what had attracted the gossip vulture's attention.

He gave Cassandra the umbrella. She briefly considered knocking the countess unconscious. But no. That would never qualify as self-defense.

"Will you join us, Lady Bartham?" he said. His voice was mild and he wore a faint smile.

Cassandra felt herself tense, while the countess took a step back.

"Oh, no, thank you. My club is meeting. I only stepped out for a moment."

She'd stalked out of the meeting in one of her temper fits, probably vowing never to have anything to do with those women again. But now she'd hurry back, the ladies would be her dearest friends once more, and she'd tell them what she'd seen.

In other words, Cassandra Pomfret was about to experience true ruination, and this time Ashmont couldn't disappear.

She felt oddly unmoved, as calm within as she appeared outwardly. Or maybe she was simply numb. The shock of being discovered. The shock of what had happened behind the curtain. The shock of Lady Bartham's saying so little. No lecture. No scold of any kind. Only pure, venomous glee.

Ashmont offered his arm. Cassandra took it. Why not?

They bade the lady good day, most courteously, and turned away.

So ridiculous. The scene seemed to be lit up in Cassandra's mind like a play in a theater. She saw the curtain swishing open in the instant she and Ashmont jerked apart. She saw Lady Bartham's face: surprise, almost instantly succeeded by delight. Her voice, so sweetly poisonous.

Laughter bubbled up. Cassandra told herself she never succumbed to hysteria.

But then, she'd succumbed to him, hadn't she?

The warmth and strength of his arm brought back forcibly the feel of his arms about her, the touch of his fingers on her face, the first, gentle kiss and those that followed. A part of her wanted to cry, too.

Hysteria. Not allowed.

They walked out of the room and on to the stairs and down them and through the door and out of Cremorne House. This door opened to the grounds rather than the river side.

"This is bad, yes?" Ashmont said as they stepped outside.

She looked up at him. He was biting his lip. His eyes sparkled like sapphires.

"Yes, b-but—" The absurdity of it struck her again and laughter welled up, throttling speech.

He made a choked sound. "Wait—w-wait. N-not here."

He pulled her toward a patch of garden near one of the footpaths, shaded by trees and tall shrubbery.

They'd scarcely reached it when she giggled. The giggles swelled and irrupted into shrieks of laughter. She let go of his arm and turned away and laughed. Tears streamed from her eyes. It wasn't funny. It oughtn't to be funny, but it was too ridiculous.

Beside her, he snorted, then went off into whoops.

Still laughing, she pulled him deeper into the shrubbery.

It was ludicrous. She was in the worst trouble of her life, but she couldn't stop laughing. The countess's face, like something in a pantomime. Ashmont's innocent expression and the courtly bow, as though Cassandra were presenting him to Queen Adelaide.

"C-calis-calisthenics," she managed to get out. "Oh, she is—"

"Of all w-women."

And off they went again.

At last they began to quiet, but the feelings, so unexpected, remained. She ought to be raging, and she was, at the unfairness of it. Yet mainly what she felt was the absurdity.

"I should have killed you when I had a chance," she said.

"Too late," he said. "Marry me."

ASHMONT BRACED HIMSELF.

He hated to see the laughter end. For a short time, it had felt as though they were conspirators who'd managed a complicated prank.

He only wished he'd quieted sooner, in order to fully enjoy the sight and sound of her. He wished he'd had longer to savor the rippling laughter and the wash of pink over her face and the light in her eyes and the way they crinkled shut when she laughed. He wanted to watch again the way she put her hand over her mouth and turned her head away, before giving up any attempt at propriety.

He wanted to see her laughing mouth, the one he'd kissed at long last. He wanted to kiss her while she laughed, and drink in that unadulterated enjoyment, the naughty delight—whatever it was, it was wonderful.

He'd tried not to laugh. This was a dreadful situation and laughing would be callous and feckless and everything she knew him to be.

But how could he not?

To have finally, finally, got a kiss, and more. To have finally, finally, got his hands on her.

Then to be caught. Behind a curtain! Like a scene in a farce.

But she'd felt the same. She'd laughed.

And now?

She wasn't laughing.

His heart began to beat erratically and overfast.

He was aware of people coming and going, though not nearby.

From a distance came voices and the sounds of shooting. Practice areas, well away from the house. Here was mainly garden. While de Bérenger had made substantial alterations to the property, he hadn't torn up the elegant plantings, but enhanced them and tucked his exercise areas in amongst them.

There were similar, somewhat secluded spots throughout the estate. The ingenious gentleman, in the company of a cooperative lady, could get a good deal accomplished in some of them.

It would serve an angry gentlewoman well, too. At some point, either in the hasty departure after the meeting or during events behind the curtain, Ashmont had left his hat behind. She could beat in his skull, if she put enough muscle into it, without attracting attention.

She must have been thinking the same thing because her gaze moved down to the umbrella in her hand. "I cannot marry you," she said.

He felt an inner chill. He ignored it. She had every right to decline. He was an arsehole and she was an intelligent young woman.

"I know, I know," he said. "Not a good bargain. But Morris's mother is going to make a terrific scandal. At this moment, she's already hard at work."

"That I don't doubt. But I am disinclined to exchange one nightmare for another."

"Yes, yes, I understand." Couldn't listen to his brain, could he? Had to have a taste, didn't he? And now he'd had a taste, he was going to drive himself mad wanting more. "Thing is—"

"Have you any idea how infuriating this is to me? If it were you, caught in flagrante delicto—"

"If only," he said. "We only got as far as the flagrante part. The delicto—"

"That is not translated as *delicious*, or whatever your dissolute mind imagines. It means crime or offense."

"We hadn't got to that part, yet," he said. "Speaking of which—"

"We're not speaking of it."

"Your dress is still wrong."

"What does it matter? Lady Bartham will make it out to be worse than it was even before you attempted to repair it. She'll have us both half-naked and writhing on the floor."

The picture rose in his mind's eye. He made himself cover it up. He needed to think as clearly as he possibly could.

"Yes. Don't say that. Distracting. I only meant that we might make you look somewhat neater," he said. "I know you'd rather present as decent an appearance as possible when you get home."

HOME.

Mama. Papa. Hyacinth.

Your behavior reflects on her, on all of us.

Mama would be mortified. Papa would be mortified and furious.

If I detect the smallest whiff of impropriety, I will kill him.

If Ashmont declined to fight a man so much his senior, her brothers would line up for the privilege of taking Papa's place.

This was *not fair.*

Yes, Cassandra had been foolish and careless. Yes, she knew that a man could be foolish and careless in the same way without suffering any consequences, and that was the way of the world and she'd never change it.

This didn't make the problem entirely Ashmont's fault. She'd listened to inner voices she knew were unreliable. She'd heeded the voice resenting all Rules for Women, an impractical, idealistic voice. She'd heeded the call of her adolescent self, the part of her that, clearly, had not fully grown up.

She supposed he deserved some commendation for immediately offering to do what everybody would deem The Right Thing, even though this time, unlike at Putney, he was not at all intoxicated and apparently knew what he was doing and to whom he was offering.

"Thank you," she said. "You're right. Best to mitigate the damage as best we can."

"Miss Pomfret—"

"No, no, do what you can with my dress. But make it quick. My aunt will be wondering what's become of us."

He looked about him, then speedily went to work. He tugged here and smoothed there.

She was keenly aware of every movement—the breeze lifting strands of pale gold hair while he worked, his hands as smoothly efficient as they'd been when he held the reins. She remembered the way his hands had moved, adept and quick, during their fight. She didn't need to remember how they felt. She felt them everywhere still.

He stepped away and surveyed her. "Not perfect, but presentable."

She was far from perfect, further than she'd ever supposed. Even now, knowing how much trouble she was in, she wanted more of his hands and his mouth. She'd tasted forbidden fruit and it was delicious, and she was not the woman she'd always believed she was. Or was she more that woman than she'd assumed?

But no time to ponder philosophy now.

She made herself look away from him and about her. Through the shrubbery she glimpsed a pair of figures. "Time to face it, whatever it turns out to be," she said. "There is my aunt, conversing with your uncle, at the end of the footpath."

He looked that way. The two stood talking, their heads bent toward each other. "Yes, there they are."

Cassandra started for the footpath. He went with her.

They'd taken not ten steps when a servant hurried up to them. He carried the duke's hat.

Ashmont thanked him, gave him a coin, and donned the hat.

"Feel better now," he said. "A fellow feels naked without his hat."

She felt naked. Exposed. Not merely to Lady Bartham, but to herself.

He was a rake and he'd used his rake's wiles on her and she'd succumbed, easily and happily.

The shocking opening of Harriette Wilson's *Memoirs*, etched indelibly on her memory, came to the front of her mind in bold, black letters:

I shall not say why and how I became, at the age of fifteen, the mistress of the Earl of Craven. Whether it was love, or the severity of my father, the depravity of my own heart, or the winning arts of the noble lord . . .

At this moment, the defiant words made perfect sense to Cassandra. Had Miss Wilson—or Mary Wollstonecraft, for that matter—been men, nobody would have fussed about their succumbing to their desires.

The trouble was, Cassandra wasn't a man, and unlike the two famous women, she had Hyacinth to consider. Miss Wilson, certainly, had felt no responsibility to her family. But then, when Harriette Wilson set out on her career, she was only fifteen.

Your behavior reflects . . . on all of us.

"DRAT YOU, LUCIUS." Aunt Julia came storming down the footpath. "Can I not leave you alone with my niece, in a public place, for even a minute?"

"Have I done something?" the duke said, all blue-eyed innocence.

He reminded Cassandra forcibly of the Cockney boy Jonesy at this minute. Even now, when all those she cared about were threatened, she wanted to laugh.

"Do hold your tongue," she said in an undertone. "My aunt is no dullwit."

"But—"

"Don't."

"But I wasn't—"

"Leave this to me," she said.

Lord Frederick, she noticed, stayed where he was, looking on, his usual cool and unruffled self. A seasoned diplomatist like Aunt Julia, he knew when to step away from the fray.

She turned to her aunt, whose gaze traveled from Cassandra's hat to her half boots. Aunt Julia closed her eyes then opened them again, in a manner very like Papa's when words temporarily failed him.

"Umbrella fight," the duke said.

Aunt Julia transferred her attention to Ashmont, which was when Cassandra noticed that his neckcloth's perfect knot was unknotting, his coat had lost a button, and his trousers bore dirt streaks. She experienced an insane urge to put him to rights—as though that were humanly possible.

To her aunt she said, "I told you our club has been practicing methods of defense against villains, and I believed the duke might be able to advise us."

"I played the villain," he said. "Miss Pomfret is devilish good at nearly killing fellows with an umbrella."

"You may ask any of the ladies, Aunt," Cassandra said. "In fact, I recommend you do it, because—"

"We were caught," Ashmont said. "In flagrante delicto."

Cassandra stared at him. "What is wrong with you?"

"You said it meant crime," he said. "We committed the ghastly crime of being improper. You see, Lady Charles—"

"*Will* you hold your tongue?" Cassandra said. "Aunt—"

"She was all"—Ashmont waved a hand—"in disorder. I was trying to help her with her—her things, you know. We were trying to be discreet. Behind a curtain. But—"

"Behind a curtain," Aunt Julia said.

"Lady Bartham pulled it open," Cassandra said.

Her aunt put one gloved hand to her temple.

"Yes, I know," Cassandra said.

"Ashmont, go talk to your uncle," her aunt said.

"I offered—"

"Go talk to Lord Frederick," Aunt Julia said. "I must speak to my niece. Privately."

CASSANDRA WATCHED THE duke walk away, so tall and easy in his big body, as confident as any god. She saw his uncle look him over in the same way Aunt Julia had examined Cassandra.

"What happened?" her aunt said. "Exactly and truthfully, if you want me to help you."

Cassandra told her.

At the end of the painful but brief telling, Aunt Julia said, "He did not force himself upon you?"

"Did it sound as though he did?" Cassandra said. "And do you imagine he ever would, with any woman? He doesn't need to. All he has to do is stand there and gaze deeply into our eyes, and our brains collapse."

Aunt Julia's lips twitched—with irritation, no doubt. She looked away—at Ashmont and Lord Frederick, at the surrounding landscape, at the heavens—as though seeking inspiration. Finally she said, "I believe you will have to accept his offer of marriage."

Cassandra turned her gaze toward him, and found the duke and his uncle looking at her. Or maybe Aunt Julia. Or both.

She went hot, then cold, and the world about her seemed to spin. She'd thought she was prepared but she wasn't. She was like her adolescent self, believing magical things would happen. Because a magical thing had happened a few weeks ago, in Putney, allowing her to escape.

Only a deluded schoolgirl or a grown woman in a state of delirium could imagine that she or any other unmarried gentlewoman could be discovered with His Dis-Grace the Duke of Ashmont, in clearly incriminating circumstances and in spite of having done nothing so terribly wrong, and be allowed to go on her merry way. As a man might do.

Well, perhaps she was deluded and delirious.

"Aunt, I cannot marry him."

"Child, you know that woman will go straight to your mother with her tale, and it is far too ridiculous not to be believed." Aunt Julia looked away, biting her lip. "And since you admitted that you cooperated—enthusiastically—"

"It is completely unfair. Men may sow their wild oats, but we may not."

"It isn't fair, and neither is a great deal in life, as you well know. If life were fair, we'd have no need of the Andromeda Society, would we? Well, think on that. As a duchess, you can accomplish a great deal more than you can in your present state."

A duchess. *His* duchess. Were Cassandra still a girl in her teens, she'd be walking on air. But she was a woman of nearly six and twenty, who saw the world far more clearly. She saw him with painful, inescapable clarity. He was beautiful and charming and amusing and exciting.

And hopeless. A great waste. He would break her heart again. And again and again.

She couldn't do it. She simply couldn't.

"THERE HAS TO be a solution," Cassandra said, not long thereafter, as Ashmont turned his carriage into the King's Road.

At present his uncle and her aunt rode ahead, their horses quite close to each other while they talked.

"The two wise ones seem unable to devise another," he said. "Marriage solves everything."

"They look at it from a practical standpoint." What did Lord Frederick see in her? Cassandra wondered. Not Medusa, probably. He'd see good breeding stock. And possibly a young lady sufficiently tyrannical to manage his wayward nephew.

That was too much to expect of any woman.

"That isn't enough for you?" Ashmont said. "The practical advantages. The solving several problems at once, including your sister's situation."

For one of the few times in her life, Cassandra felt like a coward. Afraid of having her heart broken, she was about to risk her sister's happiness and her family's good name. At present, she wasn't even sure what her grandparents would make of matters. They were usually on her side, but she'd never encountered this sort of trouble before, the kind of man trouble other women had.

The most infuriating part was that she hadn't done anything so terribly wrong. A kiss was what it came down to. A somewhat tempestuous one—but she hadn't lost her virtue.

As though a woman's virtue existed solely between her legs.

She didn't know whether to laugh or cry. She did neither. She needed a functioning brain.

You're in charge, miss.

"I'll think of something," Ashmont said. "I got you into this."

"You had help."

He turned and smiled at her.

"Mind the road," she said. "Don't congratulate yourself on your seductive wiles. I'm not helpless, as you well know."

"All the same, I started it," he said. "And even I know it was wrong of me to take liberties with your person."

"*What?*" She turned in her seat to gaze at him, which did nothing to reduce their proximity. She was all too well aware of his powerful physique—oh, and that unfairly beautiful profile.

"The kissing," he said. "And the . . . erm . . . hands where they weren't supposed to be."

She could feel them still. To her exasperation, she wanted to continue to feel them. "Yes, well, it was wrong of me not to plant you a facer or strike you in the tender parts, but I didn't."

"Either you were tired after almost killing me during the umbrella fight or we're making progress," he said.

"*We* are not making progress."

"I'm not *completely* disgusting to you."

"Does *not completely disgusting* strike you as sufficient reason to marry somebody?"

"We got along well for a few hours," he said.

Too well. Like kindred spirits. The way she'd once imagined they would do.

A few hours of good behavior didn't transform him into the hero of her youthful imaginings. What they had in common was simple enough. He'd said it: *I'm outrageous. You're outrageous.*

A match made in Bedlam: the Gorgon and the prankster.

At that moment, the scheme came to her. She watched it unfold in her mind: a solution and a prank on Society and its infernal rules.

"I have an idea," she said.

Ashmont's heart sank.

He didn't want her to have an idea. He wanted there to be no ideas except marrying him. She didn't want to, but he would change her mind. And this time he'd do it the right way, one point at a time, if he had to.

"Does it involve killing the Countess of Bartham?" he said. "Because I can't do that. Can't attack women—that is to say, not unless they tell me to and they're armed—at least with an umbrella—"

"We shall pretend I consented to marry you," Miss Pomfret said. "We shall pretend to be engaged. We'll delay the wedding by claiming the solicitors can't agree on various articles. My father can help with that, and your uncle, too, I daresay. Of course—"

"Wait."

"—we shall tell my aunt, your uncle, and my parents the truth. It makes no sense to do otherwise. Aunt Julia and Lord Frederick are difficult to deceive, and I should hate to deceive my aunt, in any event. My father must be informed for the same reason and also because he despises you. But if it's only a temporary thing—"

"Wait."

"A few weeks ought to do it. Other scandals will arise. Better yet, you can make one. You'll do something so dreadful that nobody will blame me for breaking the engagement. What happened today is fairly mild, all things considered. We've only the one witness, vindictive though she is. It won't be pleasant, I know, but it won't last. Society likes fresh scandal."

"Miss Pomfret, I'm not saying it's a terrible idea—"

"What's wrong with it?"

"It's only that—you know—Olympia bolted, and that wasn't a month ago. And frankly, I'd rather not be jilted again quite so soon."

A short, taut, pause.

"Then what do you suggest?" she said.

"I suggest you marry me."

"*No.*"

"Why not? I'm not completely disgusting to you. I'm young. I'm solvent. I'm a *duke*, dammit."

A much longer pause, before she said crisply, "I don't trust you. The thought of putting my future in your hands fills me with horror."

"Devil take it, Miss Pomfret, the future can be arranged with the lawyers. I wish you'd seen the conditions they set for Olympia. Reams and reams. Piles of pages. I had to soak my hand in a bowl of ice after signing the blasted things."

"In other words, you refuse to cooperate."

Uh-oh. He saw ice cracking now, at his feet. "Didn't say that."

"That's what it sounds like," she said. "It sounds as though you want it your way or no way, and do you know, duke, I feel the same.

I love my family—well, most of them. I love my sister. I don't want to embarrass anybody. But it's a stupid rule and a trivial event—"

"Trivial." She'd turned his world upside down and inside out. Something had happened to him and he didn't know what, only that he was still reeling, and hadn't time to make sense of it.

"A bit of naughtiness behind a curtain," she said. "And I am not prepared to risk all my future happiness, not to mention that of my children—"

Good God. Children. They'd make children. Of course. He wanted a family.

"—on a gentleman who's done nothing in his adult life to earn my respect, let alone my esteem. As to love—"

"No, no, back to the children, because—"

"I want my children to grow up in a loving family, as I did. I want their parents to respect and esteem and care deeply about each other, setting an example. It isn't an impossible thing. It isn't unreasonable of me to want that—and I don't see why one small error of judgment must doom me forever."

"Doom!"

"Not that I see anybody else asking me, but that's no reason— that is to say, I'm *not that desperate.*"

LADY CHARLES GLANCED back at the cabriolet. "They're quarreling."

Lord Frederick did not look back. "He's going to bungle it, the great oaf."

"At least they're talking," she said. "I truly did not expect her to react so strongly. Perhaps I didn't put matters as well as I ought to have done. But really, Lord Frederick. Behind a curtain. And of all women, that woman. Utterly ridiculous. You've no idea what it cost me to maintain my composure." She let out a short, strangled laugh.

He chuckled, too.

"All the same, it is no laughing matter," she said.

"Far from it."

"I'm not at all sure anything can be done. My niece is adamant. As to my brother, I doubt very much he'll see the humor in it."

"I tell myself that this is what Ashmont needs," Lord Frederick said. "Difficulty. Disappointment. A shock to his damned conceit. Being forced to exercise his brain. But I fear he's gone too far down the wrong road to find his way back. He's never faced obstacles to getting what he wants. One doesn't learn that way."

"But he appears to have learnt something in recent days."

Lord Frederick looked at her.

"The business in Putney," she said. "Something changed. I wondered whether it had to do with his duel with Ripley."

"He was unusually subdued when he came to my house."

She nodded. "When he had a problem that truly mattered to him, he turned to you, and he did what you recommended. I don't doubt he would have kept away from London, as you suggested, for a longer time, had my niece not summoned him."

"Interesting that she did."

"She knows. In her heart of hearts, she must know."

"We do not always know what is in that place, Lady Charles. It is too often obscured to us."

She glanced at him briefly. "I shall be the first to admit that matters at present do not strike me as propitious. On the other hand, I see more progress than I should have imagined, in my wildest dreams, not a month ago."

He turned his gaze away from her, and smiled a very little. "Do you know, Lady Charles, I find myself wondering what, precisely, takes place in your wildest dreams."

THINK, ASHMONT, THINK.

Miss Pomfret's brain was large. Clearly it enjoyed more exercise than his did. He was going to have to work like the devil to keep up.

She didn't trust him. Even when promised an army of lawyers to shield her from his disgraceful and evidently still disgusting self, she wouldn't take the risk.

And this woman was fearless! He'd witnessed it how many times in the few weeks since he'd nearly killed her on Putney Heath?

Trust. Trust. How did one make trust? Five thousand nine hundred and ninety-eight points from now, but he hadn't time. He hated her plan. It was devised precisely for her to be rid of him. Once she did that, he hadn't the slightest doubt she'd never come back.

She wasn't the sort to play coquette. She hadn't a coy or missish bone in her body. She was more straightforward than most men he knew. Laid all her cards on the table.

I don't trust you. The thought . . . fills me with horror . . . Children.

Respect. Esteem. Love.

Love. Her sister. She loved her sister. What was it Keeffe had said about Lord deGriffith's rule?

Cut her up something bad.

Ashmont thought and thought some more. About her sister. About what he'd discovered this afternoon.

"Very well," he said.

"You agree with my plan?"

"I don't agree, but I'll do it."

He saw no alternative. On the other hand, he also saw a chance, a fighting chance.

He'd do as she wanted. He wouldn't be pretending, though.

Chapter 10

*T*hough the Duke of Ashmont had nothing to do with Parliament, he had an idea of Lord deGriffith's fearsome reputation, thanks to Morris. Not that the gentleman's personality was hard to decipher. For one thing, he couldn't have been more unlike Lady Olympia's easygoing father.

Lord deGriffith had a way of gazing straight through a fellow and making him feel like a worm, even when the fellow hadn't done anything wormlike yet.

He didn't approve of Ashmont, to put it mildly. His lordship had made that clear enough when Ashmont arrived to collect Miss Pomfret.

And so, considering the duke's reputation, there was no question that Lord deGriffith would be at home, awaiting her return. Possibly with pistol or sword at the ready.

Now, seeing the group ushered into his house, he wasn't likely to feel friendlier.

There was Miss Pomfret looking, despite Ashmont's efforts with her dress, as though she'd been caught in a windstorm. There was Uncle Fred. There was Lady Charles.

Even a less astute gentleman would conclude that Something Had Happened. Furthermore, everybody knew that, where Ashmont was concerned, the things that happened were all too often in the nature of a cataclysm.

And so, after the first, stiffly courteous greetings were over, when Ashmont asked to speak privately to Lord deGriffith, he wasn't surprised at the temperature's dropping further while thunderclouds gathered overhead.

Leaving his lady to entertain the company in the drawing room, Lord deGriffith invited Ashmont to take a turn in the garden.

It wasn't a large one. Unlike Ashmont House in Park Lane, deGriffith House was a narrow London town house wedged into a rather cramped lot in St. James's Square. Still, the garden offered shade and a place to walk among the trees, shrubbery, and flowers. The plantings also created a screen of sorts. Should his lordship thrust a dagger into Ashmont's neck, eyewitnesses at the windows couldn't be certain of what they witnessed.

Not that Lord deGriffith was likely to kill him quite yet. And as to that, whatever the gentleman chose to do would be slower and more painful than mere stabbing to death.

"You would not have come in all this state, complete with two seasoned courtiers, had you not news of some importance," Lord deGriffith said. "I suppose it's too much to hope you're going to announce your plans of departing for America. Too much to look forward to your making your way across the wilderness, solo, fighting indignant natives as you go. No, you're going to murder my charming fantasy, I can tell."

Ashmont told him what had happened. The truth, but shorn of lurid details.

Lord deGriffith closed his eyes, then opened them. That was the only sign of emotion. "Lady Bartham."

"Before I go on, sir," Ashmont said, "I must make one thing as clear as I possibly can. I want to marry your daughter. I've wanted to since . . ." Then he realized he couldn't continue. He couldn't mention Putney because it had never happened.

"Since when?"

"Well, you know, sir, hard to say exactly in these situations. It feels like always."

"Hmmm."

"The point is, my feelings are sincere. However, Miss Pomfret is disinclined to make the marital leap. Fact is, she said the prospect fills her with horror."

"Sensible girl. To a point."

"And so she's made a plan, and I've agreed."

Ashmont described her plan.

Lord deGriffith listened but said nothing.

"However, in the spirit of fair play," Ashmont said, "I must tell you that I intend to do my utmost to change her mind."

"You cannot expect me to wish you luck," Lord deGriffith said. "Cassandra's scheme, overall, is not an unreasonable one. Nobody but that thorn in my wife's side saw, and if the Countess of Bartham were not the venomous being she is, I should dismiss her altogether. But I do not like to see my lady upset, and she refuses to cut the acquaintance. She believes it wiser to have one's foes near at hand, where one can keep an eye on them. I cannot disagree with her reasoning. Since it seems we cannot ignore Lady Bartham, we had better spike her guns."

"Glad to help," Ashmont said. "The worst for me was subjecting Miss Pomfret to humiliation. She was in no way at fault, I assure you, sir. I behaved very badly. Should have resisted. Didn't. No excuse."

"But she cooperated."

Careful now. Matters bad enough. Letting him believe you assaulted the daughter not the way to her father's heart. Not wise, either, to let him believe she leapt eagerly into ruination.

"She was tired, I don't doubt, after the strenuous effort to kill me with her umbrella," Ashmont said.

"Too tired to push you through the window, or break your nose."

"Exactly."

Lord deGriffith looked about him. "It was wise of me to invite you out of doors. I do feel the need of air. Possibly a brisk walk of twenty miles or so to calm myself. But that will have to wait. I must compose myself as best I can, for my wife's sake, not to mention my own peace of mind."

"Sir, I'm sorry, indeed, to have caused so much trouble. I do understand your hating me. I'd hate me, too, in your place."

His lordship brushed this off. "Over the course of a long career, I have learnt to govern my feelings and look at the facts and what can be achieved. I am not enamored of this plan of Cassandra's, involving, as it does, my continuing to endure your presence. However, I must admit it's sound, and a relatively simple solution. You have my permission to proceed with it. You may by no means take this as encouragement of your suit. While you are not the last man on earth I should wish a daughter of mine to marry, you are most decidedly in the general category."

It was a blow. Ashmont had told himself to expect the worst. All the same, it was a blow. Whatever he accomplished, if anything, would have to be done against a great headwind of parental opposition.

"Understood, sir. And speaking of daughters, I wonder if you would be so good as to allow me another few minutes of your time."

"Duke, you have already taxed my patience beyond human bearing."

"Understood. But this can't wait."

THE DUKE OF Ashmont took his leave, looking pale and ill.

Still, gentlemen often looked that way after a private conference with Papa, Cassandra told herself. This didn't quiet her unreasonable conscience.

The elders held a council, from which Cassandra and Hyacinth were excluded.

Some eternity later, Aunt Julia and Lord Frederick left, and Papa summoned Cassandra to his study.

"As well as the family discussion, I've spoken to your aunt privately," he said. "I've spoken to Lord Frederick privately. It infuriates me to have spent valuable time on this nonsense, all on account of a discontented woman who likes to make as many lives as miserable as possible. I shall be late to tonight's session, and who knows what they'll get up to in my absence."

Her father rarely missed a Parliamentary session, even the noontime, petition-filled ones.

"I'm sorry to have caused so much trouble," Cassandra said. She ought to be sorry about the kiss but she wasn't, and she couldn't stop feeling the whole business was completely unfair. Now, though, was not the time to vindicate the rights of woman.

He gave an impatient wave of his hand. "Yes, well, stolen kisses. Fact of life. Girls are not always the paragons we expect them to be, and perhaps our expectations are unreasonable. I should not have minded quite so much if it hadn't been Ashmont."

"Yes, Papa. I know."

"We can expect satirical prints." He closed his eyes and sighed. Then, clearly not liking what he saw in his mind's eye, he opened them and regarded her with a sort of resignation. "Ashmont is a favorite of the satirists. Even the late King, who seemed to break records in that unenviable category, has lost place to him."

The caricaturists had mercilessly mocked King George IV for nearly all his adult life. The number of satirical prints must number in the tens, possibly hundreds, of thousands.

Cassandra had no trouble imagining what they'd make of the Curtain Scene.

"Still, the duke has acquitted himself better than I should have supposed, and your scheme has merit. I've agreed to the . . . pretense. Furthermore, he's devised a scheme of his own, also not without merit."

Cassandra did not faint. She never fainted.

She didn't cry, "No! No! Not one of Ashmont's *ideas*!"

She kept her driving face on and held her tongue while her father went on, "He will escort you to the theater tomorrow night. Your aunt will chaperon. We shall consider that the first stage of the campaign. With any luck, it should prove sufficient, or nearly, and this nonsense will be done with swiftly. Now, if you'd be so good as to send your sister in to me."

"Papa, I hope you will not punish her further because of my mistake—"

"Child, I hope I need not remind you who is head of this family."

She went out of the study and did as she was told, though she apologized to her sister for whatever additional calamity was about to befall her.

Exile back to Hertfordshire, very likely.

Not a quarter hour later, Hyacinth came running into the library, where Cassandra was trying to distract herself with Mary Wollstonecraft's book.

"Oh! Oh! Oh! Oh, Cassandra! The most wonderful thing! I told you! I told you!"

Cassandra set the book down. "Wonderful? Told me?"

Hyacinth bent and hugged her, making wreckage of the pelerine Ashmont had taken so much pains to smooth.

"He's done it!" her sister cried. "The duke's persuaded Papa to set aside the rule. It's only for a night, Papa says, and then 'we'll see what we shall see.' But, oh, I'm to go with you to the theater tomorrow night. And we're to see *The Long Finn.* Pirates!"

ON SATURDAY AFTERNOON, Lady Bartham paid a visit to her dear friend Lady deGriffith.

She was all apologies for having been the one to discover the pair, but it was better by far that it was a friend who made the discovery, for she could be trusted never to breathe a word.

In fact, since yesterday the alleged friend had breathed a word to half her acquaintance, and the news had already been brought to the attention of London's largest print sellers.

She'd long awaited such an opportunity. She'd been a member of the audience when Cassandra Pomfret had made Mr. Owsley—Lady Bartham's current protégé—look ridiculous, and thus the countess by association. That she'd stumbled so unexpectedly upon her chance for revenge, with no effort whatsoever, made it all the more delightful.

She put on her best commiserating face. To her disappointment, Lady deGriffith didn't crumple. On the contrary, she sat straighter and smiled and said, "Well, well, young men can be so insistent, can they not? But as one would expect, the duke spoke to Lord deGriffith immediately when they returned."

"Spoke?"

"Naturally, you had no way of knowing matters had progressed so far," Lady deGriffith said. "As it turns out, you were right about the flirtation at the fancy fair. I had no idea, and Cassandra is the last girl on earth to boast of her conquests."

I should hope so, Lady Bartham thought, *the girl having none to boast of.* She said, "Indeed, she is only the second gentlewoman he's ever pursued, to my knowledge. As I understand it, the first one took him months. He has known Miss Pomfret, what? A few days? Or perhaps they are better acquainted than I realized."

"Oh, they've known each other this age," said her friend. "Since childhood. They met at Camberley Place on several occasions over the years. Still, it seems to have grown serious quite suddenly." She shook her head. "These impetuous young men. How is one to withstand them? And a duke, no less. Accustomed to having his own way and willing to give whatever is necessary to get it."

Without mentioning anything so vulgar as money, she reminded Lady Bartham how very much of that article the duke had, and how wealth covered a multitude of sins—in his case, literally.

"It is a trial to a mother's nerves, I'll admit," she went on. "I was shocked indeed to learn of the depth of his regard for Cassandra and how impatient he was to make her his duchess. Even Lord de-Griffith could not withstand so much ardor. How lucky you are, my dear, in having daughters who haven't been subjected to such determined suitors."

Having been made to look like a fool, having had her daughters thus neatly depreciated, and foreseeing unpleasant conversations when she encountered her other friends again, Lady Bartham soon took her leave.

She was furious. They were lying, the lot of them, Lady deGriffith especially. So manipulative. Since they were girls together, making their debut. So clever at getting what she wanted, including other girls' beaux.

Who could wonder at her producing monstrous females? And to think of one of those monsters marrying a *duke*, however debauched he might be! It was not to be borne.

Adelphi Theater
Saturday 6 July

"WE'LL GET THEM talking about something else," was the way the duke had explained his plan for the evening.

Cassandra certainly hoped so. She knew her mother had put Lady Bartham in her place today, but damage had already been done. Caricatures had appeared in print shop windows by late afternoon. The artists, according to Aunt Julia, had portrayed Cassandra, in classical dress, prophesying the loss of her maidenhead. They'd also depicted her and Ashmont's presumably naked persons partly concealed by the curtain in which they were entangled. The usual witticisms. The usual bad puns. Jokes about athletic activities at the Stadium.

Cassandra had been a butt of their jokes before this, and she would have found it more amusing if she hadn't her family to consider.

Poor Papa! So embarrassing for him. She had to admire his forbearance.

But Ashmont deserved some applause, too. His idea was already bearing fruit.

The Adelphi in the Strand was half the size of Covent Garden Theater. Its audiences had received Mr. William Bayle Bernard's new play, *The Long Finn*, with delight. His farce, *The Mummy*, had theatergoers returning again and again. The seats not currently occupied would be filled as the night wore on and the latecomers and seekers of cheaper prices trickled in.

It was a fine night to create a sensation, and the duke had arranged everything to that end, quite as though he put on a play of his own.

One of the two private boxes above the stage doors, his was stage right. He sat in the shadow of the curtains, in the seat farthest left facing the stage—as inconspicuous as possible, in other words.

Cassandra watched the playgoers opposite train their glasses on his box and discover—good heavens!—three actual *ladies* therein. And not merely ladies, but famous ones.

Beside him sat Medusa, deGriffith's Gorgon, in all her finery of shimmering light blue silk. Next to her, in palest pink, perched the Debutante of the Season, returned to the world. Yes, he'd done it. Hyacinth had been released from captivity, thanks to him. And in the seat farthest right, the long-missing-from-Society Lady Charles Ancaster presided, in a splendid red dress with deep décolleté and diamonds everywhere.

Thanks to the box's location and the curtains, the audience closest to them didn't find out who occupied it until word made its way to them.

The news circled the building like a wave: heads turning and glasses going up to eyes, spectators rising from their seats or stretching out over the railings to stare, while the pit's occupants made a sea of upturned faces. The wave completed its circuit as the curtain rose, the cast assembled onstage, and everybody began to sing "God Save the King."

It was hilarious, and Cassandra had all she could do to keep her driving face in place.

Aunt Julia leant over Hyacinth toward him and said, "I congratulate you, duke. You have contrived to create a shocking scene without breaking any laws or even disrupting the performance."

He leant closer to Cassandra to answer. "Early days, Lady Charles."

The sleeves of Cassandra's evening dress were full, but short. Her gloves came to her elbows. Somehow he managed to arrange himself so that his coat sleeve brushed the few bare inches of her arm.

When her aunt sat back again, Cassandra said in an undertone, "You are breathing down my neck."

"It'll give them something to talk about," he said.

"You haven't given them enough?"

"Also, you smell good."

"Not hot and sweaty, do you mean?"

"On a woman, that's another good smell," he said. "Tonight you're like a garden of herbs. If I could, I'd bury my nose in your neck, at the delicious place where it curves into your collarbone. But I can't." He sat back. "I promised your father I'd get them all talking about something other than the curtain business at Chelsea, but a public display of lust is probably not what he had in mind."

"Lust." Her neck tingled where he'd been breathing on it, and inside her, there was a fluttering. The theater grew many degrees warmer.

"Still, nobody would ever believe I was wanting to marry you or any lady for your mind," he said. "I'll have to cast lascivious glances your way from time to time. And every so often, you'll fend me off with sharp words or your fan. Or both."

Beyond question she would fend him off. While being near him made her brain die a little, she wasn't completely lost to reason.

She'd grown up in the country. She'd spent a large portion of her time around horses. In adulthood she'd seen more than most other ladies her age, including married ladies, had done. Though she had no firsthand experience, she understood the basics of what went on between men and women.

She remembered how she'd felt behind the curtain, the way logic gave way to wanting. It was human nature. That was how the human race continued. Monster she might be, but she wasn't immune to that aspect of being human.

She'd experienced desire and infatuation. One infatuation in particular had tormented her adolescence, but she'd matured and freed herself of it.

Or so she'd assumed until yesterday.

She was not entirely mature. She was not entirely immune to him. Apparently, there was no vaccination for this sort of ailment. The irrational adolescent inside her wanted him to bury his nose in her neck.

He was a trap, a walking, talking woman-trap.

"Stop talking," she said, and made herself focus on the play.

It took a while for Ashmont to drag his attention to the stage. After all, there wasn't much else he could do at present. But he'd seen it before, and though he, like many other theatergoers, often attended the same plays over and over, and though he liked *The Long Finn* immensely—pirates and star-crossed lovers and treasures and murder—it couldn't compete with Cassandra Pomfret.

Tonight she was deliciously undressed, or at least less covered than usual. Only a few strategically placed bows adorned the blue silk dress. One fluttered at each naked shoulder. The one at the center of her neckline moved in time with her bosom's rise and fall. Above the neckline, silky smooth skin hinted at what pulsed within the layers of bodice and corset and chemise.

When he'd leant over her, the scent of rosemary, lavender, and Cassandra Pomfret rose to his nostrils. It continued to waft toward him from time to time, teasing. Even when he couldn't smell her, he could hear the faint rustle of silk when she moved. Breathed.

He remembered, in skin and muscle and bone, the way she'd kissed him, the way she'd felt in his arms. The heat. The thrill, beyond anything he could have imagined, let alone prepared for.

He was supposedly a man of the world. He'd discovered the opposite sex at an early age and promptly given up chastity as nonsense.

Now he was like a schoolboy with his first infatuation. Only this was more powerful by far, the feelings stronger and more disturbing. He wanted the disturbance. It felt right. All this time, years and years, he'd never had an inkling of what he'd been missing.

He needed to concentrate on the performers, not her. He lacked the temperament to resist temptation, and he couldn't afford a misstep. He'd done well to this point, but he'd better not test Fate's humor too far. She was famously capricious.

At the first interval, the group stepped out into the saloon for the private boxes and into a noisy, glittering throng. As one would expect, a large portion of the crowd swirled about Cassandra's aunt and sister. Among them, unsurprisingly, was Humphrey Morris.

Cassandra had not expected the group of admirers to be so numerous, though, and she was beginning to understand why her father had been so strict about Hyacinth's social life. Still, as long as the masses of men didn't seem to trouble Aunt Julia, Cassandra wouldn't let them trouble her.

For the moment, she stood in a small oasis of calm. At the start of the interval, Mrs. Roake had joined her and the duke, but a minute ago, he'd drawn the elder lady aside, to engage in lively conversation of some kind.

Mrs. Roake seemed as surprised by the circumstance as Cassandra, but the crowd swiftly swallowed them up, leaving her bemused.

She was enjoying herself, though, watching Hyacinth glow under all the attention. It was fun to watch the audience perform, too: the flirtations and other little games people played. She was amusing herself in this way when she noticed Mr. Owsley approaching.

Cassandra assumed he was on his way to join the stream of would-be suitors trying to get close to Hyacinth. Even when his gaze turned toward Cassandra, she supposed he was only making sure she remained safely distant.

But he did not continue drifting in the river of men. He veered off and made his way to Cassandra.

"Miss Pomfret."

"Mr. Owsley."

"What a pleasant surprise to find you here," he said.

"How strange," she said. "You were not pleased to see me a few weeks ago at your lecture."

"Ah, yes. As to that, I believe we got off on the wrong foot."

She regarded him stonily, the way she regarded the majority of men. "You dismissed what I had to say. Yes, I would describe that as getting off on the wrong foot."

He colored. "Indeed, the occasion was not auspicious. It has occurred to me since that I should have done better to explain what we are trying to accomplish."

Sometimes, really, men wanted to make her scream. She knew she wasn't the only woman who felt this way.

Voice level, she said, "You presume that I not only failed to comprehend your lecture but haven't followed the arguments for and against your bill. Or perhaps you assume that I attempted to follow them but failed to grasp them because my woman's brain is too small."

"The difficulty is, the satirists have emphasized remorselessly but one aspect of the matter."

"Satirists are not my only source of information," she said. "Neither are print shop windows and gossip. I and a number of other women, of various political leanings, read the Parliamentary reports, along with the political columns in London's news journals." She would have gone on, but at that moment she saw the sea of men about her aunt and sister part, making way for the Duke of Ashmont.

Owsley must have sensed the tide shifting about him, because he glanced in Ashmont's direction and said, "I merely wished to make the most of this unexpected opportunity. But I realize this is hardly the time or place for serious discussion. Perhaps we might speak again at another time."

At that moment, Ashmont reached her side. "Ah, there you are, Miss Pomfret." He glanced at Owsley. "Perhaps you'll be so good as to make your friend known to me."

The duke was smiling the smile more ominous than another man's glower.

To her surprise, Owsley didn't suddenly discover he had another place to be. On the contrary, he planted himself in place while his shoulders went back and his chin went up.

Very well, it's your funeral, she thought. She made the introduction.

"Mr. Owsley?" Ashmont said. "Not the one with the Sabbath bill? We must speak sometime."

Long training kept Cassandra's jaw from dropping, though she did blink once. Mrs. Roake, who had trailed in the duke's wake, gazed at him in open astonishment.

"But there's the bell," Ashmont said, "and I know the ladies of my party are anxious to learn whether the Treasure Seeker's son will live."

He offered his arm. Cassandra took it. She felt the tension in it, and realized how close, how very close they'd come to violence. Owsley ought to have had the good sense to make himself vanish, if he was the humble man of charity and peace he claimed to be. As to Ashmont . . .

They were pretending to be a courting couple, she reminded herself. While she was by no means experienced in courtship, she'd observed enough male behavior to understand that posturing and trying to intimidate potential rivals was often part of it.

Not that Ashmont needed more than the thinnest excuse to fight.

All the same, she was annoyed to realize how much the display of possessiveness had gratified her. No, that was her adolescent self.

She was no longer that infatuated girl. What she felt was only a primitive, unthinking response, all part of the instinctive urge to couple. Dogs did the same thing. It had nothing to do with reason.

When they'd taken their seats again, he said in a low voice, "So that's Owsley. I'd pictured a much older fellow. Couldn't decide if he was trying to steal my charmer or persuade her to support his bill."

"Steal your—" She broke off. She would not go down that path. "He was wasting his time. How did you know about his bill? Mrs. Roake couldn't have told you. She was as astonished as I when you referred to it."

"I was at your meeting, remember?" he said.

"You were paying attention?"

"It was deuced interesting. I'd no idea. Might have to dust off my seat in the House of Lords. Heard from Morris that Mr. Stanley brought in a bill late last night—this morning, rather—for abolishing slavery in the colonies. Didn't realize we still had that sort of thing going on. I was so astounded, I forgot I was being shaved. Started to jump out of the chair, and Sommers nearly cut my throat."

"What?" she said. "What?"

"Morris," he said. "I had to let him know Miss Lily would be here tonight, and—"

"It's *Hyacinth*, as you know perfectly well."

He smiled. "Only fair to give him fair warning. He's been a decent sort of friend to me. Can't help who his mother is. Didn't get to choose. And so I asked him what kinds of business your father was dealing with these days—you know, wanting to win a fraction of a point with him—and that's how I found out."

"You are not going to take your seat in Parliament," she said. "It's all a hum, part of this prank we're playing." Pretending to be the patient suitor. Pretending to curry favor with her father.

Marry me.

He'd do anything to get his way.

He touched her glove, near her wrist. "Sshh. Play's starting."

She wanted to lay her hand over his. She wanted to take his hand and twine her fingers with his. She'd seen her parents do this. Her grandparents. Aunt Julia and Uncle Charles. Not in any obvious way. They didn't make great displays of feeling before others. But there were moments of intimacy, affection, some special understanding.

But she and Ashmont had no special understanding. She was slipping into some kind of delirium to imagine it. A delirium he created. The beautiful face. The intimate tone of voice. His nearness was extremely damaging to rational thought.

She turned her attention to the stage as the drop rose, revealing Arnold, the Treasure Seeker's son, lying on a low bed. Martha, his mother, watched him sleep. In front sat his father, Phillip, hands clasped, gazing out in the unseeing way of a man in a trance.

She put twined hands and politics out of her mind. She hadn't seen a London play in ages. She was grateful to be here. She was even happier having her sister enjoy it with her. She was not going to lose a minute of the experience, no matter who sat beside her.

Chapter 11

*T*he curtain fell on the second and final act of *The Long Finn*, and the ladies applauded and smiled at Ashmont as though he'd personally written, produced, and directed it exclusively for them.

Miss Flower was as openhearted in her pleasure as a child. No pretend sophistication. No silly airs. Not that she needed to do anything but be beautiful.

He was beginning to understand why Miss Pomfret loved her so much. The girl wasn't remotely to his taste, but she seemed to be truly sweet-natured, and he could only wish Morris good fortune. Given the competition, he'd need it.

Next in tonight's entertainment was *The Mummy*, a farce Ashmont had seen twice before. Miss Pomfret would laugh, and heartily, and he was looking forward to that.

At present, though, the interval was starting, during which he needed to deal with Owsley.

In the normal course of events, Ashmont would simply break his face.

Politics or no—and clearly, some politics was involved—the fellow had eyed Miss Pomfret in a manner any man would recognize, and which immediately roused the inner demon.

But violence wouldn't win Ashmont any points, with father or daughter.

Fighting, which he did all the time, wouldn't earn respect. He shoved the inner demon back into the darkness.

Respect. Esteem. The things that were important to her. Those sorts of things needed strategy. He could do that. It took strategy to carry out a successful prank, and he'd had years of practice.

His present task was to find Mr. Tight-Arse Oh-So-Holy in the mob of males crowding the saloon. The man needed to learn some basic facts of life. First item: no trying to steal another fellow's girl. Not funny anymore.

Second item: Even Ashmont understood that, if passed, the Sabbath bill would undermine the Andromeda Society's projects. Ordinary people needed transportation and food seven days a week. How hard was that to understand?

As so often happened, a number of theatergoers had arrived late, swelling the crowd in the saloon. The company had grown more inebriated as well. Not the Duke of Ashmont.

Though his box held a small table of refreshments, he hadn't taken more than one glass of wine. He couldn't afford to dull his mind or any urges lower down, for that matter. Not with drink. He needed his wits about him.

Sobriety wasn't the easiest way to get through the evening when one couldn't put hands, lips, and/or tongue anywhere on Miss Pomfret, in spite of gross and intolerable temptation. Those bows, those infernal bows quivering against her skin like little blue fingers beckoning, *Come closer. Have a touch, a taste.* Still, he'd borne it through the whole second act, when the theater—or at least his box—had turned into a hothouse filled with the fragrance of rosemary and lavender and woman-scent.

He would continue to bear it. No choice. Too much at stake.

At present the bows fluttered a few feet away. Miss Pomfret stood with Mrs. Roake and another lady. They were talking behind their fans and not looking in his direction. With any luck, in this crowd they wouldn't notice what he was up to.

After a few more frustrating minutes' search, he finally spotted his prey, not far from the fireplace at the end of the saloon. Mr.

Tight-Arse Oh-So-Holy was holding forth to a small group. Outraged about the play, probably. Didn't approve of pirates, depraved fellows who robbed and plundered and pillaged and perpetrated their foul deeds even on a Sunday.

Ashmont could imagine the conversation. Smiling with anticipation, he started that way.

He hadn't taken five steps before a man fell against him. He was about to shove the fellow out of the way when he realized this wasn't one lone, clumsy drunk. A disturbance was in process in the crowd surging about Miss Flower.

Two young men pushed each other, jockeying for position, it looked like. They were not much older than the girl, and still wet behind the ears. This, combined with their having taken more drink than their young heads could withstand, meant they were working up to a fight, and blundering into others in the process.

"Puppies," the man who'd fallen against him muttered.

Ashmont made his way to the rivals without much trouble. Crowds tended to part for him. He didn't realize that the inner demon had crept to the cave entrance. He didn't realize he was smiling the Death Smile. Others did, though, and got out of his way.

He grasped the nearest quarreler's arm and said, "That's enough. You're alarming the ladies. Take it outside."

"Take your hands off me," the boy said.

"Mind your own business," his rival said.

The space about them instantly began to quiet, and more than a few theatergoers stepped back a pace or two.

The demon braced to spring. Ashmont's hands tensed, ready to punch first and ask questions later. He wanted to punch somebody, in any event. He wasn't used to self-denial and didn't like it. He needed to *do* something.

But there was Lady Charles frowning, and Miss Flower all wide-eyed, and a lot of people uncertain about what would happen next and not wanting to be hit, knocked over, or stepped on. Also a lot of drunken men who'd jump in once a fight started, and turn it into a melee. In a small, narrow room with precious few escape routes.

He'd promised Lord deGriffith he'd look after the ladies. He was responsible for the precious Miss Flower.

He paused, and his hands relaxed. These were merely drunken boys, and only two of them against one big, dangerous Ashmont.

Keeping hold of the first numbskull, he caught the other with his free hand.

"I say," said one, trying to shake him off.

"Let me go," said the other, trying to pull away.

He ignored them.

He was large. He was strong. He was a duke. Whether, being so drunk, they realized who he was, they recognized power and absolute self-assurance. Though they continued protesting, it was all words. They offered only halfhearted resistance as he lugged them through the crowd.

It was fairly easy work to take them to the door. There he let them go with a shove and said, "Don't come back." He signaled a box-keeper, to make sure they didn't.

Idiots.

He shook his head and turned around.

To dead silence.

Every face was turned toward him. Nobody moved. A few blinked. A great many mouths shaped O's.

He sighed.

Not a prayer now of getting at Owsley unnoticed, and no time to give him something to think about, in any case.

Ashmont started back to collect his charges.

Then he saw her face. Aglow. Silvery eyes alight. She was looking at him—at *him*, this time, as though he'd singlehandedly killed Scylla, Charybdis, and six or seven dragons for her.

HE'D DONE IT. *He.*

If Cassandra had heard what Mrs. Roake had been saying to her, nothing stuck in her mind but the word *Owsley*. She didn't try to find out what she'd missed. It was fortunate that the interval was ending as Ashmont made his way across the swiftly emptying saloon, because she was incapable of pursuing an intelligent conversation with anybody.

She'd watched it happen. She'd heard about riots in theaters. She'd caused riots inadvertently. But not in a narrow space like this, with a dense crowd containing so many drunken men, the majority gathered about her sister. Her aunt was here, and friends. All of them in danger.

For an instant, she'd stood frozen, seeing what was about to happen and trying to determine how she could stop it.

Then Ashmont had stepped into the incipient fray like—like the golden hero of her imaginings. Like the boy who'd stepped into her battle all those years ago, at the moment when matters could have turned either way—against her or in her favor—and she'd fully expected the former.

He could have made it worse. He could have precipitated a disaster. Instead, he'd acted with restraint, so sure of himself and what ought to be done that nobody could doubt him.

He'd stopped the trouble before it could slip into the next, unstoppable phase.

He'd made it look so simple. For him, it was. But he was one of the few men who could do it, and he'd done it, easily and quickly, before matters could escalate. His doing it made other would-be brawlers think twice.

It was but one quiet act, one which perhaps only she, or a very few others, could fully appreciate.

All she could see was him.

He offered his arm and she took it, like one in a dream, her face turning up toward his impossibly beautiful one.

"Lucius," she said, and indeed, it was as though a light had dawned. She added, her voice soft and wondering, "Well done."

He was looking down at her, his eyes so blue in that angel-devil face. "What? Those boys, you mean?"

She nodded.

He smiled, and it wasn't the cheerfully homicidal one. It was a sweet smile, almost but not quite innocent, that for a moment re-called the boy he'd been once. The boy who'd told her stories of the stars and helped her fight a monster.

The boy she'd loved so long ago.

With all her heart.

The boy, she now understood, who'd left no room there for any-body else.

SHE LOOKED UP at Ashmont with stars in her eyes, and the rest of the world dissolved. He steered her straight to the box, whose door his servant promptly opened. Ashmont closed the door and backed her into the darkest corner and took her face in his hands and kissed her.

She gasped and grabbed his shoulders. Her lips parted, and he kissed recklessly: one collision, then a tangle of tongues, enough to send heat pulsing through him and his hands racing over her neck, her shoulders, her breasts, her waist, her bottom. He forgot where they were. Didn't care.

The way she'd looked at him. He'd thought he'd died and come to life at the same time.

And now, the way she felt in his arms. Like homecoming and like the fight he'd been waiting for all his life.

It felt . . . right. Wild and right.

He needed to stop. He knew this. But not yet. He needed the feel of her, the heat and the wanting and the pressure of her body against his.

So much in the way. Clothes. Everything. The world. But this moment it was all he could have, and he went headlong, the way he did everything, not wanting to lose an instant.

Stop.

Yes, in a minute.

Stop.

The shape of her. The taste of her mouth. The fire and fearlessness.

Stop. Now.

But he had grasped her bottom and was trying to bring her more tightly against his groin. Clothes, infernal clothes. Her skirts tangled with his legs, and as he pressed against her, his foot struck a leg of the small table nearby, and glasses chinked.

Alarm bells.

He came back to the world and heard voices nearby. She made an odd, strangled sound and pushed him away.

He stumbled back and made his brain work. He guided her to her chair, and she sat, trembling, at the same moment the servant outside opened the door to Lady Charles and Miss Flower.

"Apologies for the hasty exit," he said. "Miss Pomfret looked . . . faint. Needed to . . . sit down."

She gulped. He looked at her and saw the silver glint in her eyes. He realized then what it was: the devil in her. She was trying not to laugh.

But she collected herself so swiftly and sat there so composedly, one would never guess she'd kissed him mindless a moment ago. Except for the slight flush of her cheeks and the quick rise and fall of her bosom.

Where he'd put his hands. Mostly on silk but also on a delicious swell of skin like warm velvet.

Only for an instant, the most beautiful instant.

Not enough, no, not by miles. But he'd live on that instant for as long as he had to. The scent of her skin filled his head, like some intoxicant.

"I never faint," she said. "But I will admit I became light-headed at the sight of the Duke of Ashmont behaving in a sensible and useful manner. I'm amazed the saloon wasn't awash in swooning ladies."

She was a wonder. He caught only the faintest unsteadiness in her voice, the voice like a stream in springtime, the voice that had summoned him back to the world, back to life, on Putney Heath.

"Not quite that," said Miss Flower. "But several gentlemen dropped their quizzing glasses, and any number of feet got stepped on, and a great many mouths fell open." She grinned. "That part was vastly amusing."

Lady Charles did not appear amused. She looked from him to Miss Pomfret. A lengthy silence followed.

At last she sat. "What preceded was rather too exciting. I vow, I had no proper idea of the deleterious effect Hyacinth has on young men."

"Not all of them behave in that silly way, Aunt," the girl said. "Mr. Morris started for the pair of troublemakers, but by the time he'd pushed through the crowd, the duke had them in hand. That seemed to quiet everybody else."

"Mr. Morris was so good as to escort us back to your box," Lady Charles said, "following your abrupt disappearance with my other niece."

"He's a steady fellow," Ashmont said. He didn't add more. The torrid embrace had mangled his brain. Wiser to say nothing rather than risk doing Morris more harm than good.

"So it would seem," Lady Charles said. "Be so good as to pour us all a glass of wine, duke. Hyacinth does not realize how narrowly we escaped mayhem. She has never found herself caught in a riot in a crowded theater. I have. It is an exceedingly disagreeable experience—and I am finding it uphill work to fully absorb the fact that you were the one who saved us. Kindly fill my glass to the brim."

CASSANDRA POMFRET, PROPHET of Doom, prophesied grave danger to herself.

She'd let down her guard and given in to her younger self. She'd let one moment, one small exception to a lifetime of bad behavior, crush her judgment.

All the same, she couldn't regret it.

Inside, she was flying, soaring free. Inside, her heart beat like a mad thing and her body was wildly alive, the way it had been after the fight, but more so.

She let herself feel it, for now. She wouldn't let it happen again.

For a few minutes, Ashmont had been the man she'd once believed, on the flimsiest evidence, he could be. For years the girl inside her had believed he'd become what she wanted him to be. That girl was obstinate, insisting it could happen and would happen.

It wouldn't. He wouldn't change merely because she wished it.

But he was big and strong and beautiful and she was by no means the most well-behaved woman. She was Medusa, yes, but not made of stone herself. She'd succumbed to one mad moment.

Mad, indeed. They'd practically begged to get caught. That would turn the theater on its ear. She pictured the glasses going up to peer at them, the chandeliers' light reflected in hundreds of lenses. She could see jaws dropping and hear the collective hiss of indrawn breath.

Too comical, even more absurd than the audience reaction at the evening's start. Luckily, they watched a farce, and she might laugh along with everybody else.

She laughed at the scenes in her mind, but she did watch the performance, too. How could she not? The theater was one of the great joys of London life, and Ashmont had made this night possible. He'd thought of Hyacinth, and somehow persuaded their father to release her. For that alone . . .

Did one need excuses?

Whether it was love or . . . the depravity of my own heart, or the winning arts of the noble lord . . .

One of those. All of those.

She'd conquer it, whatever it was. She hadn't any choice.

AT THE INTERVAL following *The Mummy*, Lady Charles decided that the ladies would not go out into the saloon again. Naturally, an army of gentlemen gathered outside the box, angling to be let in, but the only one granted this privilege was Humphrey Morris.

"I can't believe he's making headway," Ashmont whispered to Miss Pomfret. "As much as I like him, I should have given him poor odds. Third son. Unpleasant mother. Brothers are as bad as she is, possibly worse. One of the sisters is reputed to be an agreeable girl, more like him than the others. I should never have put my money on him."

"Don't do it yet," Miss Pomfret said. "Best not to jump to conclusions where Hyacinth's concerned. Under the soft exterior . . . well, she's softhearted, yes, but she owns a spine, and it isn't made of India rubber."

"I didn't fail to notice how she robbed him blind at the fancy fair."

"She's competitive, and more intelligent than she seems. She may be naïve and idealistic, but she can be surprisingly astute about people. If she's encouraging him, she has a reason, and it isn't merely wanting to enslave him. She isn't like that."

He feigned shock. "Miss Pomfret, are you encouraging me to encourage my motley friend?"

She glanced at Humphrey Morris, who gazed at Miss Flower as though she were the eighth wonder of the world. "Does he look like he needs encouragement?"

"Her being in his general vicinity is probably encouragement enough."

"At any rate, he behaved well enough to win my aunt's approval. You did, certainly." She turned toward him, putting her fan up to conceal all but her eyes from general view. "Two points, duke."

He drew his head back to regard her in frank disbelief. "Two."

"Anything less would be unsporting," she said. "You thought of Hyacinth and made sure she was included tonight. That can't have been easy."

In fact, it had been painful and very nearly terrifying. The *responsibility*. But it had to be done. The Duke of Ashmont wanted a family. He had to prove he could be trusted to look after them.

"Then you protected her, all of us," Miss Pomfret went on. "My aunt saw it. I saw it. Two points."

"But I was so ill behaved after." His voice was barely a murmur. "Took liberties. Would have liked to take more."

Her eyes glinted. "And I didn't plant you a facer or strike you in the tender parts. Fancy that."

"Miss Pomfret."

"I'm not sure what to do with you," she said. "Or is it myself? Never mind. I daresay the answer will come to me soon enough."

"Marry me," he said. "That's the answer."

He felt her withdraw, even though she didn't move. "I'm not that confused," she said. "Or desperate. Stop crowding me."

She swatted him with her fan in the same instant the prompter's bell rang. The fan slipped from her hand onto the floor of the box. Ashmont picked it up and gave it to her. She took it, but closed it and let it rest on her silk-covered thigh, the one nearest him.

He laid his hand over hers. She looked at it. She didn't push it away.

For a moment, he hardly dared breathe. Then he turned his hand slightly, to encompass hers. She didn't pull away.

That was all. The smallest capitulation, but enough for now. More than enough. He felt as though he'd climbed Mount Olympus.

Though the theater was well lit, their joined hands lay in the shadows, invisible to the audience. A delicious secret, like the embrace and the laughter she'd kept back.

The drop rose and the last play of the evening began.

He scarcely saw what happened onstage. All his being was concentrated on the young woman beside him, and the hand he held.

A day had passed, no more. From yesterday and the rather daunting interview with her father to this moment. It seemed so simple now. So deuced complicated at the same time.

Didn't matter. Her gloved hand, warm in his, and the mad embrace would sustain him while he did what needed to be done, whatever it was.

Eventually, the dire doings onstage drew his attention back to *The Evil Eye*, and before long, he became caught up in the play.

Even if his mind had been a degree less clouded by happiness, it's unlikely that the Duke of Ashmont would have noticed, let alone cared about, the evil eye Mr. Owsley directed at them across the theater.

CASSANDRA KNEW SHE shouldn't have done it. She knew it was highly improper at best. But when he laid his hand over hers, her heart turned over, and she thought, *Why not? It's only for now. Why not enjoy it for now?*

He can be extremely winning when he chooses, and he's especially dangerous in that mode, Alice had said.

No exaggeration.

All the same, it didn't seem fair.

There he was, in all his golden godlike beauty, sitting quietly beside her, apparently domesticated. But she knew gods couldn't be domesticated. They adopted all kinds of disguises to get what they wanted. Then once they got it, they went on to the next victim.

Unfair. A woman couldn't simply surrender to perfectly natural human impulses and still be respected.

A woman couldn't do that without disgracing the people she loved.

It was the way of the world.

He'd forgotten her easily enough years ago, she reminded herself. He hadn't even seen her that night at Almack's when she stood in front of him. During other rare and fleeting encounters, early on, at one social affair or another, to him she was merely another debutante in white muslin.

To marry him then be forgotten . . . She wasn't at all sure she could bear it.

MR. OWSLEY HAD watched the trouble unfold, but he'd been too slow to realize what was going on and too far away to act quickly enough.

He could have won further admiration from his supporters. More important, he could have changed Miss Pomfret's mind about him.

But he was too late and too slow, and her admiring gaze was directed at the dissolute Duke of Ashmont, who didn't deserve her or any gently bred maiden.

Owsley told himself to leave it alone. She'd humiliated him publicly weeks ago and dismissed him out of hand during the first interval. He should not have approached her. He should not have mentioned his bill.

But she was beautiful, the handsomest young woman he'd ever met. It was her face and figure as much as her words at his lecture that had left him tongue-tied and red-faced.

He, nonplussed by a woman! The majority of those supporting his efforts regarding the Sabbath were women. He was an attractive man, of good position and excellent prospects. He might have his pick of scores of young ladies.

But no. Of all times for Cupid's arrow to strike, it had to pierce him with a witless, self-destructive desire for Cassandra Pomfret.

She was everything he disliked in a woman: opinionated, outspoken, and willful. She'd been caught behaving most improperly with the Duke of Ashmont, and did she look in the least chagrined, let alone ashamed of herself?

No. She sat in the duke's private box as the Queen herself might sit, looking over the royal dominions. Far from humbled by her disgrace, Miss Pomfret had dismissed out of hand Owsley and anything he had to say.

He would fight this, he vowed. He would not let a senseless infatuation get the better of him.

All the same, he longed to close his hands round the Duke of Ashmont's neck and throttle him.

AFTER THE ENTERTAINMENT, the duke had arranged for his party to join Cassandra's parents for supper at the Clarendon Hotel. Humphrey Morris was a last-minute addition to the party because he'd assisted Ashmont in escorting the ladies safely out of the Adelphi, through the disorderly after-theater crowd.

Once they'd made their way through the throng, they had to negotiate the thicket of carriages. Then came the long parade of vehicles progressing at a snail's pace along the Strand.

But the duke's party made better speed than most. He was, after all, the man to whom non-suicidal persons gave a wide berth. He had servants in place as well, to ease the way. His group reached the hotel in a reasonable time, only minutes after Mama and Papa.

There Aunt Julia gave a succinct account of their experience at the Adelphi. Though she didn't spare Ashmont's quick-thinking and wise action more than a few words, Papa understood, clearly, because he sat back and gave Ashmont a considering look, as though seeing him for the first time.

After a while, and a few glasses of wine, Humphrey Morris overcame his highly unusual reticence and told some stories. Cassandra noticed Hyacinth listening intently, smiling and nodding while he talked.

Humphrey Morris? Really?

"HUMPHREY MORRIS?" CASSANDRA said. "Really?"

The two sisters sat on Cassandra's bed, talking over the evening.

"He's interesting," Hyacinth said. "He seems to know everything about everybody."

"Like his mother."

"It's different. I think Papa noticed. If I did, surely he did, though I'd never blame him for being engrossed with the Duke of Ashmont. But Papa has mastered the art of listening to several persons clamoring for attention at the same time. No doubt he's accustomed to taking in different opinions at meetings and such. He must have noticed."

"All I noticed was Mr. Morris's tongue finally untied itself in your presence."

"Papa knows how to encourage men to speak. He knows he can be intimidating."

"My love, he is intimidating on purpose."

"But he only uses it as a tool."

It occurred to Cassandra that the tool worked with his sons as well as other politicians. The method had not worked quite so well with his daughters.

"I believe Mr. Morris could be of great use to him," Hyacinth said. "I feel reasonably certain that this has occurred to Papa as well."

Cassandra stared at her sister.

Hyacinth laughed. "You're preoccupied with the duke. You can't be expected to attend to anything else. You can't have noticed the way Papa spoke to Mr. Morris or the way he listened. For my part, I have been most agreeably surprised by the duke's friend. I look forward to getting to know him better."

"But, Hyacinth, his mother!"

Her sister shrugged. "For all her complaints, Mama manages her well enough. Some ancient history there, I believe. Aunt Julia hinted at it. I'm not quite clear, and one can't ask Mama directly—but I suspect an old rivalry, to do with Papa."

"I shouldn't be surprised," Cassandra said, after she recovered from the initial surprise. One didn't think of one's parents in that way. "Lady Bartham seems to regard most women as deadly rivals, and it isn't hard to imagine her always being that way. Some women are. One finds them in every year's crop of debutantes."

"I ought to feel sorry for her," Hyacinth said. "It must be dreadful to live with so much bile. But she can be tiresome. I needn't wonder what she'll make of our theater excursion."

"She won't be pleased. Supper went smoothly. No explosions. No screaming. No constables summoned."

They'd got everybody at the Adelphi talking. The supper party would add to the speculation.

The Curtain Scene would be forgiven when it seemed the prelude to a family-approved engagement. If all went according to plan, by the time the alleged engagement ended, not much of Society would be left in London to talk about it.

Parliament would rise sometime in August, according to her father. A matter of weeks. Then Cassandra would go abroad again, back to her grandparents. Her latest outrage against propriety would fade in importance, merely another in a long line of misbehaviors.

And Hyacinth could enjoy the next Season without her sister's dark shadow spoiling everything.

Meanwhile, Cassandra would think of this as a game. A prank. She'd have fun while it lasted. She had no doubt she'd be sorry when it was over. She would miss the winning ways and the moments of naughtiness. She'd miss the duke's voice and his touch. She would probably weep and feel sorry for herself.

But she'd get over it. She'd survived before, when she was young and believed a disappointment in love was the end of the world. She'd survive this.

Bartham House
Sunday

"INDEED, MR. OWSLEY, it breaks my heart to see that girl throw herself away on the Duke of Ashmont," said Lady Bartham. "What can she look forward to but misery?"

The countess had waylaid him after church and invited him to stop for tea.

She'd heard about events at the Adelphi last night. She knew Mr. Owsley had tried to talk to Miss Pomfret and had been rebuffed. She knew her third son had been there, dangling after Miss Hyacinth Pomfret. Given the number of other gentlemen also dangling, she wasn't overly concerned about this.

She was deeply concerned about the treacherous machinations of certain persons: Lady deGriffith was behind last night's scenes, she had no doubt. The countess was well aware that last night's events were already dismantling her lovely campaign of character assassination.

"I trust that is not so," Mr. Owsley said. "Indeed, I hope it is not."

"So unfortunate. But then, Lord deGriffith has never been able to manage the girls. It is a great pity, because all Miss Pomfret needs is a patient but firm hand."

Mr. Owsley looked up from his gloom. "Do you truly believe so?"

"I have no doubt of it. The trouble is, she's been let to go her own way for too long. A shocking waste, in my opinion. Such a handsome girl, and so clever. She could be of the greatest use to her husband. But what use will Ashmont make of her? He'll amuse himself for a time, then go on to the next entertainment." She shook her head sadly.

"Perhaps he'll make her happy," Owsley said. "One must hope so."

If he was hopeful, he was looking rather grim about it.

"A most regrettable failure in upbringing," Lady Bartham pressed on. "Had she been my daughter I should have recognized her potential and groomed her to be a great political hostess."

That got his full attention.

"A rising diplomat or Member of Parliament could achieve great things with her by his side," the lady continued. "But she is not my daughter, and I can't hope to see her as my daughter-in-law. The two eldest boys are married, and Humphrey, along with a hundred other young men, is besotted with her sister."

"Miss Hyacinth Pomfret appears to be an amiable young lady," Owsley said.

Lady Bartham waved away the infuriatingly beautiful younger sister. "No doubt. But such a pity about Miss Pomfret. One can only stand by and grieve for her. Such a waste. Such a great waste." She shook her head sadly.

With these and a few more words in the same vein, she undermined Mr. Owsley's sensible intentions.

He reflected on Miss Pomfret's stunning good looks and her intelligence. He thought of this handsome young woman thrown away on the Duke of Ashmont. He maddened himself by imagining her in the duke's bed.

Meanwhile, the words *patient but firm hand* lodged themselves in his brain, along with *great political hostess* and *achieve great things*.

His hostess administered the coup de grâce as he was leaving. She gave him a poem. Titled "The Bridal Gift," it had appeared in the *Court Journal*.

Taking up the entire front page of the weekly paper, the poem painted the miseries of an ill-advised marriage. The husband depicted seemed to Owsley to bear a powerful resemblance to the Duke of Ashmont. Though it had been published months ago and was addressed to a Lady Charlotte ——, Mr. Owsley thought, as Lady Bartham intended him to do, that it might have been written expressly for Miss Pomfret.

By the time he left Bartham House, he believed it was his duty to save Lord deGriffith's eldest daughter from herself.

Chapter 12

The courtship show continued on Sunday afternoon, when they rode in Hyde Park.

All the world converged on the park on Sunday, a sound reason to avoid it, especially on a hot July day. But they were here for the crowd, Ashmont and his trio of ladies: Miss Flower, in a blue riding dress; her aunt, in green; and Miss Pomfret in a different shade of green, riding a fine blood bay.

All Ashmont had to do was be seen with them and behave as suitors did. Then everybody would begin to talk about the wild and wicked Duke of Ashmont wooing and winning the formidable Miss Pomfret—and doing it properly, under the family auspices. That would become the big story, and the Curtain Scene would wither from memory, he hoped.

Meanwhile he had to actually win her while she fought him every step of the way.

He'd slept poorly, thanks to lascivious dreams about her that ended badly. Now he couldn't even hold her hand, or any other part of her. His primary task today was keeping his temper, no trivial assignment when all about him riders were behaving stupidly, and he couldn't murder any of them.

He rode Jupiter, a large, intimidating black stallion. Like his half brother, the carriage horse Nestor, Jupiter was, in fact, a gentle, rather sensitive fellow. But he looked dangerous—or perhaps seemed so because of the man in the saddle.

Between his apparently satanic stallion and his reputedly satanic self, Ashmont had pushed his party through the crush of vehicles, equestrians, and pedestrians at Hyde Park Corner without the difficulties others faced, and to whose difficulties he added, compelling those in his way to get out of the way as best they might. Thence he and the ladies proceeded to Rotten Row.

To relieve congestion, all carriages but the sovereign's had been barred from the Row. Matters today did not seem much improved. Clumps of dandies, military men, MPs, lords, esquires, bumpkins, and what seemed to be every clerk in London clotted the bridle path.

That was only the male part of the crowd. Add to this the female contingent, the scores of riders who had no business anywhere near a horse, the maladjusted horses who had no business being ridden, the hordes of gawkers at the railings, and, to provide an extra dose of unpredictability, the children and dogs—all of this taking place in the heat and dust of a July afternoon.

He was part of a performance, Ashmont told himself. The larger the audience, the better.

"This is ghastly," Miss Pomfret said. "One can scarcely move. Mainly because of Hyacinth. No wonder my father hated letting her out of the house."

Morris's adored one and Lady Charles were now in front of them, where Ashmont could watch out for lust-crazed young men.

"She's doing us a great favor," he said. "She draws the crowds, which means more witnesses to our perfectly proper courtship."

"Lady Bartham will be furious."

"There's one happy thought."

"Maybe she'll turn up," she said. "That would make this ordeal truly worthwhile."

"Then we might gaze adoringly at each other and make her wild, because that's the way courting couples ought to gaze at each other."

"I'm not sure I'll go that far," she said. "I gazed at you adoringly last night, and recall what happened."

How could he forget?

"I took advantage," he said. "Couldn't help myself. There you were, all worshipful and everything."

"Worshipful!"

"Yes. Don't do it here. Can't answer for consequences."

"I shall do my best to be resistible," she said. "I always assumed I was expert at it. No, I know I am. It's only that you're perverse."

"And Owsley? Why can't he keep away?"

She considered. "Obstinacy? Last night was the first time I've seen him since his lecture. I wondered why he approached me. Now I suspect he wants to win me over so that I'll stop making trouble for him. He sees me as a threat. Which I am." Her full mouth curved a very little. "I and the Andromeda Society. We won't be silenced."

It was on the tip of Ashmont's tongue to point out that she'd be a greater threat as a duchess. But he'd rushed his fences last night, and she'd withdrawn. She'd kissed him so passionately. She'd let him hold her hand. But afterward her mood changed.

She'd had second thoughts.

I don't trust you.

He told himself to be patient. He had no choice, but patience wasn't something he'd practiced, and it didn't come easily.

"If you could bring him round to your way of thinking, what would you want him to do?" he said.

"Throw wholehearted support to the bill for reducing working hours for factory children."

"What about Stanley's antislavery bill?"

"According to my father, the canting hypocrites are outnumbered on that one, and it will pass easily."

"He's certain of it?" The antislavery bill wasn't the only piece of Parliamentary business Ashmont was trying to come to terms with. So much went on at Westminster, and he'd never paid attention. He'd skimmed over those parts of the various periodicals or skipped them altogether. Politics. Boring.

"Progress has been made," she said. "Several acts passed over the years. I suppose that's why— Drat the man! Where's a rat catcher when you need one?"

Ashmont followed her gaze. Riding toward them was Oh-So-Holy, on a lively chestnut mare who did not seem happy with the crowd.

"This is the trouble with men," she said. "One of the troubles. They seem not to know or care when they're not wanted. I humiliated him in public. I made it plain I was firmly against his bill. Yet here he comes. Or maybe not. Maybe he's spotted somebody else to bother."

"Did you look in the dressing glass today?" Ashmont said. "Have you any notion the effect that riding dress has on a fellow?" He gestured at his chest. "When I first saw you, I thought my heart would give out." The high-necked, tight-fitting bodice exhibited her figure to breathtaking effect. The combination of mind-shattering womanliness and masculine top hat was like to kill a fellow. "Between that and the way you ride—"

"I'm not riding. I'm spending most of my time sitting in one place, glad I chose to take Dora today." She patted the mare's neck. "She's a good, patient, even-tempered girl. As I am not. Curse the man, he *is* coming this way."

"Then let's make the most of it," Ashmont said. "We're stuck here. Can't have any fun behind a curtain. Let's find out what he's made of."

CASSANDRA DIDN'T WANT to speak to Owsley.

Her eighteen-year-old self wanted to flirt with Ashmont. She wanted him to gaze at her in the besotted way that, sincere or not, made her insides tighten.

At the same time, being in reality close on six and twenty, and aware of the rights and wrongs of the world, she also wanted to go on talking about Parliamentary business with him.

Politics. Ashmont. The two didn't go together. But he wasn't falling asleep in the saddle. He'd brought up the Sabbath and slavery bills and seemed interested when she referred to the latest factories bill.

It occurred to her that a man adept at planning elaborate pranks ought to be able to grasp the basics of political strategy easily enough. If he wanted to. If he found it challenging. If it wasn't a whim of the moment.

But here was Owsley. He was ambitious, he wasn't stupid, and he was a Member of Parliament. For the sake of the Andromeda Society, she needed to think like her father and seek either common ground or a lever for manipulation.

Polite greetings were exchanged.

Then the duke said, "Mr. Owsley, I'm glad you stopped. I've been encouraged to take my seat in the House of Lords. Not sure I'm up to it, but we'll see. To start with, something's arisen in the Commons, and I wanted your view."

There it was. Not a passing whim, apparently. Or it hadn't passed yet.

"I should be glad to be of help if I can," Owsley said. "If it's to do with my bill, I should be happy to review it with you, in detail."

"Your bill wants rethinking," Ashmont said. "Unsound. As I believe Miss Pomfret has pointed out. She and numerous other parties."

"Indeed, but these parties have overlooked the crucial matter. If existing Sabbath laws were properly enforced, the lower orders would not be forced to labor on what ought to be a day of rest and reflection."

"Good intentions," Ashmont said. "Ill-advised plan. Happy to speak of it at length another time. Help you see the flaws."

Owsley's color rose.

Ashmont appeared to take no notice, dismissing the topic with a slight wave of his hand. "I was curious about your position on other matters. The factories bill, for instance."

"Another subject altogether," Owsley said. He treated the duke to the same patronizing smile he'd given Cassandra weeks ago, at the lecture. "Too complex to admit of proper discussion here."

"Complex?" Cassandra said. "You have read the reports? You are aware of the working conditions?"

"I have not had the opportunity to study them closely," he said.

"Too busy trying to spoil Sunday for the wretches who don't have kitchens to cook in or horses to ride in Hyde Park?" Ashmont said mildly.

"I don't see how the facts could be plainer," Cassandra said. "*Everybody* has been talking about the reports."

"Not surprising," Owsley said. "The interviews with the children seem calculated to play on emotion."

And he apparently hadn't any. All his energies were given to making a name for himself and carrying on a moral crusade that applied only to ordinary people.

He was still talking, but she had stopped listening. She was disappointed. She'd hoped there was more to him than this, but he was merely another canting hypocrite.

Self-control was second nature, but today the crowd, the heat, and frustration had her temper slipping. Her hands tightened on the reins. Dora dipped her head and shifted restlessly.

"Mind your horse, sir," Ashmont said sharply. "Have a care for the lady."

The sharp tone recalled Cassandra to the moment, to where she was, and the animal she rode. Patient Dora was clearly unhappy and wanted to be elsewhere.

This was because Owsley's mare was warning the other two horses off, her ears pinned back, teeth snapping.

Keeffe's voice echoed in her head.

. . . the horses . . . need you to be calm and to know what to do.

Cassandra corrected her hold of the reins, easing Dora out of range of the tetchy chestnut.

"Come away, Miss Pomfret," Ashmont said. "Nothing to be gained here. But no, why should you retreat? He was the one who approached you. Owsley, you had your chance and you bungled it. Again. If I were you, I'd go away. And stay away."

But it was the same as last night. Owsley wouldn't give ground.

He glared from one to the other. "I at least have tried to serve my monarch and my country, while your seat in the House of Lords has done nothing but collect cobwebs."

"Not arguing that," Ashmont said. "Doesn't change facts. Nothing to say to you." He made the casual gesture of dismissal. "I recommend you take yourself off."

Owsley's face reddened. "Were I the sort of man who is easily cowed, I should never have stood for Parliament, sir, and—"

"Don't care if you're cowed or not. You're boring me."

Instead of going away, Owsley legged his chestnut mare toward the duke, challenging him. The already-vexed creature bumped Ashmont's stallion, who wisely danced out of the way. Cassandra, too, moved farther away, an instant before Owsley's mount began to throw a fit, squealing, stomping, rearing.

The chestnut bucked and spun, kicking out furiously again and again. The saddle girths gave way, and the saddle began to turn. Cassandra saw Owsley's hands flailing in the instant before the mare's shoulder dropped, and he went over and down, hard, to the ground.

And lay there, unmoving, while the angry mare went on bucking down Rotten Row.

THAT STRETCH OF the Row promptly lost its collective mind. Too many inept riders in an overcrowded section of road. Women shrieking. Men shouting. Horses snorting and squealing.

Two hacks lunged through the crowd, following the runaway while others danced anxiously in place, seeing no safe way out, and still others tried to retreat where there was no place to go.

Ashmont dismounted, handed off his reins to somebody nearby, and went to the fallen man.

An instant later, Miss Pomfret was beside him. "Back, move back!" she called out, her voice calm and sure in the hubbub. Then she was giving orders, the way she'd done in Putney Heath. A litter. A surgeon. Somebody to catch Owsley's mare.

She was the general in a battle where everybody had run mad.

The voice of command had an effect, and the crowd began to give way and settle down.

Meanwhile, Ashmont heard her aunt dispersing the crowd. After a time, the world about them quieted somewhat. When the aunt and sister joined them, Owsley was coming to his senses.

He was perfectly well, he said. He wanted to get back on his horse. He wouldn't believe she'd run away. Some of his friends arrived on the scene then, and persuaded him to see a surgeon. He hadn't broken his neck or any other obvious parts, but a concussion was possible. So were minor fractures.

Before long he was loaded onto a litter and carried to a carriage. The onlookers began to disperse.

Miss Pomfret beside him, Ashmont watched the man's departure. He was remembering Putney Heath. Accidents. How many had he caused?

"That wasn't your fault," she said.

"Couldn't say."

"It wasn't."

"I know we came within a hairsbreadth of all hell breaking loose," he said. "Your sister was nearby. Your aunt. Innocent parties. It was a miracle the mare did no other harm. I was too slow."

"Too slow! You had no room to maneuver. We had a crowd pressing in to watch the show. Two men arguing over a woman, it must have looked like. We had nowhere to go."

Ashmont shook his head. "I saw he wasn't managing his hack well. We should have left him sooner. But that know-it-all smirk. So provoking. Puritanical spoilsport."

She touched his arm. "He has a gift for raising one's hackles. But nobody else was hurt. We averted anarchy."

"We." He glanced down at her hand.

She took it away, but slowly. "Yes, you and I, oddly enough. I can see the headlines tomorrow. 'Duke of Ashmont Averts Anarchy, Aided by deGriffith's Gorgon. Hell Freezes Over.'"

We. She'd made them a pair.

We. One short, beautiful word.

His mood lifted. "All the same, I wanted to break his nose."

"But this wasn't the time and place, and you didn't. Another time, perhaps." She gave him a quick smile. "I'll help you."

"Wouldn't be sporting," he said. "Two against one."

"We'll toss a coin for it," she said.

"I could kiss you," he said.

"I feel the same. You did well."

She didn't play games. A fellow knew where he stood, and at the moment, he seemed to be floating a foot or so above the ground.

He looked about him. The crowd was closing in on them again. "But not here, obviously. Why don't I help you mount?"

A pause, then, "If you must."

"Can't promise where my hands will go," he said. "Shocking experience I've had. Temporary imbalance of mind. Not to mention all the self-restraint. My not-better self wanted to stomp on his head, even when he was down."

"I felt the same. But of course it would have been very bad ton."

They returned to their horses, which some boys were holding. Though it was half a dozen boys to two horses, Ashmont divided coins among them before shooing them away.

"They can be a nuisance," he said. "Best to keep the brats happy, though. They know me, you see, and word gets about. No matter where I go, I'm likely to find a boy—sometimes a girl—I can trust with my cattle. And in other ways."

He bent and laced his hands together, and she stepped up and onto the horse, easy and graceful, in spite of the long skirt of her dress and its yards of material and all the supporting garments underneath. She did it so smoothly and quickly, he barely had time to let his hands stray over the fabric covering her legs.

Her long legs. Her beautifully shaped, strong, lithe body. Her velvety breasts. Her mouth. Her hands.

"I don't know how much more of this I can bear," he said. "When can we get married?"

She looked down at him. "I can't marry you."

"But you said you could kiss me."

"A kiss," she said. "Not a lifetime. Don't press me. I'm in charity with you. For now."

"Last night," he said. "Only a kiss? Dammit, Cassandra—"

"A few days," she said. "That's all it's been. You've disappointed me for years. I don't trust you. Is that so hard to understand?"

She rode away.

ASHMONT DID NOT understand.

He stood for a moment, swore violently, and decided he'd had enough. He wasn't cut out for this. Patience wasn't in his nature.

He would go to the devil, that's what he'd do. Go straight to the devil.

She'd kissed him as though it were the end of the world and theirs was the last kiss that would ever happen. That's the way it had felt. Not like a game. In the next breath, practically, she pushed him away.

He would get drunk, that's what he'd do. Then he'd go to Carlotta O'Neill's place and enjoy some willing females. Then he'd go to Crockford's and lose a thousand pounds at the hazard table. He would get very, very drunk, and somebody would throw him into a hackney and send him home, where the servants would put him to bed.

That's what he would do.

What he always did . . .

Every damned time.

He blinked and looked about him—at the riders keeping a safe distance from him, at the audience at the railings, at the wide bridle path down which Miss Pomfret had gone. He watched her ride, tall and straight in the saddle. His gaze went from her bottom up her straight back and up over the veil to the top hat and above that to the sky. Above the border of trees, great swathes of blue stretched between fluffy white clouds.

He saw all these things while scene after scene flashed through his mind. Drunk on his wedding day. Too drunk to pursue his runaway bride. Drunk when he did pursue her. Drunk on the night he'd found out the truth about Ripley and Olympia. Drunk in Putney.

That was only recent weeks and that was only the drinking.

The years of wild behavior. The pranks. The fights. The brawls. The duels.

Every bloody time things didn't go his way. Or he was bored. Discontented. Blue-deviled. Confused. Pride hurt.

Every last time, in other words, he wasn't perfectly content.

And he was stunned that she didn't trust him? Indignant she didn't want to be shackled to him for life?

What an arsehole he was. What a conceited thickhead.

He was lucky she hadn't killed him when she had the chance. He was lucky she let him within a mile of her.

Her father despised him, but hadn't demanded the privilege of shooting him. The father had no doubt kept the brothers at bay as well.

Lucky.

Five thousand nine hundred and ninety-six points remaining. Not a jot less.

To be a tolerable human being. Fair enough. Even generous.

Ashmont got onto his horse and rejoined the ladies. He escorted them home in good humor. No brooding. No sulking. He was fortunate far beyond what he deserved to have come this far. He had better not forget it.

At deGriffith House, he waved off the groom and helped Miss Pomfret dismount. He took some minor liberties in the process, because, after all, he wasn't a saint.

She didn't kick him in the head.

She didn't mind the liberties, he realized. It was the marrying part she minded.

He understood now.

When she stood on the pavement, he said, in a low voice, "I do understand. About trust. Will you give me a chance to earn it?"

She opened her mouth, then closed it. She looked at him and sighed. "Duke."

"I like it better when you call me Lucius," he said.

"Don't push me. Ashmont." She smiled a very little.

"Very well. Small steps."

Her aunt and sister were walking to the door. But one of the advantages of courtship, real or pretend, was, the chaperons allowed a measure of privacy. Not much. He and Miss Pomfret would be allowed a few words before the lady was required to go in.

"This is supposed to be a pretend courtship," she said.

"I know, and you can pretend all you want. All I have to do is move a mountain or two. Push the great rock up the hill and hope it doesn't roll back down on me. What I'm saying is, I understand you make no promises. When the day comes, and you decide you've had enough of me, I'll do something dreadful, as I said I would. Then you break it off, and nobody blames you. Nobody blamed Olympia, did they?"

"But." She glanced back at deGriffith House, where her father no doubt watched from a window. "There's always a but."

"But I'm asking for a sporting chance. You know. Labors of Hercules. That sort of thing. Move mountains. Slay dragons."

"Ah, yes. You can't resist a challenge, I know."

She knew him too well, far too well.

Ye gods, this was going to be hard. Impossible.

"We'd planned to carry on the pretense until Parliament rises," she said.

While Ashmont paid as little attention as possible to Parliament's doings, he was aware that upper-class London thinned out in late summer. It wasn't much time for moving mountains.

"Yes, that's what we agreed," he said.

"Very well," she said. "A sporting chance. No promises."

"No promises."

She nodded and walked to the house.

He did not kick the nearest lamppost and swear. He did not throw his hat down and stomp on it. He wanted her and he wanted her *now*, and being unused to not getting what he wanted when he wanted it, the Duke of Ashmont wanted to kick and stomp and punch something or somebody. He didn't.

He climbed back onto his horse and rode home. There he wrote a note to Miss Pomfret's friend Mrs. Roake. He and she had had a brief but enlightening conversation last night at the theater.

Then he spent two hours in his library, looking for a book Mrs. Roake had mentioned.

He did not get drunk. He did not go to Carlotta's or Crockford's.

He began reading *A Vindication of the Rights of Woman*.

ON MONDAY, THE duke escorted the ladies to Vauxhall for the fête on behalf of distressed Poles. However, the crowd at the Rotunda, where a concert was to be held, was so immense and unruly that even he decided against trying to get in.

As they later heard, too many were let in, too many were kept out, and the resulting uproar made it impossible to hear any of the performers. Pasta and Paganini and the others might as well have stayed home, according to those who did brave the Rotunda crowd. That was the least of it. People were injured in the crush, and the pickpockets had been hard at work.

That was the earlier part of the event, though. While the Rotunda was in a state of pandemonium, Ashmont took his party through the pleasure gardens, which Cassandra hadn't visited in ages. Hyacinth was in raptures, especially in the evening, when the place was lit like a fairyland.

An immense arrangement of lamps, thousands of them, created the armorial bearings of Poland. The fireworks, too, were splendid.

And there was dancing.

When had Cassandra last danced? Not in England, to be sure. Here, potential partners gave deGriffith's Gorgon a wide berth. Even her first Season had been notable for the lack of partners. As her reputation grew, the few dwindled to none. These days she danced with dancing masters or at family gatherings with family members, often with her younger sisters.

Then the Duke of Darmstadt's band began playing the "Waterloo Waltz." She'd expected to look on, enjoying Hyacinth's joy, but Ashmont, standing beside her, said, "We must dance, you know."

Cassandra looked up into his beautiful face, into blue eyes sparkling like a sunlit sea in the lamplight.

She remembered the night at Almack's, when her heart had leapt at the possibility of dancing with him. Now her heart hurt. "Must we?"

His gaze swept over the crowd about them.

"Ah, yes, for show," she said.

"You might think that," he said.

When they took their places in the dance area, the place seemed to grow strangely bright. He bowed. She curtseyed.

He took her right hand in his left and, in spite of their gloves, she became acutely aware. Of everything. His hand was warm and strong. The instant it clasped hers, all the old feelings, and the new ones, came wildly alive and seemed to dance inside her.

Then his right hand was at her back and she was setting her left hand on his shoulder . . . and they began to turn and turn again, and she was dizzy when they'd hardly begun.

The world about them seemed to dissolve in a fog that blanketed faces, voices, everything except the music. She and he seemed to dance in one small, sharply clear space, as though they were the only ones, and all else was part of a distant landscape. At the same time, a part of her was vividly aware of everything about them: the whirl of colors, the sparkle and flash of jewels, and the other couples who turned and turned, circles within circles.

She knew, too, because Keeffe had taught her to keep aware of her surroundings, that others were watching.

Their dance was for the onlookers, all for show.

It didn't feel that way.

During a waltz, there was no changing partners or holding somebody—anybody—else's hand, even briefly. No separation. One was locked in one's partner's arms all the while one turned and turned in circles of other dancers.

She was in his arms. The air about him was warm, and it pulsed with masculinity, a blend of scents and something less nameable that felt like power, encircling her, so that she seemed to breathe him in with every step.

It was all for show but it felt as though they'd been meant to do this for a very long time. It felt as though she'd always belonged in his arms.

It felt like happiness.

They danced more than once, and she saw Aunt Julia dancing with Lord Frederick, and Hyacinth with Humphrey Morris. Her parents, who'd come separately, were dancing, too, looking into each other's eyes in a way that left no doubt of their attachment. It was a magical night, and it wasn't until Cassandra was home again, preparing for bed, when she realized.

With its shaded walks and private nooks and other places where a couple might disappear for a time, Vauxhall offered countless opportunities for misbehaving.

Ashmont had not taken her to any of these places. He hadn't taken a single liberty. He hadn't even tried.

THIS IS GOING *to kill me*, the Duke of Ashmont thought.

After seeing the ladies home, he did not relieve the strain by going out and getting drunk. He didn't go to Carlotta's or Crockford's.

He went home.

He went on reading the book.

Esteem. Trust. Respect.

It was going to kill him, but he had to do it.

—A marriage is said to be on the tapis between the Duke of Ashmont and the eldest daughter of Lord and Lady deGriffith. In the circumstances, we are reluctant to comment on the curious rumors circulating in recent days regarding unseemly behavior on the part of this pair. We note only that the duke and his intended have enjoyed several outings under the auspices of Lady Charles Ancaster, whom all of Society rejoice to welcome back to London. The renowned beauty Miss Hyacinth Pomfret was present on these occasions.

—On Sunday, Mr. Titus Owsley, a sponsor of the controversial Sabbath bill, was thrown from his horse in Hyde Park, the result of a broken saddle girth. Though he suffered several contusions and a possible concussion, we are happy to state that great hopes are entertained of his recovery. In consequence of the accident, a dangerous tumult ensued in the crowded bridle path. This was swiftly subdued, and further calamities averted, we are told, by the timely actions of the Duke of Ashmont, Miss Pomfret, and Lady Charles Ancaster.

—*Foxe's Morning Spectacle*
Tuesday 9 July 1833

Tuesday morning

MR. OWSLEY HAD bungled. It was the galling truth. For reasons he could not ascertain, his brain grew clumsy when he was in Miss Pomfret's vicinity. But then, whenever he was in her vicinity lately, the Duke of Ashmont was as well, with all his ducal superiority, waving Owsley away as though he were a fly.

This was twice he'd tried to get her attention and made a spectacle of himself.

And a wreck, this time.

He lay on a chaise longue in the parlor of his rooms at the Albany. Beside him stood a small table bearing some investigative reports, his *Book of Common Prayer*, and the hand mirror with which he'd been torturing himself since Sunday. He threw aside the Tuesday edition of *Foxe's Morning Spectacle* and took up the mirror.

Every bone and muscle ached, but at least they didn't show. His face looked as though a carriage had run over it. Jaw swollen near right ear. Patches of disgusting blue-green-yellow-black disfiguring his smooth features. Scrapes and scabs.

At least his nose wasn't broken, no thanks to the vicious mare. Not that one could blame her for objecting to the Duke of Ashmont. All the same, the bad-tempered beast had come within a hairsbreadth of breaking her owner's neck. If he failed to sell her in the course of the week, she'd go straight to the knackers.

Owsley set down the mirror and reached for the stack of reports. He read six pages of one, then threw it down.

The factory matter was complex, as he'd said. Doctors did not agree with one another about the children's health. Being dirty, ragged, and ignorant did not make the little ones virtuous. Children lied. Call them up before a commission of enquiry and they swelled with self-importance and made themselves out to be more pitiful than they were. Ought they to be idle, then? Ought they be let to play all the day long? What would their families gain by that? What would the children learn from that? To beget more idle children, and more poor for the parish to support?

That's what he should have said.

It would have made no difference. Nothing he said would have made a difference while the Duke of Ashmont loomed nearby.

Mr. Owsley took up the poem Lady Bartham had given him.

> *I'd give thee patience,—to endure the bleak and bitter day,*
> *So dim to thee, so bright unto thy truant far away;*
> *Patience,—the long dark dreary hours of absence to beguile*
> *That thou may'st dry thy tears at last, and meet him with*
> *a smile.*

It was so clear to him that this was what Miss Pomfret's future held. An intelligent lady, who'd lived abroad—why couldn't she see?

How could she see, with that great, hulking duke in the way?

But how was Owsley to get him out of the way?

Chapter 13

On Tuesday, Ashmont escorted the ladies to the Cosmorama in Regent Street. To nobody's astonishment, Morris Tertius turned up.

The Cosmorama, which provided what some called a glorified peepshow, was a regular resort for London's idle classes. Its viewing room offered a Gallery of Europe on one wall and a Gallery of Asia and Africa on the other, with seven scenes in each gallery. The scenes changed every month or so.

The other attractions included a refreshment room where cakes and ices were served and flirtations carried on, and a space for concerts and other performances.

The views were the main attraction, though. One moved from window to window to look through the magnifying lenses at the paintings. These were cleverly lit and arranged in a way that made them seem three-dimensional and, some of them, in motion. Two persons could peer through a window at the same time, if they stood quite close.

With Lady Charles nearby, that was a ticklish maneuver. But she hadn't been here in years, and the images were all new to her. While she was engrossed in, say, "The Exterior of St. Peter's at Rome," Ashmont could hover near Miss Pomfret and inhale an alluring mix of herbs and skin scent. With no breeze to disperse it in the viewing room, the scent swam in his head and made him dizzy.

More than once, he realized his face was dipping within an inch of her neck.

She didn't whack him with her catalogue, as she ought to do.

But she didn't mind a bit of naughtiness. She wasn't a perfectly proper lady. He was beginning to understand the whys and wherefores of this somewhat better, thanks to his reading—though he often had to read passages two and three times over. The concepts were not easy to digest. Sometimes it was like reading a foreign language. But he persevered, and light had begun to dawn.

Thanks to his current studies, and the fact that he wasn't *completely* brainless, he knew better than to let his mouth touch her skin.

He was going to behave properly if it killed him. Which it probably would. But no matter. He had a challenge to meet.

He crushed his frustration and made himself step away.

People came and went. Not a great many. The afternoon's heat had sent much of upper-class London to spas and parks and yachts. Those who did come to the Cosmorama tended to move on quickly to the refreshments area.

"Bored?" Miss Pomfret said.

"On the contrary," he said. "Too exciting, the combination." He nodded toward the little window. "Eruption of Vesuvius and you."

"'Mount Vesuvius,'" came Miss Flower's voice, in an odd accent. "'During the last Eruption; Fire and Smoke is seen in full Motion.'" She rolled the *r*'s and added extra vowels to the ends of the words. Ee-rroop-tee-oh-nee. Fire-ah. Moe-tee-oh-nee.

Miss Pomfret smiled. "That's her extremely Italian accent."

"Now you," said Miss Flower.

Miss Pomfret looked down at the catalogue in her hand. In an exaggerated Greek accent she read, "'The City of Athens In which is seen the Temples of Theseus, Adrian; the Acropolis; the Beautiful surrounding Country of the Peloponnesus, et cetera.'"

Lady Charles, across the room, chuckled.

"My turn again," said Miss Flower. She beamed at Morris, who staggered under the force of her smile.

"'La Mer de Glace, or, the Glaciers in Savoy,'" the girl announced, in an overdone French accent, pronouncing the *r*'s as though she had a violent head cold. "'Zee Immense Masses of Ice are seemingly r-r-rolling from the Stupendous Mountains.'" She made a series of mincing sideways steps, pretending to roll by the little window.

The men, who'd stood slack-jawed for a time, broke into whoops.

Then, naturally, they had to join in. They did dumbshows. Adding theatrics, they rescued victims from glaciers and ran from molten lava. The quartet took turns reading the descriptions, mimicking the Duke of Gloucester, the King, Lord Brougham, Lady Jersey, the Princess Lieven, and others. The Pomfret sisters were first-rate mimics.

Their show attracted an audience, with people drifting in from other parts of the building to guess who was being impersonated and try to interpret the dumbshows.

"This is a good time to leave," Lady Charles said. "Before we're asked to do so."

"Shall we try the Colosseum next?" Ashmont said when they'd reached the pavement. "Shall we see if the ladies can get us pitched out of that one?"

"Not likely," Miss Pomfret said. She moved to walk beside him and lowered her voice. "I'm amazed my aunt let it go as far as she did. Young ladies are not supposed to make spectacles of themselves. We're not to be observed having fun in public."

He'd never thought about that, until very recently. He'd always thought of respectable young women as boring. He was only beginning to realize they weren't given much choice.

"It was delightful," he said. "Your sister—rather more to her than meets the eye."

"As I believe Mr. Morris appreciates."

"The same applies to you," he said. "Your Princess Lieven was perfect."

"You haven't heard my Duchess of Kent yet."

He didn't get to hear it that day. At the Colosseum they met up with a party of Fitzclarences—the King's illegitimate offspring—and some legitimate minor royals, all of whom fawned over Lady Charles and Miss Flower.

"So much for getting tossed out," Ashmont said to Miss Pomfret in an undertone. "Got to be on best behavior now. No antics."

"You cannot be intimidated by royals," she said. "They were never exempt from your pranks, as I recall."

"That was before," Ashmont said. "I'm in bad odor with the King. Wants to hang me by the yardarm. I've fences to mend."

The Duchess of Ashmont had to be welcome at Court.

And so he set out to charm and disarm. It had to be done, and he knew how to do it.

THE CHARMING AND disarming continued for a week, during which the ladies kept Ashmont busy.

They visited the Zoological Gardens of the Regent's Park. They attended concerts and benefits. The opera. Yet more charity affairs.

On Saturday, Miss Pomfret's friend Mrs. Roake took her to the monthly meeting, no ruffians being required this time.

On Sunday, they rode in Hyde Park again, and once again, somebody dismounted unintentionally. But somebody in the park was always falling off a horse or getting run away with, and this accident, for once, had nothing to do with Ashmont.

On Monday they attended yet another fancy fair, this time at Vauxhall, where, happily, the sisters hadn't to manage a stall and, better yet, dancing had taken place in the evening. Miss Pomfret wore a pale orange dress, like the color of apricots, with a sinfully low neckline edged in lace. Designed to torture a fellow, in other words.

Her eyes sparkled in the lamplight. Her silk skirt brushed against his legs while they went round and round. He had her in his arms, and she fit there as though she'd been made for him.

She was made for him. He knew that. Persuading her was the challenge.

One of the challenges. Remaking his reputation was another. The Duchess of Ashmont had to be welcome everywhere. Her husband couldn't be a pariah. He had to find a place for himself, and it had to be the kind of place a difficult, troublemaking duke fit into somehow.

He had any number of burnt bridges to rebuild, and possibly some new ones to construct.

Knowing she wasn't happy with her current life didn't make the work easier. He'd rather be there, at her side, all the time, trying to make it more agreeable for her, but he couldn't.

He couldn't accompany her on morning calls, for instance. The aunt or the mother took the sisters on the endless visits ladies were obliged to pay, and which Miss Pomfret told him she despised.

"We sit and talk of nothing," she complained on Tuesday night. "Too many bored women with nothing to do except gossip or drone on about inconsequential matters. Even Hyacinth finds it tiresome. She says she lets it wash over her, like noise in the background. I wish I could do that, but what washes over me is a longing to create a disturbance."

That night they occupied a box at the Haymarket Theater. She wore a dress the color of amethysts, again cut diabolically low, with lace floating about the neckline, like icing on a delicious cake. He fantasized trailing his tongue along the neckline. He made do with holding her hand, and now and again letting his arm or leg brush against hers.

On Wednesday night, he had no similar delicious torture to look forward to. The family were attending a dinner to which Ashmont had not been invited.

He couldn't remember the last time he'd been invited to a private gathering of the bon ton. He knew why he'd been expunged from invitation lists.

Nobody trusted him. Hosts never knew what would happen. Explosions. Screaming. Invasions of domestic animals or circus performers.

Thus Wednesday evening found Ashmont free to torment himself by imagining other fellows at that dinner ogling Cassandra Pomfret's décolletage and having the kinds of fantasies he did.

He was in his dressing room, reviewing papers his solicitor had left with him, when the note arrived.

deGriffith House
17th Instant

Dear Ashmont,

Mrs. Roake has notified me of a situation wanting my
attention, which obliges me to pay a call to a part of
London my parents would not approve of my visiting.
Normally, Keeffe accompanies me on these missions. The
neighborhood is merely poor, not necessarily dangerous.
That is to say, it is no more dangerous than most other
parts of London. However, since a woman cannot travel
alone without being subjected to masculine attentions she
doesn't want, and since making this clear to men takes
time and effort I cannot spare, I require you to take Keeffe's
place.

From Mrs. Roake's house, where I shall change into suitable attire, I shall take a hackney to Furnival's Inn, Holborn.
There you will meet me at ten o'clock in the morning. Dress
as plainly as you can. The residents have reason to fear and
dislike aristocrats in their midst.

Our task is not hazardous. It is the kind of simple errand
I often perform on behalf of the Andromeda Society and it
is urgent, else I shouldn't risk it now, when Hyacinth's life
is finally what it ought to be.

Cassandra Pomfret

Morning of Thursday 18 July

"Bleeding Heart Yard?" Ashmont repeated when Miss Pomfret
told him their destination. "Why go there yourself? You could have
sent me."

"All six feet and some of you, in all your ducal glory, sauntering into the place?" she said. "We try to do our work without calling excessive attention to ourselves."

They were walking along Holborn, a busy, noisy street whose passersby paid them little heed. Miss Pomfret wore a brown dress of simple print whose sleeves were many degrees less swollen than the usual and whose decoration consisted of a fragment of lace about the collar. The hat was austere: no lace, flowers, or bows, except the one tied under her chin. No umbrella today. She'd been delayed setting out from home, she'd told him, and in her hurry to change, she'd forgotten it at Mrs. Roake's.

"But I dressed as you ordered," he said. He wore a suit of clothes he used when he needed to travel incognito.

She gave him a sidelong glance. "The weather gods have been kind. Under overcast skies, in what for you is shabby attire, the Greek deity quality dims somewhat. But you don't carry yourself as you ought. You're still too much the lord of all you survey."

"Right. Forgot about that." He let his shoulders sag and his chin droop and adjusted his stride. "Will this do?"

Another quick, sidelong survey. "Not bad for a duke. All the time you spend at the theater, I suppose, and the hobnobbing with actors—and actresses. That and frequenting low places. But don't speak."

"I can alter my accent, you know."

She shook her head. "You think you can. But they always know. I've had to practice with a strict tutor."

"Keeffe."

"Who else? Still, women do have an advantage. We're trained to adapt to others' wishes, which makes it easier to change our posture and walk. This gives me the freedom to concentrate on my speech. I recommend you keep your mind on not walking as though you own the place, although for all I know, you do."

"Not in Bleeding Heart Yard, I don't think."

They turned into Ely Place.

"You still haven't told me why we've come here," he said.

"To forestall an eviction," she said. "I volunteered for Holborn, as I usually do when I'm home. The people who live here aren't the problem, usually. It's the property owners, their managers, and their rent collectors. Some are overzealous. Some cheat the tenants, who can't afford lawyers or don't know they need one."

"I see."

He did, unfortunately, all too clearly. He'd done a great deal of reading in recent days, which had brought troubling discoveries. Now, to learn of people who didn't know their rights and had no means of obtaining them . . .

"Are you ill, Ashmont? Too much carousing last night?"

He didn't realize he'd paused and put his hand to his head. He took his hand from his temple and laughed, but he couldn't laugh off the feeling, as though some weight lay on his skull. "You make my head hurt. And my heart. It's rather . . ."

Overwhelming. He looked about him at the ancient, soot-darkened buildings looming over them. "It isn't something I've thought about."

"Neither did I, until I met Mrs. Roake and discovered the club and simple ways to make myself useful."

You must collect yourself and try, for once in your misbegotten life, to make yourself useful.

She'd said that weeks ago, the cool, clear voice penetrating his haze of drunken misery.

He'd survived that day in Putney, possibly the lowest point of his life, and managed to be somewhat useful. He wanted to be useful, yes, for once in his life. He simply wasn't used to this, that was all.

"One small part of London," he said, half to himself. "So many lives inside. Places like this everywhere. Somebody overzealous. Somebody cheating people who can't protect themselves."

Not something he'd ever considered. This wasn't a world he paid attention to. He was uneasy, and he wanted to sit down in a quiet place with a glass of wine and make sense of it. He couldn't. Not now. Had to carry on. She could.

"It's better to do something than to do nothing." She went on walking, and after a moment, he caught up with her.

THEY WERE LATE.

Mrs. Pooley stood on the cobblestones, her few belongings strewn about her. Holding one child by the hand and another balanced on her hip, she gazed helplessly at a man walking to the other end of the yard.

"Oh, no, Mr. Crummock," Cassandra called after the man. "You don't throw a woman and her children out of their home and run away."

He wouldn't have done it if Mr. Pooley had been here, but Mr. Pooley wasn't here. Out looking for work, probably.

Crummock paused and turned. He was a great bull of a man, dressed, not elegantly, but better than most of the yard's inhabitants. They were nearly all in view, watching.

"Don't you be starting trouble with me, missus. I been as patient as I ever could with 'em. More'n four months behind, they are, and the one pays my wages ain't in the charity house business."

Ashmont started toward the man. "You did this?" His voice was mild and he wore a faint smile. "You threw their possessions into the filth of the yard?" He gestured at the worn clothing, cracked dishes, utensils, and other pitiful odds and ends.

Cassandra caught herself as she was about to grab his arm. She'd told him to hold his tongue. He was here for show, no more. Having a man nearby changed the balance of power.

But she was aware of people watching. Men coming out of their workshops. Women standing in doorways or looking down from open windows.

They paid no attention to her. They were fixed on Ashmont and waiting to see what he'd do.

She folded her hands and waited, too. If matters went awry, she'd simply have to deal with it.

"They wouldn't go," Crummock said. He seemed to shrink in size as Ashmont neared.

"You threw out their things," the duke said. "Onto the stones and dirt. A woman and two children."

"They don't pay, mister. Sir. They owed since Lady Day. It's my job to collect the rents. I been back time and again, and they put me off. Can't do it no more."

"We're waiting for Mr. Pooley's wages," Mrs. Pooley said. "He been owed them for months. He isn't here. Gone to look for work. Never got paid for the last job he took. I been taking in mending and washing. We wouldn't ask for charity. What we want is time to get right again. It's all we can do now to feed the children."

Ashmont's gaze slid over her, the children, and the collection of belongings scattered over the cobblestones. He clenched his hands.

Crummock took a step back.

Ashmont closed his eyes and opened them again. He unclenched his hands. "Mr. Crummock," he said in the same mild voice.

Even Mrs. Pooley retreated at the sound, an ominous quiet before a storm.

The rent collector looked about the yard. He couldn't expect sympathy or allies. He could make a run for it, Cassandra thought, but he must realize he wouldn't get far with Ashmont in pursuit.

The man clutched his rent book to his chest. "Mister—sir—I got my job to do."

"Yes, and what you will do now is collect all the articles you've tossed out, like—like rubbish," Ashmont said. "A family's possessions. You will collect those articles and you will carry them back to Mrs. Pooley's rooms. You will help her put her household in order once more. You will apologize for disturbing her."

"Apologize!"

"You will apologize, Mr. Crummock. Then you will return to me and we'll discuss business."

Crummock's face reddened. Though the yard lay in the shadows of the surrounding buildings, though no sun beat down on him, sweat trickled down the side of his face. He studied Ashmont for a time. The duke still smiled. He seemed quietly at ease. But he was a duke. And he was Ashmont.

Nobody here seemed to have any idea who he was, but everybody must sense, as Cassandra did, danger throbbing in the air. The yard was still. Even the workshops had fallen silent.

Crummock walked back and began to collect the family's possessions.

ONE THING AT *a time*, Ashmont counseled himself. First, he had to keep his temper. Second, he had to think.

By the time Crummock had carried the Pooleys' household possessions back to their rooms and helped Mrs. Pooley return them to their rightful places, Ashmont had devised a plan of sorts. He borrowed the rent collector's book and wrote his solicitor's name and direction there.

"Call on him tomorrow," he said. "He'll arrange matters with your employer."

When the rent collector left, Ashmont made himself deal with the family. He hadn't any choice. Miss Pomfret had not uttered a word since he'd gone after Crummock. She said nothing now, only waited, as calm as a stone statue.

Mrs. Pooley looked frightened. The children simply stared, great saucer eyes following his every move.

Though the rooms were ancient and decrepit, the high ceilings hinted at better days in some long-ago time. Once, this had been part of a great house. It was no longer great, but this part of it was clean. Mrs. Pooley was shabby but not slatternly. Except for the breakage Crummock had done—and which he'd pay for—the place was neat. Even Sommers would approve.

"I know you don't want charity," Ashmont said. "But a loan wouldn't be taken amiss, I hope. To carry you through the interval. Until we can see about Mr. Pooley's wages and further employment."

Miss Pomfret approached then. She took out her purse and

counted out the money she'd brought. Ashmont added something rather more substantial, which he assured her was a loan. Mrs. Pooley wiped her eyes with the corner of her apron. He looked away.

To his relief, the women moved aside to talk quietly.

To his alarm, the smaller child, who'd been set down on a threadbare piece of rug or blanket—it was hard to say what it was—crawled to Ashmont, and levered herself up by grabbing his trousers. He took her up, and after a moment's panic about what to do with her, finally rested her on his hip, the way her mother had done. She weighed nothing.

They had nothing.

He wanted to weep.

She makes men cry, Morris had said.

Maybe they ought to.

ASHMONT AND MISS Pomfret made their way out of Bleeding Heart Yard and into a tangled conglomeration of yards and courts. He wasn't at all sure where they were, or why they'd come this way, but she seemed to know, and he followed her lead. For the moment he had all he could do to absorb what he'd seen and the sorrow and anger churning inside him.

He was dimly aware of the rain, the light drizzle quickening into a steady pelting as they continued. The dim byways grew darker still, and finally he said, "Are you lost?"

She grabbed his arm and pulled him into a doorway. "Yes," she said. "Yes, I'm lost. You undermine me at every turn."

A leaden weight settled into his gut. "What have I done? Why didn't you tell me?"

She looked up at him, but it was too dark in the doorway to read her expression—not that her beautiful face was easy to read in the best of circumstances. "Do you remember that day at Camberley Place? The party for the children, when you fought Godfrey Wills?"

"Of course I remember. How could I forget?"

"Ah, but you forgot me."

"Not altogether. What do—"

"I loved you. I was eleven years old, and I loved you for what you did. I went on loving you, though, when there wasn't a reason."

"I don't—"

"I believed you'd grow up and be a hero, somebody fine and noble and true. I waited and hoped and waited and hoped. But it never happened. You disappointed me, again and again. At last I gave up waiting and hoping."

He was chilled now. "I didn't know."

"How could you know? After that day, you never saw me, even when I was there. Almack's. I stood in front of you and I might as well have been furniture."

No. No. But it was true. He didn't remember, and he knew she wouldn't lie, exposing herself like this.

"And after a time, I gave up," she went on. "I had other things to do and others to believe in. But now you do this."

"I didn't mean to spoil your plan."

"You were *splendid* today, don't you understand?"

He understood nothing anymore. The world was all awry. A woman and her children with everything they owned lying in the dirt. Hundreds, thousands of women like that. He wanted to hit somebody.

Now this. She'd loved him and he hadn't known or cared. He'd hurt her, the elfin girl she'd been and the young woman she'd become, repeatedly. He'd been oblivious, too busy with his own pointless life.

She grasped his shoulders and shook him. "Today you were everything I ever wanted you to be. Oh, Lucius, what am I to do with you?"

"Wait." His spirits had lifted and sunk and risen again at a dizzying rate. They rose once more. "You're not disappointed. I'm . . . splendid."

She flung her arms about his neck and kissed him.

Not tentatively. When was she ever tentative? She kissed him hard on the lips. She kissed his cheeks, again and again. She kissed his chin. Her fingers slid up his neck into his hair.

The day had darkened, and the narrow way they'd entered was darker still, the buildings closing in on them. Rain pattered against windows and splashed onto the cobblestones. He didn't know where he was. It didn't matter.

He brought his hands up to cup her face. In the doorway's shadows, her eyes were unreadable, but he wouldn't have understood, in any case. "This is confusing."

"I'm so proud of you," she said. "And now I'm in love with you again, and that won't do at all."

Happiness broke out, like an inner burst of sunshine.

"It will do very well." He kissed her all over her rain-slicked face, again and again—cheeks, eyelids, eyebrows—and pushed her bonnet back to kiss her forehead. He covered her lips with his, and savored the softness and welcome he found there. So little and yet so much.

He'd waited for what felt like forever and he expected to wait another forever. But for now, he let himself grow drunk on the feel of her mouth under his. Her mouth, so soft and full and so free with words plainly spoken. She kissed in the same direct way. She let out a quick, impatient sigh, and her tongue flicked over his lips.

His heart lurched and he forgot any good intentions he might have had. He let her in, and the world went away. Her mouth was cool and sweet, like the river at Camberley Place in springtime. Like that place it felt like refuge, home, belonging, and he hungered for it. Within, he was never quiet, it seemed, and now, his feelings a rioting mob, he longed for the sanctuary she seemed to promise. She was the storm and the haven from the storm, this unpredictable and passionate woman.

He slid his hands down her neck, where the lacy collar tickled his fingers, then down over her shoulders, her arms. They weren't swallowed up in immense pillowy sleeves today. No enormous lapels or layers of lace concealed the womanly curves. He slid his hands over her breasts, all too firmly encased in bodice and undergarments. What lay beneath was velvety and warm, he knew. He knew what her skin smelled like: lavender and rosemary and Cassandra.

She made odd little sounds, and pressed herself closer. She dragged her hands over his shoulders and arms, over his back, and down, pulling him to her. He brought her as tightly against him as he could, his swollen groin pressing futilely against layers of skirt and petticoats. His hand slid down over her skirts, following the line of her hips. Her legs, her long legs. He'd let his hands slide over her riding dress that time and they itched now for more: garters to untie and silk stockings to slide down and soft skin to caress.

He grasped her skirt, and started to pull it up. Rain splashed onto the back of his leg, and through the uproar consuming him, reality intruded. He remembered where they were.

Somewhere in Holborn. Standing in a doorway in a maze of streets and lanes and courts and alleys. A public place.

It was raining. He remembered the rain in Putney, beating down in the courtyard. He remembered waiting. He'd been waiting for her . . . for how long?

He'd have to wait longer still. But not too much longer, he hoped.

He brought his hands back to her waist. He broke the kiss and pressed his forehead to hers. "Wait," he said. Gasped.

"Yes."

They remained that way, forehead to forehead, while rain cascaded from the building above and splashed up from the pavement.

"We can't," he said.

"I know. But I love you madly at this moment."

"I know. Hard not to. So lovable."

She drew back and looked up at him. "You knew what to do."

"In a doorway? With a beautiful girl? What half-wit doesn't?"

"In Bleeding Heart Yard."

"Obvious." What he wanted at this moment was not to think about what he'd seen and what he'd felt. His world was unraveling.

"No, it wasn't," she said. "Not to do it perfectly, as you did.

Oh, Juno, I could slap you from here to Land's End. All these years. I knew you had it in you. But you are the most aggravating man."

"Does that mean you don't love me anymore? That didn't last long."

"Ashmont, for heaven's sake."

"Did I get a point, in any case?"

"I am greatly tempted to strangle you."

She pulled away and straightened her bonnet. Not very well. He tried to push her hands away, so he could do the thing properly, but she jerked away from him.

"It doesn't matter," she said. "It's raining. No one will notice. I must get back. Mama's carriage will go to Mrs. Roake's to collect me, and I'll have to change before it arrives. And return to my family. That life. After this brief escape. What have we to do today? The blasted aquatic fête on the Thames. When will we be done with this curst pretending? It doesn't suit us, Ashmont, either one, and it only makes everything more complicated."

"We could stop pretending," he said. "We could marry."

"Don't. Not now. I need to . . . think. Collect myself." She turned away from him and left the doorway. She walked quickly, but he caught up in a few strides. His heart thudded with the riotous feelings, now compounded by anxiety, balked lust, and self-loathing.

"Cassandra."

"When you do what's right, it makes all the rest—all the waste of yourself—all the more galling," she said. "I wish I'd left you lying in Putney Heath and simply dealt with it myself and endured the consequences. Instead I go from joy to despair and back again. Again and again. It's maddening. I've become a woman I despise, maudlin and irrational."

She'd kissed him so passionately. He'd answered passionately.

She said she loved him madly. Was that what it was? Madness? Certainly it was maddening, stealing moments together, snatching at every straw she offered him. She'd upended his world, and now it lay strewn about him.

Like the Pooleys' belongings.

It was too much: the child, too small, practically weightless, who'd simply assumed she was safe with him. The two children whose parents had been cheated and taken advantage of while they only tried to live decent lives.

It was more than he could make sense of at this moment. He couldn't put a sentence together. Words and images tumbled through his mind. These last few weeks. All that had happened since the morning in Putney. But it stretched back further than that, and he hadn't known.

All these years she'd been there, somewhere in the dim background of his useless life. He'd never noticed her, and she'd loved him, and he'd disappointed her again and again.

An instant passed, or maybe months. It was all the same to him. Then they stood at the entrance to Furnival's Inn once more. The rain continued steadily, unaffected by the doings of two unhappy people. They were drenched, but this was a warm summer day, and they weren't delicate creatures.

He remembered her, soaked through in Putney, because she'd gone for a doctor. She'd gone out in a storm for Keeffe, who was so important to her. She loved her sister dearly, but Keeffe was her Blackwood and Ripley, the one she'd trust with her life, the one who'd helped give her life direction and a measure of freedom. He'd made her life tolerable, in other words.

She hadn't really needed Ashmont today. Any male would do, to keep the men from bothering her, all those men who believed it was perfectly acceptable to accost women who had the audacity to walk about London unaccompanied.

She could have managed today's business on her own. If he'd stayed in the background, as she wanted, then perhaps all of this would have been easier to endure. For her. For him.

He was doing the same as he'd done with Olympia: charming and disarming and wearing down her resistance without a thought to who she was and what she wanted. He'd understood nothing of Olympia's character, wishes, dreams. Who she was hadn't mattered. He'd wanted a wife and she fit the requirements and he'd simply set out to obliterate the barriers.

He was doing it again, and this time with a woman who'd come to mean everything to him.

Not five weeks had passed since Putney Heath. Not nearly enough time to undo the decade and more of hurt and disappointment he'd inflicted on her. Not nearly enough time to prove himself. He was a spoiled, shallow, thickheaded man who'd refused to grow up and take responsibility for himself.

Small wonder he was causing her so much confusion and anguish.

He took her to the hackney stand and handed her into the coach.

"You're right," he said. "This is maddening."

He gently closed the door and walked away.

He had work to do.

Chapter 14

*I*n spite of the rain and the consequent delays in making her way across London, Cassandra was ready and waiting when her mother's carriage came to Mrs. Roake's house to collect her.

She had no time to confide in Hyacinth. Cassandra hadn't even time to think about what had happened.

They had to dress for the water party, and that took longer than it should have done. The trouble was, they hadn't yet found a replacement for Gosney, and Colson, the maid Cassandra shared with her sister, had twice as much to do in the same amount of time.

As a result, nothing went as smoothly as it ought, and the sisters had no opportunity to talk privately until they returned, late that night. By then, Cassandra was too weary and out of sorts to do more than climb into her bed.

At least Hyacinth had enjoyed the entertainment. Though they didn't travel on the Lord Mayor's barge, they sailed near enough, on Lord Eddingham's yacht, to share in the water procession to Richmond.

There was music and a banquet, but the noise made Cassandra's head ache, and she had no appetite. She spent most of her time taking in the pretty views along the river of great houses and villas, many of whose gardens had been lit for the occasion.

Parties seemed to be in progress all along the route. The evening was beautiful, but she couldn't enjoy it. Her mind was filled with images from Bleeding Heart Yard: Ashmont going after Crummock . . . the way Mrs. Pooley had looked at Ashmont, as though he were a guardian angel . . . Ashmont panicking about the toddler, yet taking up the trusting child.

Trust.

Cassandra wanted to be home and quiet, making sense of it. She wanted to be doing something further for the Pooleys. She wanted to talk to Ashmont. Instead, she shared a luxurious boat with people to whom she had nothing to say.

The following day didn't improve her mood. Lady Bartham called, with Mr. Owsley in tow.

After shredding the reputations of various persons at the gatherings she'd attended in recent days, the countess said, "I understand the Duke of Ashmont did not join your party yesterday. I should have thought he would have taken you on one of his boats. But no, I forget, he has a great deal to do, preparing to leave London."

Cassandra took care not to react during morning calls. The only way to get through them without committing a social crime was to hold her tongue and keep her driving face firmly in place. With Lady Bartham this was crucial. Like so many discontented persons, she hated to see those about her happy.

"Naturally a duke has a great deal to do," Mama said. She did not try to catch Cassandra's eye. She was not a politician's wife for nothing.

"I'm told he intends to set out for Southampton for the regatta," Lady Bartham said. "My son Humphrey happened to mention it last night when he stopped by Lady Thurlow's ball. I gather he will accompany the duke."

Translation: Your daughters' suitors are abandoning them for boat races.

If the countess was hoping for signs of dismay, she was disappointed. Cassandra, Hyacinth, and her mother merely regarded her with mild interest.

"How pleasant for them," Mama said. "Regattas can be so exciting. We must wish them every success."

"I'm sure it's a harmless pastime," Mr. Owsley said. "Healthful exercise in the sea air. Competition in itself is by no means unwholesome. As I understand, the wagering at regattas is not nearly so egregious as it is at horse races. Sadly, the criminal element has infected those to a distressing extent."

Lady Bartham shot him a warning look. "I believe the duke and Humphrey mean to continue from Southampton to Goodwood," she said.

The Goodwood races, held at the Duke of Richmond's estate in Sussex, would begin at the end of the month and continue for four days.

Owsley took the hint. "Naturally one assumes the Duke of Richmond will ensure fair play and keep out the undesirable element."

Then why would he let in Ashmont? Cassandra wanted to say. She exchanged glances with Hyacinth, who must have read her mind, because her blue eyes sparkled with amusement.

She was enjoying herself, Cassandra realized. To Hyacinth, this sort of verbal sparring was a game. Small wonder she fit into the beau monde so well. She let the pettiness, jealousies, and ill will wash over her, as she'd said. It was a gift Cassandra didn't possess.

"How devoted Mr. Morris is, to keep his mama apprised in so much detail of his plans," Hyacinth said.

"Humphrey always tells me everything," Lady Bartham said. "Indeed, it can become difficult, keeping abreast of his many activities and interests. They change so often."

Translation: You are no more than a passing fancy.

"How fortunate for him, then, to have friends with the means to race yachts and travel anywhere at a moment's notice," Mama said.

Translation: Your Humphrey is merely a younger son, with no fortune or prospects to speak of.

"Mr. Morris exerts himself to be agreeable," Hyacinth said. "I have never heard him utter a disparaging remark about any of his friends. I cannot wonder at their wishing for his company."

There it was: Where Cassandra confronted, her sister disarmed.

But Cassandra wasn't her sister and never would be, and to her the visit seemed to go on for weeks. Certainly it dragged on for longer than the usual quarter hour of a morning call. But none of Lord deGriffith's womenfolk would allow themselves to appear in the least ruffled, and the Countess of Bartham was obliged to take her leave without having visibly raised any hackles, and not even sure who had won the verbal fencing match.

As she was preparing to depart, however, she drew Mama and Hyacinth aside to whisper something, and Mr. Owsley approached Cassandra.

His back blocking the others' view, he placed a small folded note on the table nearby.

"I hope you will do me the kindness to read this in private," he said in an undertone. "I give you my word of honor that it contains nothing any young gentlewoman would be ashamed to read."

He moved away too quickly for her to respond, had she wanted to. But she simply sat, mask in place, refusing to react to anything.

She regarded the note beside her. She didn't want to touch it. Then she reminded herself that he was nothing more than one annoying man among multitudes. She tucked the note into the pocket hanging inside her skirt.

"THEY KNOW SOMETHING I don't," Lady Bartham told Mr. Owsley as her carriage set out from St. James's Square. "They wouldn't take the news so calmly otherwise."

They'd displayed not so much as a flicker of surprise. Lady de-Griffith, in fact, had looked amused. As to Miss Pomfret, one might as well try to read a cobblestone.

"But Mr. Morris told you—"

"Yes, yes, but there must be more to this than meets the eye."

"Do you believe it's a . . . prank of some kind? But to what purpose?"

To make a game of me, Lady Bartham thought. *Again*.

She said, "When does the Duke of Ashmont need a purpose for

his pranks? Something is amiss. How I wish I could be sure he leaves tonight! Until he's gone from London, Miss Pomfret cannot be safe."

CASSANDRA WAITED UNTIL she was with her sister in the sitting room they shared to tell her what Owsley had done.

"How curious," Hyacinth said. "Do you think he's drafting a new bill, and wants your approval?" She laughed.

"That I doubt very much." Cassandra took out and unfolded the note.

Within a blank piece of paper was folded a page of the *Court Journal* dated the twenty-seventh of April of the present year. A poem addressed to "the Lady Charlotte ——" filled the front page. Somebody—Owsley, no doubt—had crossed out "Lady Charlotte ——" and written "Miss P——" next to it.

"A poem?" Hyacinth said.

Cassandra glanced over it, and paused at "I'd give thee Patience,—to endure the bleak and bitter day, / So dim to thee, so bright unto thy truant far away."

Then she went back to the beginning and read the thing through, her sister at her shoulder.

When they'd finished, they looked at each other.

"Good heavens," Hyacinth said. "Is this Mr. Owsley's idea of a love note?"

"More like a prophecy of doom." Cassandra read aloud:

"I'd give thee Patience,—to sustain the still more weary night
When round thee swell the harp-notes, and the lamps are
   blazing bright,
And to thy rival's whisper'd words he bends with raptur'd ear,
Nor marks amid her showering smiles thy one lone silent tear!"

"I remember this," Hyacinth said. "It appeared while the influenza was raging. Everybody wondered which Lady Charlotte was meant, and some argued that it was a pseudonym. As to the errant husband, we had no shortage of candidates."

"That I don't doubt," Cassandra said. "But Owsley can mean nobody but Ashmont."

Her sister read aloud:

> *"I'd give thee Patience,—to speak on, in gentleness and peace,*
> *Though answer'd but with silent scorn that longs to bid thee*
> *cease;*
> *Patience,—to check the rising flush,— the sob, —the choking*
> *sigh,—*
> *Patience,—to live unmurmuring on, though it were bliss to die.*
>
> *"I'd give thee Patience,—to receive within thy sacred door*
> *One whom thou know'st as dear to-day, as thou thyself of*
> *yore;*
> *One whom he bids thee smile to greet, and welcome as a guest,*
> *And emulate the graceful smiles in which her looks are drest!"*

On it went, stanza after stanza, in the same vein: the mistress flaunted, the children and home scorned, the wife's patient nursing met with complaint and ingratitude.

It was true, beyond a doubt, of the plight of all too many women, even those who didn't marry known libertines.

And there in plain black and white were expressed her deepest fears: of a broken heart, abandonment, neglected children.

Not her fears alone, but those of so many women, because men were granted all manner of license, while women were taught to suffer in silence.

She stared at the newspaper. "I wasn't taught that," she murmured. "Or if I was, the lesson didn't take."

"Cassandra?"

She looked up from the troubling stanzas at her sister. "This isn't me."

She walked to the window and gazed unseeingly out. She saw in her mind's eye instead: Ashmont with the child. She and Ashmont laughing in the shrubbery. Herself in the demi-mail phaeton—she, driving it, because she could. She was capable and she did it. Ashmont fighting with her—and she, fighting back, unafraid, only determined to win.

She shook her head. "Who did I think I was?"

"I don't know," Hyacinth said. "I don't know what you mean."

"This." Cassandra shook the piece of newspaper. "This isn't me. Mr. Owsley must be deranged, and I must be as well. Patience? I? Endure the— What is it?" She looked down. "'Bleak and bitter day'? I, beguiling 'the long dark dreary hours' of Ashmont's or any other man's absence?"

Hyacinth smiled. "You, allow a rival under your roof, let alone smile and welcome her? If you did, you'd read Mary Wollstonecraft to her, and bring her round to your way of thinking, and he'd find himself out in the cold."

"And this: 'to live unmurmuring on'—in quiet submission to caprice and cruelty, in other words. I, mute and submissive? I should suffocate him with a pillow while he slept, and say it was heart failure. I should never submit to be treated like this. No woman ought to endure it."

"Have they a choice?" Hyacinth said.

Men had all the power. They owned everything. Women didn't even own their children. They couldn't fight back. The law was on the side of men.

Cassandra looked down into the garden, where Papa had taken Ashmont that day. Lord deGriffith could be puzzling at times. He could be wrongheaded and infuriating. Yet she doubted very much that he would have agreed to the plan for a pretend courtship had he truly believed Cassandra was in any danger of being hurt. From his perspective, Ashmont was the one in danger.

In the right circumstances, she could knock him down, her father had said of her. He wasn't wrong.

She looked down at the newspaper page she held. "What a fool I have been, a fool and a coward. Thank you, Mr. Owsley, for pointing this out to me. You've done me a great favor. Now I know what to do."

"And that is—?"

"I shall write a letter."

It took Cassandra a while to organize her ideas, but at length she put down what she needed to. Not allowing herself time for second thoughts, she went to Keeffe's quarters to arrange for discreet delivery to Ashmont House.

There she found a note waiting for her.

Ashmont House
18th Instant

My dear Miss Pomfret,

You need relief from me. I see that finally. Sorry to be so slow, but my brain, you know. Lack of exercise. I need to do something—not sure what yet, but I trust it will come to me in time. Leaving Town under cover of darkness—a touch of drama never hurts. The world will say I've slunk away to my usual depravities. If you've had enough of me, this will give you the excuse you wanted, to break off our supposed engagement. Your sister's life is back where it ought to be, and yours will be soon enough, with Keeffe so close to recovering.

In other words, I've no excuse to go on plaguing you, or only the thinnest of excuses, and it's time to face the fact. "No promises," you said, and I ask none. Must find my own way, without adding to your difficulties. I haven't given you time to breathe since that morning in Putney. Past time I do it now.

A

Ashmont House
Evening of Friday 19 July

SOME YEARS EARLIER, after one of Their Dis-Graces' drunken card parties, several drawers in the dressing room had fallen or been pulled out and the contents spilled and trampled on. Sommers had wept for two days, then declared his nerves couldn't take it anymore.

Architectural changes being easier than replacing Sommers, Ashmont rebuilt this side of the first floor, creating a light closet between his bedroom and the dressing room. His clothes were now stored there, and nobody except Sommers was allowed to touch them. He had been touching them for some hours today, because he was packing for an extended journey.

A moment ago, he'd stepped out of the closet in order to deal with a footman hovering at the door. Ashmont was only partly dressed, and in no hurry to complete the process. He sat at the small table before the fireplace, where a cold collation had been laid out for him. He was about to pour a glass of wine when Sommers came back.

"A gentleman has called, Your Grace," the valet said.

"Told you I wasn't to be disturbed, unless it's an attorney."

He had told the servants he was not at home to anybody but Morris, and wasn't to be bothered with messages unless they came from his solicitor.

The Pooleys' problems were simple enough, on the face of it. Ashmont had carried out more intricate pranks. However, getting to the bottom of matters had turned out to be slow work.

Yesterday he'd gone back to learn the name of Mr. Pooley's previous employer. Then he had to find the employer, who turned out to be working for somebody else. Before long it became clear that lawyers and agents were needed, if the business was to be settled in a satisfactory way, preferably not in Chancery. As much as one wished to, one couldn't grab these fellows by the lapels and lift them off their feet and give them a good shaking. Actually, one could, and one had done so, but the technique didn't seem to clarify matters.

It had taken his mind off Cassandra Pomfret for a time, though. It had distracted him from the distress he'd heard in her voice.

. . . wish I'd left you lying in Putney Heath . . . I go from joy to despair and back again . . . I've become a woman I despise.

"Your Grace?"

"No exceptions. Except Morris. Wasn't Morris, was it? Or one of my friends?" Not that Blackwood was likely to turn up. Still at Camberley Place. And Ripley and his new bride were busy transforming a bachelor household into one for a family.

"No, Your Grace. But the gentleman said the matter was urgent."

"They always say that. Tell the porter to send him about his business. I should like to dine in peace."

Sommers went out. Ashmont returned to his meal and tried to find his appetite.

PERHAPS, AFTER ALL, this wasn't the best plan, Cassandra decided after the third rebuff from Ashmont's porter, but it was the only plan she had. Furthermore, when did Ashmont ever allow himself to be kept out when he wanted to get in?

She adjusted her top hat, smoothed her gloves, and set out to reconnoiter. He owned most of this part of London, and his house and grounds occupied no small portion. Eventually, though, she found a set of gates between the stable yard and the walled garden. Keeping to the shadows, she was able to approach the gate without attracting attention. Then, it was a matter of lock picking without getting caught or scaling it without breaking her neck. Odds decidedly not in her favor.

She was lurking in a gloomy corner, watching for the right moment, when a man emerged from one of the outbuildings, went to the gate, and unlocked it. The gate was heavy, and opened slowly. Holding her breath, she slipped in behind him and quickly concealed herself in the shrubbery. He glanced back, but this wall faced east, out of reach of the setting sun and concealed by mature plantings. He went on making a circuit—patrolling the grounds, apparently, though not as thoroughly as he ought to do. Had he been Keeffe, he'd have caught her before she was through the gate.

Ashmont's security measures needed improvement. Some irate husband or abandoned mistress could break in and cut his throat and slip away again without raising any hue and cry.

First things first. The duke's watchman was making his rounds, and she needed to concentrate on getting in. A few of the first-floor windows overlooking the garden were lit and open to the warm July night air. She drew closer.

The stables and houses surrounding the property made a buffer against the bustling streets bordering this part of Ashmont's estate. While they wouldn't completely mute the early evening din of Park Street and Park Lane, they helped create an oasis of calm. She was able to hear voices coming from one of the open windows. Though she couldn't make out the words, she recognized Ashmont's, and her heart went into a wild flutter.

Still here, then.

Very well. No turning back now.

THE OFFICES WERE in the west wing of the house. Judging by the sounds Cassandra caught, the servants were taking their dinner. While this didn't eliminate the risk of being detected as she ran up the back stairs, it reduced the chances. In any case, she crept inside unhindered. Once inside, the odds were in her favor. If they tried to stop her, she'd raise strong objections, and Ashmont would hear her.

That was the plan, at any rate.

She made her way cautiously to the first-floor rooms where she'd last heard his voice, and stepped into the first one. A bedchamber. His, judging by the size and furnishings. Empty. The voices she'd heard became clearer, from the next room, it sounded like. A dispute about coats, with the other voice sounding tearful. That must be Sommers, the valet.

"It doesn't matter, where I'm going," Ashmont said. "Go, take your dinner. We won't leave for hours yet, and I want to be let alone in the meantime."

"But Your Grace's red under-waistcoat—"

"Can't think what I'd need it for. Go to dinner. Or read a book. Whatever you like, only go away. I'm sick to death of waistcoats. You'll drive me to travel in my dressing gown."

The valet mumbled something. Then footsteps came toward Cassandra, and she pressed herself against the wall behind the door. But the footsteps changed direction, and she heard another nearby door close.

Time now.

ASHMONT THREW OFF his dressing gown and pulled off the waistcoat Sommers had objected to.

"Your Grace cannot wear that," Ashmont mimicked his valet in a low voice. "Because if I do," he answered in his own, "don't you know, the world will come to an end. Rain of frogs. Ghouls rising in the churchyard."

He heard a gasp, and spun toward the sound. A man stood in the doorway of the light closet. Though the room was far from brightly lit, it was clear he wasn't Sommers or any other servant.

Ashmont didn't pause to think or ask questions. He lunged—and a walking stick blocked him, and an unforgettable voice said, "If you try to kill me, I'll make you sorry."

He backed away and the voice's owner stepped out of the closet's doorway and into his dressing room.

He watched, heart thumping, while she—for it was *she*, and no other—straightened her hat, smoothed her neckcloth, and brushed the sleeve of her coat. "If you'd spared a minute of your precious time to see me, I should not have been obliged to break into your house."

Ashmont only stood gaping at her and waiting for his heart to slow down.

His gaze moved from the top hat down over the brown coat, colorful neckcloth and waistcoat, and striped silk Cossack trousers. Cut full at the thigh and tapering to the ankles, they accommodated her shape, as did the layers of shirt, waistcoat, and coat, with its nipped-in waist. In most circumstances, one would assume she was a young man. He'd assumed it, and now he wondered how he could have done so, even in the shadowy light.

"I could hardly come as myself," she said.

He found his voice. "You shouldn't have come."

"You left me no choice. As it was, the odds were good you'd run away before I could get to you. Ashmont, if you must go to Southampton, you must, but—"

"Southampton? I'm not going to Southampton."

"Oh, direct to Goodwood, then."

"What in blazes are you talking about?"

She relayed the tale she'd had from Morris's mother earlier in the day.

"Morris made that up," he said. "I told him I didn't want anybody to know where I'd be—Camberley Place, actually, but it makes no matter. Didn't you understand my note? Admittedly, I'm not the most coherent—at least according to Blackwood—but—"

"You're running away," she said. "You've given up on me."

"That isn't what—"

"Not that I blame you. But your timing is execrable. I had only this day realized— No, I am not going to explain my thinking. You'll fall asleep before I'm halfway done."

"Not likely to fall asleep with you standing there in trousers. I can practically see your legs."

"Don't be silly. The trousers are lined with cotton. Not at all transparent."

"I can see more of your legs than when you wear a dress and two hundred petticoats underneath."

"Never mind what I'm wearing. I came—"

"Never mind? Never mind? You're wearing silk *trousers*—and I can see—I can see practically *everything*."

Her gaze slid over him, up and down, then up, to linger on his neckcloth. Which was when he realized he was in his shirt—his underwear. A more delicate fellow would have blushed. If he was blushing, it started well below his face, and his trousers covered the excitement. Somewhat.

"Ashmont, you're becoming hysterical. It isn't helpful, when I am working so hard to be calm."

"I'm not hysterical. I'm a man, and you are wearing—"

"I wrote you a letter," she said, chin jutting. "I should have sent it in the usual way, but, clearly, there wasn't time for circumventing propriety. And so I came to deliver it in person, in case it wasn't perfectly clear and you had any doubts of the meaning, but above all, to make sure you got it."

From inside the waistcoat she withdrew a letter. "I wrote it before I saw yours, but that changes nothing." She lifted her chin. "I will not take back a single word."

She gave it to him.

He took it and tried to take in what was happening.

She was here. In his house. This was she, only a few feet away.

He stared at the letter. His heart still thumped furiously.

This letter had lain against her breast, only a thin layer of linen between it and skin, and it was still warm, and faintly imbued with her scent.

In fact, the air about him seemed filled with the scent and sight of her. In trousers. Silk trousers that brushed against the long, *naked* legs underneath.

Not now, he told himself.

He was so tired of *not now*. And the letter. That couldn't be good news. He wanted to tear it to pieces.

Coward.

She'd risked life, limb, and reputation to deliver it personally.

He moved nearer to one of the gaslights and unfolded the letter.

deGriffith House
19th Instant

Dear Ashmont,

This day has brought a blow to my amour propre, with
specific reference to my intellect. I might say, with the hero-
ine of Miss Austen's great book, Pride and Prejudice, "Till
this moment I never knew myself." Now that I do, we must
thank Mr. Owsley, who was so charitable as to foist upon
me a poem.

Ashmont looked up, chilled. "Owsley."

"One must give credit where it is due," she said. "Credit or in-
famy. That judgment I leave to you."

She wore the majestically calm expression. Though Ashmont had
learnt to read subtle changes in her regal face, these were impossible to discern in the shadows where she stood.

He returned to the letter.

The poem caused me to reflect upon what has occurred
since you staggered into my life some weeks ago. I wrote
a list of these occurrences, to make of tumultuous feelings
a semblance of order. The items came to me at last in the
mode of Shakespeare, no doubt because I found it easier
to regard events of my recent life as though observed on a
stage. Let us title the play "What Manner of Man Is This?"
Or, better, perhaps, "What Manner of Woman Am I?"

1. Thou hast broken my groom.
2. Thou hast broken my carriage.
3. Thou hast driven my maid to flee.
4. Thou hast played unfairly on my and Keeffe's feelings
   with thy gift of a precious painting.

5. *Thou hast made an almighty stench in the Hanover Square Rooms by bringing within its sacred precincts a juvenile delinquent known as Jonesy, among other aliases, thereby causing me inappropriate mirth.*

6. *Thou hast taken will-melting advantage of my joy in the unprejudiced and helpful manner of thy fighting.*

7. *Thou hast included in thy plots and schemes my beloved sister, e'en unto bringing her a suitor of whom she had no need but who amuseth her.*

8. *Thou hast set Society agog with all thy mischievous doings, and disarmed me with laughter.*

9. *Thou hast kissed me in a wanton manner and taken liberties too numerous to mention. On several occasions.*

10. *Thou hast made me love thee, against logic and good sense.*

These are ten sensible reasons to hate you. And yet . . . and yet . . . there is Number Ten, and all the trouble in a nutshell. I began loving you a long time ago for no sensible reason, and cannot seem to stop, or to care whether it is sensible or not.

Yours sincerely,
Cassandra Pomfret

CASSANDRA STOOD AT the window, looking down into the garden while he read her letter.

He cleared his throat.

She looked toward him, her heart racing. "Questions? No? Then I had better be going." She made a slight adjustment of her hat and briskly smoothed her gloves. "Gates to climb. Hackneys to summon. I am pretending to be in bed with a sick headache, and

Hyacinth is nursing me, forbidding anybody to disturb me. Fortunately, my parents are attending a reception. Mainly politicians and plotting, which means it will go on for some time." She started to turn away.

"Wait," he said.

She paused.

"What does this mean, exactly?" he said.

"What does it mean? What does it mean?" She gazed at him in disbelief, then realized it wasn't a good idea to stare at him for too long, because he had barely any clothes on, and she might be blushing, which was annoying.

She wasn't missish. It wasn't as though she'd never seen any of her brothers in a state of undress. But he wasn't her brother and this was altogether different. Through the fine linen of his shirt, she caught glimmers of gold . . . hair . . . on his chest and lower down.

"Yes, what does it mean?" he said.

She stomped toward him. She took the letter from his hand and pointed to the lines above her signature. "There." She stabbed the paper with her finger. "How much plainer must I make it?"

"Love."

"Yes. I believe I mentioned that some time ago."

"But you hate me, too."

"Not as much as I ought to do. For heaven's sake, Lucius. Must I draw pictures? How thick can a man be? No, never mind. I know the answer to that."

"I only meant, shall I go away or would you rather I didn't? Because, you see, you can be a trifle confusing sometimes. For a simple man. And I made up my mind I wouldn't give you any more cause to be unhappy. Or to despise yourself. I was going away to give you time without me here, looming over you constantly and trying to sweep you off your feet. And to give me time as well, to think . . . about my life. And also in hopes that absence would make the heart grow fonder. Not my heart, because if mine were any fonder it would explode or melt or disintegrate in some fashion."

She melted then, brain, heart, knees, everything. "Oh, Lucius."

"Ah. Not 'duke.' Not 'Ashmont.' Perhaps, then, I needn't leave, after all."

She stood near enough to feel his body's warmth. She couldn't help leaning into it. His neckcloth tickled her cheek. She turned to get closer to the warmth and strength of him.

His arm slid round her waist. "Perhaps not."

"This is very trying," he said. "I can feel parts of you I oughtn't to feel. No corset."

"I worried it would call too much attention to my bosom, and the clothes wouldn't fit properly."

"Yes, probably best not to call attention to your bosom." He slid his hand lower. "No petticoats." His hand moved lower still. "And there . . . is the most beautiful bottom in all the world."

She was a redhead, yes, but not given to blushing. Now she seemed to be made of glowing coals.

"You would know," she said. "Having made extensive surveys."

"This isn't— This is too much for a man of no willpower." His hand slid over her hip, and he groaned. "No drawers. Oh, Cassandra. We must get you home."

"Yes. No. Forgot about drawers. It wasn't easy and I was in a hurry." She really ought to push his hand off her hip. She didn't want to. His big hand slid over her bottom and down and . . . *there*, between her thighs. Sensations rocketed through her, as though her body were filled with shooting stars.

"I have to stop," he said. Before she could catch her breath, let alone feel what she was feeling, he took his hand away and planted it firmly on her back, pressing her closer.

She tipped her head back. "You may kiss me. We can do that. We've done it before."

"When you had clothes on."

"I have clothes on."

"Not enough. And even when you did have clothes on, layer upon accurst layer, matters spun out of control very quickly."

She gazed into his eyes. In this light they were the color of the

Adriatic. She wanted to sail away on that sea. She wanted to lose herself in him.

He knew it. And he wasn't going to let her.

"I believed once that you would grow up into a hero, fine and noble and true," she said.

"I know. Sorry."

"I wasn't wrong," she said. "You only took longer than expected. You're being heroic now. I ought to be as well."

"Not very heroic. I don't want you to leave."

"I don't want to leave."

A long silence, while her senses swam with him: the scent of his skin and a faint trace of cologne or soap mingling with the starch of his neckcloth . . . the fine linen shirt that was no more than a veil over his shoulders and arms and chest. She brought her hand up to trace the muscles of his arm, and he sucked in his breath.

"Dammit, Cassandra." He tipped two fingers against the hat brim and tipped it off, onto the carpet.

"That's no way to treat a good beaver hat," she said.

"I'll buy you another. After we're married. You can wear it sometimes. It'll be fun."

"After we're married? You haven't asked yet."

"Only a hundred times."

"That wasn't asking. That was—"

He kissed her.

Chapter 15

*T*he floor dissolved under Cassandra's feet, and she seemed to be in a whirlpool, spinning and sinking in sparkling waters. She grasped his shoulders, catching hold of him as she'd been wanting to do for most of her life, it seemed. He'd always been out of her reach. This was because he was unreachable, beyond help or hope—or so she'd eventually persuaded herself.

But he wasn't, not in the way she'd supposed. She had hopes for him now, and he'd given her reason to trust him, but she trusted herself, and that was most important.

Trusting, she took the moment as it came.

She was in his arms, where it seemed she'd always been meant to be, and once in his arms, she didn't know how to hold back. She didn't try. She answered his kiss in the way she'd learnt from him, a soft, insistent, intensifying pressure of the lips.

Later she'd wonder how it could be: How could mouth slanted over mouth create starbursts of sensation, happiness, longing, and a thousand more feelings, a galaxy? But now she simply felt and acted, giving in to her senses.

She gave in to the taste of him, cool and sweet as a stream in springtime, and heating to become warm and fiery, like brandy. She drank him in, the kiss deepening while the world spun and glittered.

Magic.

That was what it was. That was what she'd always seen in him. As beautiful, unreasonable, and untamable as any mythical deity, he simply dazzled her.

He broke the kiss and cupped her face in his hands. "Marry me."

"Are you incapable of *asking*?"

He stroked her jaw with his thumbs, and she felt herself dissolving. She gripped his shoulders to keep on her feet. "You don't play fair. Where are my knees? I had them a moment ago."

He gave a short laugh, and slid his fingers to the back of her head, slipping them into her hair. "What is this?"

She'd pulled her hair toward the front of her head and piled it there, in a style she'd seen on fashionable Frenchmen and the occasional English dandy. The hat helped subdue its volume. It would pass as a man's coiffure if one didn't inspect it too closely.

"In case I had to take off my hat. I couldn't wear a woman's coiffure. Don't spoil it. So many pins. And a cartload of pomatum to keep it from springing loose."

"Why is this so exciting?" he said. "You, in trousers and neckcloth?"

"Because you're perverse?"

He pressed his temple to hers, one hand cupping the back of her neck. "Because you're you," he said softly. "My beautiful, wild girl, will you marry me?"

Because you're you.

Her heart seemed to shatter then, into diamond shards. "Yes."

"Yes," he said. "Yes." He kissed her ear and trailed kisses along her jaw. He loosened the neckcloth, and she should have protested. Tying the blasted thing was an exercise in physics and higher mathematics. But there was his mouth on her skin, grazing her throat, and the sweetest warmth was spilling from somewhere within, from her fast-beating heart. The heat spread downward, to settle in the pit of her belly and make her ache.

He unbuttoned the coat and waistcoat and slid his hands over her breasts. She wore no chemise. The shirt was her chemise, and it might as well have been made of mist. She shivered, her skin prickling under his touch, her breasts tightening. She forgot how to breathe.

She dragged her hands over his back and down to his taut waist and down farther. He made a choked sound, then, "We really must stop," he said.

"I know. Oh, but Lucius." She could not get enough of touching him, of wondering at him. Warm muscle tensed under her hands. His skin's scent, mingling with starch and the faintest hints of some spicy male fragrance, filled her head and made her dizzy and wanting . . . more. She pressed closer.

He tipped her head back and kissed her full on the lips once more, and the kiss dragged her deep and deeper still, until she was in a place where there was no one but him. She rubbed herself against him, as though she could burrow into him.

He made a sound, a low growl, and picked her up and carried her to the sofa. He pulled off her coat and waistcoat. He drew off the mangled neckcloth and threw everything carelessly onto the carpet. Her breath came faster, and heat danced over her skin, while something else, a feeling whose name she didn't know, tugged at her inwardly and made her ache, everywhere, it seemed, but not in pain. This was a different kind of ache, a powerful current that pulled her, and one she didn't want to fight.

He kissed her, and she sank back against the sofa cushions, drinking him in, as though the kiss could soothe whatever it was—a pulsing need for more. And more. Awareness shrank to this: the man surrounding her, holding her, kissing her, and the current pulling her toward something further, something felt but distant, indescribable.

She grasped his shoulders and moved her hand up over his braces to the neckcloth, and pulled it apart, as heedlessly as he'd destroyed hers. She slid her hand along the column of his throat and down over the opening of the shirt, caressing skin lightly dusted with silky, pale gold hair.

She moved her hands downward along his shirt, over his big chest, hard and smooth and warm. Her finger grazed his nipples, and he gasped, but he didn't push her away, and she let her hands stray farther down, over rippling muscles and hard belly and lower still . . .

His hand closed over hers. "I don't think—no—yes." Then he

drew her hand down over his groin. Under her palm, beneath the flap of his trousers, his breeding organ swelled and throbbed.

She caught her breath. She knew what this was. She was neither ignorant nor oblivious. She'd seen dogs, horses, and other creatures in the act of coupling. She'd seen salacious prints. She marveled, all the same.

"This is the first time you've done that," he said thickly. "I pray it's not the last. But let's . . . savor the moment." He gave a short, choked laugh.

"Oh, Lucius."

"We truly need to get married," he said. "Soon."

"Yes."

He took her hand away and kissed her again, a long, deep, dark kiss that sent her swirling into the whirlpool again.

"We must save something for the wedding night," he said when at last they remembered to breathe. "But in the meantime, I should like to lead you into temptation. Because I'm hopelessly debauched, as you know."

"Yes." She was aching all over, squirming. She wanted to be closer. Needed to be closer. She tried to pull him down over her, but he braced himself on his elbows.

"I should like to be debauched," she whispered. "Truly, I should."

"I cannot tell you how much I look forward to that."

"Now?"

He drew in a deep breath and let it out again. "Let's take this in steps, yes? Let's begin as all good stories begin, with the prologue. Let's say you know nothing."

"True enough." She comprehended the principles. She understood, in theory. She had no experience. She'd never even kissed another man in that way. She'd never wanted to.

"Being untutored," he said, "you lie there, in all your seductive innocence, while I have my wicked way with you."

Her pulse escalated and her breath came fast. "Yes."

"I wish you would not keep putting me off in this way, my girl. You'll force me to use my wiles upon you."

"Yes," she gasped. "For heaven's sake, Lucius. Do something before I do something—and you know it'll be awkward at best. I have no expertise in these matters."

Another choked laugh. "Did I not tell you to lie there?"

"I do not care for your dictatorial manner— Oh, sweet mother of Hercules." He was kissing her breast and his tongue flicked over her nipple, under its useless shield of linen. Then he was suckling her, and she felt the tug in the pit of her stomach then all the way to her curling toes.

She dragged her fingers through his hair, destroying whatever artfully careless arrangement his valet had made. He caressed with his hands and his mouth, roaming freely over her torso, claiming it for himself, as though there could ever be anybody else. He slid down, and then his hands were moving over her belly and down over her legs. He paused, and sighed. And ran his hands down her legs.

"Your legs," he said softly. "Beautiful, long, strong legs."

He unfastened the buttons of her trousers, and drew them down, and swore softly at her shoes. But he had them off quickly enough. Then the trousers were off, dropped on the floor with other garments. He untied her garters, and slipped the stockings from her feet.

She lay there, exposed to him from the waist down and barely covered from the waist up. She was shameless, clearly, because she felt no shame at all. She loved him and wanted him. And she trusted him.

His hands, his big, clever hands glided over her belly and down her legs, and he sighed.

He slid off the sofa and began to kiss his way up her right leg, starting with the toes and moving up over her ankles, and up, to linger at her knees. Then up again, kissing the outside of her thigh then the inside, and then his hand was on her most private place, stroking, and she was shaking with need. The heat she'd felt before was nothing to this, tiny fires dancing over her skin and inside her, pulling her toward that distant place.

Then he put his mouth there and her mind went dark. There was only the sparkling whirlpool and sensations, pulling at her harder and harder, until she seemed to fly up and into the heavens, into the stars. She let out a cry. Then he was kissing her again, coming up over her belly and breasts and at last to her mouth. She grasped his head, and her eyes filled with tears.

A long, long kiss, while she floated back to earth.

Then, "Oh," she said, her voice broken and hoarse. "What have you done?"

A long moment passed while she listened to his breathing, fast and hard, then gradually slowing, and while she slid her hand over his chest and felt his heart thud against her palm. After this time, while the world began to return, he said, "Now don't you wish you'd married me the first time I told you to?"

HE OUGHTN'T TO have done it, but Ashmont was no good at being noble and self-sacrificing. He was a man hopelessly, helplessly, over head and ears in love, and the world ought to make allowances. Not that he cared whether it did or didn't.

She loved him—he had it in writing—and he needed no other approval.

She'd said yes, and nothing else mattered.

Now he had no choice. He had to be noble and self-sacrificing, like it or not, and get her home . . . undetected. She'd taken an appalling risk. Even marriage wouldn't smooth over this sort of outrage against propriety: coming to his house, of all men, and dressed in trousers!

The satirists would have a Roman holiday. They'd been having a fine time with him for years—and with her, on occasion. But all the jibes that had gone before would be nothing to this. Her family would be utterly humiliated. Her father would become a joke to his colleagues. Her sister . . . that didn't bear thinking of.

And Ashmont couldn't bribe all of London to make it go away.

He let his gaze travel over her—the smooth skin and perfectly shaped breasts and the sweet curve of her belly under the man's shirt. The linen, pushed up, left the coppery triangle between her legs exposed.

Her legs. As perfect as everything else about her, and strong, as she was. She rode and drove and fought, and she knew how to scale a wall. A hoyden, people must have called her when she was a young girl. They probably still did. But that was an obnoxious epithet meant to make women feel ashamed for wanting exercise and freedom. So unfair.

He wouldn't have realized this several weeks ago. But a book had opened his eyes. Now, a part of him ached for her and for what she must have endured, trying to grow up while holding on to her true self, in a world that didn't approve of her. Small wonder Keeffe was so important to her. He understood her and encouraged her. No doubt he'd helped toughen her as well.

"I regret nothing," she said, "and most certainly not rejecting that ridiculous offer. You were not remotely ready to marry."

He oughtn't to tempt the devil in him again, but he laid his hand—lightly, lightly—over the coppery curls, which he ought to have left untouched. But he had no regrets, either. She was as open and direct in lovemaking as in all else, and what man could ask for more than that? He knew beyond any question that he'd given her pleasure, and he felt smug about it. His own physical release could wait. "And this?" he said.

"Certainly not. Are you mad? How could I regret such a thing? I only regret not having experienced it sooner and often."

"With me."

She shrugged and smiled the smallest smile, the slightest upturn of her lips.

"With me," he repeated.

She lifted an eyebrow.

"Because," he said, "other fellows won't do it, you know. They're not depraved enough. So it's me or nothing."

She laughed and sat up and threw her arms about his shoulders. "Thou amuseth me, sir."

"Yes, well, I'm an amusing fellow, everybody says. But we've had our fun for tonight and greatly as I regret it, we must get you dressed and home."

Her grey eyes widened. "Home."

She looked wildly about her, and at last her gaze lit on the clock on the chimneypiece. She let out a long, unsteady breath. "Not so late, then. It felt— It was like a long, beautiful dream. And the windows are fully dark. But now I must wake up."

She started to get up from the sofa, but he signaled her to stay where she was. He drew down the shirt to cover her, more or less. He collected her garments and brought them to the sofa and played valet, restoring trousers and stockings, waistcoat and coat.

"This is exciting," he said, as he slid her foot into a shoe. "I've never dressed a man before. Don't even dress myself, generally."

"I'm not a man. I thought you'd noticed that about me."

"That's why it's exciting," he said. "If you were a man, and if I were your valet—oh, no. Doesn't do to think of that. Sommers's life is not an easy one. Still, we'd better tackle the neckcloth. Now you may stand."

She rose from the sofa, and his insides did odd things, as though a team of jugglers tossed them about, while his unsatisfied cock bounded up, ever hopeful.

She was a young man again, but she wasn't remotely a man. She was unmistakably Cassandra Pomfret, who laid all her cards on the table, and who'd taken a shocking risk to make sure he knew she loved him—and why.

The thought made him want to cry and to laugh at the same time. And to throw her down on the sofa and have an early wedding night. He made do with a smile.

"A neckcloth is no joking matter," she said. "I had only the one, and you've no idea the palpitations I underwent, terrified I'd spoil it beyond help. As to help, I had no diagrams, only Hyacinth to guide me, and the two of us in terra incognita, with only the dimmest recollection of our brothers' convolutions to guide us."

"I'd trust Sommers with my life, but the sight of this neckcloth would cut him to the quick." Holding the midpoint of the cloth at the front of her throat, Ashmont brought one end round the back of her neck to the front, then brought the other end round in the opposite direction. "Not enough starch, to begin with. But it would have been limp by now in any event, which leaves only one choice: the waterfall or coachman's knot." It was the simplest of cravat-tying methods.

"From what you've said about your valet and what I overheard this evening, he seems to be highly strung. Was he always that way or is it you?"

"From what I've seen, these fellows come either highly strung or unexcitable." He brought the neckcloth round again. "He's the former, to be sure. But when it comes to what I may and may not wear, he's a terror. Won't let me leave the house if I'm not up to snuff. Chin up."

She lifted her chin. "Yet he let you out in that drab—for you—suit of clothes yesterday."

"I explained where I was going and said it was delicate, and he did his best to accommodate."

Ashmont set about creating the allegedly simple knot. He bungled it, because this wasn't another fellow he was helping, and because he'd already had his hands on the magnificent female form underneath the masculine attire, and his hands wanted to go back there. Not to mention what his manly urges were urging down below.

Her cool voice penetrated the mental muddle. "He sounds like a good man."

"A very good man. I usually do as he tells me, but tonight I was blue-deviled. There, up on the wall. Cruikshank. How well he captures these states."

On the wall hung a series of works by the well-known illustrator: *The Blue Devils, The Headache, Indigestion,* and *Jealousy*.

They always seemed like perfect company to him when the moods struck—although jealousy had been an unknown state until he'd set his sights on her.

In *The Blue Devils*, a disconsolate fellow in his dressing gown sat with his feet on the fender while a host of tiny beings tormented him. One tempted him with a noose. Another offered a razor. Along the floor a funeral procession marched. Behind him on a shelf, a book of domestic medicine lay beneath a copy of *The Miseries of Human Life*. Upon this book stood an artist painting a scene of conflagration. On one side of the fire painting was a shipwreck. The work was hilariously accurate.

Her gaze traveled beyond the Cruikshank set. "I see you have an interesting collection of erotic prints. Before I took the wrapper from the painting of Keeffe and Amphion, I suspected it was in that category."

"The thought crossed my mind." While they talked, he'd finally arranged the allegedly simple waterfall correctly, more or less.

"That'll do," he said. "With any luck, nobody will get a close look at you. Now, all we have to do is get you home with nobody the wiser."

She stepped back and walked to the horse dressing glass and studied herself. "I'd assumed I could simply deliver the message as a young gentleman, then return via hackney, as I came. But the business became more complicated than anticipated, and then I planned only how to get into your house, not how to get out again." She brushed a piece of fluff from her coat sleeve.

They'd be wed. Soon. Otherwise they were sure to get into serious trouble. She was as daring and single-minded as he was, although she had, for the most part, employed these qualities in more productive ways than he had done.

"We need a confederate," he said. "Blackwood is still at Camberley Place. Ripley is busy rearranging his life. We'll have to bring Sommers into our confidence. He may be highly strung, but he's loyal and discreet."

Meanwhile

MR. OWSLEY HAD taken Lady Bartham's hint. He, too, couldn't rest easy until he was sure the Duke of Ashmont was gone from London.

The man couldn't be trusted. His and the rest of Their Disgraces' pranks were notorious: a dinner at which men with speech impediments were required to recite poetry, another for which the dukes had replaced the mirrors with distorting ones.

They'd arranged for cartloads of rotting fish to be delivered to one victim. Other targets had found hordes of people at their doors, answering ads the dukes had placed: for brides, fiddle players, trained monkeys, dancing dogs, musical donkeys, and assorted other trained pets. They'd used a sling to hoist a goat into Almack's during a Wednesday night assembly. They'd brought a bull into a china shop, to test the old adage, they claimed.

That was only a fraction of their so-called larks.

From what Owsley had heard, the most puerile of these alleged jokes were Ashmont's work. As Lady Bartham had said, this supposed departure might easily be part of another prank.

This was what brought Mr. Owsley to the environs of Ashmont House. He was determined to find out what the accurst duke was about.

He was not in the least ashamed of spying on the Duke of Ashmont. On the contrary, Mr. Owsley deemed it his duty to do so, for Miss Pomfret's sake.

He loitered as close to the house as he could, dawdling in Park Street, wandering into the mews opposite the gardens of Ashmont House, and lingering in the shadows near the stable yard. From time to time, when well concealed by darkness, he took out his spyglass for a closer look at the house. Some of the windows were lit, and once or twice he saw a figure pass in those overlooking the garden.

Upon returning to the stable yard area, he had confirmation of a sort. Some stablemen were talking about Surrey and readying the traveling chariot. Very well. While the duke wasn't headed for Southampton and Goodwood thereafter, he was going away. Good news and good riddance.

Mr. Owsley was preparing to give up his vigil, and all would have been well if he had done so. However, he turned back to glance up once more at the lit windows of Ashmont House. There he saw two figures.

Unable to believe his naked eyes, he lifted the spyglass to them and watched, riveted, until the pair left the window.

THE FIRST PROBLEM was sneaking out of Ashmont House. It wouldn't do for any of the servants to get a good look at the strange young gentleman the porter had turned away, or to wonder how that gentleman had entered Ashmont House.

When the lady returned here as his duchess, she must be regarded with unequivocal respect. Ashmont wouldn't have servants speculating or tittering behind her back. And when some were let go—this wasn't an *if*, being inevitable when a man married—they mustn't have any ammunition for spreading tales about her.

That alone was no small order.

For similar reasons, he and Cassandra couldn't use one of his vehicles. For one thing, stablemen liked gossip as much as anybody else and, for another, Ashmont's carriages were too distinctive.

But he enlisted Sommers, and after some turbulence of spirit and agitation of delicate nerves, the valet helped them make their escape.

He promised to create a diversion, and he must have made a spectacular one, because Ashmont and Cassandra passed easily down the main staircase and out of the saloon on the ground floor. Thence they made their way to Grosvenor Street, and found a hackney not long thereafter.

When they'd settled into the coach, and caught their breath, Ashmont said, "Now all we have to do is get you home unobserved."

"I've a way in via Duke Street," she said. "The trouble is the servants. They're everywhere and very difficult to elude. Three times I was nearly caught as I tried to leave."

He sat on the seat opposite, mainly to keep his hands off her. He and she had a tendency to forget where they were, and he truly didn't want to make any scandals for her family. Still, he couldn't help but lean toward her and take her hand. "You took a great risk."

Greater than they'd faced in his house, assuredly. His wasn't a family home. He hadn't servants prowling the corridors constantly.

Ashmont House, in fact, was far too large for one man, no matter how often and how extravagantly he entertained. This was why its owner more or less lived in the corner comprising his bedroom and dressing room. Bachelor quarters.

"Ah, well, I like to live dangerously," she said.

He squeezed her hand. "I do love you."

"How can you help it? I'm so lovable." She laughed.

"I'm trying very hard not to kiss you."

"Yes, it would be better not to think about that. I had no idea that kissing could damage the brain so extensively."

"Ours is a special case," he said. "I give it all I have in me. Can't seem to do otherwise."

She let out a shaky breath, slid her hand from his, and sat back in the seat.

"Let's put our brain boxes to work planning how to get me into my parents' house without scandalizing the servants," she said.

He sat back, too, and looked out of the none-too-clean window. This time of evening was busy, with carriages traveling to parties or carrying late arrivals to the theater.

The theater. Performances.

The plan came to him as vividly as any scene on the stage. He told her.

"That will do," she said. They agreed on various signals.

"Then tomorrow, I call on your father," he said.

"Yes." A pause. "No."

"No? I thought—"

"Everybody believes we haven't seen each other since Wednesday. You were supposed to be leaving London. When, exactly, did I change my mind about a pretend courtship? My father will ask questions. We have to be prepared."

She was right—and it was a good thing one of them could still think. He only wanted to marry her as quickly as possible.

"I'm very glad one of us has a large brain," he said.

"Yours is perfectly functional," she said. "The trouble is lack of exercise."

"Do be quiet," he said. "I'm exercising."

He told himself they had time to form a plan. Perhaps a mile or so lay between their respective houses. At this hour the hackney, like other vehicles, would be slowed to a walking pace for the most part.

At last, as the coach was turning into Piccadilly, she said, "I have an idea."

"This one had better not involve wearing men's clothes—and by the way, how did you come by them?"

"My brother Anselm, for a family theatrical. I think the Cossack trousers were a purchase he regretted. He didn't mind their being tailored for me and he definitely didn't want them back."

"Sommers would not let me own a pair," Ashmont said.

"I think they look better on women, actually."

"So do I. Please keep them. For after we're married. For private . . . erm . . . theatricals."

"Private, indeed. If anybody recognized me in these—not in an amateur theatrical but traveling the streets of London—"

"Let's not think about that," he said. "We simply won't let it happen. Tell me your idea."

Meanwhile

IT WOULD NOT be too much to say that Mr. Titus Owsley was shocked out of his wits. Of all the accusations one might hurl at the Duke of Ashmont, the last Owsley would have considered was what he'd witnessed. After all, the duke flaunted his mistresses—in the very same box, for instance, that had a few weeks earlier held Miss Pomfret and two ladies of her family. The duke was a known habitué of Carlotta O'Neill's den of iniquity and others nearly as famous.

Though the two figures left the window, Owsley remained gazing in disbelief at the place where they'd been. While he'd believe the Duke of Ashmont capable of anything, this was beyond comprehension. Was it a joke? A game? Did he know Owsley was watching? It would be like Ashmont to play such a prank. More likely than . . . no, it was impossible.

If the duke belonged to that category of . . . men, one would have heard whispers. One would have caught a hint, a sly reference here and there. Beyond question, Owsley had kept all his senses alert for some time now, seeking hints. When a man lived as openly and shamelessly as Ashmont did, it was nigh impossible to discover dark secrets.

"It's a trick," Owsley muttered to himself. "Or a game of some sort being played in that house. How do I know who else is there?"

And so he waited and racked his brains and stewed over the problem. There had to be a connection between what he'd observed and the volumes of the duke's far-from-secret history.

By this time darkness had fallen, and the streets were busy. Periodically he took out his watch, pretending to be waiting for somebody, though for all he comprehended of the watch's face, it might as well have been a seashell.

He was staring at the timepiece for what felt like the hundredth time, and wondering whether he was becoming too conspicuous, when he saw two masculine figures emerge from the duke's garden and hurry toward Grosvenor Street. As the pair passed under a gaslight, he recognized the Duke of Ashmont's tall figure. The other was not quite as tall, and there was something familiar in his walk.

Once, Ashmont glanced back, but Owsley kept his head down and crossed the street. Heart racing, he followed them into Grosvenor Street and watched them walk to a hackney stand. The duke spoke, and the other fellow answered, and Owsley stopped, so suddenly that he stumbled.

He couldn't make out the words but the voice . . . He knew that voice. How could he forget it?

Mr. Owsley, in recent weeks some pieces have appeared in the London journals.

I don't see how the facts could be plainer.

He would not mistake that voice had he heard it among a hundred. Hers had the same effortlessly compelling quality her father used so brilliantly in the House of Commons. She'd inherited her father's mind as well.

Lady Bartham's remarks echoed in his mind: . . . *should have groomed her to be a great political hostess . . . achieve great things with her by his side.*

He clenched his hands. He'd dared to believe so. Until now.

Cassandra Pomfret was the other figure he'd seen in the window. She was the one Ashmont had kissed so passionately.

She, ruined. What had possessed her to throw away her future, her good name?

But no, he could not, would not believe it. She could not possibly hold herself so cheap. But why had she been there? How had she been lured into a situation so dangerous? She was daring. Everybody knew this.

"No," he told himself. "It is impossible. She would never . . . I don't believe it. There's another explanation." Yet intelligent women made ghastly mistakes like this time and again. The streets were filled with women who'd allowed themselves to be led astray.

No, not she. Impossible. It made him sick to think of it—of that handsome young woman in the duke's arms— No, he would *not* think of it.

How long had it been since he saw them in the window? Not an hour. For all he knew, half an hour could have passed. Less? Had it only seemed like more? Why had he not read his watch properly? He had no idea what time it was, even now.

He watched the duke summon one of the hackneys. He watched the pair climb in. He took note of the hackney's badge number. He watched the coach drive away.

As soon as it began to move, he hastened to the stand, claimed another coach, and told the driver to follow the other vehicle.

Then he took out his watch and at last noted the time.

Chapter 16

$\mathcal{A}$ short time later, after one stop at an establishment in St. James's Street, the hackney paused at the corner of Great Ryder and Duke Streets to discharge the Cossack trousers–wearing person. The vehicle then turned left into King Street, where it disgorged its remaining passenger.

Bottle in hand, the Duke of Ashmont stumbled from the coach into St. James's Square and staggered toward the center of the square. There, in a fenced-in enclosure, in the middle of a pool of water, King William III sat upon his horse.

DeGriffith House stood in the northwest corner of the square. Ashmont positioned himself by the fence opposite King Street. He had his hat tipped at a drunken angle, so that the gaslights threw his face into shadow.

He took a swig from the bottle and began to sing, at the top of his voice:

> *"The Dey of Algiers, when afraid of his ears,*
> *A messenger sent to the Court, sir,*
> *As he knew in our state the women had weight,*
> *He chose one well hung for the sport, sir.*
> *He searched the Divan till he found out a man,*
> *Whose ballocks were heavy and hairy,*

And he lately came o'er from the Barbary shore,
As the great Plenipotentiary.

"When to England he came, with his prick in a flame,
He showed it his hostess on landing,
Who spread its renown thru all parts of the town,
As a pintle past all understanding.
So much there was said of its snout and its head,
That they called it the great Janissary,
Not a lady could sleep till she got a sly peep,
At the great Plenipotentiary."

On this warm July night, windows of the houses facing the square were open. Figures came to the windows and paused there, looking down at him. He went on singing lustily.

CASSANDRA, MEANWHILE, HAD made her way to the house. She'd been able to slip in from the garden, thanks to her sister's leaving one of the tall windows unlocked. That hurdle overcome, Cassandra hurried up the stairs, composing an excuse in case she was caught. It was an incoherent excuse, because, really, she had no acceptable one for being dressed in her brother's clothes and sneaking out in the evening.

But she'd counted on Ashmont, and she knew he wouldn't fail her.

All the household staff ought to be riveted to the front windows by now, or as near to them as they could get.

She dashed into her room, where her startled sister bolted up from a chair and dropped the book she'd been reading.

"Thank heaven," Hyacinth said. "I was terrified that something had happened to you."

"Something happened, assuredly," Cassandra said. "Help me get out of these things and into a dressing gown, as quick as you can."

As she was wrestling herself out of the coat, they heard from a distance the sound of a familiar voice singing. His voice carried splendidly.

"He's done it," Cassandra said.

"Done what? Who?"

"Ashmont. Creating a diversion. Oh, Juno, he can't be singing what I think he's singing."

The clothes came off swiftly. Men's clothes were so much simpler. Their lives, too. But then, they were simple creatures, by and large. She shed waistcoat, trousers, and shirt, then hastily threw on a nightgown, and over it her dressing gown.

"We must go look," she said. "Everybody in the square is doing so, I'll wager anything." Mainly servants, she was reasonably certain. Their masters and mistresses would be out at this hour.

She went with Hyacinth to the drawing room, which overlooked St. James's Square.

Below them, hat tilted low over his forehead and holding onto a lamppost with one hand and a bottle with the other, the Duke of Ashmont was singing at the top of his voice:

> *"The next to be kissed, on the Plenipo's list,*
> *Was a delicate Maiden of Honor,*
> *She screamed at the sight of his prick, in a fright,*
> *Tho' she'd had the whole Palace upon her.*
> *O Lord, she said, what a prick for a maid!*
> *Do, pray, come look at it, Cary!*
> *But I will have one drive, if I'm ripped up alive,*
> *By the great Plenipotentiary."*

"I'm not sure I understand," Hyacinth said.

"That's probably for the best," Cassandra said. "I had better let him know I'm in safely."

She opened the window and stepped out onto the narrow balcony. "Stop your noise," she called, "or I'll summon a constable."

He looked up at her and waved the bottle.

"Yes, yes, you've delighted us for long enough," she said. "Go serenade someone else."

He laughed and let go of the lamppost. Moving into the shadows, he made an elaborate bow, then staggered into King Street and out of sight.

AFTER WALKING ABOUT the neighborhood for nearly an hour in a misery of indecision, Mr. Owsley at last returned to his rooms. There he wrote a short note to Lady Bartham, asking to meet with her on a highly confidential matter.

Accordingly, Saturday morning found the pair in St. James's churchyard, where the only possible eavesdroppers were belowground.

Mr. Owsley was sobbing. "I thought I had found my partner for my life's journey, but she has thrown herself away—"

"You're absolutely certain it was Miss Pomfret?" Lady Bartham said. Another woman might have sobbed, too, in frustration, but she was made of more obdurate material. "You stood at a distance, on a dark night. So easy to be confused."

"It was she. I should know her voice anywhere. And once I heard the voice, I understood why he—she—had seemed familiar. It was she, beyond a doubt, though she contrived somehow to walk in the manner of a man."

"You had had a shock."

"Not enough to blind my senses. Certainly I tried to make myself believe it wasn't she. But that became impossible. There is no mistaking her, particularly her voice. A feminine version of her father's."

"Her father. Ah, yes."

Her ladyship had discovered only last night that Humphrey would not be traveling with the Duke of Ashmont after all, because he'd had a note from Lord deGriffith appointing to meet with him today.

"He might have a place for me," Humphrey had announced, to his father's great astonishment. While Lord and Lady Bartham loved their children, they had never regarded Humphrey as one likely to rise in the world, let alone one to be taken under Lord deGriffith's wing.

"I can scarcely believe it," he'd said. "But it seems I've made a good impression, although I can't say how, exactly. I rather suspect Miss Hyacinth had something to do with that, although again, my mind can't take it in, quite. Me, of all fellows. But she has been so kind." Thence he'd launched into a rambling speech about her numerous perfections.

This made no sense to Lady Bartham. Hundreds of men sighing after her and Hyacinth Pomfret chose *Humphrey?* Not a troublesome son, by any means—his two older brothers were more of a trial—and not unattractive. But even Lady Bartham would not go so far as to call him *dashing*. Or in any way exceptional. A third son! *Her* son.

Bartham, naturally, had been delighted. This spared his having to stir himself on Humphrey's behalf. He had his hands more than full with the elder two.

Lady Bartham was not delighted. It did not take her long to discern whose hand was behind this. After she'd visited deGriffith House yesterday, Lady deGriffith must have gone straight to her husband and used her wiles on him, to keep Humphrey dangling after Hyacinth. As though the girl needed more suitors!

That was it. Not the girl, but her manipulative mother.

While she boiled with outrage inwardly, the countess was all concern and sympathy outwardly. She only glanced now and then at the crumbling headstones and thought about what an agreeable world she'd live in, if only certain persons might soon lie beneath them.

"You upset yourself needlessly," she told Owsley.

"Needlessly! She's ruined! Beyond the pale."

"That I strongly doubt. Miss Pomfret has hoydenish tendencies, as you well know. She only went to his house to stop him from leaving London. It is the sort of reckless thing she'd do. Once there, she persuaded him not to leave. This is simpler than you'd think. She need only give him a taste of what he might hope for if he stayed and married her. Minor favors, no more. But if you are too fainthearted to take her in hand—"

"A soiled dove!"

Lady Bartham sighed mentally. Men could be so tiresome. They might do as they pleased in that way, but their brides must be virgins. As though that sort of thing couldn't be managed on the wedding night. She could name a score of women who had lost their maidenheads before the wedding.

"I do not see that young lady giving away the prize lightly," she said. "As I said, it's most likely she's allowed a few favors in token of future marital rewards. At the very worst, she is simply another Magdalen. A man of conscience would wish to save her and bring her back to decency."

She watched him wrestle with himself. Lust struggled with male vanity. He couldn't bear for Ashmont to be the first . . . but Owsley wanted her. Oh, he wanted her badly. He was as lovesick as Humphrey, stupid boy.

No matter. Whatever else happened, that bold, self-willed girl would not become a duchess.

"Never mind," the countess said. "I'll get to the truth myself. What was the number of the hackney coach? And what, precisely, was she wearing?"

Early that afternoon

Ashmont frowned at his reflection in the horse dressing glass.

Sommers had selected a single-breasted black wool tailcoat, worn with a single-breasted, white striped silk waistcoat, white trousers, and black ankle boots. The neckcloth was white. "I should have thought one of the blue tailcoats or the green frock coat the right thing. This is rather . . . black and white."

"Subdued, Your Grace," Sommers said.

"Right. Want to impress him with my sobriety. As though he'd believe it."

The pronouns referred to Lord deGriffith, with whom Ashmont intended to meet today.

But first, the rendezvous. Ashmont glanced at the clock on the chimneypiece. Plenty of time yet to get to St. James's Park. There he was to meet Cassandra and whatever entourage she'd been able to arrange this morning.

His gaze shifted to the window, beyond which hung a grey day. "I don't like the looks of that. If it rains, we'll have to put it off. Can't have ladies walking in the rain. We didn't plan for it, though it's as likely as not. We hadn't time last night to think of everything."

Ye gods, last night, last night.

Ashmont still half believed it was a dream. That she'd taken so great a risk to tell him she loved him . . . her willingness and openness . . . her trust. His throat tightened.

"Not sure I measure up," he said.

"I daresay Lord deGriffith will think not, Your Grace. However, as I understand, fathers of daughters tend to regard all suitors with suspicion, if not outright loathing."

"You were heroic last night, Sommers. I'll have to raise your wages again. A pity I can't bestow a title."

Sommers cleared his throat. "The staff have seen it before, Your Grace. A fit of despair. A threat to leave without notice—or better yet, to cut my throat."

"Audience in tears."

"Audible sobbing. At last I am recalled to a sense of duty. I had four footmen hovering over me in the greatest anxiety. I am, as you know, something of a mentor to the staff, keeping them up to the sartorial mark on their half-day-off excursions. Most of us like to cut a fine figure, and I am deemed a Delphic oracle in that regard."

"You are a Delphic oracle, in that and other regards."

Sommers was no Keeffe, certainly. Not a mentor or bodyguard. But he was as much of a confidant as Ashmont had, and beyond a doubt had been, at times, all that stood between Ashmont and utter chaos. There was something settling to the mind about wearing the right neckcloth, properly tied, and a suit of clothes suited to the occasion. Sommers was the ballast in the whirlwind of Ashmont's life.

But a man needed a wife, the right wife, to be the sun, and keep him in a steady orbit. There would be explosions, meteors, and sun storms, he didn't doubt. He and Cassandra were strong-willed people. But as long as she was the center of his universe, he could weather any upheaval.

At last the final smoothing and fussing was done, and Ashmont was at leisure to pace the dressing room, waiting for the agreed-upon time, an hour hence.

He waited five minutes before anxiety overcame him. "She might arrive early. She's dealing with others. No predicting when they'll set out, and it's hardly ten minutes' walk from deGriffith House to St. James's Park. They might arrive and be gone by the time I get there. Better go now."

He grabbed his hat and walking stick and hurried out.

DESPITE THE GLOOMY day, Cassandra easily persuaded her mother to accompany her and Hyacinth on a walk in St. James's Park. After all, if it rained they were only within a few streets of home.

The rain held off, and early in the afternoon Cassandra, her mother and sister, and a pair of tall footmen reached the park about the time she'd planned. Ashmont, who'd promised to keep watch, timed his arrival perfectly.

The ladies were strolling along one of the footpaths toward the lake. He turned up where theirs joined another path, near the water.

At sight of him—impeccably dressed, graceful, and unreasonably handsome, Cassandra's heart performed almost painful acrobatics. She knew he'd be here. He'd said he would come, and she trusted him, as she'd trusted him last night, in so many ways. All the same, the happiness bubbling up inside included a small portion of relief.

"How unexpected," Mama said with a glance at Cassandra. "Mr. Morris told his mother you were leaving London."

"A momentary impulse," he said. "But I came to my senses. I had more important and enjoyable business to attend to in Town. What great luck it is to find you here."

His blue gaze went to Cassandra, and instantly her mind went straight to what had happened between them last night. Her body went there, too, the muscles tautening and tensing while the day grew many degrees warmer.

"Miraculous, I should call it," Mama said drily. "I should never have thought of coming out to walk today, but Cassandra insisted that she and Hyacinth needed exercise and fresh air."

"My sister and I were disturbed last night by a drunken lackwit singing bawdy songs in the square," Cassandra said. "It was difficult to sleep afterward."

"Appalling," Ashmont said. "There ought to be a law about that sort of thing."

"What law can we possibly need when my eldest daughter is about?" Mama said. "She could not leave it to one of the neighbors, or the servants, to deal with the rascal. No, she must step out onto the balcony *en déshabillé*—for all the world to see—and see to him herself."

"All the great world were out at their entertainments," Cassandra said. "Servants made up the audience, and they only stood by to enjoy the show. Furthermore, I should like to know what sense there is in rising from a sickbed and spending an hour dressing, only to tell a sot to sing somewhere else?"

"No sense at all, I suspect," Ashmont said. "By the time you'd finished dressing, it would be time for breakfast. Ladies' attire is so complicated."

"You would know," Cassandra said.

"Really, child," said her mother.

"Am I to pretend that the duke is a model of decorum?" She rolled her eyes. "So many rules. Did you know, duke, that once upon a time, and by no means was it ancient times, ladies received gentlemen in their boudoirs in very much what I wore when I went out to silence our entertainer, and nobody thought twice about it."

"That was in your grandmother's time," Mama said. "No woman of repute would do it today. Kindly change the subject—and pray do not tell me I began it. I thought we meant to walk, and here we are, standing." She glanced up at the grey clouds thickening overhead. "We had better take our exercise while we can."

"Would you do me the honor of allowing me to join you?" Ashmont said.

Mama took a long, hard look at him, then Cassandra. "Since you clearly came with that purpose, who am I to spoil your stratagems? I am far too discreet to ask how you managed to turn up on the spot at precisely the same time we did. These matters can always be managed, with determination."

"Lady deGriffith, I could not be more determined."

"A man ought to know his own mind. I will not hold your momentary indecision about the appeal of horse and boat races against you. We are all subject to an occasional wandering of mind."

She took Hyacinth's arm and let Cassandra and Ashmont walk ahead.

Once they were no longer within easy hearing range, Ashmont said, "I think she suspects we plotted this."

"I suspect that she and my father had their own way of managing these matters during their courtship," she said. "As long as they don't know where I was last night, I'm not anxious, not on my own account. The trouble is, if they find out, they'll know Hyacinth was my accomplice."

"No, no. We'll find a way to make me your accomplice. Or the instigator. And they're not going to know about last night. How could they? Also, as soon as you like, you'll be a duchess, and you can arrange your sister's social life. How soon, by the way, can we get this deed done?"

"As soon as my father will allow it."

She couldn't marry without her father's permission. She wouldn't. She'd never be so irrational as to commence her marriage estranged from her parents. For all the difficulties she had with them, her family was dear to her. Furthermore, even the best marriages faced difficulties, and women, having so few rights, needed as much support as they could muster.

"But first I need your consent," he said.

"I gave it last night."

"I want it here, in broad day, under chaperonage, when neither of us is in a state of high emotion. I want it at a time when your mind is quiet and you haven't just taken the most stupendous risk for the most undeserving fellow, and might at any moment be discovered."

She threw him a sidelong glance. That was to say, she meant only a glance, but he caught her gaze and held it, his blue eyes glittering, and for a moment she was nearly blinded by it: the way he looked at her, and the nearly unearthly beauty of his countenance, and the strength and grace of his tall physique. She remembered looking up at him long ago and marveling, while he told her stories about stars. The glittering being she'd regarded with awe— Was this the same one, and was he truly hers?

Yes. The same but become a man, altogether human, with the full complement of human flaws.

She said, "You are undeserving, certainly, but you seem to be the best I can do."

He came to a halt. "In that case, Miss Pomfret, would you do me the very great honor of consenting to be my wife?"

She had paused with him. Now she looked up into his sky-blue eyes, and something within her seemed to fly up to whatever Olympus he resided upon. "Yes," she said. "I believe I will."

CASSANDRA AND ASHMONT had planned all—excepting weather—to a nicety, they believed. First, the accidental meeting in the park, when Ashmont and Cassandra would settle matters between them. Then he would accompany the ladies home and ask to meet with Lord deGriffith.

It had never occurred to either of them that her father would not be at home.

The first raindrops began to fall at the precise moment he and Cassandra shared their hopes with her mother.

"Oh, that is too bad," Lady deGriffith was saying. "Why was I not given a hint? Lord deGriffith has gone out for the day. A meeting." She glanced at Hyacinth. "But we will be home in the evening. I'll arrange it. But do be aware that I can say nothing until you speak to Lord deGriffith."

"Oh, Mama!" Hyacinth said. "You must say something. You will at least encourage Papa to look kindly on the duke."

Lord deGriffith was the head of his family. Yet at this moment it became clear to Ashmont which of the pair was the sun, and which the orbiting planet.

"Very well," Lady deGriffith said. "I believe I may say that I am not displeased. Will that do?"

"Mama!" Hyacinth cried. "Can you do no better? Really?"

The rain began to fall harder then, and Lady deGriffith unfurled her umbrella. "It will have to do for now. These matters are properly left to the head of the family. Come along, girls, duke." They hurried along under umbrellas to St. James's Square. Since Ashmont could hardly hang about the house all day, he had no choice but to leave them there.

He'd wanted to get it over with. He knew the meeting would be difficult. Lord deGriffith loathed him. But after all, perhaps this was better. Ashmont would have more time to prepare his speech, as well as answers to the hard questions his lordship would undoubtedly pose—if, that is, the gentleman was willing to hear him out and didn't throw him out of the house.

As Ashmont made his way home in the downpour, reasons for throwing him out of the house piled up in his mind. In other times, he might have stopped at Blackwood House or Ripley House, and let his friends tease him over a glass or ten of wine.

Not today. Those days were behind him.

"Behind me," he murmured. The rain beat down on his top hat and spilled from the brim. He was not quite wet through, but getting there. And yet the day . . .

He paused and looked about him. Only two days ago Cassandra Pomfret had told him he was splendid. Last night she'd taken shocking measures to demonstrate her feelings . . . then let him take shocking liberties. Today, while in full possession of her reason and not influenced by kisses and caresses and other lures, and in the sobering presence of her mother and sister, she'd said yes.

Lady deGriffith would put in a kind word with her husband on his behalf, and that would make Ashmont's way a degree easier. Not easy, by any means. He labored under no illusions. Where

Lord deGriffith was concerned, the way would be bumpy, dark, and abounding in pitfalls.

That was as it should be. The bulk of Ashmont's old life was behind him and the new was in process, full of obstacles and uncertainties. He was ready for whatever came. In fact, being a fighter at heart, he looked forward happily to the challenge.

Midafternoon

As she usually did on Saturday afternoons while they were in London, Mama joined her sisters for tea. Today the ladies gathered at Aunt Elizabeth's.

Cassandra and Hyacinth, meanwhile, were in their sitting room, talking about the prospects of their respective beaux, although Hyacinth would not acknowledge Humphrey Morris as a beau.

"I enjoy his company," she was saying, "and I know he can be of use to Papa. But as I told you some time ago, I'm in no hurry to marry. Truly, I don't feel ready to think of any gentleman in those terms. Certainly I should like to know what Papa thinks of him, in the event he decides to take Mr. Morris on. After that it will be some time before we know the verdict."

"If he can survive working for Papa, he'll show stamina and resilience at the very least. And if our parent can tolerate him for any length of time, that will tell us something about the gentleman's personal qualities as well as his character." Cassandra smiled at her sister. "You're cautious. Unlike me."

"I'm eighteen," Hyacinth said. "And unlike you, I have not been following the gentleman's career for a great part of my life."

Though it was mainly from afar, Cassandra had followed Ashmont's mad career for some sixteen years, more or less. Not that she'd devoted all her energies to waiting and hoping. Even in her idealistic youth she'd set out to make her own life and find her own way. Even during the worst of her infatuation, he'd never been the center of her universe. More like a distant star.

That was the trouble with the ghastly poem Owsley had given her: The lady in the poem lived the narrow life Mary Wollstonecraft had deplored. It bore no resemblance to the life Cassandra had made for herself, thanks to her grandparents and Keeffe.

"At least I know the worst about him," she said. "That's a great deal more than most brides can say."

"We're guarded so closely, it's nearly impossible to tell what a gentleman is truly like. How many hours, altogether, does the average young lady spend in a gentleman's company before they're wed? She has no idea how he takes his coffee or tea, let alone what he's like when he's disappointed or angry or suffering from a cold or dyspepsia. We go into marriage knowing practically nothing—his dancing ability, his manners in public, his dress, his looks. All superficial. All we know of his personality is what he shows while wooing, when he displays himself at his best."

"That won't be my case, quite," Cassandra said. "If, that is, Papa consents."

Hyacinth wasn't so lost to reason as to say he wouldn't reject Ashmont out of hand. She knew how their father felt about the duke. While the feeling had softened a degree from utter loathing, Lord deGriffith still regarded him in the way any keeper of hens regarded hawks and falcons. She said, "If he doesn't?"

Colson appeared in the doorway. "If you please, Miss Pomfret, I'm to tell you Lady Bartham is here and wishes to speak to you."

LADY BARTHAM KNEW Lord deGriffith would be out of the house for the afternoon, luring her starry-eyed son into his political coils. She knew also that Lady deGriffith would join her sisters for their weekly tea party.

One couldn't ask for a more fortuitous set of circumstances, offering more than sufficient time to prepare. Following her meeting with Owsley, she did a little shopping in Piccadilly, stopping at Hatchards, Fortnum and Mason, and other establishments. Then she climbed into her carriage, returned home, and changed her dress into one more suited to the occasion, crimson, with a fine cashmere shawl of black and white.

During these leisurely preliminaries she considered several approaches and settled on three, depending on the reception she met.

Miss Pomfret came downstairs promptly. She did not appear wary. She wore her usual expression, which was to say, no expression. A china doll was easier to read. But Lady Bartham didn't need to look for clues. She held all the cards.

They exchanged courtesies.

"You will wonder why I wished to see you, particularly," Lady Bartham said.

"I assumed you had something particular to say to me, since neither of my parents is home, as you are doubtless aware," Miss Pomfret said. "A secret, is it?"

Though Lady Bartham was far from unfamiliar with the girl's blunt speech, she'd grown accustomed to the seen-but-not-heard Miss Pomfret she'd encountered here lately. The directness took her aback, though she didn't show it.

"How perceptive you are," she said. "I daresay it is a secret, for the present." She withdrew from her reticule a folded note. "I considered asking you to walk with me in the garden, for privacy, but I supposed you might hesitate when you didn't know what the matter was."

She held out the note. Miss Pomfret stared at the folded paper for a moment, then took it. She opened it and read. Her expression didn't change.

"I see," she said. "You wouldn't have given me this merely for information. You want something. The rain has subsided. We shall walk in the garden."

THE NOTE WAS to the point:

Your adventure last night was witnessed. You wore a top hat, coat, and Cossack trousers. You were observed in the window of Ashmont House, in the embrace of the Duke of Ashmont. You were seen and heard later, in Park Street, climbing into hackney coach No. 317. The direction given the driver was the intersection of Duke and Great Ryder Streets, close by your home.

Chapter 17

*I*t took a moment for the words on paper to become real. Cassandra stared at them with the sensation of being in a dream. It made no sense. It wasn't possible. And then, yes, clearly it was possible, because here she was, reading it again, and the words didn't disappear, and all the world remained as it had been minutes before. In the garden a few persevering birds, past their springtime mating enthusiasms but not yet taciturn, chirped in the shrubs and trees.

What a curious thing it was to have one's greatest anxieties realized like this, out of the blue. How had Lady Bartham found out? It was unlikely she'd seen for herself, though not impossible. But no, she would have had to skulk about Ashmont House for at least half an hour, perhaps an hour or more, on a Friday night, when she might be skewering reputations at any of half a dozen entertainments. And why hang about waiting for Ashmont to do something gossip-worthy? That made no sense. She must have had a spy. Did others know, apart from the spy?

The questions tumbled over themselves in Cassandra's head, though the answers hardly mattered now. The lady walking alongside her on the garden's gravel path knew. That was enough. She'd have no trouble informing the entire world, and in no time.

The rain had stopped a short time ago, leaving the air cooler but heavy with humidity.

Life felt heavy at this moment, weighed down by a crushing sense of responsibility. A few hours earlier, Cassandra's spirits had soared impossibly high, all the way to Olympus, to touch true happiness. Now she felt like Icarus, wings melting, plummeting into the sea.

"Obviously your sister helped you," Lady Bartham was saying. "You couldn't have done it without her. On that count alone your father would not be pleased." She smiled. "An understatement, as you must realize, unless you are lost to all natural filial sensibility."

Your behavior reflects on her, on all of us.

But this went far beyond appearances. Papa would be furious and worse, hurt. To him, what Cassandra had done would constitute a betrayal of trust, and he would not be wrong.

"I'm aware of the consequences," she said. "Perhaps you will be so good as to tell me what you want. It seems pointless to ask why you've done this or how you came by the knowledge. I should simply like to know what you hope to accomplish."

Lady Bartham only smiled. "Well, then, let me match you in directness. It would give me no small satisfaction to make your duplicity and shame known to the world. However, other considerations make me willing to offer an alternative. I will consign the whole matter to oblivion on two conditions. First, you will never see the Duke of Ashmont again. You will break off with him immediately and irrevocably. I strongly recommend you decide upon a change of scenery and return to your grandparents for a few years. That would be best for everybody."

She paused, waiting for a response.

Cassandra regarded her unblinkingly. "You said two conditions."

The lady's gaze shifted upward toward the windows. Hyacinth looked down on them from the window seat of their sitting room. Lady Bartham met her gaze briefly, then returned to Cassandra.

"Second, Miss Hyacinth will break it off with Humphrey."

"So far as I know, there is nothing to break off."

"Don't try to play with me, Miss Pomfret. You will find yourself outmatched. How much longer do you imagine I will allow you to make me your dupe?"

"Is that how you view it?"

"I know what I interrupted at Cremorne House. But you and the duke conspired to twist plain fact into falsehood, to make me look ridiculous. To be sure, I do not hold you entirely to blame. He's corrupted your mind. If you suppose he will make you happy, you are sadly deluded. He had all in train to leave London—"

"Taking your son with him."

"Humphrey is a grown man, and yes, I had rather he wasted his allowance at races than become entangled with your family. If your sister throws him off, in no uncertain terms, working with your father will lose its allure."

"I see." Cassandra did not see. Not very well, at any rate. She was fighting shock, bewilderment, grief, rage, despair, and other emotions, too many to count or name.

You're in control, she told herself.

She wasn't. She was at sea, drowning. She'd thought her greatest concern was her father's rejecting Ashmont. She'd concentrated on how best to bring Papa round. She'd assumed that her anxiety about last night was groundless, as Ashmont had assured her.

. . . they're not going to know about last night. How could they?

Somehow, somebody had found out and given this spiteful woman details obtained in only one way. The informer had been on the spot, and she and Ashmont had failed to notice.

"And the one who told you this?" she said. "Will that person be silenced as well?"

"You needn't be anxious," Lady Bartham said. "If I say the information is to be buried, it will be buried. You're not the only one with shameful secrets. However, if I say it's to be broadcast, it will be, and this time there will be no turning the tables or devising schemes to trick and deceive and manipulate."

"All this," Cassandra said, "because you did not like the way matters turned out. The pain you'll give others is of no consideration."

Her parents . . . All that Cassandra had imagined before, about Putney and about being caught behind the curtain would come true, but on a massive scale, infinitely worse. What she'd done this time went well beyond those improprieties. She might as well have been caught in the act.

She'd visited a man's house. She'd worn men's clothes. She'd been seen kissing a famous libertine. That alone was sufficient to make her soiled goods.

She didn't care what the world said about her. But she wasn't the one who'd pay for what she'd done. It was her parents and her sister, first and foremost, who'd bear the burden of shame, which they in no way deserved.

Nobody's fault but Cassandra's. One impulsive act. That was all it took to ruin everything.

"Do not delude yourself that marrying Ashmont will wipe the slate clean," the countess went on. "If, that is, he'll have you, now he's had you already. He'll continue as he's always done, but you'll be an outcast, unwelcome at Court, unwelcome everywhere. It would be as though he'd married a courtesan or a divorcee. You'll have less influence than you do now."

Cassandra knew of such cases. Lord Holland and his divorced wife had had to make their own society, and those who visited them at Holland House were almost exclusively men of similar political leanings.

"You'll be shunned and despised," Lady Bartham went on. "Even your little club of radicals won't want you. Your shame will taint them."

For women who wanted to go about their good works quietly, notoriety like this would make Cassandra a liability.

"And what do you think will become of your children?" Lady Bartham laughed. "And as to children—you dare to speak of the pain I'll inflict. Have you truly no notion of the pain you've inflicted upon your family, year after year, with your undutiful behavior? Innocent, are you? Driving about in your chariot with that hideous jockey at your side. Spouting the despicable philosophy of a bluestocking harlot. Playing into the hands of an unscrupulous debauchee. Now you drag your innocent sister into it—though how long she remains innocent, if in fact she has remained so, is an interesting question."

"Pray do not insult my sister. She's done you no harm."

"Has she not? But that is neither here nor there. What I want is simple enough. You drive recklessly through your life, mowing down any rules not to your liking and any persons who happen to be in your way. I will not be mown down, nor will I see any member of my family dragged under your wheels."

The countess took out her pocket watch. "It will take you no time at all to send a message to the Duke of Ashmont. Doubtless you know where to find him and how to reach him. However, your sister's message to Humphrey might not reach him before tomorrow, depending on how late your father keeps him. I shall give you until three o'clock tomorrow to carry out my conditions."

Three o'clock. Not twenty-four hours before this woman set out to kill her parents' happiness and her sister's future.

"If by that time I do not receive clear proof of your having done as I require, I shall provide the contents of that note, with further specifics, to *Foxe's Morning Spectacle*," the lady went on. "I shall also share the interesting details with all my intimate acquaintance."

"And this will give you pleasure, will it?"

"A pleasant enough task, when you've done all the heavy work for me."

That was true enough. Cassandra had fashioned the noose to hang herself.

"Do not for a moment think I will hesitate," Lady Bartham said. "Your father will not have my son, and your mother will not triumph over me. You will never be a duchess, Miss Pomfret. You may never be a wife. What a pity it is that you couldn't resist temptation and take Mr. Owsley when you had the chance."

"I had rather someone with better taste in poetry."

"Now there will be no one. You may look forward to being viewed by any decent gentleman with revulsion, and by the indecent ones as—well, let's leave that unsaid."

"Why? You've said so much. Why stop now?"

Lady Bartham smiled. "Three o'clock, Miss Pomfret. I shall see myself out. I know the way."

Ashmont House
An hour later

ARMS FOLDED, EYES narrowed, Keeffe gazed about him at the Duke of Ashmont's dressing room. "Nice place you got here, Your Grace."

"It's small, but we like it. If you're here, I can only assume Miss Pomfret is in trouble."

Ashmont had arrived home from harassing his solicitor to learn of a disturbance belowstairs. The disturbance now stood before him: Keeffe, apparently free of his rib wrappings, with the glint of challenge in his eye.

"No, I was only taking the air in the neighborhood. Yes, Your Grace, it's her, like you guess so clever. Not but what this is a fine place to visit, and your servants got themselves on the right side of things quick enough—soon as one of 'em worked out who the little crippled fellow used to be. Then they was as genteel as a cove could ask."

He nodded at Sommers, who stood, clearly torn. Here was a common, twisted little person in His Grace's own private dressing room, where even certain of the staff dared not venture. On the other hand, this common, twisted little person was no less than Tom Keeffe, of whom even the youngest of Ashmont's employees stood in awe.

Servants were by no means immune to the lure of the turf, and this was one of its living legends. Unlike members of the racing community, they had no axes to grind. He was a celebrity.

After the briefest hesitation, Sommers returned the nod.

"I reckon I can talk in front of him?" Keeffe said.

"Yes, yes, or I'd have sent him away the instant I saw you," Ashmont said calmly, while the inner demon began to pace at the mouth of the cave. "What's happened and who is it she wants me to kill?"

Keeffe told him about Lady Bartham's visit.

Ashmont swore.

"My miss come busting into my place in a temper and tole me she couldn't write any letter, she was that wild. But her hands was tied, she said, and she didn't know how to kill the lady quick and easy on her own. And so she sent me and wants to know, would you come along?"

"Not sure I can help murder a lady," Ashmont said. "Want to, yes." Desperately.

"Not in that waistcoat, Your Grace," said Sommers.

"My miss is that cut up," Keeffe said. "Never seen her thrown like this before."

"Yes. My fault. Should've been more careful. How the devil could anybody—" He shook his head. "No matter. Sommers."

The valet had already moved into his sacred domain. He emerged with a red waistcoat and black cravat.

"Ah, good," Ashmont said. "Won't show the blood."

"His Grace likes his little joke," Sommers said.

"Well, it don't do to moan and groan and rant and rave, does it?" Keeffe said. "It's bad, but you'll pull her through. Or she'll pull you through."

"Both," Ashmont said. "We're a pair now. The lady said so."

"Matched well enough," Keeffe said. "Both of you headstrong and reckless and ready for a fight, like I tole her. Not that it's up to me."

"It won't be up to Morris's annoying mother, I promise you. Sommers, let them know I want the cabriolet."

KEEFFE BESIDE HIM, Ashmont drove to the jockey's quarters, where they found Cassandra still pacing and stewing. At sight of him, she stopped and drew a deep breath. Then she walked to him and laid her head on his chest.

"I cannot think clearly," she said.

"I'm not so gifted in the thinking department myself," he said.

"I have looked at the matter in every way."

"Including telling me to go to the devil?"

She tipped her head back. "I have waited and hoped for years. I made a life for myself without you, but I believe it will be a great deal more interesting with you. You haven't a prayer of escaping now."

"Relieved to hear it."

He'd make any sacrifice for her. He knew he'd give his life for her. It would be easier, in fact, to give his life than to live it without her.

"We might have to go into exile in Siberia," she said, "but I will not let that woman dictate to me. It's vindictiveness, pure and simple. A weapon dropped into her hands, and she has no scruples about using it. She hates me. But I've had time to think about what she said. It's more than likely she made everything out to be worse than it is. In any case, I doubt it's simply me. She has a grudge against my parents."

She told Ashmont what Lady Bartham had said, as much as she could remember. "I tried to make myself calm, but I made a bad job of it."

"She did everything she could to throw you off balance," Ashmont said. "Couldn't chance your being clearheaded and getting the better of her."

"It's the guilt," Cassandra said. "I knew it was wrong to go to you. I knew it was dangerous. But it was necessary—rules be damned."

"No arguments from me," Ashmont said. "As to wrong and dangerous—practically an invitation. Hard to resist. And then there was me. How could you resist me?"

"I reckon I'll step out of the place now," Keeffe said. "Getting too thick in here for me. Need some air."

They looked at him.

"Sorry," Ashmont said. "Forgot you were there."

"That's dangerous," she said. "When people forget he's there, very bad things can happen."

"Ah, but he has the knack, doesn't he?" Ashmont smiled at the jockey. "I never acquired that one, the making-yourself-invisible trick."

Keeffe looked up at him and laughed. "You. Invisible." He laughed again, tickled.

His cackling laughter somehow made everything a degree less dark. This was a man whose body had been left in pieces. He'd survived. Here he was, laughing.

Ashmont turned to Cassandra. "We got ourselves into this fix. We'll get ourselves out of it. But I have a feeling it's not going to be pretty."

"No." She shook her head. "To begin with, we have to tell my parents the truth."

SHE'D PACED KEEFFE'S compact parlor, back and forth from the chimneypiece, with its portrait of the beloved horse and his rider, to the door. She'd paced in the other direction, too, from window to wall.

No matter what schemes Cassandra devised, no matter what desperate measures she considered, the one thing she dreaded most kept appearing, like a great, angry bull blocking her path. She had to tell her parents what she'd done. If matters went awry, if Lady Bartham wasn't true to her word—so many ifs—Cassandra couldn't let them find out from anybody else.

"I can't let them be taken unawares," she told Ashmont. "The thought is unbearable. I'm not ashamed of what I did. I don't regret it. I'm only sorry on their account, and Hyacinth's. They've done nothing to deserve this. It isn't their fault, but they'll be blamed and they'll suffer. The least I can do is prepare them."

"Does your sister know?"

She closed her eyes briefly, remembering the expression on her sister's face when Cassandra told her. A series of expressions. Disbelief. Concern. Indignation.

"She knew what it signified for her," Cassandra said. "But what does that extraordinary girl do? There I am, so overset I can scarcely speak, and she puts her arms about me and says, 'That dreadful woman! She's wrong, you know. She's made it out to be uglier than it is. That's what she does. You must step back, the way you do, and pretend she's a troublesome horse, snapping and biting for reasons you don't understand yet. But you will, and when you do, you'll find a way.'"

"Miss Hyacinth ain't wrong," Keeffe said.

Cassandra looked at him.

"You know it well as I do. There's some horses as has been let to get too vicious or made to be so from being handled bad. Some of 'em get beyond what anybody can do for 'em. They get to a point where you can't get through to 'em, no matter what. But most of 'em got reasons, 'n' you can work it out of 'em."

"You know that woman's reasons," Ashmont said. "She told you. She didn't want your father to have any hold over Morris Tertius. She doesn't want him near your sister—near any of you, it seems. A grudge, you said."

Cassandra remembered Hyacinth saying something about an old rivalry between Mama and Lady Bartham. To do with Papa. "An old one, apparently."

"All the more reason to enlighten them," Ashmont said. "If this scheme doesn't work, she'll try another."

"Yes, they need to know. I'm only concerned that Papa will try to kill you."

"And who could blame him?"

"I, for one. Youngish dukes in possession of all their teeth and passable good looks are in short supply."

CASSANDRA'S PARENTS ARRIVED at deGriffith House within minutes of each other.

Naturally, Tilbrook would inform them who awaited them.

By the time the parents entered the drawing room, Humphrey Morris trailing in their wake, thunderclouds were already forming over Lord deGriffith's brow.

"If we're being met by a delegation, I must conclude that an Incident has occurred," said Papa. "Since you form part of the delegation, duke, the reasoning man must deduce that the Incident is of no small proportions."

"Maybe I'd better go," Humphrey Morris said. "Family council and all that."

"On no account," Hyacinth said. "I see no reason for you to be excluded."

Lord deGriffith looked at her. "Not you, child. Surely, this hasn't to do with you." He said it in the manner of Shakespeare's Julius Caesar, with his dying words, *Et tu, Brute?*

"It does, unfortunately," Cassandra said. "But I'm the cause. Mama, please sit down."

"Yes, do, my dear," Papa said. "We had better conduct this conversation in my study. Cassandra. Duke."

They followed obediently into his study. But before he could close the door, Lady deGriffith, Hyacinth, and an obviously reluctant Humphrey Morris entered.

The thunderclouds thickened. "Did I not say Cassandra and the duke?"

"You cannot expect us to sit in the drawing room, on tenterhooks," Mama said.

"Why not? This is hardly the first occasion when I've withdrawn to speak to one of the children or a visitor."

"My dear, here is the Duke of Ashmont, and here is Cassandra, and neither of them glowing with happiness as I had expected, given certain hints I received earlier today. Here is Hyacinth, wishing Mr. Morris to remain. Naturally, something has occurred, clearly not of a pleasant nature. A council seems to be in order. A family council. I am your helpmeet. I shall help."

With that, Mama took the chair nearest his desk.

Everybody else remained standing, like a lot of criminals at the magistrate's court.

The judge did not sit, but stood behind the fortress of his desk, like one preparing to withstand an assault.

As well he might. After all, here was Cassandra, and here was Ashmont, two outrageous persons. If they weren't glowing with happiness, as Mama said, something outrageously bad had occurred.

Cassandra approached the desk and held out Lady Bartham's note. "Lady Bartham gave me this a short time ago."

The lady's third son started at this, and flushed, but said nothing. The look he sent Hyacinth might have meant a thousand words or nothing at all. Cassandra was in no state to interpret.

She watched her father's expression darken as he read it. He started to crumple the note, then thought better of it, and passed it to her mother.

"Oh, my," said Mama. "Really, Cassandra."

Her father had his hand to his temple.

At that, Cassandra, who never gave way to tears, even when bullies harassed her, felt her throat close up and her chest heave, and then she was sobbing violently. In front of everybody.

Ashmont moved to her.

"No," Papa said. "If you touch my daughter, I cannot answer for the consequences."

Ashmont put his arms about Cassandra and held her. "It's all right," he murmured. "We'll make it right."

Before Papa could explode or throw something heavy at him, Cassandra's mother spoke. "Mr. Morris, a small glass of brandy for my daughter, if you will be so kind."

Hyacinth's would-be beau leapt to act. Ashmont pressed the glass into Cassandra's hands. She took a sip, then started to rub away the humiliating tears. He gave her his handkerchief.

She wiped her eyes and collected herself.

"I beg your pardon, Papa," she said. "Excess of emotion. Not a bid for pity, I assure you. The note is true. I did what it said. I do not regret the actions themselves."

"Good grief, Cassandra."

"I would convey a false impression if I said otherwise. However, I very much regret not considering the consequences for my family. As you told me some weeks ago, my behavior reflects on everybody."

"You remembered but you didn't heed me."

"No, I didn't. Still, we took great precautions not to be caught, and it was only the worst possible luck that a spy was in the vicinity. Why that person was there I cannot say. It makes no sense to me. It cannot be a coincidence. On that night of all nights, to have somebody watching. I thought perhaps it was one of the newspaper people. They have the most to gain by spying on Ashmont. But why then give their discovery to another instead of going straight to the press?"

"At present, the whys of the matter do not concern me," Papa said. "Except the one to do with you. Ashmont—"

"You are not to suppose he lured me," Cassandra said. "In fact, he was trying to get away from me. But I couldn't let him go before—before I made my feelings clear."

"For heaven's sake, Cassandra, could you not wait? You are too impulsive."

"Yes, I am impulsive. But to wait? For how long? We had come to an impasse, and he was going away, and he might be gone for months. Perhaps you can wait months in such a case, to learn whether your feelings are understood and then whether they are returned. I could not."

Her father shook his head and turned to her sister. "And you, child? I know your sister could not have managed all this skullduggery without your help."

"Yes, I helped, Papa," Hyacinth said. "I should have done more if I could. I did not like to let her go alone, but I should only be in the way if I went with her."

Their father appeared as close as she'd ever seen him to wild-eyed. "Did it not occur to you that this was *wrong*?"

Hyacinth shook her head. "It seemed wrong for them to be kept apart because of a misunderstanding. If I'd believed it was wrong, I shouldn't have helped. I believed it was right."

Papa sat down. He closed his eyes, then opened them. Apparently, the view did not improve in the interval. He was trying to remain composed, Cassandra understood, but the way his fingers curled and the light in his eye when his gaze fell upon Ashmont told what a struggle that was.

Hyacinth shifted her attention to Humphrey Morris who, clearly, was trying desperately to understand what had happened.

"I helped my sister disguise herself and sneak out of this house in order to visit the Duke of Ashmont last night," she said.

Mr. Morris's mouth formed an O.

"She was dressed in my brother Anselm's clothes," Hyacinth went on. "They were seen. The witness informed your mother, who has offered to expose them."

"*Wh-what*? My mother?" Mr. Morris blinked several times.

"Miss Hyacinth, my abject apologies. I will speak to her immediately. This is—"

"Don't recommend it," Ashmont said. "Might make matters worse, accidentally. She might take it ill, you know."

"Take it ill! Take it ill! I shall damn—dashed well take it ill. Lord deGriffith, I assure you—"

"Pray do not assure me. You underestimate my intelligence if you suppose I should for a minute believe you had anything to do with this."

Apparently, Mr. Morris had passed the first character test with Papa. At this moment, he had probably passed another.

"Actually, he does," Ashmont said. "He's part of the conditions."

"The *what*?" said Mr. Morris.

Ashmont briefly outlined the conditions for suppressing the information.

"This is the outside of enough," Mr. Morris said. "The kind of thing I'd expect from one of my brothers, nothing but trouble my whole life. But *she*. Good gad, I hardly know what to think. She never offered the slightest hint of disliking . . ." His gaze went to Hyacinth.

"Oh, I doubt she truly dislikes me," Hyacinth said. "I suspect it's something else."

"Well, it's nothing to do with my father, that's certain." Mr. Morris returned his attention to the judge. "He was pleased as he could be when I told him I'd meet with you today. But it's all of it rather thick, don't you think? What's m' mother care who Miss Pomfret likes or doesn't? I wonder if she's taken some kind of turn. Had a shock. Nerves all ahoo. Talking strange, like when old Birdwell started imagining his laundry maid was putting poison in the starch. But is she old enough to go senile?"

"Mr. Morris, perhaps you will pour yourself a glass of brandy," Mama said. "Ashmont? One for you?"

"Not at present, thank you, Lady deGriffith," he said. He still had his arm about Cassandra's shoulders, despite the black looks Papa sent his way.

"Tea, then," Mama said. "I could do with a cup. So soothing, yet at the same time stimulating to the senses. Hyacinth, my dear, be so good as to ring."

WHILE THE TEA was in preparation, Ashmont found himself studying Lady deGriffith. He couldn't say why, but at the moment she held his attention. She sat calmly enough—calmer than anybody else—observing and listening.

Any of a score of mothers, in these circumstances, would have been weeping and dropping into fainting fits.

He supposed Lady Bartham would have liked to see that. But would she suppose that Cassandra would have the courage to face her parents with the truth?

He had no idea. Women were complicated. He remembered his uncle saying something about the usefulness of listening to women.

Until recently, Ashmont had never, actually, listened. So many words and usually confusing.

Cassandra had changed that. Now he listened with all his might, noting the smallest change in expression. If he'd thought about it, he would have realized that the listening started with her, but then somehow spread out to other women.

The book that Mrs. Roake had suggested clearly had something to do with this change. It had made him take notice of a great many things.

And so he noticed that Lady deGriffith, who ought to have been the most distraught person in the room, seemed to be the calmest. At present she was murmuring something to Lord deGriffith, who had moved his chair slightly to be nearer to her, and was leaning toward her, his head bent, his brow knit.

He muttered something in answer. She spoke again. More muttering. She said something else.

. . . *the woman who strengthens her body and exercises her mind will, by managing her family and practicing various virtues, become the friend, and not the humble dependent of her husband.*

He'd read the passage over and over. He'd had to read so many passages in the same dogged way, as he'd rarely studied in school, to understand and digest and remember.

This woman was the friend of her husband.

A friend. His gaze moved to Cassandra, who'd drawn her sister aside to share some thought or reassurance or apology.

Whatever they might be talking about, the sight of the two heads bent together, the fair and the redhead, touched something inside him and warmed the place.

This was a family. A loving family.

He'd wanted a family without having much idea of what it was.

This was what it was.

How could she help but want to protect them? He wanted to protect them, too.

At the moment, he didn't know how he'd do this. But he hadn't any doubt a scheme would come to him. They always did. Eventually.

The tea arrived, and even before they'd begun to drink, while Lady deGriffith was still pouring, Ashmont had the curious sensation of a change in the atmosphere.

He looked up to find Lord deGriffith's sharp grey gaze upon him once again, but this time, it seemed somewhat less murderous and somewhat more—what? Resigned? Speculative? Impossible to say, except that he seemed more the politician now and not quite so much the vengeful father.

"Ah, then, that's better," Lady deGriffith said into the quiet. "Difficulties seem to fall back into proper proportion, rather magically, over a cup of tea."

"All I see at present is a matter of her word against ours," Cassandra said. "When you pare away the threats, real and imaginary, it comes down to this could happen and that could happen. The question is, can she make it happen? Can she make it impossible for any of us to show our faces in Society again? Can she cause Hyacinth to be tarred with the same brush as I? Will the world blame you, Papa, for having a wanton hussy for a daughter?"

"Yes," said Lord deGriffith. "It can be done. A dedicated smear campaign can destroy a career."

Cassandra stared at her father, her grey gaze bleak. "Might this destroy yours?"

"Not likely."

"But it won't be pleasant," she said.

Her father shrugged.

"Not pleasant?" Morris said. "Miss Pomfret, I don't like to distress you, but it'll make Lord deGriffith's job a deal harder. This sort of thing gets out, the satirists have a festival. Then there's people laughing behind your back, that sort of thing. As bad as boys at school—you know, making remarks about a fellow's sister. What's a gentleman to do? Call them all out? He'd be fighting every dawn for months."

"Should he be so fortunate as to survive the engagements," Lord deGriffith said. "And should he be so fortunate as to survive his wife's wrath, were he to undertake them."

"Makes it deuced hard to get any proper work done," Morris went on, "when people are making puns and jokes at your expense. It's a low thing to do, and I wonder at my mother. I still think I ought to talk to her, at least find out what maggot's got into her brain."

And here Miss Flower smiled upon him, and lo, his face became suffused with crimson.

That girl, Ashmont thought, could do anything she liked with poor Morris. But then, Ashmont was in much the same case with her sister.

"That is very good of you, Mr. Morris," Lady deGriffith said. "But it will not be necessary." She put down her empty teacup and rose. "I shall speak to Lady Bartham myself."

Lord deGriffith sprang from his chair. "Jane."

"This time she has gone too far," said she. And out of the room she went.

Chapter 18

Cassandra's father hurried out of the study after her mother. Cassandra heard their voices and footsteps gradually recede. Then one set of footsteps returned. They were not her mother's.

Her father came to the study doorway. "I will speak to Cassandra. Duke, you will wait. Mr. Morris, I had hoped to continue our conversation, but as you see, family matters have arisen. You are welcome to wait, though I cannot say how long the wait will be. Hyacinth, be so good as to show these gentlemen the billiard room, and have refreshments sent to them. Regardless what it does for your mother's faculties, I doubt that a cup of tea suffices, in the circumstances."

"Sir, I'd like to speak to you first," Ashmont said.

"You will speak to me second," said Papa. "My daughter comes first. Kindly do as I say. My patience is shredded to its last thread."

Ashmont looked to Cassandra for confirmation. She nodded. He went out with the others.

Her father walked back to his place behind the desk.

Cassandra stood in front of it, hands folded at her waist. "It might be wisest to disown me," she said. "I don't know why this didn't occur to me sooner. It would solve a host of problems, and spike Lady Bartham's guns in the bargain."

"I will not disown you," he said. "Among other things, my mother would never forgive me. She would call me puritanical, and overfastidious, and those are the kindest terms. But I shouldn't do it, mother or no mother. You are my daughter, and you should have to do a great deal worse than this for me to cast you out. Not that you are to consider this a challenge."

She wanted to run behind the desk and hug him, the way she'd used to do when she was a child. She only swallowed the lump in her throat.

"I do not approve," he said. "I do not like it. I especially do not like the fellow on whose account you got yourself into all this trouble. But it seems to me that, at the very least, you act in accordance with your principles. As your mother has pointed out to me on many occasions, we do not treat women justly. We expect a great deal too much or else a great deal too little, and we judge them far more harshly than we judge men. This is so. But this is the way of the world, child, and that I cannot change."

She only nodded. Her throat hurt. She'd wept once already and couldn't bear to do it again. She did not want pity or even sympathy. He'd given her understanding, and that was more than enough.

"So." He bowed his head and studied the floor for a time.

She waited.

He looked up. "Do you truly love the rakehell?"

"Yes. That's why I went to his house. To tell him so."

"And I daresay you believe he's reformed."

She considered. "To a point. He's in the process, at any rate."

"But enough to be acceptable."

"Yes." She wanted to tell him about Bleeding Heart Yard, but her father had had enough upheaval for one day. Another time. Maybe in a year or two.

"You know, my dear, I only wish for you to be happy. I fear you will be hurt."

"Papa." She let out a small sigh. "Really. Do consider. Of the two of us, who is more likely to be hurt, in the event Ashmont behaves badly?"

"Promise me," he said. "Promise me you will not suffer him to show you any less regard than I show your mother. Promise me."

She smiled. "That's an exceedingly high standard."

"It's the only standard I can tolerate. Promise."

"I promise, Papa."

"Very well. You may send him to me. I might as well try to accomplish something while your mother does whatever it is she means to do."

"You don't know, Papa?"

He lifted his shoulders. "You know as much as I do. Yet I find myself feeling, quite strongly, that I would not be in Lady Bartham's shoes this day, for any consideration."

IT DID NOT occur to Lady Bartham that Cassandra Pomfret would do the sensible thing and admit her shocking behavior to family members. Being everything but straightforward herself, the countess failed to imagine any other route but guilty secrecy.

She was enjoying the picture her mind painted, of the rebellious hoyden suffering in silence, squirming in shame and misery, when a servant told her that Lady deGriffith had called and wished to see her.

She had a moment's instinctive alarm, that the lady had come on her daughter's business. But this was so unlikely as to be laughable. Meanwhile, the prospect of carrying on a conversation with her dear friend, all the while privately chortling over what she knew and what she'd done and the power she held over the family, was too delicious to resist.

She found her friend waiting in the entrance hall, having declined to be taken to the drawing room.

After the usual exchange of greetings, Lady deGriffith invited her to drive out with her.

"Drive?" said Lady Bartham.

"A turn in the park. I realize you will wish to prepare to dine at

Lady Jersey's tonight, but it's early yet, and I shan't make a great claim on your time." Lady deGriffith lowered her voice. "I wish to consult you on a delicate matter."

Delicate matters were Lady Bartham's stock-in-trade, and this was irresistible: more secrets to do with Lord deGriffith's family. Her cup overflowed.

She sent for her hat and shawl, and in short order she sat in her friend's barouche, en route to Hyde Park.

They passed the first few minutes of the journey in ordinary chitchat, as etiquette required. Lady deGriffith talked about her weekly tea with her sisters. She would miss these gatherings, she said, when the family returned to Hertfordshire after Parliament rose. But then, she had other family get-togethers to look forward to in the autumn and winter.

Lady Bartham didn't hurry her to the point. She had plenty to entertain her: what she knew and what Lady deGriffith didn't. The future, when all her friend's schemes would explode right under her nose, and her daughters would return to Hertfordshire husbandless. That was only the beginning of the countess's happy fantasies.

"But to the business that brought me here," Lady deGriffith said. "A painful business, I am sorry to say."

"I pray you will not hesitate to tell me. What are friends for?"

"What, indeed? We have known each other for how long, my dear?"

"Why, we were girls together at Miss Biddleton's School for Young Ladies."

"So we were. It's for the sake of that long friendship that I called on you today. About my daughter."

Lady Bartham felt a momentary uncertainty, a prickling of concern, but only briefly. There were many confidential matters one might discuss concerning daughters. The youngest, Helena, was away at school, but children got into trouble at school. The other two—could one of them have found herself in a family way? That would be too delicious for words. "Ah, yes. One of your charming daughters."

"I recall your mentioning that Mr. Humphrey Morris tells you everything."

"I have always encouraged my children to speak freely to me," said Lady Bartham. The two elder ones scarcely uttered two words to her in the course of a month. Not that they were known for their conversational skills.

"Always best, I believe. My children are confiding as well. Cassandra, for instance."

At last Lady Bartham's antennae quivered. "A handsome girl. So independent. One who goes her own way." Inevitably the wrong way.

"So true. Not at all easy to predict what she will do. If she were in trouble, for instance, would she confide in her parents?"

"I cannot say. Perhaps it would depend on the kind of trouble."

"If she found herself being blackmailed, for instance."

The carriage's hood was up, which meant one couldn't see the two footmen in back. The coachman in front was plainly visible. But the ladies would have to raise their voices in order for any of these servants to eavesdrop, and ladies did not raise their voices.

Lady Bartham did not raise hers, nor did she attempt to jump from the carriage. She told herself she was a match for any woman, especially this one, who couldn't manage her daughters.

In any event, she held all the cards. Lady deGriffith could only have come to plead for her daughter. That would be amusing. "Blackmail is an ugly word."

"For an ugly business," Lady deGriffith said. "A curious business, too. When monetary gain is not involved, one must ask, What *is* gained? Let me give you an example. Suppose Person X demanded that a young woman, who is no relation to Person X—not that person's own daughter, certainly—break off with Gentleman A. What could the blackmailer hope to gain?"

The words *blackmail* and *blackmailer* rang in Lady Bartham's head. A mental image arose of her standing in the dock of the Old Bailey. She blocked it out. "I am no lawyer. I could not possibly say."

"Use your imagination, my dear," said Lady deGriffith. "I can imagine several motives." She sighed. "Sadly, none of them raise much sympathy. Some are rather pathetic. *Petty* would not be too strong a word. Or *childish*. For instance, I might guess that the blackmailer simply couldn't endure seeing a young lady she doesn't approve of become a duchess. Or perhaps this has nothing to do with the daughter. Perhaps the key is the girl's parents? A resentment festering some forty years. Or perhaps I have let my imagination run away with me."

"That is all too likely."

"You may be right. Who would ever believe that a happily married woman of high rank would *still* nurse a grudge—forty years later—because the gentleman she fancied during her first Season fell in love with her friend instead?"

Lady Bartham went icy cold, then hot. She hadn't simply fancied Lord deGriffith. She'd been wildly, madly in love. She'd gone so far as to write a love letter to him, which he'd sent back, with a gentle, tactful note, claiming to be unworthy, and wishing her happiness.

All the tact and gentleness in the world could not soothe her wounded vanity. Thanks to indulgent parents, she had been used, all her life, to having whatever she wanted. Since she could not have it this time, she ascribed the defeat to her friend's cruelty, deceit, and machinations.

She was years beyond blushing, fortunately. "It is absurd, patently absurd," she said.

"Yet it is precisely the sort of unpleasant little tale that Society likes to feast upon. Especially those who might feel some resentment against the grudge bearer. It would be a pity if, say, in response to a salacious story about her daughter, a mother let that sad little tale slip."

"Forty years." The countess waved her hand. "Ancient history. Who would care?"

Everybody. Every enemy Lady Bartham had made, and everybody happy to turn enemy. They'd feast upon any embarrassing tale about her, no matter how trivial, even one forty years old. Especially one forty years old that could only make her appear childish and spiteful.

Lady deGriffith shrugged. "Merely a thought. There are a number of responses to blackmail. One is to fight fire with fire. Then it would become interesting to discover whose flame blazes highest, would it not?"

Lady Bartham was beginning to see the path ahead, and the sight was not agreeable.

"It would be a fascinating test of influence, do you not think?" said Lady deGriffith. "Who is better liked? Who might garner more sympathy? Who has relatives who can make or break a person's standing at Court with a few words?"

"An intriguing question."

Lady deGriffith turned her gaze to the passing scene. "How pleasant it is to have Lady Charles Ancaster back," she said absently. "She is at Windsor until Monday, I believe. Their Majesties can't seem to get enough of her. Lord Frederick Beckingham accompanied her. I wonder where that will lead. Ah, there is the Serpentine."

Lady Bartham looked out at the park as well, seeing nothing but Lady Charles and Lord Frederick whispering about her to the King and Queen, and the whispers traveling through the Court.

One word from Lady Charles, and invitations would stop coming, to Court events and all others to which royals were invited. Then, as word traveled the aristocratic circuit, the other invitations would stop coming, too.

"We've nearly completed our circuit," said Lady deGriffith. "Unless you would like to go round once more? I shall not be wanted for some time. My husband has business with Mr. Humphrey Morris, which apparently will continue into the late afternoon, possibly the evening. But it is important business. As you are aware, Lord deGriffith contemplates engaging your son as a secretary. I understand Lord Bartham expressed some pleasure at the prospect. Let us hope nothing occurs to prevent the engagement. I should hate to see Lord Bartham disappointed."

One blow after another, every one aimed true.

For the most part, Lord Bartham let his wife do as she pleased.

But he deeply resented her interfering in what he deemed men's business. He would never raise a hand to her, or even his voice. But if he found out she'd tried to thwart Humphrey's employment with Lord deGriffith, he would react fiercely. He would curtail her allowance, stopping her ability to shop and entertain. Once or twice, in cases of extreme displeasure, he had sent her back to Yorkshire.

"Thank you," Lady Bartham said. "One circuit is sufficient."

"Are you quite sure, my dear? As I said, I am at leisure."

"So kind of you. Another time, perhaps. I seem to have a headache."

"Ah, then you will want to return home and be quiet."

Lady Bartham met her gaze. "Yes, it seems that would be best."

"Yes," Lady deGriffith said. "I believe it would."

THE DUKE OF ASHMONT emerged from Lord deGriffith's study, looking, as Humphrey Morris put it, "Like he'd gone ten rounds with Gentleman Jackson, then another ten with Tom Cribb."

This was a slight exaggeration. As His Dis-Grace re-entered the billiard room, he dragged a hand through his hair and looked about him in bewilderment, as though he'd been days in a deep black hole and the light, even the pale light of this uncertain day, blinded him.

"This is what comes of so much thinking," he told Morris. "Have my eyes crossed?"

"Stimulating," Morris said.

"What?"

"Lord deGriffith. Stimulating. Kept me hopping, I'll tell you."

"You're going to work for him? Truly? Couldn't you find something easier? Like—oh, I don't know. Lion taming. Wrestling pythons."

"*She* thinks I can do it," Morris said. "She said I was wasting my talents. What talents, I wanted to know. And she smiles and tells me I'm too modest. But about Miss Hyacinth."

"What about her?"

"Any idea why she wanted me there, with all that family confabulation going on, and mighty personal, too. I didn't know where to look, I was that embarrassed. I mean, your private business and all that. And Miss Pomfret's, too."

Ashmont considered. It wasn't easy. He felt as though his future father-in-law had tossed his brains about with a pitchfork, then raked them over for good measure.

Women are told ... that ... should they be beautiful, Mrs. Wollstonecraft had written, *every thing else is needless, for, at least, twenty years of their lives.*

"Maybe Miss Hyacinth wanted you to know who she was," he said finally. "Not merely the most beautiful girl you've ever seen."

"Ashmont? Is that you? Or has another being taken over your brain?"

He turned to the doorway, where Cassandra stood.

"What brain?" he said.

"That's all right," she said. "Papa does that to everybody. Gentlemen, mainly."

"Stimulating," Morris said.

"So it would seem," said Cassandra. "The duke remembered my sister's name."

"What time is it?" Ashmont said. "What day is it?"

"Still today. But my mother is back. I heard her come in, and ran down to find out how her errand went." She glanced at Morris, who blushed and mumbled something.

"Apparently it went well," Cassandra said. "She told me I was not to be anxious. It was all settled. And that is as much as she would tell me. She's gone to talk to my father. He may discover a little more."

"All settled," Ashmont said. "Like that? She wasn't gone—what? An hour? I've lost all sense of time."

"Something more than that," Morris said.

Cassandra went to Ashmont and smoothed his hair. The simplest gesture. She'd never done it before, and here she was, doing it in front of people. Well, Morris, but still.

"I know you're disappointed," she said. "You would have liked to make an explosion or break noses. I'm disappointed, too. I had visions of breaking into the house—"

"In Anselm's Cossack trousers—"

"—and rifling her belongings, looking for something incriminating."

"Another time, maybe," Ashmont said.

"But this feels right," she said. "Mother to mother. Done quietly. The way the Andromeda Society prefers to work. Woman to woman."

"Woman to woman," Ashmont repeated. The world had grown a great deal more complicated than it used to be. And a great deal more interesting. He thought, perhaps, there was a good chance he'd never be bored again.

"But one thing," Morris said. "You know, it's well and good, woman to woman, and to tell the truth, I'd rather not wrangle with my mother if it isn't necessary—though I would if it was. But if they've settled it between them, I reckon it's to do with them more than us. The thing I want to know is, Who was the spy who told her?"

"It might have been anybody," Cassandra said. "Ashmont, I meant to tell you, before all this crisis began—I ought never to have been able to get into your garden last night. The man who patrols your grounds was not as observant as he ought to be. If that had been Keeffe, I should never have made it into the house."

"Then I'm glad it wasn't Keeffe."

"As am I. But the fact remains, somebody was able to get close enough for a long enough time to spy on you. If that person had meant to do you harm, what would stand in his way?"

"Sommers. You should see those irons of his. Or if he happened to have the razor handy. Or he could garotte the intruder with a cravat. I wouldn't be surprised."

"Nor would I," she said. "But you had better talk to Keeffe."

"Later," he said. "First I want to talk to you. Aren't you interested in what your father said to me?"

THEIR CONVERSATION WAS cut short by Cassandra's father. His wife having reassured him that nothing more needed to be done regarding Lady Bartham, Lord deGriffith decided he'd had enough for one day.

Most especially he'd had enough of Ashmont.

Like it or not, His Dis-Grace was going to be his son-in-law, as soon as the lawyers finished wrangling. Since his lordship intended his side to take no prisoners, the fight would be fierce. However, it would also have to be short. Given the events of the previous night, he saw no alternative. If he tried locking his daughter in, she'd get out. If he tried sending her to a convent, she'd escape. If he sent her back to his parents, Ashmont would follow.

While Lord deGriffith's initial loathing had softened to intense dislike, he was, after all, a man who could see when it was time to cease opposing and begin negotiating for the best position. In short, since the deed must be done, then "'twere well / It were done quickly," as Macbeth put it.

This is why only a very short time passed before Ashmont went to the mews to talk to Keeffe. Remembering Cassandra's comments about intruders and assassins, and at any rate uncertain what to do, now that Lady deGriffith had settled matters without violence or housebreaking, he decided he might as well deal with this piece of unfinished business.

"Well, you know, I was thinking about that very thing," Keeffe said when Ashmont told him.

Indeed, he'd appeared in contemplative mode when Ashmont entered. The jockey sat before his fireplace, arms folded, gazing at the painting above the chimneypiece.

"I was thinking my miss got in too easy, like she said," Keeffe went on. "Then I was thinking about the one keeping an eye on you. Is it a regular job? I wondered. Just the once? Or, since he got something this time, maybe he'd come back again, hoping for more."

"She's worried I'll be assassinated."

"Wants to save the job for herself, I reckon," Keeffe said. He lifted his mangled body from the chair. "Whyn't I go have a look."

"Now?"

"No, not until dark. For now you can take me round the corner and treat me to a tankard or two while we talk it over."

Mr. Owsley had not, originally, intended to return to Ashmont House. He'd gone first to Bartham House, to learn what Lady Bartham had done with the information he'd given her. He was told that her ladyship was not at home.

This he very much doubted. It was too early for her to have gone out to Lady Jersey's. But "not at home" wasn't always meant to be taken literally. She might be ill. She might simply be ill disposed to see visitors, even him.

Not being able to speak to her and learn what she'd done, if anything, and whether she'd been successful, he grew uneasy and uncertain. He wasn't sure he'd done the right thing. Maybe he ought to have dealt with the matter himself. Or not dealt with it. He could have simply turned his back on Miss Pomfret and any possibility of a future with her. Perhaps it had been ungentlemanly to report her shame to another woman. But he had been so wretched!

He was wretched still. If not for the Duke of Ashmont, he wouldn't have made so many mistakes. If not for him, provoking, arrogant man that he was, Owsley wouldn't have said the wrong thing, again and again. Then Miss Pomfret would not have come here and ruined herself.

Or what if last night he'd been wrong? What if it was as Lady Bartham had said?

These and other equally incoherent thoughts drew him back to Ashmont House at nightfall. There he lurked, as he'd done the previous night, hardly knowing what he was watching for, but feeling he had to be there.

He returned to the place where he'd watched the two figures in the window. Several of the windows overlooking the garden were lit, as they'd been last night. A form passed once, then returned. Then there were two forms.

His heart pounding, he took out his spyglass and peered through it. He took a step closer.

And tripped over a walking stick. He stumbled, but hastily righted himself. And found he wasn't alone. A group was gathering about him.

This part of the stable yard was ill lit. The light from Park Street cast most of it into shadows. Still, there was light enough for him to make out figures, all men.

A Cockney voice said, "Well, look what we've got here, Your Grace. A peeping Tom."

"Filthy, sneaking bastard." The spyglass was knocked from his hand. He heard it clatter to the ground as a fist drove into his belly.

ASHMONT HAD BEEN wanting to hit somebody ever since Keeffe had appeared in his dressing room with the news about Cassandra. He couldn't hit a woman, even Lady Bartham. He couldn't break into her house. Lady deGriffith had taken care of that.

The trouble was, hitting Owsley wasn't satisfying. He didn't hit back, only doubled up, sank to his knees, let out a loud groan, and fainted.

His stablemen, who'd been alerted to the investigation, gathered round to watch the fun.

"Damn the fellow to hell," Ashmont said. "One blow and he's down."

"Not the worst idea," Keeffe said. "Did he ask, I'd recommend it."

"Someone bring a lamp," Ashmont said. "I want a look at what we're dealing with."

The lamp was brought near.

Ashmont gazed at the man for a time, shaking his head.

"You know him, Your Grace?" Keeffe said.

"Yes."

"Gentry cove."

"Yes."

"What d'y' want to do with him?"

"Throw him in the river."

"Well, you're a duke. Hard to hang. 'N' the river don't tell tales."

"I *want* to throw him in the river. But I'm reformed now, and so—"

Owsley groaned.

"—I've got to deal with it in a bloody civilized fashion."

ASHMONT HAD OWSLEY taken back to the house, to the anteroom at the back of the ground floor. The man looked ill, but that might have to do with getting caught behaving in a swinish manner.

All the same, Ashmont ordered brandy and soda, and sent away all servants. This left him and Keeffe on guard, but Owsley didn't strike him as the sort of man who'd like the odds.

"Maybe you could explain to me," Ashmont said mildly, "why I shouldn't throw you into the river, with stones sewn into your pockets and a gag in your mouth. And don't tell me it would be wrong. You're in no position. Do you know the trouble you've caused, with your little spying glass?"

Owsley remaining sullen, Ashmont told him.

Over the course of the narrative, the MP's sulks gradually altered to stunned disbelief. "I didn't know. I never thought— No, it can't be as you say. Lady Bartham wouldn't do such a thing."

"She did, and you gave her the ammunition." Ashmont looked at Keeffe. "What sort of blackguard passes on stories that blacken a lady's name?"

"I dunno, Your Grace. The kind as belongs at the bottom of the river?"

"Was it gentlemanly of you?" Ashmont asked his prisoner.

"You! To talk of gentlemanly behavior. That's a laugh."

Ashmont considered. "Fair enough. I ask you then, Was it sporting?"

After a moment, Owsley said, "No, no, it wasn't. Nor gentlemanly, either." He rubbed his head, though it ought to have been his gut that ached. "This is not right. I am not right. This isn't like me."

"Oh, it's very like you," Ashmont said. "It's all of a piece with your Sabbath bill and not getting behind a bill that would actually do some good. You're wrongheaded."

"I! You should not have let the lady inside your house. Had you behaved as a gentleman, I should have had nothing to tell anybody. Had you only gone away—"

"Wouldn't do you any good. She doesn't want you. She doesn't want your poetry."

Owsley's head jerked back, as though he'd been punched. "She told you about that?"

"She told me you gave her a poem. She told me it made her realize she liked me. You started it, you sanctimonious blockhead. You settled it for her. That's why she came here."

Owsley closed his eyes. He said nothing for a long time.

Ashmont looked at Keeffe, who shrugged.

At last Owsley let out a long breath. "I see. I have allowed myself to be played, like a—"

"Barrel organ?" Keeffe said. "Or maybe it's more like the organ grinder's monkey?"

"Yes."

Ashmont moved to the window and looked out into the garden, mainly a large expanse of varying degrees of darkness.

He did not know what to do with this man. He would have known, say, a month earlier. He would have fought him. At dawn at thirty paces.

Or maybe he wouldn't have done something so civilized. He would have fought with his fists, the way he'd tried to fight Ripley. The way he'd fought scores of males, on the smallest provocation.

This wasn't small.

But the method didn't strike him as useful at present. Owsley would still be a sneaking jackass, with an even smaller brain than Ashmont's. Hell, he made Ashmont feel like a genius, another Newton or one of those other big-brained fellows.

He turned back to Owsley.

"We had better settle this like gentlemen," Ashmont said.

Owsley went white.

"Not that," Ashmont said. "Drink your brandy, damn you."

Hand trembling, Owsley brought the glass to his lips and drank.

"You will give me your word of honor as a gentleman," Ashmont said, "never to breathe even a hint of this business to anybody. You won't utter a word about it ever again to that poisonous snake of a female. I doubt she'll be wanting to bring up the subject at this point, but bile might get the better of her. She seems to have plenty of that. But if she does bring it up, you won't know what she's talking about. You'll stare at her as though she's sprouted horns—which, by the way, wouldn't surprise me. Is that clear?"

Owsley nodded. "I'll be happy never to speak to her again."

"Good idea. Then I have your word?"

"You have my word."

"Then we're done," Ashmont said. "Although I recommend you discover a strong urge to travel to foreign parts. Soon. And stay away for a long time."

"But my constituency—"

"They'll muddle along. Somebody else will take your seat. You're young enough yet. Find another career. A rich wife. I don't bloody well care what you do, only keep well away from me—and my duchess. You heard that, right? My duchess. You keep away from my family or I won't be so filled with loving kindness next time."

Chapter 19

—We understand that the matrimonial alliance between the Duke of Ashmont and Miss Pomfret, eldest daughter of Lord deGriffith, will take place in a few days.

—*Foxe's Morning Spectacle*,
7 August 1833

*T*he wedding took place at St. George's, Hanover Square, on the following Saturday. This was eight weeks to the day, and very close to the hour, after the Duke of Ashmont crashed into Cassandra's life.

A dejeuner followed, attended primarily by family members but also by a handful of illustrious persons, including the Duke of Sussex. His Royal Highness was charged with reporting to his brother the King his impressions of the state of the Duke of Ashmont's morals as well as any Incidents, explosions, screaming women, visitations of domestic animals, or other untoward events.

The wedding proceeded in the normal way, however, and the breakfast was notable only in the early disappearance of the newlyweds, who had a journey of some three or four hours ahead of them.

Ashmont wanted to spend his wedding night, not in his own house, but at Camberley Place.

"Where I first met you," he'd told Cassandra.

He'd arranged it all ahead of time, and sent his own servants to prepare part of the house for them, since Lady Charles had left only a small staff.

The newlyweds dined in the house, but when evening fell, he led his duchess not upstairs to their bedchamber but outside, to the fishing house by the river.

"Exactly where I met you the first time," he said, as they reached the ancient building.

He heard her catch her breath. "You remember."

"Yes. An elfin girl, turning round and round, looking up into the heavens, her face bathed in starlight."

"Oh, Lucius," she said softly.

He took her hand and squeezed it, then looked up at the night sky. "Not sure I can recapture the conditions, though. There are limits, even to what a duke can do. I distinctly remember ordering the Milky Way. Ought to be here by now."

The day had been cloudy, and the stars twinkled but dimly. Still, what stars there were and the waning moon offered light enough to see her.

"We can pretend," she said.

He drew her into his arms and kissed her, a long, searching kiss. They'd had almost no privacy in the weeks since she'd sneaked into his house. Three weeks of balked lust, with an intimate interlude in the carriage on the way here. As interludes went, it had been rather chaste. He hadn't wanted to hurry. He wanted everything to be perfect.

This was their wedding night. They'd never have another. They could take their time.

After a long, sweet time, he gently broke the kiss and drew away. He took her hand and led her a few feet along the level ground by the fishing house. This was the place where he'd found her spinning, arms spread, face to the heavens. This was the place where he'd told the elfin girl stories about the stars.

There was a large basket in the place now. And a bucket filled with ice, holding a bottle of champagne.

"Oh, Lucius," she said. "You planned this."

"For my duchess." He knelt and opened the basket. He took

out a rug and spread it on the ground. He patted the rug, and she sat. She drew up her legs and folded her arms on her knees and watched him.

He took out the glasses and laid them on the rug. He drew out the champagne bottle and opened it, and the pop sounded like thunder in the quiet.

The world about them wasn't utterly still, though. Water burbled over rocks in the river. Leaves fluttered in the light breeze of a late-summer night.

He filled their glasses. "Here I first met you," he said.

"And soon forgot."

"Better for you that way."

"I know that now." She raised her glass. "I'll drink to it gladly."

He drank and the sparkling taste seemed to dance in his mouth.

"And here you shocked me out of my wits by taking my side against another boy," she said.

"No boy ever defended you before? No, you're trying to be sweet."

"I? Sweet?"

"But the odds weren't right," he said. "All those boys against one girl."

"If Alice had been by, there would have been all those boys against two girls. But she was in durance vile. I forget what her crime was."

"And the other girls?"

"Safer to be neutral. We weren't proper girls. The others didn't want to be like us."

"'. . . scrupulous attention to a puerile kind of propriety,'" he murmured.

"Say again?"

"Nothing. Thinking. How to seduce you."

"Yes, that will be terribly difficult." She drank. "Shall I get tipsy and help you? I might take off all my clothes and dance naked in the moonlight."

"Do you know, I haven't the smallest doubt you'll do it. But you might want to wait for more moonlight." He looked up. "Damn. It seems this is the best we're going to get."

He swallowed the last of his champagne. She did the same. "Such a wonderful drink," she said. "I always thought that ambrosia, the drink of the gods, must be champagne."

He stretched out on his side, to lean upon one elbow. "I wish you would come here," he said. "Closer. Or I'll come to you. You *are* a duchess. And I'm yours to command."

She set down her empty glass on its side in the grass beside the rug and moved closer to him. She lay down, and looked up at him, and he saw all the stars he wanted in her eyes.

He bent his head and kissed her, deeply and deeper still. Oh, she tasted like ambrosia made especially for him. He tasted champagne and Cassandra and fire and ice, tempest and tranquility.

There was a kind of peace in having her storming alongside him. Boadicea. Fearless and loving. So loving. Who, looking into her stony grey eyes, would have guessed at the depths of passion behind them, and the depths of affection.

He lifted his head, and traced her jaw with his fingers. "I love you," he said.

"I know."

"And I love the way you hate me."

She smiled and slid her fingers through his hair. "The ways. Ten ways."

"Then I'll have to love you ten ways. And ten times ten."

"Yes," she said, a sigh of a word.

He drew his hands over the contours of her face, the fine arch of her eyebrows, the curve of her cheekbones, the line of her jaw. He followed the outline of her neck and shoulder. Like her character, her features were strong, but soft, too. He changed his position to slide his hands over her breasts and her belly and down. All this while he traced mainly the way her clothing shaped her. But this, too, was Cassandra. And then there was Cassandra underneath.

He began to undo her clothing, layer by layer. The belt and the dress fastenings, and the sleeves that needed to be detached from the little clouds that filled them. And at last he could pull the dress over her head, a flurry of silk, while she laughed, but softly.

"So much work," she said. "Yet how well you do it. There are advantages to marrying a man of experience."

"No, no. This is the first time."

"With me."

"The first time like this." The first time it truly mattered. The first time it was a precious moment.

The corset came next, and the sleeve puffs, and petticoat. Then he paused, and traced her again, his hands following her shape under the fine linen chemise and over her belly and legs with their thin pantalets and the silk stockings below.

"Closer now," he said. "Closer to the real you."

"I should like to be closer to the real you," she said.

Preoccupied with her, he'd forgotten. "Right. Only fair." He freed himself of his coat, with her help. She untied his cravat without help. The waistcoat followed.

"Oh, Lucius," she said, and she drew her hands over him as he'd done her, her fingers trailing over his face and down his throat and over his chest and his belly and without hesitation lower still, where his cock shoved against his trousers. "It seems you're ready," she said.

"I've been ready since I woke up this morning. I've been ready for weeks. But I want this to be as perfect as it can be."

"Ah, well, then." And she let her head fall back again and stretched her arms above her head and said, "Do as you wish with me, Your Grace."

The wanton pose wanted to undo him and throw his careful plan into disorder. He had to remind himself that this was the only wedding night they'd ever have. He slid down and kissed her foot, her ankle, and trailed kisses up her lower leg to her knees and upward still, to the place where the pantalets opened, at the sweet junction of her legs, but the chemise still veiled it.

By this time he was trembling, and she was, too.

"Lucius," she said. "This is torture. Beautiful torture, but torture all the same."

The chemise came away, and all the rest, and then there was nothing but Cassandra, as she was. He flung away the rest of his clothes, trying not to be hasty but unable to quite manage. He drew her into his arms and kissed her, deeply and hotly, and received the same in return. A long, wild kiss in the nighttime, while their hands moved over each other, learning, memorizing, reveling.

"So beautiful," he said. "Oh, Cassandra."

"You, too," she said. "Come, make me truly your wife."

The words blazed through him, and he obeyed. Feverish caresses now—the perfect swell of her breasts, the elegant curve of waist and hips, oh, and the soft wetness of her most womanly place.

He caressed her until she was moaning, then laughing and saying, "Oh, come now, Lucius. Make me yours completely. I can take it."

He poised himself at the place, then bent to kiss her at the same time he entered her, as carefully as he could. But no, his cock had its own ideas, and no patience, and he felt her quick, sharp gasp against his mouth. But he was inside her, and it was tight and warm, and thinking was nigh impossible.

He could barely manage a few words. "Sorry. Did it hurt?"

She laughed, but he thought he heard a sob in it. "Oh, Lucius. I thought . . . Oh, is there more?"

He laughed, too, perhaps like a madman. But his body was moving already, desire and instinct gaining the upper hand. He moved carefully at first, but as she began to find the rhythm of it, he grew bolder.

After this there was only the movement of two lovers. Only they two, joined, and traveling together, riders on a wondrous tempest. Her muscles tensed, holding him and releasing, and holding again, and with every shift of movement he rode higher and higher, until he felt her shudder around him and heard her cry out, not words but cries of pleasure. Then it was his name she said, like a breath, a whisper, a secret. *Lucius.*

His heart seemed to break and come together again, and he thundered on to a moment of pure happiness, and the world went black. Then it exploded into sparkling shards, like diamonds. Like a shower of stars. He drifted among them, and slowly came back to earth.

THEY LAY FOR a long time, hearts pounding, skin glistening with sweat. Cassandra held him, her arms tight about his strong back. She had never dreamt of such closeness. Not simply the joining of their bodies, but of something deeper still.

She lay holding him, while their breathing slowed, and the world slowly drifted back. She had her eyes closed, holding on to the moment and savoring the feel of him, the powerful muscles and the surprising smoothness of his skin and the scent of him. She pressed her face into the hollow of his shoulder and the scent filled her head and made it spin. But it was already spinning. With happiness and pleasure and some strange kind of peace.

He moved, and carefully withdrew from her.

She was sorry. It felt so wonderful to have him inside her, even for the time it hurt. But not very much. She was strong and agile. She rode. And he had done everything to make it easy for her, taking his time when she was quite sure that was difficult for him. After this it would be much easier, her mother had assured her when she came to talk to her about conjugal relations.

"It gets better," she'd said. "If he's a considerate man, as he seems to be. I do believe he will care for you very well."

"Mama said it gets better," she murmured. "I wonder how it can get better than this."

He grinned and kissed her. "I'll see what I can do."

He moved off her then, and she felt cold, though the night was mild. But he drew her close, tucking her against him, then pulled the rug over her, as though he knew.

And she was about to say, How did you know, when she opened her eyes fully, and looked up, where he wasn't anymore.

"Lucius," she whispered, though there was no reason on earth to whisper. "Look up."

He turned a little and tipped his head back and looked up. And laughed.

The clouds had blown away, and the sky was filled with stars.

"It's about damned time."

"Yes," she said, looking from the stars to him. "Yes, it is."

HOURS LATER, THEY returned to the house, where Cassandra bathed and changed into a proper nightdress.

She had a new lady's maid to look after her. Mademoiselle Fougère's English skills were unimpressive, but her skills in dressing and hairdressing were of the highest order. Equally important, she was unflappable. She had lived through Paris's most recent revolutions as well as the cholera epidemic. Sommers had found her not long after she left her previous employer, an English lady of retiring disposition. Fougère had given notice because, she told Sommers, the work was not stimulating, and the house was very dull.

"I believe you will find that is not the case in Her Grace's household," he'd told her.

Fougère didn't purse her lips in disapproval when her mistress returned from wherever she'd been, wrapped in a grass-stained rug, under which her attire was in a haphazard order and her carefully arranged hair in wanton disarray.

This merely increased the maid's respect for the English couple. They were not bourgeois. As well as being handsome enough for his striking wife, His Grace was, apparently, an inventive and amusing lover. His French was passable, while his lady's was impeccable. The duchess knew Paris, too, and not merely the obvious places, where all the English aristocrats went.

All in all, Fougère felt her position was more than acceptable. She demonstrated her approval by making her mistress as enticing as possible—not that it was any great labor—and discreetly withdrew thereafter, leaving the lady to await her bridegroom.

Cassandra waited, marveling at what Ashmont had done already, to bring her here and create a magical first night of marriage in a place that held so many fond memories.

She and Alice had taken refuge in the fishing house many, many times, after the boys had gone back to school. She knew Alice still came here from time to time, especially in the last three years, when all the family worried about Aunt Julia. Alice had stayed in the fishing house not long ago, in fact, shortly before Ripley married Olympia.

Blackwood had been there recently, too, but returned to London for his friend's wedding. Matters between Alice and him had not seemed at all improved.

"Frowning, on your wedding night?"

She looked up. Ashmont stood in the doorway. He wore a dressing gown of deep blue velvet, with dark red piping. Apart from the red slippers, he seemed to be wearing nothing else. The neckline of the robe revealed a fine sprinkling of golden hair. He had a book in his hand.

"I was only woolgathering," she said. "You are holding a book."

He looked down at it. "Oh. Yes. Forgot for a minute. You're even more ravishing than you were in your wedding dress. And out of it. And in the traveling dress. And out of it. Do you know, I'm beginning to believe you must be ravishing all the time."

He came to the bed. "I thought I'd read to you."

She stared at him. "This is our wedding night."

"Yes, but we had the ceremonial deflowering already. And may I say I was never so petrified in all my life. Never did that before."

"You mentioned it was your first time. You did well for a beginner."

"Thank you."

That was why he'd gone so slowly and carefully. To make it as enjoyable for her as he could. A considerate man.

Who'd have guessed?

Cassandra Pomfret, for one. She'd known he could be more, so much more, and he'd been proving her right . . . oh, for weeks now.

He came to the bed. He set the book on the bedside table, unfastened the dressing gown, and threw it onto the nearest chair.

"Warm night," he said.

She let her gaze travel down his long, lean, muscled body, gleaming in the candlelight. A golden Apollo. While she studied him, a part of his anatomy began to swell.

"No, no, that won't do," he said.

"I believe it will."

"No, I had this all planned. I'm going to read to you."

"My dear, I never doubted you could read. You don't have to prove it."

"No, I want to read to you. Been waiting. Planning."

"You had an idea," she said.

"Yes." He sat down on the bed beside her. "Make room for the duke, please."

She moved aside.

He settled into the bed, plumping up pillows behind her and behind himself. He took up the book.

She couldn't tell what it was. It was contained in an expensive leather binding, with a gilt design but no title or other identification.

"Just lean back and listen," he said. "I think you'll like it."

She liked being next to his nakedness. She liked his wanting to amuse her. She settled back against the pillows. "I'm ready."

He began to read.

"AFTER considering the historic page, and viewing the living world with anxious solicitude, the most melancholy emotions of sorrowful indignation have depressed my spirits, and I have sighed when obliged to confess, that either nature has made a great difference between man and man, or that the civilization which has hitherto taken place in the world has been very partial."

Cassandra sat bolt upright. "That is Mary Wollstonecraft."

"So it is." He went on reading, not page after page, but what she discovered were marked pages. He'd read the book. He'd found passages he wanted to share with her.

She wanted to weep.

"Ashmont."

He went on reading.

"Lucius."

He turned and looked at her. "I didn't understand what you were about," he said. "I asked Mrs. Roake, because somebody had mentioned the book at the club meeting, and it seemed important to the ladies. She told me I was more likely to have it in my library than to find it in a bookshop, since it was rather old and not read much these days."

"It was well regarded in the author's time," Cassandra said. "But after she died, her husband wrote an honest memoir of her life, and it wasn't a proper life, and so people turned against her."

"The sort of thing she writes about."

"Yes." She looked up at him. "You read this to understand me better?"

"You. The other ladies. You were so sincere and determined. About what you were doing. I was all at sea."

"We don't agree with her on all counts," she said. "But who else has captured our position, our education, the world we live in, so aptly?"

"Don't know. I've only read this one. A few times, to understand, because it's not my usual thing. No murders, for instance. No cutthroats or brigands or star-crossed lovers or even a servant pretending to be a mummy."

She pressed her cheek against his arm. "I didn't think it was possible to love you more. It's easy enough to go about knocking people down and defending honor and all that. But to read *A Vindication of the Rights of Woman*—I could swoon, and I never swoon."

He smiled down at her, the glacier-melting smile. But he saw her now, truly saw her, as no other man did or probably ever would. He'd taken pains to see her truly.

"You mustn't make me weep," she said. "I did that once, a few weeks ago, and that's enough for the decade."

"Don't want to make you swoon or weep. What I was hoping was, enough of this, and you'd be climbing all over me, and the second bedding could go a trifle less cautiously than the last."

"I see." And she did see. The moon and the stars and the Milky Way. Everything she'd dreamt and hoped and more. "Read on."

> "Women are told from their infancy, and taught by the example of their mothers, that a little knowledge of human weakness, justly termed cunning, softness of temper, *outward* obedience, and a scrupulous attention to a puerile kind of propriety, will obtain for them the protection of man; and should they be beautiful, every thing else is needless, for, at least, twenty years of their lives."

He said, "That was one that knocked me on my beam-ends. What? I said. What? No. What?"

She couldn't wait. She reached for him. "Come," she said. "Put away the book. I'm going to climb all over you."

"But there's more."

"I know. But you've made the most extraordinary sacrifice for me, and I must express my feelings."

"Does this mean I get a point?"

"Yes. All the points."

"Truly? Already? No, you're making it too easy."

She studied his face. He was serious. "Very well. One point."

"That's more like it. Later we can talk about the points you owe me. For my clever impersonation of a drunk, for instance, to create a diversion. And disposing of a villain, though he wasn't much of a villain. But your mother did all the heavy work there. My contribution was paltry. Maybe only half a point."

She threw back the bedclothes and clambered into his lap. His rod came to attention. She smiled. "Can we count later?"

He threw down the book and wrapped his arms about her. "Good idea."

She loved him then, as she'd always done. She'd never stop. And neither, she was absolutely certain, would he.

Author's Notes

FOXE'S MORNING SPECTACLE is a fictional publication, which first appeared in *Silk Is for Seduction*. The *Court Journal Gazette of the Fashionable World* is not.

RIPLEY AND OLYMPIA AND OTHERS. *A Duke in Shining Armor* tells their story, and introduces some of the secondary characters featured in *Ten Things I Hate About the Duke*. Lady Bartham first appears in *Dukes Prefer Blondes*. The street child Jonesy makes his first appearance in *Scandal Wears Satin*, where Sophy Noirot christens him Fenwick, cleans him up, and gives him a job. He reappears in *Vixen in Velvet*. In *Dukes Prefer Blondes* we learn he was previously known as Jonesy, the name he goes by in *A Duke in Shining Armor*. Since the latter, like *Ten Things I Hate About the Duke*, takes place two years earlier than the Dressmakers series, I use his earlier alias.

SABBATH BILL. This appeared in various forms over the years. I've substituted my fictional Mr. Owsley for the non-fictional Sir Arthur Agnew, who sponsored the 1833 version that earned the scorn of *Figaro in London* (a precursor to *Punch*) as well as many less radical publications. The bill died one of its many deaths somewhat earlier in real life than it does in my book.

THE WHITE LION INN. The large coaching inn near Putney Bridge (aka Fulham Bridge, depending on which nineteenth-century author one is reading) appears in various accounts of Putney as the Red Lion, the White Lion, and the Putney Hotel. I went with the White Lion, the name it has in its 1889 incarnation. Whether Cassandra or Ashmont would recognize the name is debatable. I know they wouldn't recognize the late Victorian building.

FANCY FAIR. Like several other large social events mentioned in the story, the Grand Fancy Fair and Bazaar for the Benefit of the Society of Friends of Foreigners in Distress actually happened. It did take place over four days at the Hanover Square Rooms on the dates specified. It was definitely jam-packed and ladies fainted all over the place. A description may be found in the *Court Journal* of 22 June 1833, which is online.

ASHMONT'S ARRIVAL AT DEGRIFFITH HOUSE. This is taken from a description of the dashing, real-life Count d'Orsay in *Fifty Years of London Life: Memoirs of a Man of the World*, by Edmund Hodgson Yates, Harper & Brothers, 1885, which is available online.

THEATER MATTERS. The Adelphi is still there, albeit in a form my characters wouldn't recognize, the building having undergone several transformations over the years. The theater was not darkened on Monday nights. *The Long Finn* was a highly popular play by the highly popular American-born playwright William Bayle Bernard. To the best of my knowledge, it wasn't printed. What I have is a photocopy of the microform of the British Library's handwritten copy, thanks to the efforts of my indefatigable research assistant, Pamela Macaulay. If it was printed, and you know where a copy might be found, please email me. Bernard's *The Mummy*, on the other hand, may be read online at Google Books and HathiTrust. It's possible I poached the royal box at the Adelphi for my duke. Despite the abundant detail provided online about this particular theater, I discovered no way to be certain about the boxes over the stage, nor yet the saloon. In this, as in many other cases, I arranged the architecture to suit.

THE POEM TO LADY CHARLOTTE. Titled "The Bridal Gift, Addressed to the Lady Charlotte ——", this lugubrious item did appear as described, in the *Court Journal* of April 1833.

BOUDICCA VS. BOADICEA. *Boadicea* is the name most commonly used through the nineteenth and much of the twentieth century. "Boudicca, or Buduica (we do not know exactly how to spell the name, but neither, presumably, did she) . . . For Roman writers, she was a figure simultaneously of horror and fascination. A warrior queen, intersex, barbarian Cleopatra: 'very tall in stature, with a manly physique, piercing eyes and harsh voice, and a mass of red hair falling to her hips,' as she was described centuries later by someone who could not possibly have known what she looked like."—Mary Beard, *SPQR* (2015)

MARY WOLLSTONECRAFT. While perhaps not a feminist in today's sense of the word, she was certainly one for her own time. *A Vindication of the Rights of Woman* is still in print and available online as well.

THE PLENIPOTENTIARY. The ribald lyrics to this drinking song appear in *Merrie Melodies*, many editions of which can be found online.

MONEY MATTERS. Until 1971, English money wasn't based on a decimal system. It went like this:

Twelve pence in a shilling (*bob*, in slang)

Twenty shillings in a pound or sovereign (a *glistener*)

Twenty-one shillings in a guinea

There were numerous smaller and larger units of these denominations, such as:

Ten shillings in a half sovereign.

Five shillings in a crown.

For more, please see Wikipedia's article on "Coins of the Pound Sterling," under "Pre-Decimal Coinage."

As to value then compared to value today, this is a tricky subject, as you'll discover if you search online. Multiplying by seventy to one hundred will give you a *very* rough sense.

You'll find topics like these covered in my website blog in more detail, with pictures. Subscribing to the blog will not only bring story background and other interesting historical material to your inbox, but will keep you up to date with book deals, book progress, and other matters as well. Illustrations for my books appear on my Pinterest page, too. If your question or concern isn't answered in these places, please feel welcome to email me at author@lorettachase.com. I do my best to answer, though this tends to take much longer than it ought to do.